CHRONICLES OF THE
CLANDESTINE KNIGHTS

CURSE OF THE VALKYRIE

BY TONY NUNES

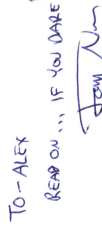

TO - ALEX
READ ON ... IF YOU DARE!
Tony Nun

Nunes Brothers Productions

Special thanks to Steve Nunes for his contributions, Christine Nunes and Anna Nunes for their work on the project. Thanks also to the following: Gabriel & Susanah Ruhl, Skip Ronneberg, Brad Karhu, and Craig Parker.

Questions & comments to
Tony Nunes
P.O. Box 5304
Chico, CA 95927
www.clandestineknights.com

Chronicles of the Clandestine Knights:
Curse of the Valkyrie
© 2005 by Tony Nunes
All rights Reserved
Printed in the U.S.A.

Maps & Illustrations by Michael Nunes
Cover by Renee Boyd

ISBN-13:   978-0-9773963-0-6
ISBN-10:   0-9773963-0-4
Library of Congress Control Number 2005908763

Nunes Brothers Productions

For Antonio D. Nunes
World War II Veteran and member of
A Generation of Heroes

And for Aunt Connie…

CONTENTS

Chronology of the Astorian Realms

100?   The Seven Astorian Tribes separated themselves from the Morbidites and Trepanites and settled the Astorian Realms.

216   The Ethereal Region war; the Trepanites subjugated the Morbidites.

226   The Astorian Tribes defeated the 1st Trepanite invasion.

273   The Astorian Tribes defeated the 2nd Trepanite invasion.

335   The Plague swept the Astorian Realms and the Ethereal Region. As a result, 10% of the Astorian population and 25% of the Ethereal population died.

402   Morbidites seized control of Ethereal Region and enslaved the Trepanites.

407   The Astorian Tribes separated into seven tribal regions. Cyril Astor established the kingdom of The Dales, and formed the Knights of Astor; Henri Roberval established the kingdom of Montroix; Viktor Barove established

the kingdom of Barovia; Vladimir Vyatka established Vyatkagrad (later know as Gyptus), Vyatkagrad settlers were primarily of Gypsy heritage. Other tribes often felt they were 'gypped' in business dealings with those from Vyatkagrad and started calling the residents 'Gypsies.' Vyatkagrad was soon labeled as 'Gyptus' and the name stuck. Joshua Esdraelon established the kingdom of Syros; Karl Kronshtadt established the kingdom of Kelterland; Augustus Xylorius established the kingdom of Xylor.

518   War of the Jeweled Cities. The seven tribes united to defend Gyptus from an invasion of sea faring plunderers.

561   War of Kelterland. The seven tribes united and defeated a Morbidite invasion.

577   Ravenshire established its own kingdom. It became the hub of trade for the whole realm and a land of mixed heritage from all the tribes.

603–5 1st War of Ravenshire. Ravenshire defeated Barovia and seized part of the eastern plains.

684–7 2nd War of Ravenshire; Ravenshire defeated an invasion by Kelterland.

687   The Ravenshire Knights are established.

744   The Seven Tribes united for final time to repel a Morbidite invasion.

836   1st Astorian War lasts five years. Six tribes united against the Kelterlander's attempt to take control of the realm. From this point on relations are strained between Kelterland and other tribes. Open travel into Kelterland from other territories diminishes greatly.

904 The Trepanite Campaigns: 110 years of skirmishes against Trepanites who fled slavery in the Ethereal Region. The Trepanites barbaric practices and cannibalism made them unwelcome wherever they went. Each territory raised its own forces to deal with the Trepanite menace. The Trepanites were eventually forced back into the Ethereal Region where they became tunnel dwellers in order to avoid contact with Morbidites. The Ravenshire Knights became a recognized and respected force throughout the realm.

1014 With the end of the Trepanite Campaigns few from the realm venture to the Ethereal Region. Morbidites maintain unfriendly posture to Astorian Realms; they do not invade again. The repulsive Morbidite practice of human sacrifice kept them from trade and voluntary contact with Astorian tribes. Rumors suggested a great evil enveloping the Ethereal Region, a rumor assisted by the Morbidite and Trepanite reputations. Only a few brave adventurers journeyed to the Ethereal Region, most of which never returned. Knowledge of the region faded and was soon mixed with legend, folklore, and outright fantasy.

1179 2nd Astorian War; six tribes united against another Kelterlander bid for conquest of the realm. Eventual truce, but Kelterlanders maintained control of eastern mountains of Syros, and Astoria-capital of the Dales along with the territory between the two rivers; Excelsior became the new capital of The Dales.

1255 3rd Astorian War; Kelterlanders attempted once again to conquer the realm, and again were defeated by the other six tribes who united for the third time.

1282 Novak was born on October 11 to Oskar and Elise Reinhardt.

1283   Zephyr was born on January 17 to Gustav and Katrina Arrisseau. Cad was born on June 18 to Basil and Lara VanKirke. Scorpyus was born in November and abandoned. Liesel Verazzno and her adult son Vasilli took him in.

1290   4th Astorian War began; earlier allegiances were forgotten and much envy was harbored against Ravenshire for its prosperity. Though Ravenshire had always came to the aid of its neighbors in times of war, famine, and pestilence, the other tribes left Ravenshire to fend for them selves. Even the Dales, long time allies of Ravenshire, collapsed under political pressure from the other realms and did not send aid.

1295   The Ravenshire knights are betrayed and massacred.

1296   The fall of Ravenshire to Kelterland; tribes did not unite; this was the beginning of the end for the six tribes.

1298   Cad, Scorpyus, Novak, and Zephyr officially formed the Clandestine Knights and made the small Isles, Jade Inish and Skerry Inish as their bases of operations. Abandoned by the superstitious Kelterlanders as haunted, the tiny islands became a refuge for a small band of friends who wished to reclaim Ravenshire.

1301   The fall of Xylor to Kelterland; remaining tribes still did not unite. In the Dales, the house of Astor sent out a call for assistance, stating remaining tribes must unite to fend off Kelterland's lust for realm domination. King of Montroix rejected their request and signed a neutrality treaty with Kelterland. Gyptus, Barovia, and Syros pledged troops but were unable to stop Kelterland's mighty war machine.

1306   The fall of the Dales to Kelterland; Kelterland was all but unstoppable. Kelterland ruled its conquests with a strong hand. They put their subjects to high taxes, and mandated Kelterland customs and practices.

1311   March 3, the Clandestine Knights were hired to find Hyacinth Blue.

March 13, the Clandestine Knights arrived in Xylor.

March 20–24, the long dormant rebellion against Reddland erupted; Reddland was overthrown and rebels seized control of Xylor.

April 8, in violation of the neutrality treaty, Kelterland marched on Montroix.

June 6, Kelterland began a reprisal against Xylor; Valkyrie's arrive.

MAP OF ASTORIAN REALMS

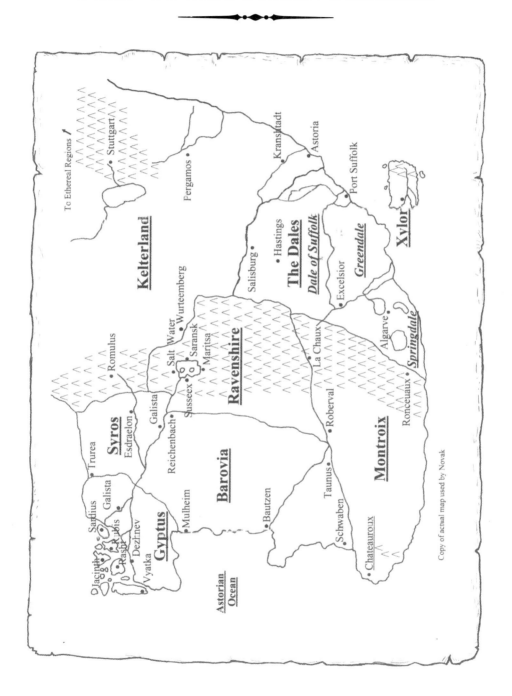

To Ethereal Regions

Stuttgart

Pergamos

Kranstadt

Astoria

Port Suffolk

Kelterland

Hastings

The Dales

Dale of Suffolk

Greendale

Xylor

Salisburg

Excelsior

Salt Water

Wurteemberg

Romulus

Saransk

Maritsa

Ravenshire

Algarve

Springdale

La Chaux

Galista

Susseex

Syros

Esdraelon

Reichenbach

Roberval

Ronceuaux

Barovia

Montroix

Trurea

Mulheim

Bautzen

Taunus

Galista

Schwaben

Sardius

Gyptus

Dezinev

Chateauroux

Jacinth

Rubis

Rasit

Vyatka

Astorian Ocean

Copy of actual map used by Novak

MAP OF RAVENSCLAW

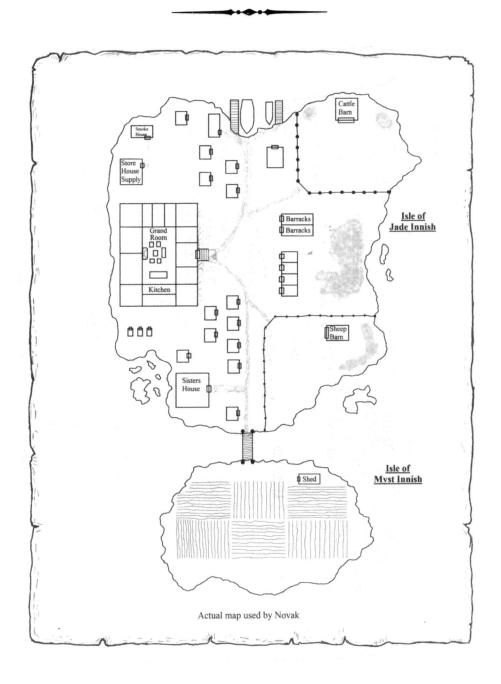

Actual map used by Novak

PREFACE

FREEDOM IN XYLOR was bought at a great price. Through muscle, sweat, and the shedding of blood, liberty was gained for a forlorn people. Precious blood was shed by the finest society had to offer, and yet the times were full of evil. It was a time when danger lurked behind every corner and every shadow held death. Dark days lay ahead of that first victory, days that tried the souls of men. Most others would have abandoned us in our desolate state: but not the four strangers from Ravenshire. They were faithful and loyal when others had failed.

I've often thought about the Clandestine Knights in the years since they first appeared in Xylor. It has been said 'for days such as those are heroes born.' I regard that as true. For it was in our darkest hour that the four blazed brightest. Obedient to their calling, they and their friends restored peace to a corrupted land. To maintain that peace would require further sacrifice. It was a burden four strangers continued to bear. And history didn't care.

There are still those who would say a true Knight is born of nobility and is well educated in the social graces. I have to disagree. Knights are forged by fiery trials. They are ordinary people who respond courageously to extraordinary circumstances. They stand against tremendous opposition to do what is right. How can you ever thank them?

All I can do is to tell their story…

"…and precious shall their blood be in His sight."—Psalm 72:14

PROLOGUE

—————•◦✦◦•—————

"SWORD! SWORD!" SCORPYUS'S weapon flew, spiraling from his hand and landed in a patch of grass near the trail. Scorpyus, now defenseless, cried out for assistance. There was a throbbing sensation in his hand caused by the explosive dislodging of his weapon. His burly opponent could hit as hard as Novak. His attacker relentlessly hacked away with his blade in a bloodthirsty search for flesh. The menacing man's sword tore chunks from the earth near Scorpyus's feet and whistled through the air about his face and body. Frantically the stout man tried to carve a limb from his flighty foe. Scorpyus ducked and dodged, barely keeping a half second ahead of death. Much to the stout man's dismay, Scorpyus was too agile to land a hit on. It was worse than trying to catch a fish with your bare hands.

Zephyr craned her neck toward the sound of her friend's plea for help. She saw Scorpyus fling his arms up and jerk his torso back just as a blade swung by his mid-section. Scorpyus didn't wear armor. He instead relied on lightning speed for his protection, and his stout opponent was taxing every bit of it.

"Scorpyus, here!" She pulled her own sword and flung it through the air, over the head of his attacker toward Scorpyus. It sailed end over end clattering to rest on the trail. Her aim was off by ten feet. She contemplated loosing an arrow at the man but feared she might hit Scorpyus as he was circling and sidestepping in a most unpredictable manner. Behind her Cad and Novak were busy with two other opponents.

Scorpyus dove for the sword, sliding supine for a few feet and quickly rolling to his back. He sprang to his feet in time to block his attacker's downward blow. Now the fight was back on an even field. Scorpyus moved in on his burly, brown-toothed foe, his burgundy tabard flapping about with his motions. He brought his long sword into his opponent from every imaginable angle only to have it blocked. His attacker, relying heavily on his large shield and armor, proved to be a formidable adversary with better fighting skills then expected. What he lacked in oral hygiene, he made up for in stamina. Scorpyus usually tired out his opponents rather quickly by keeping them swinging wildly at places he once stood. The brute he now faced was up to the task.

Cad locked swords with his attacker and pushed the short, stubby man back. The man braced his sword with both hands keeping Cad's blade inches from his face. Cad pushed his way in close; so close he could feel the man's hot panting breath on his brow. A fishy garlic stench assaulted his nostrils. Cad tried to force his blade into the short man's neck but they were locked in a gritty stalemate for the moment.

The stout man's pudgy face protruded from his chain mail hood, and Cad couldn't help but notice how ugly the man was. Perhaps obscenely hideous was a better description. The man was obviously a rough sort, and had much combat experience. He looked like the type one would expect to find camped out at a tavern near the docks. With several grotesque scars on his cheeks and chin, it looked as if he had taken a few blows to the face. But most gruesome of all was that the man lost the front half of his nose. Two black holes stared Cad in the eye filling him with nausea. The flesh around his nose was jagged. It looked as if rats chewed it off instead of it being cleanly severed in combat.

"Bloody aye mate, you're a freak." Cad repulsed, tried to push the man away. The enraged man braced himself vehemently. Furious from Cad's insult he was determined not to move.

"What's the matter? Is momma's pretty boy fearing me?" The man growled with a gravely voice.

Cad brought his knee hard into his opponent's belly causing the short man to let out a guttural grunt and step back. A thick mist sprayed from the two black holes in the man's face, showering Cad.

"Get a mask for those, mate. Did your face catch fire and some bloke put it out with a rake?" Cad wiped his mouth and goatee with his sleeve as he raised his shield to block his opponent's retaliatory blow. Snorting like a bull, the man swung violently at Cad. He didn't like smart mouths, and besides, Cad was wearing a cuirass and greaves that would go well with the short man's chain mail.

Novak was fighting a man who kept circling around like a sheep dog. Each time Novak took a swing, the agile man would run around to the side just out of sword range and poke at Novak with his spear, all the while hooting and hollering. The man was jittery and jumpy like a nervous cat, but very fast. Whether he was trying to attack from behind, or just stay out of the way of Novak's two-handed sword was not known. Either way, Novak was getting impatient with the run and hide game. If the agile man thought his wooden shield was going to protect him forever he was mistaken. It already showed signs of being damaged, and running in circles was not a fighting technique that led to victory. Novak decided to take his time and study his opponent in case it was a ruse.

Zephyr took in the late afternoon scene not having an opponent to fight. She watched, confident her friends would have this latest threat dispatched shortly. With her forest green cap and short cape, and her brown tunic and boots she looked at home in the wilderness. Minutes earlier she and her friends had been walking the wooded trail to Sage when three highwaymen looking for an easy heist jumped them. Thievery had seen a sharp increase following the recent change of power in Xylor. Many thugs were emboldened by the temporarily unorganized new government. Unfortunately for the would-be-robbers they unknowingly picked the Clandestine Knights as their next victims.

Zephyr watched intently as her friends fought with their attackers. Even though the fight seemed to be going well, she felt uneasy in the pit of her stomach and she didn't know what to make of it. As usual, there was a cool breeze on the island of Xylor but Zephyr felt warm and flushed. She hoped she wasn't coming down with an illness.

There was a slight rustle in the bushes twenty feet to the left of the trail. Zephyr eyed the area where the noise came expecting to see a chipmunk scurry about. Nothing appeared so she turned her attention back toward the fight. Then she heard it again and this time it sounded a little farther away. Just north of the trail amidst the trees was a thick patch of manzanita brush. Something was definitely there, and this time it sounded bigger than a chipmunk.

Zephyr moved a little closer to get a better look. A bead of sweat ran down her cheek and she ran the back of her hand across her brow. Her forehead felt warm and moist and her shoulder ached when she moved her arm. In fact, all of her joints ached a bit. Her neck felt stiff, and the discomfort seemed to travel down her spine to her hips. Putting the pain aside she peered into the brush trying to discover what was making the noise. To her side she still heard the clanking of swords and she took a quick glance to make sure her friends were doing all right. All was going fine. It looked as if her friends were wearing down their attackers.

She took two more steps closer to the brush then froze when she saw a branch move; whatever it was had to be the size of a deer. Her heart pounded in her chest as she glared into the bush.

Then there was another noise! It was the faintest sound of metal scraping against brush. Zephyr's eyes grew wide with a sick realization. There was no deer in the bushes. With a curse, a man suddenly sprang from between the branches of manzanita with a bow drawn. His clothes were filthy and he had a wild growth of hair on his head and face. Leaves and twigs protruded from his tangled locks. The man looked right at Scorpyus.

The world suddenly ground to a halt, and everything became slow motion. The sounds of the forest were replaced by a dull thumping sound echoing in Zephyr's ears. Zephyr felt like she was neck deep in thick mud. Her arms and legs seemed to weigh a ton, and to move required great effort. She turned to warn her friends of the danger as yet another man with a battle ax emerged from the undergrowth. He bounded agonizingly slow toward the melee. Something was wrong. Her friends and their opponents were fighting in slow deliberate motions as if they were underwater. Zephyr drew in a deep breath and shouted a warning. It took an eternity to get it out, and when her voice left her throat it sounded low and distorted.

Zephyr saw an arrow glide slowly through the air and burry itself deep in Scorpyus's back. Scorpyus gritted his teeth and arched backwards before he toppled heavily to the ground.

"No!" Zephyr's voice came out in a deep groan. Her peripheral vision washed out, and everything seemed to be tainted in a brownish hue. The sound of a bell chiming rang through her head. The bell was clear and crisp, unlike the dull thudding of swords clashing and muted footsteps. It struck Zephyr as peculiar that there would be a bell chiming in the forest.

Cad's gaze shifted towards the manzanita. Zephyr felt sick. She saw Cad's nose-less attacker raise his sword and bring it down. Cad's attention diverted to the new attackers coming from the brush. Though the man's action seemed painstakingly slow, she could do nothing to warn Cad. A quarter time nightmare unfolded before her eyes and a feeling of complete helplessness came over her.

Cad let out an agonizing groan when his arm was severed. The limb floated through the air and bounced off the ground, a sword still clenched in its fist. Zephyr panicked. She tried to run to her friend's assistance but her legs were paralyzed. Her heartbeat throbbed in her ears and she could hear herself breathe. Her breath sounded like a blacksmith's bellows, deep and throaty. Her eyes screamed out to God for the nightmare to end.

Zephyr watched helplessly as the two men from the bushes and the ones that had been attacking Scorpyus and Cad, now all turned their attention on Novak. In a lumbering slow motion they bounded toward the hulking Novak and surrounded him. Her friend braced himself for an attack from all sides.

Zephyr felt faint and wanted to vomit. Tears welled up in her eyes and began cascading down her cheeks. Her knees became wobbly, and she could feel herself trembling like a leaf. She sank slowly to the ground; the atmosphere felt thick and heavy. She tried to go help Novak, but her feet were heavy and her strength sapped. In agonizing despair she could only watch as Novak was lost in the swarm of swinging arms that slowly engulfed him. Was this how it was going to end? Something was terribly wrong here. None of this made sense. This wasn't supposed to happen. Abnormalities abounded for which Zephyr was powerless to overcome. Darkness swallowed up her vision. The circle of light shrank and shrank until it became a pinpoint and then eventually disappeared.

Zephyr felt a stab in her side, and didn't care. She could do nothing to defend herself. Her body was paralyzed. Slowly she closed her eyes and resigned herself to her fate. She didn't want to live knowing she did nothing to help her friends. With them gone she had no desire to live. She may as well join them.

Zephyr felt another stab at her side and sank further and further into a murky unconsciousness. There was another jab and she could feel herself weeping, her chest heaving in small quick breaths. All of a sudden a pinhole of light formed in the middle of the blackness and grew larger and larger. Soon the light was so bright she had to squint, its rays radiating out in all directions. It was so incredibly bright she wanted to shield her eyes with her hand but couldn't move.

A peace came over Zephyr; a peace she never felt before. Was the light heaven? She felt another poke in the side. It didn't hurt. In fact she could barely feel it. Nothing mattered anymore. Soon she would be with her friends in a better place.

Zephyr heard a voice. It was calling her name! It was calling her from the light. No it was trying to call her away from the light. She didn't want to go back to the forest and fought it with all her might. The voice was insistent but Zephyr didn't want to listen. She didn't want to leave the light, especially now with her friends gone.

I

"HEY," CAD WHISPERED as he poked Zephyr in the ribs through her cell door. She lay on a small pile of straw, her short cape rolled up as a makeshift pillow. The straw did little to soften the hard stone floor of the jail cell, but it was better than nothing.

Cad looked through the cold gray bars separating his cell from Zephyr's. His friend was having a nightmare, whimpering as she tossed about on the floor, her copper hair dark with sweat. She had been sick for several days, and eaten little. Cad was worried how much more her petite frame could take.

"Wake up." Cad poked her harder this time. Zephyr's eyes shot open with a startle. Immediately she squinted at the bright sun shining in her eyes from the solitary window in the stone cell wall.

"Where are we?" Zephyr turned toward Cad trying to blink him into focus. Her face was moist with perspiration, and extremely pale.

Cad released a sympathetic sigh. "We're in jail, in Kelterland. Don't you remember?" Somewhere in the distance a large bell chimed.

Zephyr swallowed. Her mouth was dry and her tongue ached with thirst.

"Here, you better drink a bit." Cad ladled out some water from a wooden bucket in his cell and held it through the bars for Zephyr. She forced herself to sit up, her joints achy and her neck and shoulders stiff. She pulled her knees up, her soft leather boots scraping across the stone floor. The move took all the energy she could muster and left her light headed.

Zephyr drank greedily finishing the contents of the ladle with a deep sigh. Cad quickly refilled it.

"Still feeling pretty bad, ay?" Cad watched her drink down the second ladle.

Zephyr wiped her mouth with the back of her sleeve and gently lowered her body back down to the stone floor. She repositioned her short cape under her head.

"Oui, but I do not feel as bad as yesterday. I pray this illness will pass quickly. I cannot stand much more of this." Zephyr's normally dazzling green eyes were dull and sunken with dark bags underneath them. Her cheeks were slightly drawn and her full red lips were now pasty white. She struggled to stay awake but found the task impossible.

"Well go on and get your rest. There's not a bloody thing we can do now anyway." Cad surveyed his dismal surroundings. He and Zephyr were in 8'x6' cells, each furnished with only a wooden bucket of water with ladle, a battered wooden plate for a daily meal, and a pile of straw to sleep on. Utensils were viewed as potential weapons so prisoners ate with their hands. Prisoners used a clay jar to relieve themselves in. If they were lucky a guard would empty the jar regularly, but right now it seemed to be a non-priority. Cad's jar hadn't been emptied in three days, and the air in the jail was becoming fetid. This added to the scent of disease and decay that wafted through the place.

Gray bars made up three sides of his cell. The fourth wall was of stone with a two-foot hole cut in for a window. The window was barred, and open to the outside air. In the day it provided some relief from the thick air of the jail. At night however, it provided a way for the cold air to enter. Chattering teeth and shivering limbs accompanied all slumber.

There were eight other cells to Cad's right. Zephyr's was the only cell to his left. She was in a corner and had one of the only cells to have two stonewalls instead of one. Ten additional cells were across the way from Cad, a wide corridor separated them.

The jail had a rat problem, but it was more evident at night. The pests would scavenge any uneaten food. In the absence of scraps, the rats would settle for chewing on one of the prisoners. Most of which were often too ill to ward them off. Cad made Zephyr sleep close to the bars so he could keep them away from her. At first, when one of the damnable rats ventured into Cad's cell, he would grab it by the tail and slam it against the floor, then toss it out the window. Lately he had been bartering the dead rats to those who wished to supplement their diet. Cad wasn't that desperate yet, and with a looming death sentence, he saw no reason to be. He gladly traded two or three rats for a piece of crusty bread, usually to those facing a long stay in the prison.

Their daily meal consisted of a chunk of spoiled meat heavily salted to mask the foul taste, and a piece of stale or moldy bread. Often times Cad had to soak the bread in water in order to be able to eat it.

They lived in squalid conditions, and disease was rampant. Dampness clung to the walls in a murky slime and mold was ever present. Some prisoners developed a deep hacking cough that often proved fatal. Others contracted maladies caused by a poor diet. Already two men in Cad's vicinity died in the short time he had been in the jail. There was plenty of disease to go around. So far Cad was one of the two lucky ones in his cellblock to avoid illness.

Cad and Zephyr had been in their cells for several days. They had been captured in Xylor and shipped to Kelterland to stand trial for treason. Both were accused of participating in a rebellion that overthrew the Count of Xylor, a liege of the King of Kelterland, thereby undermining Kelterland's claim to the territory. Half of the island's inhabitants counted the demise of the Count as a blessing. Luther Reddland, the Count of Xylor, had ruled the island for ten years. The few who opposed his bid for power and warned others of trusting the charismatic stranger had been silenced. They either fled Xylor or died in mysterious accidents. Thus Luther's opposition soon diminished.

Despite being appointed Count by the King of Kelterland, Luther violently asserted his power. He had been granted some autonomy, and allowed to maintain his own Royal Guard rather then be occupied by a contingent of the King's Brigade. Xylor was the only territory conquered by Kelterland that allowed such a luxury. It spoke volumes of Reddland's friends in high places. It also saved Kelterland considerable resources and manpower.

The Royal Guard insured Reddland's power hold on Xylor. Thousands died in the struggle and few dared to challenge his authority. The occasional outbreak or revolt was soon crushed. Anyone even remotely suspected of being part of a rebellion was swiftly put to death. As Luther continued to rule the people began to fear his authority. Most Xylorians could relate stories of public executions, mysterious disappearances, even the arrest of whole families. More than one family had been burned out of their home. Luther was sure to punish any crime swiftly and ruthlessly and very few were pardoned. Often he engaged in random killings as a means of controlling the populace. What Luther didn't know was that a formidable rebellion had been brewing. That rebellion succeeded in overthrowing Reddland and his murderous regime. Reddland soon met the end he dealt out to countless others.

Cad, Zephyr and the other Clandestine Knights had been hired to find a rare medicine for an anonymous wealthy customer. They were in Xylor on the quest when they unknowingly became entangled in the rebellion. Upon being made aware of the situation, they agreed it was a worthy cause and decided to help. They soon discovered Reddland was the wealthy customer and that fact made the decision all the easier. Cad and Zephyr had been captured while assisting the transitional government. They were now sentenced to death without the benefit of trial, and awaited their fate in the dank jail of Astoria, a coastal town in Kelterland. Novak and Scorpyus managed to elude capture. Cad hadn't heard from them and wondered if they even knew where he and Zephyr were. Cad feared the worst. He prayed Novak and Scorpyus would find him in time. Cad rose from the filthy cell floor and went to the window. The fresh air felt good on his face, and revived him a little. Pigeons cooed from their roost somewhere up above. Cad looked out into the free world with a longing. The stone structures of the downtown area stretched forever. Astoria was the largest and wealthiest coastal town in Kelterland. The town had already made a fortune on the shipping and fishing industry when a cadre of minors discovered a vast treasure trove of riches in the nearby hills. The diamond mines of Kronshtadt fueled the local economy with an obscene amount of abundant wealth. The famous city was one of the jewels of the Kelterland Empire.

Horse drawn carts rolled down the streets of Astoria, and people mingled about in the mid-day sun. Everything was a bustle of activity in the city with a reputation for never sleeping. Every imaginable from of entertainment, the finest clothing, or type of merchandise was available for the right price in Astoria. Every sort of person could be found there, be it good, evil, strange, normal, or bizarre. The place was filled with those who came to seek their fortune, and those who already found it. The finest architecture and most elaborate landscaping the world had ever scene existed in this fascinating city. The city was beautiful, but also contained a seedy and dangerous underside. One could come to Astoria and take in the finest life had to offer. However, if one wasn't careful, the city could swallow you up and leave nothing for the buzzards.

Down the street Cad saw a gentleman help a lady from a wagon, both well dressed in the latest fashions. A teenage boy was selling apples from a handcart as a man in a white apron swept the boardwalk behind him. An angry man with a meat clever was chasing a stray dog, a string of sausages dangling from its mouth, away from the butcher shop. Men on horseback, ladies out shopping, and soldiers from the King's Brigade all went about their daily business. It was unnerving to be so close to the normal way of life, and yet be so far removed. Cad had only to turn around to be reminded of his bleak fate. He spent most of his time at the window gazing at the city with its distant rolling hills and white cloudy sky.

Cad heard hammering in the distance. From what he was able to piece together, scaffolding was being built in the town square for his and Zephyr's execution. He knew their time was running out. He prayed Novak and Scorpyus were on their way to rescue them. In a town of this size with so large of a contingent of the King's Brigade the odds didn't look good. Nevertheless, Cad had the utmost confidence in his friend's abilities. It would have been near impossible to catch the wily Scorpyus. He was an expert at vanishing and evasion. Novak was another story. Cad liked to joke about Novak and his occasional incarcerations; usually caused by his explosive temper. He had every confidence his friends would assist in this dire moment if they were at all able.

"Ahh!" A scream pierced the cellblock.

Cad was startled and turned to see a thin gaunt man hop to his feet and scurry to the side of his cell.

"It bit me! The cursed rat bit me!" The man bellowed on the verge of insanity.

"I can't take it any more! They're eating us alive!" The man slowly sank to the floor sobbing uncontrollably. He looked as if he had been in prison a while, his clothes had nearly rotted off his body. He had long stringy, matted hair and a long stringy beard.

Cad himself had not had a bath or shave since he was arrested. His charcoal gray tunic and breeches were by now heavily soiled, and his goatee was turning into a full beard. Dried blood stained his collar from an undressed laceration on the back of his neck. If one of the prisoners wanted to bathe they had to use their daily ration of drinking water. At one bucket a day, water was a scarcity.

The wooden door at the end of the hall opened and slammed against the wall. Three armed men from the King's Brigade entered Cad's cellblock and headed straight for him and Zephyr. One was carrying shackle irons, and another jangled a set of keys. They stopped at Cad's cell first.

The men wore the black surcoats with silver piping of the King's Brigade. Heraldry consisting of a red two-headed serpent emblazoned on both the back and front of the surcoats. Baggy gray breeches tucked into mid-calf high boots extended from beneath the surcoats. Each was armed with a sword and wore the traditional chain mail hood and coat with supporting plate greaves and gauntlets. Troops from the King's Brigade looked to be made up of a rougher sort of character than the Royal Guard in Xylor. These three were not carrying their shields, but wore the dark gray helmets with an extending nasal brace to protect the nose. All three had grown accustomed with their assignment at the jail, and appeared bored.

"Let me see your hands." One man ordered Cad to place his hands through the slot in the cell door that was also used for passing food in and out. When Cad complied the soldier placed shackle irons on his wrists.

"Now step back." The man unlocked the door and the other two men grabbed Cad by the arms taking him from the cell. Once out of his cell he thought about attempting an escape but he wouldn't leave Zephyr. Cad decided he would wait until he was outside to make his move. He hoped his friends would be there to help.

The guard with the keys went to Zephyr's cell.

"On your feet," The man ordered. Zephyr remained motionless on the ground.

"She's very ill mate. I don't think she'll be up to walking." Cad offered.

"We'll see." The guard unlocked Zephyr's cell door and walked in cautiously. He kicked her in the thigh to rouse her awake.

Zephyr shifted her leg and let out a slight moan. "What?" She peered through slits in her eyelids at the figure standing over her.

"I said, on your feet."

Zephyr forced herself to sit up. It was a difficult feat. With trembling arms she retrieved her short cape and fastened it in place. She paused for a moment to recover from the activity. Zephyr panted slightly, her cool and clammy face looked at the brooding guard. Awareness of what was transpiring set in.

"Is it time already?" She glanced worriedly at Cad who replied with a single nod. A cloud of desperation came over her.

"But, I…" Zephyr looked to Cad searching for some sign in his eyes everything would be all right. There was none. She pulled her damp hair back from her face and struggled to stand.

"Oh, for the love of Balar. We haven't got all day!" The guard cursed and called angrily upon Balar the dual headed serpent god of the Kelterlanders. He shackled Zephyr in wrist irons, then jammed her cap under her belt and jerked her to her feet roughly.

"Let's go!" The guard gripped Zephyr's arm tightly and forced her along. She teetered down the hall bumping into cell doors as she went. It angered the guard who responded by striking Zephyr in the face.

"Beating her won't help, you bloody idiot!" Cad strained against the two guards who held him back.

"Shut up!" A guard backhanded Cad snapping his head to the side. Cad shoved one of his escorts against a cell door with his shoulder, and pushed him hard against the bars. The other tried desperately to free his friend who was gasping for breath. Cad's struggle was in vain. Within seconds two more guards entered the cellblock, running for the ruckus.

"You two take her. She won't walk."

The two new guards each took one of Zephyr's arms and walked her down the corridor. She stumbled and almost fainted. The guards half carried half dragged her. Zephyr would not be allowed to be late for her execution. The other three concentrated on Cad and brought him quickly under control. They gave him a few shots to the ribs and then continued escorting him down the corridor.

Cad and Zephyr were led down stairs through the dimly lit prison. All along the way cries could be heard from other prisoners, moans echoed down hallways, and wails came out of the darkness. The stench of the lower levels was unbearable and far worse then the level where Cad and Zephyr had been. Disease and decay hung thick in the air. The lower levels had fewer windows, which gave the prison even more of a dank, depressing feel then it already had. The lower area also looked to be older. Cad realized the top two stories must have been recently constructed to expand the jail. Most of the inmates were men, but there were a handful of women scattered around. Apparently Astoria made no distinctions between male and female prisoners, treating them all the same.

Cad squinted in the morning sun after he was shoved through a doorway into an alley. Zephyr was forced along behind. The guards walked them down the alley and into a huge courtyard. Gray stone buildings, many elaborately adorned with large pillars ringed the rectangular courtyard, and several streets led to this central location where most of the town business was carried out. On this day hundreds of people gathered to watch the execution.

Cad peered out into the crowd as he was led to the scaffold. Soldiers from the King's Brigade stood shoulder-to-shoulder forming a protective barrier around the scaffold in order to keep spectators at bay. The eager masses were ready to see some excitement. In a city where there had to be a thousand things to do, people queued up to watch an execution. Many dressed for the occasion as if they were attending a social event. Cad wondered at the oddity. What possessed people to take time out of his or her day to watch someone be killed? Didn't they see enough during the war? Here were young couples, families with children, businessmen, old and young alike, all acting as if they were attending a summer gala. The courtyard was packed full. Enterprising merchants worked the crowds selling food and drink. No doubt pickpockets worked the masses as well. Cad shook his head.

On the scaffold stood a well fed man dressed in a regal purple coat and breeches. The coat sported fancy gold stitched embroidery. Underneath the coat he wore a black velveteen vest that covered a frilly white shirt. Pudgy hands extended from lacy cuffs. His curly black hair was covered with an ornate cap. Cad learned from one of his guards that this was the lord mayor of Astoria.

The mayor was a ruddy-faced fellow with a long mustache waxed to a point. He held a scroll clenched in his fist, and strutted the stage with an air of superiority. Beside the mayor stood and aged and stoop-shouldered man in a hooded brown cloak. He had a gray beard and penetrating eyes peered out from the hood. He gave Cad a hostile stare.

Also on the scaffold was a large man wearing a black cloak with a hood over his head covering his face. He stood ready in front of a block of wood holding an axe. The guards walked Cad and Zephyr up the eight stairs to the top of the scaffold.

"What are we going to do?" Zephyr whispered to Cad. The walk to the courtyard had raised her level of alertness. Of course fresh air and fear also played a part.

Cad swallowed hard. "I…don't know." He scanned the crowd looking for a friendly face but found none. If he was to make his move he would have to do it soon, but where would he go? There was a ring of soldiers around him not to mention hundreds of people. The situation looked grim. If Scorpyus or Novak were in Astoria he didn't know where. The previous weeks had been very harrowing and anything was possible. Cad had no idea what transpired since the night of his capture.

A murmur circulated through the crowd as the prisoners were walked up to the scaffold, and many onlookers wagged their heads disapprovingly. Each stood on the tips of their toes or craned their necks to get a better look at the condemned. Some started to push and shove, trying to work their way closer to the action. They were met with scowls from the soldiers who formed the protective barrier.

The lord mayor stepped forward and raised a hand to quiet the crowd. A hush fell over the gathering and he continued, unrolling the scroll.

The mayor read in a loud voice.

"By proclamation of King Phinehas Faust of Kelterland, supreme ruler of this land and all her territories, these two prisoners, a Cadwallader VanKirke of Ravenshire, and a Zephyr Arrisseau, also of Ravenshire, are hereby sentenced to death for the following crimes against the kingdom:

1. They willfully and intentionally, by force of arms, took action and lead the overthrow of the King's representative in the territory of Xylor, murdering Luther Reddland the Count of Xylor.
2. They engaged in and lead a revolt resulting in the murder of over one thousand soldiers of the Royal Guard, and injury to scores of others.
3. They conspired with a rebellion whose actions included theft of property belonging to the kingdom, injury to Royal personnel, and a general disruption to the lives of the kingdom's citizenry.

4.   They disobeyed the laws and injunctions forbidding the
     practice of other than the state sanctioned religion for
     the territory.
5.   They participated in the intentional burning of the
     King's property, namely a warehouse at the port of Xylor.
6.   They displayed irreverence to Tanuba, the official
     goddess of Xylor, going so far as to purge the island of
     all things bearing her image or name."

"For these high crimes of treason, Cadwallader VanKirke
and Zephyr Arrisseau will now be executed publicly. Let this be a
reminder to all that the King does not tolerate treachery against
the kingdom and her peoples." The lord mayor shook his head
approvingly at the gasps that rose from the gathering at the
reading of the charges. Clearly, many were shocked to think the
two standing shackled before them were responsible for wreaking
so much havoc. Cad, not having a shave, the luxury of a bath or
a change of clothes was starting to look as if he could have been
guilty of such things. For many it was hard to believe that the frail
and petite Zephyr could have been a part of a huge conspiracy.
Some surmised it must have been Cad that led Zephyr astray into
the depths of the underworld. Women had to be careful around
such rough and unsavory men or their end would be just as
appalling
   "And now Felix, High Cleric from the Temple of Balar will
have a moment with the prisoners before they are put to death."
The mayor stepped back and the stoop-shouldered man in the
hooded brown cloak came forward.
   Cad looked at the cleric with disgust. "You may as bloody
well save your breath. I'll be having none of your snake religion."
   "Do not haste toward an arrogant decision my young man.
You shall have but one last time to renounce your God in the
hopes of finding mercy with Balar the deity in whose land you
now find yourself." Felix had a low whispery voice that sounded

like wind moaning across the top of a clay jar in a storm. It was a voice that belonged in a nightmare.

"Blessed be the Lord God forever." Cad stated flatly and looked away from the cleric. He left little doubt as to where his allegiances lay.

"Suit yourself, but you will come to regret your inflexibility shortly. Your narrow mindedness is the reason you are in this position in the first place, and yet you fail to see the error of your actions." Felix glared at Cad his dark eyes boring holes into him.

"On the contrary old man, it is you who are blind to your present state. The one true…" Cad's head snapped violently back as a guard backhanded him.

"You will show respect for the High Cleric and address him as such!" The guard demanded of Cad.

"*This can not be happening!*" Zephyr thought to herself. Tears welled up in her eyes as she scanned the crowd for some hope of rescue. Scorpyus and Novak probably couldn't make it to the mainland. She prayed they were all right where ever they were.

Cad turned back to the cleric, blood oozing from the corner of his mouth. He remained silent. He didn't see any way he could escape. There were too many guards, and there were too many people. Maybe he would have a slim chance alone, but there was no way he was leaving Zephyr. He would die before leaving her and it looked like he would indeed.

"Perhaps the female will show more wisdom, and be willing to accept the reality of her current status here in Kelterland." Felix would waste no more time on the defiant Cad, and went to Zephyr.

"Peddle your bloody lies elsewhere old man!" Cad's parting remark was met with another blow to the chin. He glared at the guard, anger bubbling to the surface.

"What about you young lady? Are you willing to perish defying the god of this land? I encourage you to be wise. Don't be resistant like your unfortunate friend here. Beg for mercy from

Balar and renounce your God." Felix's monadic voice droned to those on the scaffold.

The crowd was becoming restless, and shifted to see what was happening. Those in the front were able to hear the dialogue, but those farther back had no idea what was being said. Much to their amusement they did know Cad upset one of the guards.

"Monsieur, I cannot do this thing you ask. Far be it from me that I should ever renounce my God. I would sooner die first." Zephyr was polite, even to those who would see her harm.

"And die you shall." The mayor stepped forward again having run out of patience and anxious to proceed. Felix placed a hand on Cad's shoulder and whispered something in his ear. Cad listened then shrugged the Cleric's hand from his shoulder.

"We are ready to proceed. Guards, place the first prisoner in place at the chopping block." The mayor proclaimed in a loud voice so all gathered in the courtyard would be sure to hear.

A wave of excitement swept over the gathering and then all fell silent. Many of those in the front rows shook their heads with displeasure at Cad as he was placed into position at the chopping block. Cad took one last look out into the crowd. A man selling food from a wagon was off to his right. Business was at a stop for the man as all eyes were on those on the scaffold.

Zephyr was agonized by what was happening and her chest heaved with sobs as Cad knelt before the chopping block. The guard placed Cad's neck squarely in the middle of block. It looked as if Cad were hugging the block with the chain from his shackles draped just above his head.

Cad faced the right toward his executioner, staring at the man's feet. He would face the next moments fearlessly like the true warrior he was. He would not give his captors the satisfaction of seeing him weak. He was confident God would see him through. People in the crowd waved their fists at him. He refused to look at them. Cad quietly prayed as he fixed his gaze on the executioner's feet.

Zephyr was scared and frantic inside. She felt she would be trembling if her body could have mustered the strength. Tears trickled down her cheeks and burned a trail to her chin. How did life come to this? She was only twenty-eight years old. Just over a week ago life was good. She and her friends helped a people reclaim their island from the oppressive Kelterland. The Kelterlanders annexed Xylor ten years earlier after a long and bloody war. All Zephyr and her friends did was help make things right, and now she was about to watch one of her friends be killed.

"Cad, save yourself!" Zephyr knew Cad would have tried to escape had it not been for her. She felt she was too ill to run long enough to escape. Cad's chances of escaping while carrying her were nil.

"S'il vous plait, go on! Do not worry about me, save yourself!" Zephyr pleaded for Cad to try to save himself. She felt terrible he would rather die then abandon her now.

"Must we both die? Cad, S'il vous plait; go now," Zephyr pleaded with her friend amidst a shower of tears.

"Shut her up." The mayor ordered. A guard clasped his hand over the sobbing Zephyr's mouth. She heaved uncontrollably.

"It'll be fine." Cad tried to reassure his friend.

"Proceed." The lord mayor signaled the executioner, who was clearly perturbed by the delay. The hooded man positioned himself and raised his razor sharp axe.

Zephyr closed her eyes unable to witness the carnage. The last thing she wanted as she left this world was the memory of Cad's death going through her mind.

"Oh, God…Oh, God." Zephyr sobbed and squeezed her eyes tight. She felt weak and dizzy. Her vision became a blur of memories as she collapsed on the scaffolding. In a traumatic daze, scenes flashed through the portal of her mind, her sub-conscious trying to protect her from the evil reality of her fate. Insanity was being beat back by a brain unwilling to surrender. For the moment she was back in Xylor; back before this heart-wrenching turn of events. She and all her friends were having a discussion around the table, laughing, joking, and enjoying a good time. Her memory of that day was so vivid it was as if she were still there. Footsteps sounded around her but Zephyr refused to believe they were there. Instead she drifted farther and farther back into her memories, back to that day of warmth and friendship. She heard the thud of the ax come down and fainted.

II

———◆•◆•◆———

NOVAK FORCED HIS razor sharp blade deep into the flesh until he came to bone. With a flick of the wrist he severed a sizable piece of meat.

"This is good ham; my compliments to the cook." Novak spooned some lentils onto his plate and grabbed a piece of bread. He had been out on patrol with Cad all morning, and the hot meal was well received. On his way back to his seat he dipped his tankard into a cask of cider at the end of the banquet table to refill it. He was relieved to be drinking something besides tea, which was the traditional beverage of Xylorians. The herbal brew was grown locally, and was a blend of three different tea leaves. It was called Astorian Black, and very popular in the Dales as well. Though quite good, Novak had grown weary of drinking it at every meal.

When Novak sat across from Zephyr she decided to rib him. "Did you not see the ladle hanging from the cask?"

"Ya, is that what that was? I thought it was a cup with a long bent handle. And I already have one, so..." Novak brought a round of laughter to the small gathering. "What I need is some milk. There are cows everywhere; why not milk?"

"How do you like the cider Cad? I was just getting used to the tea." Scorpyus added. He favored Gyptus Bitter tea. The Astorian Black tea served in the rest of the realm was a little too weak for his tastes.

Cad shrugged his shoulders. "I'd rather have a spot of tea myself. I never was able to develop a fondness for apples."

"I like cider." Zephyr added while sipping from her cup. She eyed Novak's plate.

"There is more up there if you want it. You don't have to steel it from me anymore." Novak teased.

"I tell you I am not hungry; and besides I would not steal your food even if I was hungry." Zephyr feigned a miffed expression. She knew where this conversation was headed.

"That is not true. You stole my bread once." Novak exclaimed.

"I did not!" she retorted

"Ask Cad and Scorpyus." Novak pointed to the pair who both nodded their heads in the affirmative.

"That's true mate." Cad added. "Remember when Novak tripped and fell down the stairs at Ravensclaw? You ran to him rather quickly. We thought you were going to help him up, but instead you took the piece of bread out of his hand and ate it."

"I did not want it to get ruined by falling on the floor." Zephyr laughed hysterically, recalling the event. The others joined in the laughter of the memory. It was a story Novak liked to tell.

Emerald sat next to Novak and watched him eat. His fork looked so tiny in his large hand. She enjoyed what little time they had together. Having finished her meal she pushed her plate away.

"That was delicious." She looked across to Scorpyus. "Is it true that in Gyptus they put butter in their tea?"

"I've only been to Gyptus once but I believe they do. My grandmother put butter in tea when she made it. Either way Gyptus Bitter is the best." Scorpyus was of Gypsy heritage and many people assumed because of that, he must know all about customs in Gyptus, land of the Gypsies.

"Oh, I didn't mean to…" Emerald didn't get to finish her sentence.

"Ahh, don't worry about it," he waved a hand at her. "It's a common mistake."

At the head of the table was Thadus, the new leader of Xylor. He was a rugged man in his mid forties, and had been guiding the Xylorians for the last three months in their efforts to restore order after the overthrow of Reddland's oppressive regime. It had been a daunting task fraught with much difficulty. The sleeves of his white cotton shirt were rolled up to the elbow to reveal thick, hairy forearms. He stroked his graying beard thoughtfully as he looked around the table at his gathered guests.

To Thadus's right sat his older brother Bartus. Bartus was a thin, frail man with wispy gray hair. Until recently he lived under a pier at the docks. After his land was seized and his wife and daughter murdered, he lost the will to live and became a vagabond. Through a series of events he was brought into contact with the Clandestine Knights, and consequentially back into the rebellion shortly before the overthrow of Count Reddland. Bartus was still recuperating from the severe flogging he received at the hands of Reddland's men. He had nearly been killed and the road to recovery had been long and hard. He sat stiffly in his chair, the flesh on his back yet tender.

Next to Bartus sat Novak, a muscled hulk of a man. At six foot six and two hundred and forty pounds, Novak dwarfed Bartus making him look like a child. In his black tunic and bronze cuirass he looked every bit the warrior he was. His knuckles were deeply scared; evidence of the numerous fist poundings he administered. Novak's deep resonating voice fit his stature, but underneath his imposing frame was a true warm-hearted friend to those who knew him. Only highwaymen and their ilk had reason to fear Novak.

Novak's muscled stature drew much attention from the maidens. His boyishly unkempt brown hair and deep blue eyes further added to his appeal. Lately, however, Novak had been keeping company with Thadus's daughter Emerald…much to the disappointment of a few Xylorian maidens.

To Novak's right sat Emerald, a beautiful blond in a blue dress. She had been working with Doc, tending to the recovering soldiers from the battle that ushered in the rebel victory. Most were ambulatory enough to care for themselves, but there was still a few who needed daily attention.

Emerald and Novak had grown closer over the last few months; her pale blue eyes met his at regular intervals throughout the luncheon. Thadus looked at his daughter approvingly, warmed by the fact that Emerald found some long overdue happiness. The relationship was far from certain, but he decided to give his daughter advice in the matter nonetheless. He warned Emerald about the burden carried by the wife of a soldier; much less a Clandestine Knight. For now Emerald was more then willing to accept the risks, and yet Thadus sensed some real soul searching in his daughter. He could read the worry in her countenance every time Novak went on a patrol, and see the relief in her eyes every time he returned safely. Novak was a God fearing man, and Thadus approved of his daughter's choice. If she could live with the dangerous lifestyle Novak led, then he was content to let things run their course. The battle for Xylor's freedom wasn't over yet. The coming months, possibly even years would surely test her resolve in the matter. Thadus prayed all would work out well in the times to come.

At the foot of the table sat Abrams, pastor of the newly reopened Hyssop Creek Oratory. It took the better part of two months to refurbish the oratory back to its former splendor. Abrams oversaw the project, he himself laboring countless hours with its construction. Services were held in the open air in the interim.

Abrams was a fit man in his early fifties. His graying hair and neatly trimmed beard gave him an air of distinction. He wore a brown thigh length coat over a white cotton shirt and charcoal trousers. Thadus relied heavily on Abrams for strength and friendship during this trying time. Governing Xylor was a tremendous responsibility and one he didn't take lightly. Abrams was full of wisdom on how to treat people and smooth out relations with citizens who had been loyal to Reddland. Abrams excused himself from involvement in making political decisions, preferring to keep to the spiritual side of matters, and offering advice only when asked. Thadus appreciated his prayers and input. The two went back a long way and had been through much together.

To Thadus's left sat Zephyr. She was a sprite of a woman with carnelian locks pulled back along the nape of her neck; her eyes were of a brilliant jade. At home in the outdoors, she was a natural born tracker and an accomplished archer. Zephyr was the only female member of the Clandestine Knights, and one of the few women who could hold her own with her three gifted male counterparts. As such, she was often times the voice of compassion and mercy for the group. She was the perfect balance to Novak's charge and attack attitude, Cad's logic and analysis, and Scorpyus's suspicion and inquiry.

Sitting next to Zephyr was Scorpyus, dressed in a black and burgundy tunic. His olive complexion, black hair, and dark eyes announced his gypsy heritage. His lean, chiseled, six-foot frame contained the speed and agility of a panther. Relying on his swiftness, Scorpyus seldom wore armor. He was quite knowledgeable in the art of herbal remedies; a skill his grandmother taught him as a child. Scorpyus handled most of the fact finding and surveillance for the group. He and Zephyr recently arrived back in Xylor from one such fact-finding mission in Kelterland.

Next to Scorpyus sat Cad. With his goatee, blond hair and brown eyes, Cad held an air of fashionable regality about him. He came from a family of architects, and had it not been for the conquering of his homeland of Ravenshire by Kelterland, he may have continued in the family tradition. As fate would have it, he would learn to use a sword and become a warrior instead. Cad had three years of education, a rarity in Ravenshire, and had taught his fellow Knights how to read.

A beautiful brunette walked into the room, wearing a plain green dress. She had a soiled apron tied around her waist, and came to the head of the table. Her eyes caught Scorpyus looking at her and she responded with a coy smile.

Scorpyus leaned over to Cad. "Who is that? She seems familiar." He kept his eye on her as she leaned down to speak with Thadus.

"Don't tell me you don't recognize Natasha. She tended to you for several days when you were wounded."

A flash of recognition shone in Scorpyus's face. It had been three months since then, and at the time he was barely conscious having suffered a vicious leg wound.

"That's right. How could I forget? It has been a while."

Cad watched his friend take in the dark haired beauty. "She's quite attractive." Scorpyus nodded in agreement.

"How's your leg by the way?"

Scorpyus massaged his right thigh. "It's still a little sore. But I've got most of my strength back thanks to all of that walking I did in Kelterland. How is your wound?"

"I'm fine mate. My wound was minor. Others fared much worse…" Cad's voice trailed off. The battle for freedom against Reddland's oppressive regime still haunted Cad. Never had anyone seen such carnage. The atrocities done to the rebel wounded by some of Reddland's men were beyond evil; they were from the pits of hell. Cad had gone over and over in his mind how he could've avoided that dark day. Logically there was no way anyone could have foreseen such hideousness, but Cad nevertheless felt somewhat responsible. He was one of the commanders of the rebel army, and the rebel battle plan had been his idea. Knowing scores of wounded were mutilated and cannibalized was a heavy burden. It would be an event that would haunt those who had seen it for the rest of their lives.

"Cad and I were fortunate Scorpyus," Zephyr added. "It is Novak who worried me terribly." Novak had been wounded seriously in the side and it was a miracle he was still alive.

"I'll say," Cad was still amazed at the incident. "But the bloke is as strong as an ox. After a few weeks of lying on his bum he was up and about like nothing happened."

"Oui, that is very true."

Scorpyus could only agree. His muscular friend made a fantastic recovery. God definitely still had plans for Novak, and wasn't ready to call him home.

The three watched their big friend chatting quietly with Emerald. Natasha retrieved a tray from the food table and started clearing away plates and silverware. She glanced at Scorpyus as she set about her work.

"Is Natasha working in the kitchen now?" Scorpyus wondered.

Cad nodded. "Yes. Emerald and Doc are caring for what few wounded are left and Natasha was reassigned to the kitchen. She's a hard worker; likes to keep busy."

Scorpyus caught Natasha's gaze and nodded with a smile, somewhat intrigued. Natasha continued clearing away plates, glancing up periodically. Before she got to Scorpyus's place setting, Thadus tapped his fork against his cup to get everyone's attention. The small gathering fell silent, and Natasha paused in her work.

"I'd like to get this meeting under way. I have a speaking engagement with the Xylorian businessmen's group shortly. They want to know what I intend to do about this nasty blockade that is keeping their wares on our docks." Thadus reported grimly then turned to Natasha. "Please, if you don't mind, I'd appreciate it if you would finish up after the meeting."

"Oh, not at all." Natasha set her tray on the food table and started back for the kitchen closing the door behind her. Scorpyus watched her all the way. He smiled when he felt Cad elbow him in the arm.

Thadus smiled warmly at those gathered. "First I'd like to say welcome back to Scorpyus and Zephyr. I look forward to their report on Kelterland, but first I would like to open with a word of prayer. Abrams, would you do the honors?" It was Thadus custom to have Abrams pray before each meeting. He did not take his position as Xylor's leader lightly and continually called upon God to give him the wisdom to conduct a fair and equitable government the people could trust.

"Certainly," Abrams paused while everyone bowed their heads. "Dear Heavenly Father, it is written, 'Except the Lord build the house, they labor in vain that build it: except the Lord keep the city, the watchman waketh but in vain.' We ask that you indeed build and keep watch over this house that would become the new Xylor. Our prayer is for the return of Xylor to its former splendor and morality. We thank you for the removal of the oppressive regime of fear, terror, and needless killing. We ask that you grant Thadus the wisdom and discernment to know what to do in these pivotal days. Grant us all the courage to do what we know to be right. I pray for the safety of those gathered, as well as for those who are assisting Thadus in this good work. I also pray for those who oppose us; that they would come to see the light and know of your abundant blessings on those who chose you. May your will be done in all things, we ask in Jesus name, amen."

The others gathered all said amen in unison.

"Thank you Abrams, and now we shall get started." Thadus turned to Scorpyus and Zephyr. "Tell us about Kelterland. Were you able to learn anything about what the Kelterlanders have in store?"

Zephyr spoke first. "Oui. As you already know a blockade is preventing trade between Xylor and the other territories. Scorpyus and I found out it is not easy to get through the blockade, but it is not impossible. I tell you monsieur it would be very difficult to get to Kelterland in anything but a small boat. The King's navy is preventing any ship coming from Xylor to dock at their ports. Anyone caught pirating goods to or from Xylor will be put to death."

Thadus furrowed his brow. "It is bleaker then I imagined." The others, except Scorpyus, nodded in agreement.

Zephyr continued. "The price of spices has increased three fold. Scorpyus and I saw first hand what happens to those caught smuggling. Three men were executed on the day we arrived."

"But yet the smuggling continues." Scorpyus cut in. "If there is a shilling to be made, someone will take the risk. Mostly it is very small shipments brought in by rowboat at obscure points on shore. The ships can't get close enough to dock themselves because of the rocks. Once it's boated to shore it has to be carted to town, sometimes over several miles."

"I am told your friend Dantes only unloads three of four row boats of goods at a time. He has to keep moving because of the patrols." Zephyr had not met Dantes and relied on what she heard about the man.

"Dantes is a good man. I pray he keeps his wits about him." Thadus praised his old friend who risked everything to trade for necessities needed in Xylor. Many things could be done without, but clothing and medicines had to be traded for on the black market.

The news worried Emerald. "How long can we rely on smuggling? Sooner or later the risk will be too great."

Cad pondered the problem in his head. "Thadus, what goods do you see coming into shortage."

"Well, I should think we wouldn't starve. There is enough ranching to provide adequate food, and we have plenty of wood in the forest. The only two important commodities I foresee falling into shortage are cloth and raw material to make swords and armor. All of our cloth is imported, and we'll need material to forge weapons to equip our troops."

"I wouldn't worry about weapons," Novak shifted in his chair. "Between what Reddland had stored here at the compound, and what we seized from his defeated troops, we should have enough military supplies for a long time."

"So all we have to worry about is keeping the people in clothes?" Zephyr asked.

"A clothing shortage is the least of my concerns." Thadus looked around the table. "We can make due with what we have for some time. What I am worried about is the local economy. Many Xylorians depend on exporting their goods in order to earn a living, especially the spice growers. How will those who depend on sales to the mainland markets keep their families fed without their wages? That is the biggest hardship to be borne from this blockade."

All those gathered took in what Thadus said. If the people started to starve there could very well be a revolt. Many would gladly surrender if it came down to starvation; it would be hard to blame them.

"Well then, we better find a solution to this problem shouldn't we." Cad stressed.

"If the Kelterlanders suffer another defeat, more people will be encouraged to run the blockades." Novak offered his opinion.

Thadus let out a deep sigh. "Let me speak with the local businessmen first about this. I'll have a better idea of where they stand and how long I have to come up with a plan. Maybe they will have suggestions."

Abrams sat silently listening until now. "I have faith everything will work out in the end. God will bless your efforts."

"Thank you Abrams, for your words of encouragement. I pray you are right." The subject weighed heavily on Thadus.

"Continue on Scorpyus. What else did you find out?"

"After the first day, Zephyr and I parted ways so we could cover more ground. I wanted to find out when we could expect Kelterland to strike back. I think we all know it is just a matter of when, not if they send troops." All those gathered knew this to be true.

"As you all know the king's brigades are being kept quite busy maintaining order in the occupied territories. The four of us can attest to the fact that Ravenshire has always kept the King's soldiers busy," Scorpyus remarked proudly. "They won't be able to divert many troops from the occupied territories if they want to keep them under control."

Zephyr broke in. "I must tell you Kelterland recently invaded Montroix. The king's men are facing strong opposition. This has forced them to use their reserve brigades. I do not think they will be able to spare any men from this front."

Zephyr's news took her audience by surprise.

"My word, Kelterland has invaded Montroix?" Abrams was wide eyed in shock.

"When did this happen?" Cad inquired.

"About a month before we left Ravenshire." Zephyr stated.

"Five months ago!" Thadus was utterly taken aback. "It looks as if this blockade has stopped the flow of news as well."

"How much land do they want? When will they ever stop?" Emerald couldn't understand what drove Kelterland to want to conquer the world.

"They will never stop unless someone stops them." Novak stated the cold hard truth.

"Well then, this should keep them busy for some time." Thadus hoped.

Scorpyus shook his head. "No, I'm afraid not. Kelterland has raised another legion of troops for the king's brigade. They are being trained as we speak. I have heard they are even conscripting men from the conquered territories and pressing them into service as laborers, fletchers, blacksmiths, and other troop support positions. Kelterland is a very wealthy nation, easily able to afford an army."

"How do you know these new troops will be sent against Xylor?" Thadus asked.

Scorpyus's brow furrowed at the question. "I know because it was my job to find out. I assure you the troops will be on their way as soon as they are trained."   "Reddland's overthrow has caused a furor in Kelterland. It is the talk no matter where you go." Zephyr confirmed Scorpyus's last statement.

"When can we expect them?" Cad inquired.

"Two, maybe three months."

"Well then, we have a little time." Thadus was somewhat relieved. Emerald had a scared look on her face. Bartus fidgeted nervously.

"Do you know…I mean…how many troops?" Thadus asked.

"In the vicinity of four thousand," Scorpyus watched the numbers register. Bartus went pale, and Cad let out a whistle.

"Oh my, four thousand men! How will we ever stand a chance?" Bartus was chilled to the bones by the news.

Novak rolled his eyes. "There you go again Bartus. Why don't you look for the hope in the matter? The troops will be green and untested in battle."

"That is of little comfort."

"So do we just wait until they show up?" Thadus inquired, hoping to hear something to put his mind at ease.

"Give us a few days to think of something. We'll be ready for them somehow." Cad stroked his goatee, not exactly sure what the answer was yet, but the wheels were turning.

Thadus stood up to excuse himself. "Very well then, keep me posted. We'll have to finish up later. I must be going. Let's meet back tonight at dusk." Thadus opened the door.

"Alright, that's about all I had anyway." Scorpyus took a drink of cider.

"I'll walk you to town." Abrams got up and walked out with Thadus.

"Good-bye father." Emerald waved as Thadus and Abrams left. The others quickly waved also.

"Good work you two," Cad smiled. "Zephyr, I hear you also went to Ravenshire."

Zephyr's face lit up. "Oh, I tell you it was good to be home if even for one night. I decided to stop after I passed through Montroix to seek word of the invasion. Everyone on the island says hello. I have two letters." Zephyr handed Cad a letter from Ingrid, Novak's sister. Scorpyus received one from Zenith, Zephyr's sister.

"How's Izzy doing?" Scorpyus asked while reaching for his letter.

"Oh, Scorpyus, she misses you terribly. She worries about you and is praying for you every day. She sends her love, and wanted to know when we were going to come home."

"You didn't tell her about me getting wounded…"Scorpyus asked.

"No, I did not say anything about that, but do not think she did not try to find everything out." Zephyr laughed remembering Isabella's relentless questioning.

"Thank you. My sister has enough to worry about. What does Zenith have to say?" Scorpyus waved the folded parchment.

The smile slowly sank from Zephyr's face. "I guess you will have to read her letter to find out." Scorpyus didn't push the issue.

"What did my sisters have to say? Are they all doing fine?" Novak was eager to hear from home, his deep voice sounding excited.

"I tell you this; they miss you Novak. They wanted to know if the three of us were watching out for their baby brother."

"Watching out for me?"

Emerald chuckled. "I can't picture Novak as a little brother."

Cad laughed. "He's twice the blooming size of his sisters. Yes Novak, watching over you is right. Someone has to keep your bum from sitting in the jails of this world."

"Hey now wait a minute," Novak raised his hand in protest. "I'm just trying to keep your rescue skills polished."

Zephyr laughed. "Oh, and Cad, I must tell you; Megan has been relentlessly practicing with her bow. I tell you she is quite good."

Cad shook his head knowing full well where Zephyr was going with this information. "My sister can be so stubborn. I told her she was daft to consider joining us. She thinks everything is a bloomin' adventure, that girl. I've tried talking her out of it but she won't have any of it."

"She has made up her mind. I told her I would ask you." Zephyr grimaced.

"I can't allow that. It's far too dangerous."

"I do not know what to say, Cad."

"Your sister has always been a handful and almost as bull headed as you are," Novak added. "Once she's made up her mind…"

"Megan has no idea what she's asking. There are a lot of nasty blokes out there. I don't want to be constantly worrying about her."

"If we turn her down she may act on her own." Scorpyus raised a haunting possibility.

Cad was perplexed. On one hand Megan would always be his little sister. However, she was a woman now; a woman with a strong will of her own. Cad was both scared to death of the prospect and proud at the same time. He knew this day would eventually come. Megan had always been full of spunk and looked up to Cad. He had always been able to put her off because she was so young, but she was twenty now.

"What did my mum say about this?"

"I tell you Cad she is worried sick. Yet if Megan must involve her self in the struggle for freedom, she would rather have her be with us where we can look out for her."

Cad stroked his beard and let out a deep sigh. "Do you think she could handle herself Zephyr?"

"Oui, she is very skilled with a bow, and has been practicing with a sword. She can ride, and has been preparing for this moment for some time."

"I don't think she'll take no for an answer. I don't see as I have much choice but to let her help us; just not right now."

Novak nodded his head in agreement. "You're right. She won't be turned down. We could use the help; besides, we can start her off slow and help her along until she gets experience."

"I know," Cad resigned to the fact. "A lot of the rebel troops are less qualified. It's just that she's my little sister."

"I feel for you Cad. Thank God Isabella is very content to stay out of this." Scorpyus was sympathetic.

"I told Megan it could be months before we were able to contact her again. I just wanted you to be prepared the next time you see her." Zephyr said.

"It is a sign of the war torn land we live in." Emerald added. "No one is truly safe as long as Kelterland is out to conquer and control us all."

No one could argue with that. The land hadn't been safe since the start of the war when the Clandestine Knights were children. With a rebellion uprising it would become a lot more dangerous before it would get better. The future was so uncertain life had to be enjoyed to the fullest. Each day was a blessing to be cherished. Every last drop of joy had to be wrung out of each moment. Those gathered at the table knew better than most the end was always near.

Emerald and Novak started to chat amongst themselves. Zephyr filled Scorpyus in on how their friends were doing back in Ravenshire.

Cad held his letter to his nose. It still bore the sweet smell of perfume. For a moment he was lost in thought fondly remembering the last time that particular scent graced his nostrils.

It was the night of Novak's sister's wedding; the last night Cad spent in Ravenshire. Ingrid wore the perfume that night. Oh how Cad longed to see Ingrid. He pictured her sandy brown locks and her soft, ivory toned skin. She had deep blue eyes like her brother. It often amazed Cad how his fair, and delicate Ingrid could be a blood relative of the rough and muscled Novak. God creates a wondrous variety indeed.

"Are you going to read the letter, or inhale it?" Novak jibed.

The remark brought Cad back from his reminiscing. He still had the letter pressed close to his nose. The others got a chuckle from the remark.

"I think I will." Cad stood from the table and went to a corner of the room for a little privacy.

"Let me know if *my* sister has any messages for me." Novak pretended to be perturbed. "How do you like that? She writes Cad and not her own brother."

"Je regrette, I was not in Ravenshire long. I was on my way back when asked to deliver the letters." Zephyr explained. "I am sure the others prepared letters but did not get them to me in time as I left long before the break of day." The others nodded their understanding.

"What about you Scorpyus? Aren't you going to read yours?" Novak asked. Zephyr looked away when he asked the question.

"I think I'll save it for later." Scorpyus looked at Zephyr wondering if something was the matter. She seemed relieved he was going to wait to read the letter. Scorpyus was expert at analyzing subtleties in behavior and naturally suspicious. Zephyr avoided eye contact until the subject was changed.

Novak stood from the table. "I don't have to take a patrol out till this evening. Emerald and I are going to take a look at the hedgerow maze and gardens. Do you two want to go?"

"Novak has put it off long enough." Emerald laughed. "I've been wanting to see it for some time."

"Oui, that would be nice." Zephyr agreed.

Scorpyus shrugged his shoulders. "Why not? The last time I was there I had to hurry through them. He laughed at the memory.

Cad broke the red wax seal of his letter as the others chatted at the table. He could hardly wait to read it. He immediately recognized Ingrid's smooth flourishing handwriting.

My dearest Cad,

It seems like ages since we've last seen each other. I must confess I miss you terribly. Must you be away so long? I pray all is going well with you, and that you will return shortly. It seems like an eternity since you were here. Each day I long to look out my door and see you walking up the path, like you did so many times when you were here. I remember when I used to inquire of Novak about the knights in order to make sure I was home when you were to come over for a meeting. I eagerly anticipated those meetings. Imagine my complete surprise when you arrived one day for no other reason than to call on me. Novak told me that since our father had died, you asked his and my mother's permission first. I am grateful they agreed. I wouldn't have wanted to be on Novak's bad side. Not a day goes by I don't thank the Lord for that day. I know we have been courting for barely nine months, and for four of those you've been away, but it feels like much longer. Zephyr told us somewhat about the battle. Knowing that you all are in such danger puts life into perspective. All the little inconveniences of life no longer matter. All that matters is cherishing the good moments we are given in this war torn world. I think about the times we've shared, and about what you said that last night before you left for Xylor. It is what sustains me until your return. I pray you will return safely to Ravenshire, and that it will be soon. I pray for the others as well. Please be careful and take care of each other. Last of all; remember the question you posed before you left? I think I can now say without a doubt that I am capable of carrying such a burden. I look forward to hearing from you soon.

Love always, Ingrid.

P.S. Tell Novak all of us miss him very much, and that we want our brother returned safely. Tell him I love him and to stay out of trouble. Thank Scorpyus for me for helping Novak escape that prison ship.

Cad was beaming by the time he finished his letter. Now he missed Ingrid more then ever. He could not wait for the day he would be able to return to Ravenshire, if only for a visit. Perhaps if things were going well enough in Xylor he would be able to slip away for a few days.

Cad's reminiscing was abruptly interrupted when Cyrus burst into the room with some urgent news.

"Oh, there you are. The sentries told me I would find you here." Cyrus had a rough growling voice. There was an intense look of uneasiness on his face. In his late thirties he was an experienced soldier who at one time was a member of the Royal Guard. He resigned his post and started helping the rebellion when he became a Christian several years earlier. He was introduced to the Clandestine Knights shortly after their arrival in Xylor, and quickly became a trusted friend who helped command the rebel troops.

"What is it Cyrus?" Cad inquired.

Cyrus took a deep breath. "It's probably nothing, but I felt I should notify you at once just in case. The north patrol has failed to return. I arrived back a while ago with the south patrol. They should have returned before I did. I dispatched a rider to Sage, and he learned the north patrol also failed to make their rendezvous there."

Worry spread on the faces in the room, and a nagging uneasiness filled the air. Everything had been going smoothly since the rebel victory over the Royal Guard. This was the first unusual incident.

Emerald didn't quite grasp the seriousness of the matter. "There has to be a good explanation for it, right?"

Novak explained the situation. "The north patrol takes the trail around the north side of Xylor to where it curves around to Sage. Then they take the main trail back to Xylor. The south patrol takes the beach trail along the south part of the island, and it is twice the distance and a rougher trail. The north patrol should have been back long before Cyrus; and they didn't even make it to Sage yet."

A wave of nausea swept Emerald. "Oh no! What could have happened? She feared the worst.

Bartus started rattling in his chair. He had always been timid, but since his recent torture at the hands of Reddland he was even more jittery. "Something's wrong. I just know it."

"Maybe the chaps came across some trouble. Not everyone is happy with the changes around here," Cad offered before turning to Scorpyus. "Have you heard any talk from the Tanuba loyalists or other dissenters?"

Scorpyus had been heavily employing his many 'techniques' of obtaining information.

"There are certainly those who would do us harm. Drakar is trying to assemble a force for a counter coup, but so far has been unsuccessful in gathering a following. The opposition seems to be content in waiting for Kelterland to act. They are confident the Kelterlanders will be victorious."

"That doesn't mean a few blokes won't get impatient and try something on their own." Cad remarked.

"True," Scorpyus thought a moment. "Maybe the lost patrol deserted."

"I can't believe that," Cyrus was adamant. "I've known Sergeant Maddox for years. He is a good man. He would never desert, nor would any of the men. They risked everything to fight the battle with Reddland. They wouldn't quit now."

Cyrus had a point. If the men were dedicated enough to endure the week of carnage in battle against the Royal Guard, they weren't going to flee now.

"You're probably right." Scorpyus conceded.

"At any rate, we have to find out what happened." Cad leaned forward in his chair and stroked his goatee.

"Since you two have the evening patrols," Cad pointed to Novak and Zephyr, "Scorpyus and I will go find out what happened." Everyone agreed with the plan. The whereabouts of the north patrol had to be discovered. All hoped and prayed for a logical explanation in the matter.

"Shall I ready more men to go with you?" Cyrus asked.

"No. Scorpyus and I will work quieter and faster on our own."

"You two promise me you will be careful." Zephyr added.

Scorpyus gave Zephyr a wink. "You don't worry about us. Just keep an eye out around here. If we aren't back by nightfall cancel the evening patrols. Let's assume there is a reasonable explanation this until we find out otherwise."

Before Cad and Scorpyus could leave Natasha entered the room with a tray and started clearing the tables. She was obviously perplexed.

"What is it?" Scorpyus could tell Natasha was a little upset. "Are you worried about the patrol?"

Natasha looked sullen. "No, that's not it…what patrol…it's just …something happened before I came here. I don't want to bother you all with it. You have enough to worry about."

"What is it? You are among friends madam." All gathered nodded their agreement to Zephyr's statement.

Natasha let out a heavy sigh. "I feel sort of silly for bothering you with such a trivial matter; especially in light of how busy you all are. But…I can't get this out of my mind." Natasha unintentionally kept her audience in suspense. All gathered patiently awaited her reply as she nervously bit on her lip.

"A little girl, about three years old, was abandoned outside the compound gates. A cloaked woman rode up on horseback and set the girl down, barely stopping before riding off again. The little girl was crying out to her mother as she rode away. It was the most pitiful sight."

"Oh that's awful!" Emerald exclaimed.

"The mother is probably fleeing the island, no doubt resistant to the changes." Cad cast a glance toward Scorpyus. His explanation made some sense. Many Xylorians were afraid of the new government despite the efforts of Thadus and the extreme efforts undertaken to treat the citizenry in an honest and forthright manner. Many others were ardent loyalists to Reddland. Uncertain times often pushed people into making hurried decisions.

"Fleeing the island?" Natasha hoped there was a better explanation to abandon a child than that. "What's the poor little girl to think when she gets older and find's out she was abandoned like an unwanted dog?"

Scorpyus rose from his chair and addressed Cad. "I'll get the horses ready." He had a somber expression on his face and didn't bother to say good-bye or offer any customary parting remarks to his friends. Natasha watched him depart and felt a little hurt by the sudden cool treatment.

"Did I say something wrong?" She could tell by the looks on Cad, Zephyr and Novak's face that something was wrong. Emerald, Cyrus and Bartus looked puzzled about the whole event.

Cad explained as delicately as possible. "Well Natasha, you had no way of knowing this so don't feel bad…but Scorpyus was abandoned as a child also. He was a few months old when his sister and…they were left at a burial pit outside of town. They were discarded like trash. You've done nothing wrong."

"Oh, I am so sorry. I didn't mean anything…"

Novak cut Natasha off. "Scorpyus knows you didn't mean anything by it. You were just relating a tragic event. We all have things in the past…"

"I must apologize." Natasha rushed from the room anxious to settle her conscious of the matter. She had to know that Scorpyus understood she regretted any bad memory her remark may have caused.

"I'll give them a little time. A few more minutes before we set out on our search for the missing patrol won't hurt I hope." Cad finished his cider and leaned back in his chair.

Zephyr was concerned for her friend but knew something more. "I am afraid this is the start of a melancholy day for Scorpyus. A little bad news is yet to come his way."

Cad and Novak glanced at each other wondering what Zephyr meant. They were curious but confident that all would be answered in due time.

A young hostler in his early teens greeted Scorpyus. "Good afternoon my lord, shall I saddle your horse?"

Scorpyus shot a quick glance around before realizing the stable boy was addressing him. "You don't have to do that. I can saddle my own horse."

"No my lord, it is no problem. It is the least I can do to repay you."

"You owe me nothing. Thadus is the one responsible for giving you a job." Scorpyus was impressed with the boy's politeness but had never seen him before and didn't know how the boy could owe him anything. If the young man was grateful for having a job, he was thanking the wrong man. Scorpyus walked by the lad, going to the stall that held his horse. The boy persistently followed at his heels.

"Please my lord, allow me. It will be but one small token of my gratitude for what you and your friends have done." The lad squeezed past Scorpyus and into the stall. He immediately started brushing down the steed.

"If you are referring to my friends and I coming to the aid of the rebellion, it was as much our fight as it was yours. As believers we are all in this together." Scorpyus assumed the boy was a believer as he was working for Thadus. He started to bridle his mount.

The lad paused from grooming the horse. "But my lord, there is something you do not know. Reddland murdered my parents and burned down our house shortly before the rebellion succeeded in overthrowing his reign. He pressed my brother and me into service for him. We can never repay you and your friends for avenging our parent's death. Please allow me to be of service to the rebellion in some small way, especially to you who have helped me more than you could ever know. Please my lord, allow me now to be of assistance, if only as a stable hand. Perhaps some day I will be able to do more."

Scorpyus knew what it was like to have loved ones murdered at the hands of a tyrant, and what that did to the survivors. He knew what it was like to burn with a desire for revenge. Channeling that desire to serve the common good was the only option open to a true believer. Otherwise one would become another Reddland. Scorpyus saw a bit of himself in the boy. Who was he to stifle the boy's desire to serve?

"Very well, but on one condition," Scorpyus replied while relinquishing the reins to his mount. "Don't call me 'lord'. I am far from worthy of that title, and there is only one who is."

"Yes my…sir." The boy was grinning broadly. He set about his task with great enthusiasm.

"Will you saddle Cad's horse also? It's the one in the end stall." Scorpyus wasn't accustomed to having someone else saddle his mount. He was very particular about how he cinched up the saddle, and wanted to be sure of his mount in all regards.

The boy nodded his willingness and was beaming with pride. To be working with the Clandestine Knights was a thrilling prospect. He fancied himself someday being like them. He saw their lives as being filled with adventure and intrigue. Had he been a witness to the carnage of the previous months battle he would have realized the unglamorous side of being a soldier.

Scorpyus went to the stable doorway and watched the boy work for a while. He prayed there would be a better future in sight for the next generation. Deep down though he felt there would be a long road ahead before that would happen.

Scorpyus pulled out the letter he received from Zenith. Perhaps this would be a good time to read it. He held it to his nose. The letter smelled a little musty, and a little like a horse. Breaking the seal he opened it and started reading the neatly formed letters.

Scorpyus,

I know I should tell you this in person but I don't know when you will return, and to wait to tell you is not right either. I know we only started our courtship shortly before you left Ravenshire, and I will cherish those moments forever, but your absence has brought me to face the reality of it all. I have worried incessantly these past few months you have been gone, and have been barely able to eat. Wondering about your welfare has disturbed more than a few nights sleep. Even though I care for you deeply, I don't think I can bare the strain of knowing you may never return from one of your missions. Worrying about my sister and the others has been troublesome, but with you it was different. I can't live life knowing that each time we say goodbye it might well be the last time I ever see you. I hope you can forgive me for embarking on this course with you, but I honestly thought I could handle it. I never meant to hurt you, and I pray all goes well with you. I felt you should know as soon as possible.

I also wanted to tell you about Talon before you heard any rumors. Talon and I have been courting for the last three weeks. He is a good man with a stable job. As he is a Fletcher, he faces far less danger then you and the other knights and that's what I need in my life right now. With all we've been through with the war and the killing, I just couldn't go through with us. You must believe me Scorpyus, I really wanted to; it was all I dreamed about for so many years. Forgive me for being delicate in this matter, but I just couldn't go on. I wanted you to hear it from me. I owe you at least that.

Yours truly,
Zenith

Scorpyus reread the letter then slowly folded it and tucked it into a pouch on his belt. Before he could react to the news he was startled by Natasha. She saw him reading the letter and waited until he was done before approaching.

"Bad news?" Natasha judged from the look on Scorpyus's face that the letter wasn't glad tidings.

"No…it's ah, just a letter from home." He forced a grin to his lips. "What brings you to the coral? Are you going riding?"

"No, I…" Natasha looked shyly downward. "I wanted to apologize in case I offended you somehow…you know, with the remark about the abandoned child. You left in such a hurry I thought I may have said something wrong."

"No, I'll be fine. I just feel for the little girl. It won't be easy for her knowing her parents didn't want her. She's another victim of war."

Natasha looked deeply into Scorpyus's eyes. She could see a certain sadness behind that penetrating stare. Scorpyus could also see sorrow in Natasha's eyes.

"Are you alright?" Scorpyus inquired.

"Yes…I only wanted to make sure it wasn't something I said."

Scorpyus grinned genuinely this time. "Well thank you for your concern, but you didn't say anything wrong. Besides, I don't think I could ever get mad at you."

Natasha warmed at the compliment. "And I thank you. Well I must be getting back to work. Go with vigilance tonight."

Scorpyus nodded. "I will." Natasha turned to leave.

"Oh, and one more thing," Scorpyus waited for her to turn. "Maybe I'll see you when I get back."

Natasha smiled. "Hopefully," she replied and walked back toward the kitchen. She passed Zephyr coming along the path. Scorpyus watched Zephyr walk up to him.

"Did Cad decide not to go after all?"

"No, he is still going; I just wanted to talk to you before you left."

"Is it about the letter?"

Zephyr let out a heavy sigh. "Zenith told me she was going to be writing you that letter. Je regrette…I am sorry Scorpyus. Zenith was confused. She did not know what to expect. It is not you she can not live with, it is your job."

"That's understandable; either one of us might not come back. The last few months have taught us that." Scorpyus shrugged the whole incident off.

Zephyr knew Scorpyus well enough to know he was disillusioned by the day's events and was putting on a brave front. "Do not take it to heart. Tomorrow is a new day. I know things will get better."

"I'm fine. I escorted Zenith a few times, nothing more. Talon…is a good man. He is a good choice for a woman who needs reassurance and stability. In our line of work, I could never provide that. Deep down I knew Zenith was too tender to withstand the harsh realities of a life of worry. I should have listened to my instincts."

"You do not have to pretend nothing bothers you." Zephyr tried to reach out to her friend.

"I'm not." Scorpyus looked past Zephyr and changed the subject. "Where's Cad anyway? We should be going soon."

"I could go with Cad if you need some time alone." Zephyr offered.

Scorpyus rolled his eyes. "Zephyr, I'm fine. I'm ready for this mission."

"Are you sure you are not too preoccupied?"

"Yes."

Zephyr wasn't convinced. "My father once told me there are two kinds of heroes; those who believe in a cause so strongly, they would never swerve from the path of duty even if it meant laying down their life; and those who were just willing to lay down their life. Which one are you Scorpyus?"

"Your father left out a lot of variables."

"You did not answer my question."

"I'm not a hero."

Zephyr was getting a little perturbed. "Scorpyus, you know what I mean."

"What if I said it depends on the day?"

"This is not a game. I am serious about this."

Scorpyus placed a hand on Zephyr's shoulder and looked her directly in the eyes, holding her gaze. Her eyes were welling up with tears of concern. "Thank you for caring. You are a true friend, but honestly Zephyr I'm fine. I assure you my instinct for survival is intact."

Zephyr wiped a lone tear that managed to spill over her eyelid. "I do not want you to feel bad. We all care about you."

Scorpyus was moved by Zephyr's loving heart. Friend or not, she was a beautiful woman with soft green eyes that could melt the coldest ice. Her life had been no easier than his and yet she was trying to comfort him. The fact that Zephyr could remain so compassionate through all she had been through was a testimony to her sweet and gentle character. For the first time Scorpyus understood the depth of her compassion. He wiped a tear from her cheek.

"Zephyr, you truly are a winter rose."

Zephyr furrowed her brow. "What is it you mean by that?"

Scorpyus explained. "In a bleak and desolate place you are the lone bright spot, the one thing of beauty. You always see the best in situations and people. It is a gift I myself lack. Don't ever change."

Zephyr smiled broadly at the compliment. "Merci." She embraced her friend. "Make sure you and Cad come back."

Scorpyus smiled warmly. "We'll come back."

Zephyr looked into Scorpyus's eyes and saw something she had not seen before in all the years she had known him. Behind that penetrating stare she saw a flicker of longing; perhaps a deep felt desire to be needed. It took her by surprise, and much to her confusion it stirred something deep within her. As quickly as it came it vanished and Scorpyus's face was back to its trademark glare.

Zephyr didn't know what to think. For one brief moment she saw something more of her friend then she knew existed. The idea, for some reason, troubled her in an enticing sort of way. She wondered if it were possible to ever really know all there was about someone. If the eyes are the windows to the soul, was this a new room?

The two held the embrace longer then was prudent, and were slightly awkward when they were finished. Both were a little shocked about the spontaneous display of affection. That had never happened before. Before they could dwell on it, Cad rounded the corner of the stables.

"Sorry I took so long. A few chaps cornered me with questions about the evening patrol. I told them to wait until our return. Of course I had to explain why. That took longer then I expected."

"Yeah, they better wait until we get back; just in case." Scorpyus glanced into the stables. His horse was ready and the stable boy was about finished with Cad's.

"So you think they are in trouble?" Zephyr said with a hint of worry.

"I think they were attacked; either by a group of Reddland loyalists or by a band of cutthroats. They probably have a few wounded and are now in Sage having them treated. It's the most logical conclusion. We know they didn't get lost." Scorpyus stated his theory.

Cad nodded while stroking his goatee. "I fear you are right. They came upon trouble. I hope no one was killed. I just didn't want to worry Thadus until we knew exactly what happened to them."

"Maybe a horse went lame and they didn't want to leave a man behind." Zephyr offered.

"There's that winter rose again." Scorpyus gave Zephyr a knowing smirk. She looked down demurely at the remark.

"What? A rose?" Cad was puzzled.

"It is a little inside lark between Zephyr and myself." Scorpyus explained.

"Oh," Cad still looked puzzled. "Well anyway, I should hope if a horse went lame the Sergeant of the patrol would have sense enough to dispatch a rider to inform us of that. It would blooming well save us a wasted trip and a lot of worry."

The stable boy led two horses out the stable doors. "Here you are my l…I mean sir."

"Thank you." Scorpyus grabbed the reins to his mount and swung into the saddle. "Well Cad, shall we?"

"Let's put our wonder to rest." Cad climbed into the saddle. "See you soon Zephyr."

"Hurry back and God speed."

Cad and Scorpyus gave Zephyr a quick nod and kneed their mounts onward. Hopefully the mystery of the lost patrol would soon be answered.

III

————•◆•————

CAD AND SCORPYUS rode carefully along the road, twisting their way through the crowds on their way to the north trail. She watched their every move from a second story window, her jaw clenched tight.

"Here are two of them now." She closed the shutters making sure to keep a narrow opening by which to watch Cad and Scorpyus.

Seeing the two made her blood boil. They were responsible for all that had gone wrong in Xylor. They were the cause of much grief and suffering. Oh how she wished they were dead. To watch them die an agonizing death would be a pleasure. Dying quickly would be much too good for these peasant class instigators. It wouldn't be long now.

She watched Cad sit atop his dapple-gray mount, a shield held firmly in place. Look at him in his cuirass and gauntlets, with his neatly trimmed blond hair and goatee. He exuded a pompous hatred for the people around him, probably lording his status on all those whom he could. Who was this man anyway? He's nothing more then a mercenary, a hired thug as far as she was concerned. He's riding about like he owned the town.

Scorpyus rode next to Cad on a black horse with white stockings. She fixed her gaze on him now, the veins in her temples bulging. She particularly hated Scorpyus. Gypsy trash had no reason being in Xylor. They were always up to no good. When they weren't playing a mandolin or dancing for coins, they were stealing you blind. This one went even farther. He hooked up with a band of highwaymen, no doubt engaging in confidence games as a sideline. His penetrating eyes shifted all around, probably looking for another victim. He and his fellow cadre of paid assassins would pay for what they did, and those who hired them also.

She watched Cad and Scorpyus ride by her window. They looked so smug it made her sick. Her stomach was in a knot of hatred and vengeance. Her muscles were taught with vile disgust for what she was seeing. In due time their meddling in others affairs would return to haunt them. Things would change soon. In fact they were already changing. Suddenly she realized she had been digging her fingers into the windowsill. So much so she had torn one of her finger nails back, and it was now bleeding. She squeezed her finger forcing a big drop of blood from under her torn nail. Raising her finger to her mouth, she closed her eyes as she sucked the blood from her small wound. Vengeance would taste just as sweet, and it was coming soon.

Scorpyus turned around and scanned the streets and buildings carefully. Xylor was busy at mid-day, a bustle of people everywhere.

"What is it?" Cad turned in his saddle realizing his friend was taking an unusually long look behind.

Scorpyus continued to scan the surroundings. "Probably nothing; I just had the feeling someone was staring at me."

Cad turned for a look of his own. "With so many people it would be hard to tell."

Scorpyus studied the crowd a moment longer before turning around. "I hate it when I get that feeling, when your hair stands on end."

"There are many enemies of the new government. Of course lately we've been getting looks from admirers as well. All thanks to Thadus and his March Octave; what with him making heroes out of us." Cad added.

"This was different. It was enough to send a chill down your spine; like being in the presence of evil or something."

"I hope you're wrong Scorpyus."

Cad and Scorpyus rode through the residential part of town on their way to the north trail. The north side of Xylor was wealthy. There were several estates with lavish landscaping and ornate fences. Most impressive were their real glass windows. Riding through this area reminded Cad that several people acquired much wealth under Reddland's regime. Perhaps there could be some discontent to account for Scorpyus's bad feelings about the place.

On the northern outskirts, an appropriate distance from the nicer homes, were several small scattered shacks where the poorer folk resided. Most of the homes consisted of nothing more then four walls with a roof and door. Some had a shuttered square cut in the wall to serve as a window. A few had a makeshift fence about their property. Almost all had some form of vegetable garden and livestock such as chickens, goats and sheep to supplement the diet of the occupants. One of the fenced properties had been burned to the ground. The residue of a farmhouse with blackened stones from a fireplace was all that remained. Two wooden crosses pieced together from scrap lumber marked two graves. Someone placed flowers on them recently. Certainly these people would welcome the change in Xylor, Cad thought.

Once Cad and Scorpyus were on the north trail they picked up their pace. The trail wound through Xylor's lush and fertile forests. Tall pines bordered the trail keeping it in a cool moist shade. Birds fluttered about and squirrels scampered around being sure to keep a safe distance from the horses. The trail would have made for a nice relaxing ride under other circumstances.

"Bad news from home, ay?" Cad broke the silence. He knew Scorpyus well enough to know something was wrong. Cad pieced together that it had something to do with the letter. He was concerned for his friend, and the curiosity was eating on him.

"Zenith decided to have Talon court her. I can't say it's unexpected. In actuality she made a wise choice for herself." Scorpyus scanned the surrounding forest looking for any sign of the unusual.

"How can you say that? Surely you must be a bit disappointed."

"Come now Cad; we both know Zenith isn't made for the worry. Deep down I knew that, but I had to risk the venture. She was worth taking the chance with and we had a nice few evenings. Now we both know it's not meant to be. She was honest. She just can't do it. She's not like Ingrid. Count your blessings."

Cad nodded in agreement. Scorpyus was right about Zenith, and he was right about Ingrid. Cad knew he found a treasure more precious then rubies in Ingrid. It looked as if Novak found one in Emerald. He only wished Scorpyus and Zephyr could find someone also. It was one of the few comforting things in the war torn world.

"Well, in due time Scorpyus…you never know." Cad tried to reassure his friend.

"Right now we've got so many other things to think about, I don't have time to contemplate women." Scorpyus laughed. "What about you Cad? Are you and Ingrid going to marry someday?"

"I must say I've been thinking about an engagement. After the battle with Reddland's troops I realize how precious and short life is. I always knew I suppose, but that last battle was a revelation. I wanted to wait for the proper time, a time with more peace and security, a better time for a family. I now fear it may never come, not in our lifetime. It feels like we've seen nothing but a procession of graves. We sure haven't missed out on the blooming trials and tribulations of life. Why should we miss the few good things that come our way?" Cad surveyed the trail for signs of the missing patrol as he spoke.

Scorpyus thought long and hard on what Cad just said. "You know Cad, that's the most sense I've heard anyone make in a long time."

"Thanks," Cad smiled. "And you're right about Zenith. She would never have been able to withstand you being gone so much, especially if she ever found out exactly what you do on your spy missions. The poor girl has been through too much. She needs stability. You do have a good sense about these things."

Scorpyus had an ability to read people with some accuracy. Being always suspicious, always questioning motives and a keen observer of human behavior had its benefits. Unfortunately, as Scorpyus found out on a few occasions, taking a suspicious tone with genuinely trustworthy people was often hurtful.

"There have been times when I've taken my hunches about people too far, and you can never take that back."

"I should think your sister is glad you take your hunches as far as you do." Cad remarked.

Scorpyus shot Cad a whimsical glance. "Izzy? What do you mean?"

Cad raised his eyebrows slightly surprised. "Surely you haven't forgotten mate."

Scorpyus searched his memories. He followed several hunches concerning his sister Isabella. "Are you referring to the time that shyster tried to pass off a mediocre mare as a quality horse. I guess I did save Izzy twenty shillings on that deal"

"No, that's not it." Cad shifted in the saddle. "Remember two years ago when Morpheus courted Isabella. You always had a bad feeling about that chap. As it turned out you were right. At first I thought you were being over protective of your sister. When you asked me to go with you after our Christmas feast and follow Isabella and Morpheus on their walk I thought you were daft, but thank God you were suspicious."

Scorpyus nodded back and forth as the memory came back. "Yeah, I remember." Scorpyus analyzed that incident again.

"You know Cad; I did have a bad feeling about that man. It was nothing I could say specifically; it was just a sick feeling in the pit of my stomach. I wanted you to go with me when I followed them so I would have a witness in case I was right. I didn't want it to be my word against his."

Scorpyus grew quiet a moment before he continued. Cad listened patiently.

"When I saw Morpheus try to force himself on my sister… and Izzy pleading for him to stop…" Scorpyus jaw tightened up in anger as if he were still seeing the events transpire.

"I swear this Cad; no one, I mean no one is ever going to put Izzy through that again. When Morpheus starting pressing his advantage, it was like I was reliving that day when my grandmother was killed, and Izzy was…" Scorpyus swallowed hard. "She had that same sound in her voice, that trembling, tearful waiver. It makes me sick to think about it. I'll die before Izzy has to go through that again."

"Isabella is fortunate to have you as a brother." Cad said.

"She's the only family I have left. It's been me and Izzy since we were little."

"Unfortunately for Morpheus he picked the wrong lady to act ungentlemanly with. I should think for weeks to come, each time he tried to talk or smile, that chap would remember the cost of his transgression." Cad replied with a knowing smile.

Scorpyus flew into a rage when he saw Morpheus force his advances onto his sister and ended up tearing the man from the bench he was sitting on, knocking Isabella over in the process. Before Morpheus knew what was happening he had received a hearty beating without putting up much resistance. Scorpyus wasn't proud of loosing his temper; but he offered no regrets for defending his sister. Isabella was embarrassed by the episode, mainly because Scorpyus was right once again. Morpheus knew he was in the wrong, and much to his credit even apologized for the infraction saying he didn't know what came over him. Scorpyus was quick to point out the three pints of ale Morpheus consumed had a lot to do with it. That was the reason he followed Morpheus and his sister in the first place. He, like all the Clandestine Knights, had witnessed enough rapes, murders, thievery, and general mayhem at the hands of inebriated persons that they had grown to hate alcohol for the rottenness it brought out in those who consumed it. Besides all that, in their line of work, the Clandestine Knights needed every shred of speed and skill that an unclouded mind could bring. It was a matter of life and death.

Scorpyus and Cad continued up the north trail looking for any sign out of the ordinary. So far there was nothing to suggest what happened to the missing patrol. If there was an ambush, there was absolutely no evidence of it. Yet a growing uneasiness crept over the duo. The woods were strangely silent of the usual sounds of birds and squirrels. All that could be heard was the slight breeze cutting through the tree branches in a gentle rustle.

Cad craned his neck to the treetops. "Not a blooming bird to be seen."

Scorpyus reined his mount to a halt and Cad followed suit. Both strained to hear any sound the woods had to offer but heard nothing. The clear blue sky was visible through the treetops.

"There doesn't appear to be a storm coming our way. I wonder where the animals are." Scorpyus shifted nervously.

"I don't like the feel of this." Cad replied while subconsciously clasping the hilt of his sword and shifting his gaze from tree to tree. "And to think Megan wants to join us." It was the moments like this that gave Cad cause to think twice about having his sister along.

Scorpyus nudged his mount along at a slow canter. He kept his attention focused on the right side of the trail while Cad kept his attention focused on the left. That old familiar feeling of fear oozed to the surface. Feeling their hearts pounding in their chest, their pulse in their temples, and their breath sounding abnormally loud, they surveyed their surroundings. Controlling their fear had become a way of life. With their senses at their peak they cautiously continued slowly, ever vigilant for danger.

"Megan has become quite the archer." Scorpyus replied. "Surely you must have seen it coming. Every time we go back to Ravenshire after an adventure, Megan sits in rapt suspense listening to all of our stories."

"I almost wish I'd told her some of the less then savory things we have been privy to see on our 'adventures.' Maybe then she would want to stay home." Cad and the others never told in any detail about any of the danger they faced or death they witnessed. Their family worried enough without the details.

Cad and Scorpyus continued several hundred yards down the trail. Three miles out of Xylor Cad spotted something on the ground on his side of the trail. He dismounted to investigate.

"What is it?" Scorpyus asked keeping vigilant.

"It's a hoof print." Cad inspected the area around the hoof print carefully. "It looks like they may have left the trail here and headed north."

"Can you say for sure it was the patrol and not a party of hunters of something?"

"It looks like about six horses."

"It doesn't make sense." Scorpyus surveyed the area all around. "I don't see any sign of an ambush or attack of any sort. Why else would they leave the trail?"

"I don't know, but the chaps left in a blooming hurry. They were at a full run by the time they were ten yards out." Cad mounted his horse. "What ever the reason, I think they went that way." He pointed in a northerly direction.

"Well let's go find them."

Scorpyus and Cad tracked the hoof prints northward at a cautious pace. The woods became noticeably thicker the farther they went. The trail from hoof print, to broken sapling, to disturbed patches of moss was easy enough to follow. Bark was scraped off trees, and there was the occasional twig, partially broken and dangling from a coniferous branch. A novice could track this party through the woods.

"The sign is so blooming easy to read it's as if it were done intentionally." Before Cad finished the sentence he and Scorpyus halted their mounts in their tracks. A curious possibility presented itself. Both listened intensely to an eerily silent forest, the only sound being the creek of leather and the infrequent snort of their mounts. The dead stillness was unnerving.

Scorpyus whispered. "It could be a trap...unless they were fleeing in a panic."

Cad mulled it over in his head. "If it's not a trap, then what could have made the patrol flee in such chaos as to be practically running into trees? And if they did flee, whoever or whatever made them run could still be out here."

Scorpyus's eyes darted from tree to tree. The silence of the woods was now deafening. Both men took in their surroundings, methodically searching for something to quell their apprehensiveness. Cad could see his breath in the cool forest air, still no birds or small animals about. His mount shifted its weight and let out a snort, unconcerned about current events.

Scorpyus suddenly shot Cad a glance. From somewhere far ahead came a sound.

"Did you hear that?" Scorpyus whispered.

Cad nodded. "It sounded like a horse whinny."

Scorpyus slowly dismounted and unbuckled his sword from around his waist. He handed it to Cad. "I'll take a look."

With Cad wearing a cuirass, grieves, and plate gauntlets, Scorpyus would be much quicker and stealthy. Besides, sneaking around undetected is what Scorpyus did best. Scorpyus pulled his dagger and padded off toward the sound.

Scorpyus crept in the general direction of the whinny. All along the route was the same easy to read sign, but there were no clues as to what or who was chasing the patrol. One hundred yards from where he left Cad, Scorpyus came to a small patch of manzanita brush. Noises came from the other side. Scorpyus paused to listen carefully. There was the sound of grass being torn from the ground followed by a snort. There was the sound of flies buzzing and it sounded like a lot. Suddenly the horse on the other side of the manzanita brush made a startled whinny. Scorpyus checked the wind. The breeze was at his back and blowing toward the horse.

With his dagger at the ready, Scorpyus crouched low and crept around the manzanita patch. The buzzing of the flies grew louder. His heart banged away in his chest as he stepped lightly through the pine needles making his way around the brush.

Cad sat and waited for what seemed an eternity. What was taking Scorpyus so long? He had been out of sight for some time. All kinds of unsettling thoughts started to go through Cad's mind. What if something happened to Scorpyus? What if this was part of the trap? Cad started to look around nervously. There was nothing out of the ordinary to see. Cad shifted on his mount and looked skyward. There was nothing but tall trees stabbing into the blue sky and a lone buzzard. Cad looked back to where Scorpyus disappeared. His uneasiness grew with every passing second. The minutes whittled away at his patience. What on earth was taking so long?

With a jolt Cad was practically startled from the saddle. "Bloody ay mate! Don't be sneaking up on me like that."

Scorpyus looked as if he had seen a ghost, and was visibly shaken. His eyes were wide and his vision distant. "You'd better see this."

Worry creased Cad's brow. He dismounted and followed Scorpyus. Both led their horses to the thicket of manzanita where they tethered them. Scorpyus was silent and morose the whole way. Cad didn't have to ask him if there were any survivors.

"Does it look like they suffered a lot?" Cad inquired.

Scorpyus shook his head practically speechless. "I've never seen anything like it. All but one of the horses has been killed also. Something abnormal, something strange…I just don't know."

Cad didn't know what to expect when he rounded the thicket with Scorpyus. His jaw dropped when he saw the lost patrol. All six men were dead; two hadn't even drawn their weapons. The four that had apparently didn't use them. Cad found no traces of blood on their blades. The two men that didn't draw their weapons lay dead with their faces contorted into a ghastly, fiendish grin.

Cad inspected the corpses more closely. Their eyes were bulging, staring blankly skyward, and their flesh mottled and spotty. Their jaws were clamped together tightly with their lips curled back baring their teeth like a menacing dog. One man severed the tip of his tongue, the bloody appendage still clamped between his teeth. A white pasty film drooled from their mouth and down their chins. It looked like the dried sputum of a dead rabid dog. The soldiers arms were bent inward, their fingers twisted in a grotesque manner. It looked as if they were in the throngs of pain.

Cad was horrified. "Bloody ay Scorpyus, what in the world happened to them?"

Scorpyus shrugged his shoulders. He didn't have a clue yet. "Let's search for some answers."

They knelt beside the soldier that bit his tongue off. His pale gray skin and glazed eyes were the only thing normal about his face in death.

"Do you smell that?" Cad noticed the faint smell of flowers coming from the corpse.

Scorpyus inhaled deeply. A faint but distinct smell wafted to his nostrils. He smelled that odor before but it had been a long time ago. "It's lotus blossoms."

"Are there any lotus flowers on Xylor?"

Scorpyus shook his head and looked at Cad. "The lotus doesn't grow anywhere in the Astorian Realms. They grow somewhere beyond the ethereal regions."

"Then how is it we smell them here?" Cad wasn't going to be getting any logical explanation.

Scorpyus sniffed the air again. It was definitely lotus blossoms. He got down real close to the dead soldier to make sure the scent was coming from him, and it was. When he got close he noticed a fine white powder in the soldier's hair. It contrasted with his dark locks. Scorpyus also noticed the powdery substance on the dead soldier's skin. He touched it with one of his fingers and brought it to his nose. The white substance contained powdered lotus blossoms and some other substances Scorpyus couldn't identify. He quickly wiped his finger on the dead soldier's sleeve.

"What is it?" Cad inquired.

"It looks like some sort of poison; one that will do that to your body if you inhale enough of it." Scorpyus pointed to the twisted and contorted soldier.

Cad felt a knot in the pit of his stomach. "What kind of poison does this to a fellow?"

Scorpyus's grandmother taught him in the arts of herbal remedies and concoctions, but he had never seen anything like this before. He learned about several poisons, but none that would do this to a person. Whatever it was, it was particularly vile and toxic.

"Is it safe to breathe the air here?" Cad asked while stepping away from the soldier.

"It should be. It looks like a handful of the powdery stuff was thrown in this man's face. It's all over him. Apparently you have to inhale or ingest a fair amount." Scorpyus shook his head. "And God help you if you do."

They turned their attention to the other four soldiers. They all had a thin deep slit across their throats. It was too thin to have been made by a typical dagger. There was no indication the soldiers put up any sort of struggle, or that they even saw their attackers. It appeared they were taken by surprise. They had been frightened and ran spooked to this area by something. Whatever or whoever it was managed to kill the patrol effortlessly once they drove them from the trail.

"This doesn't make any sense." Cad was perplexed. "Two of these blokes were highly skilled swordsman. I can't see how they were taken so easily."

Scorpyus was just as bewildered and could only stare down at his fallen comrades. He didn't know them well personally, but they had become somewhat acquainted during the past few months. To see them victims of some bizarre circumstance was disturbing.

Scorpyus noticed a black image on the sergeant's forehead. "What do you make of this?"

Cad took a look. He rubbed the mark with his thumb. "It looks like a bird; a goose maybe, and it's tattooed on his skin."

"Whoever killed the men from this patrol took the time to tattoo one of the corpses? We're up against more then a rogue band of cutthroats." Scorpyus didn't like the sound of it. Someone highly trained wanted that patrol dead, and they achieved that goal rather effortlessly.

A further check of the area revealed five of the soldier's horses had their throats slit. They had then been disemboweled. Nothing seemed to be missing, and all of the soldier's weapons, clothing, saddles, and money looked to be accounted for. None of their personal effects were disturbed.

"They're a daft lot alright. Why leave one horse alive? They killed every other living man and beast on this patrol." Cad didn't like things that were illogical. He could think of no reason for the actions of whoever attacked the patrol. "There had to have been more then one of them to do this with out a struggle."

"Whoever did this knew what they were doing. They were professional; as if they were assassins."

Cad's eyes grew wide at that remark.

Scorpyus studied the scene carefully not wanting to believe what he was seeing. This was the last thing the rebellion needed.

"Hey Scorpyus, over here!" Cad found a parchment nailed to a nearby tree. He removed it and read it. It was obviously meant as a message to be found by whoever went searching for the lost patrol.

Scorpyus took the parchment from Cad who had a pensive "what have we got ourselves into" look. The text was neatly written in the common language of the realms. At the bottom was a superscription in an unknown tongue along with a depiction of a woman in a flowing white garment. She was drawn to appear as though she were flying. There was also an image identical to the one tattooed on the fallen sergeant!

BEHOLD...
Strange footsteps lurk the corridor
A stench corrupts the air
Fingers scratch your chamber door
On end will stand each hair
Dark eyes survey a weary foe
And hunt the rebel cursed
My vengeance waits to vex your soul
For blood, a blade does thirst
Frenzied rats feed on the dead
Black venom finds a vein
A bloated corpse in mottled thread
Is all that shall remain

EXSECRATUS VALKYRUS

"It's worse then we thought it would be, isn't it?"

Cad nodded in agreement. "They bloody well went through some great lengths to make sure we got the message."

"Do you think it's the Kelterlanders? Is this the precursor to an invasion?" Scorpyus was thinking out loud as much as he was asking for Cad's opinion.

"You tell me Scorp, you're our main source of information."

"I know Kelterland is training an army to retake Xylor. I know of nothing else they have planned. Thadus's men have told me nothing about any thing like this. Sure there are dissidents but…I didn't think there were any this organized…or sophisticated." Scorpyus ran his fingers over his mustache while taking in the scene.

Cad placed his hand on Scorpyus's shoulder. "We must get to the bottom of this. There is a potential for terror and chaos to sweep the island, especially among the undecided. We can't have the citizenry going daft on us."

"I'll see what I can uncover. It looks like I have my immediate future planned." Scorpyus reread the parchment and contemplated the scene. "What worries me is that whoever did this seems to want us to find them. Why else do all this?"

"Unless they want to divert us off the trail." Cad had a point. The incident was bizarre. It would take some time to analyze all the details. Perhaps the others would have some ideas.

"We better get back before they start worrying about us." Scorpyus gathered his and Cad's mounts.

Cad and Scorpyus gathered the corpses. They placed two on the lone surviving horse of the ambush, and two each on their own mounts. The dead horses they left for the vultures.

"We'll get these men a proper burial. After we tell Thadus and the others, we have a lot of work to do." Cad tied the deceased across his saddle. Leaving them for the scavenger birds wasn't an option.

"Wait a second." Scorpyus bent down to inspect a slight disturbance in the dirt.

"What do you have there mate?"

Scorpyus bent over and looked close at a strange indention. It was about the size of a man's hand and had a trace of sawdust and crushed dried leaves in it. "That's strange."

"What's that?" Cad asked.

Scorpyus explained. "There is saw dust on the ground, and leaves from a plant that I don't see growing in the immediate area."

"What in the blooming world is that supposed to mean?" Cad was growing weary of the illogical oddities.

"I have no idea; maybe nothing. Let's just get back."

Scorpyus and Cad led their horses back toward the north trail. It would be a long three miles on foot, but both were grateful to be walking. It was preferred over being one of the six riding back to town.

IV

———————◆•◆•◆———————

THE SHOREBIRD INN was a modest wooden structure situated a short walk from the docks. Sailors, dockworkers, and many travelers visiting the island passed through the inn's large carved oak doors. Hospitality and comfort awaited the weary visitor inside. The two-story building consisted of a large restaurant and tavern downstairs, and thirty guest rooms upstairs. Its small but functional rooms were usually rented, and its tables were always a buzz with activity at meal times. Ale flowed steadily from the inn's tavern.

By mid-afternoon the patrons and guests would normally have been on their days activities, leaving only a few stragglers behind to keep the bartender busy. With the recent blockade, the inn was abnormally busy for this time of day with those who were in need of work. A few lucky ones would find an odd job here and there to sustain them. Many others weren't as fortunate, and were starting to become restless waiting for their new leader Thadus to solve the problem. The growing dissent over the blockade combined with the usual roughnecks and instigators found at taverns, turned the inn into a fertile field for anyone wishing to stir things up.

Braydon Mendax was addressing a gathering at one end of the bar. He was man in his early forties with dark wavy hair and shifty eyes. A short man with a nasally voice, he was often the center of the latest gossip. Today was no different. He was filling in the gathering on the latest happenings in Xylor.

Braydon flailed his arms and waved his hands enthusiastically as he spoke to stress his points. His short frame was fitted in a nicely tailored white cotton shirt and black pants. Smooth, supple hands extended from the sleeves of his long gray sea coat with gold braids on the cuffs. Braydon was not a man accustomed to hard physical labor as his uncalloused hands bore witness. His tailored clothes and somewhat plump frame attested to the fact that he was able to afford some of life's little luxuries. They were comforts that none in his audience could boast of.

"I tell you, I saw it with my own eyes." Braydon blared to his eager listeners.

A man in the front shook his head in disgust. "I'm not surprised," he growled. "I always knew they was hypocrites. Them religious folk always are. That's why I don't bother with any of their nonsense myself."

Braydon smiled. "I am in full agreement with you sir."

"Now let me get this right," a skeptic in the back of the group, added. "You said you saw one of them grab this little girl by the ears and drag her into the compound. And Thadus stood by approvingly?"

A disapproving murmur resonated through the crowd. Many shook their head in disbelief unsure of weather or not to believe this report. Comments and questions flooded Braydon's way.

"I hoped Thadus was going to be different then Reddland."

"Where were the girl's parents; letting her be treated like that?"

"I don't believe Thadus would allow that. He's a good man."

"Was it the gypsy one that did it? Or that big one?"

"What do they want with a little kid?"

Braydon held up a hand to quiet the crowd. "I know how you all feel. I couldn't believe it myself. I am as shocked as you are. I too had high hopes for this new regime, but…I don't think its Thadus's fault. He's a good man. It's just that…" Braydon made sure he had everyone's full attention.

"It's those mercenaries he has. They're a bad influence… probably threatening him. And Abrams…who knows what kind of ideas he is putting into Thadus's head."

"Those mercenaries helped rid us of Reddland." A voice offered up.

"True enough, but what if…just what if…" Braydon held up a finger as if to point and shook his hand. "What if they helped for no other reason then to someday help themselves? Right now they stand unopposed. The Royal Guard was their only real opposition."

Voices started shouting forth theories on the matter. Those that were loudest were actually heard. The crowd started talking over one another.

"Now I've met one of them…the girl…and she seemed to me to be a decent young lady, very polite. I think they really want to help us."

"She's mighty pretty too."

"I'll say!"

"You're thinking with your eyes again Ivan."

"The big one's the reason they outlawed Tanuba."

"I was there when he smashed the statue!"

"That muscle bound lad just does what he wants."

"The one called Cad is a warlock. I heard he has power over fire."

"You men are all wrong. They're our friends. They're trying to help us."

"That gypsy one isn't. He killed my brother with a rake in Reddland's stables."

"Gypsy scum!"

Braydon held up his hands. "Please, please, one at a time. You all have valid ideas. Maybe they are our friends. Then again maybe they aren't. They've changed a lot of our traditions. They're all following Abrams's teaching now, even Thadus. Most of us know their religion is a bit fanatical. They aren't tolerant like we are."

"So what are you saying we should do?" A man in front asked, suspicion in his voice.

"I'm not suggesting anyone break any laws." Braydon paused for effect. "But...we all should do what we have to do to ensure we don't go from Reddland's regime to something worse. Dragging a little girl by her ears...that sounds worse to me."

"Worse my foot. I saw Reddland kill a family once." An older man shouted.

"That doesn't mean we have to tolerate another repressive regime." Another said.

"Maybe Braydon is right. Why let them get too comfortable before we do something."

"You're all fools!" A burly man spouted. "Kelterland is sure to send troops and re-establish control of Xylor. Nothing we do will matter. You'll only be getting yourself killed for nothing."

"Maybe now is the time to take a stand."

Braydon stood back and watched the gathering, content that he had stirred them up to the possibilities he saw for Xylor's future. He wasn't a fan of Thadus and Abrams. They were too religious for his tastes, then again most people were. And the four newcomers scared him. He would never act against them himself. He fancied himself as a leader...a leader who delegated the dangerous work to those more capable while he watched from the wings. He was a thinker not a fighter.

Amidst the heated discussion the bartender walked up to Braydon with a message. "An admirer wants to buy you and the group a round of ale. She told me to tell you she was impressed with your argument."

Braydon looked about the room. There were no women in sight except for a few ladies clearing tables in the nearby dining area. "What admirer would that be?"

"She's right over…" The bartender pointed to a corner table that was now deserted. "Well where'd she go? She was just there a second ago."

"What did she look like?" Braydon was curious.

The bartender thought a moment. "You know, I can't really say. She wore a burgundy scarf. I didn't really get a good look at her. To tell you the truth I never paid her much attention till she waved me over and paid for a round of ale."

"Is that so?" Braydon seized the opportunity. "Listen up everyone! How about a round of ale? Barkeep, fill their tankards!"

Cheers and whoops filled the tavern. Those assembled thanked Braydon, some slapping him on the back. He did nothing to dispel the impression that he was responsible for buying the ale. He never *claimed* to have purchased the round; but someone had to take the credit. Since the mysterious woman was gone, Braydon would say nothing to give the credit to whom it was due. Instead he stood back and basked in the adulation of grateful drinkers.

Dusk came upon Xylor like a thief in the night, systematically snuffing out the last rays of sunlight. Shadows of the evening crept across the streets swallowing them whole. Cyrus looked to the sky and saw a thin sliver of moon. It would be a dark night.

A nervous tension weighed heavily on Cyrus. He wondered if whatever caused the death of the lost patrol would strike again tonight. Cad seemed to think so. The regular north and south patrols were canceled until answers could be found. With all efforts concentrated within the city, it was hoped the odds of finding those answers would be increased.

Cyrus removed his helmet and slicked back his thinning hair. It had been a long day. Since Cad and Scorpyus found the patrol the rebellion had been busy. Hopefully it was quieting down.

Cyrus heard a shout and turned to see a child being chased by a man with a bushy moustache. The child was around ten years of age and looked terrified. The man was obviously angry and was waiving an axe handle like a club.

"Hey, hold on here!" Cyrus snatched the child as he ran by, and then stood between the boy and the irate man. "What seems to be the problem?"

"I'll tell you what! That thief stole a piece of salt pork and an apple from my store." The man jabbed the axe handle in the boy's direction. The child cast his eyes downward at the accusation.

Cyrus stooped down and raised the boy's chin to look him in the eye. "Is that true? Did you steal from this man's store?" Cyrus already knew the answer. He could see the apple in the boy's hand. If he wasn't mistaken, the big bulge in the lad's pocket was the salt pork.

"Yes, sir." The boy's voice trembled when he spoke. His eyes were as wide as a full moon.

Cyrus let out a deep sigh. He felt for the child. The boy was thin and wispy, and looked to be extremely hungry. He was also respectful unlike the typical delinquent.

"Where are your parents?" Cyrus inquired as the shopkeeper waited patiently.

"My father left us three years ago because of the war. My mother is home. She's been sick for awhile."

Cyrus's heart went out to the child. This was not an isolated incident. A number of people had fled the island in the wake of the rebellion's victory. How they could abandon their families was beyond comprehension. Anyone who could do that wasn't a real man as far a Cyrus was concerned.

Cyrus turned to the shopkeeper and handed him a shilling. "How much does he owe you? Is that enough?"

"Why yes, it's more then enough." The shopkeeper was surprised by the gesture, and his anger left him.

"Good. Put what's left over on account for the boy. He'll be in to spend it later, but I'm going to have a talk with him first."

"Very well." The shopkeeper thanked Cyrus and shook his hand, relieved that the situation had been taken care of to his satisfaction. His confidence in the new government rose considerably over the incident.

After the shopkeeper left, Cyrus turned to the boy who was now smiling. "You're not let off that easy. A shilling is more then a fair days wages, especially for a boy. How do you intend to make this right?"

The boy stared up at Cyrus wide-eyed and nervous, "I don't know sir."

"Well I'll tell you how," Cyrus said. "You're going to turn up at the compound bright and early tomorrow morning to work off that shilling. We can always use help in the stables. Be sure you come by. I don't want to have to track you down. If you don't show up I may have to arrest you. Do you understand?"

The boy nodded his head up and down rapidly. "Yes sir, I won't give you cause to arrest me. I'll be there."

"Good. If you do a good job, I may just let you work as much as you want…for pay of course."

"Thanks mister." The boy smiled.

"One more thing; where do you live?" Cyrus asked while giving a stern look.

"Down this way about a half mile by the fork in the road." The boy pointed in the general direction.

Cyrus smiled and patted the boy on the back. "You run along now, and tell your mother a doctor will be by to see her at first light."

"Thanks mister!" The boy grinned broadly and scurried off.

Before Cyrus could contemplate the event, he heard a scream from far down the street. It sounded like it was near the docks.

Without missing a beat he ran in the direction of the scream. A few people were already starting to gather near an alley, craning their necks to get a look into the darkness. A man comforted his wife who held a kerchief to her mouth in shock.

As Cyrus got closer to the disturbance he saw Cad running toward him from the opposite direction, no doubt having heard the same scream. A woman recognized Cyrus and ran up to him.

"Oh, thank God you're here. A man has been murdered in the alley." She was on the verge of hysteria and was fanning her face with her hand.

"Well let's stay calm. We're here now, and we'll take care of this." Cyrus reassured the woman and nodded to Cad as he arrived.

"What do we have, mate?" Cad asked.

"This lady says a man has been murdered in the alley." Cyrus pointed down the darkened corridor. Cad squinted but couldn't see anything.

"Did anybody see what happened?" Cad inquired of the small crowd that had gathered.

The lady with the kerchief spoke up. She was visibly shaken. "I did I think." The woman was trembling; her husband placed an arm around her shoulders for support.

"What is that supposed to mean?" Cyrus furrowed his brow.

"My husband and I had just left our shop through the alley door where we get deliveries and came to the street, when I went back to get something I had forgotten. Before I could open the door I heard this horrendous thump right behind me. When I turned around…" The woman broke down in tears, sobbing heavily.

"It was so awful."

"Go on madam, when you are ready." Cad shot a glance to Cyrus.

The woman dried her eyes with her kerchief and sniffed gently. "When I turned around there was a dead man lying on the ground. His face was all contorted in a ghastly horror."

"Did you get a look at who did it; who may have struck this man down?" Cyrus asked.

The woman shook her head, a look of wonder in her eyes. "That's just it. There was no one in the alley with me. I was alone."

Cad stroked his goatee as he evaluated the woman's truthfulness and sanity. "You didn't see the man before he was killed?" The murderer was no doubt lying in wait which would account for the lady not seeing him. However, if the victim fell right behind her, surely she must have seen him.

"No, I was alone." The woman stared in a trance like state as she thought back on the episode. "One second I was alone, the next this man lands with a thump right behind me. It was as if he fell from the sky."

Cyrus shot Cad a bewildered look. "Fell from the sky?" He looked down the alley a moment, and then to the sky. It suddenly dawned on him what may have happened.

"We'll handle it from here." Cad sent the woman off, and tried to encourage the small gathering to disperse. He pulled Cyrus aside.

"Are you thinking what I'm thinking?"

Cyrus was studying the tall three story buildings on either side of the alley. "If you're thinking the man fell or maybe was pushed from the roof, then yes."

Cad smiled. "Right again mate. Let's get to the bottom of this."

Cad and Cyrus walked cautiously down the alley until they came to the dead man's corpse. His face was contorted into a bizarre horrified expression. The man was not a soldier in the rebellion, and looked to be in his fifties. His apparel was that of a man of some wealth; not an extremely rich man, but by no means a peasant. At first glance there were no traces of blood or an obvious wound. Both men bent down to examine the corpse more closely.

There was a swan drawn on the man's left cheek, and a powdery substance on his face, especially around his nostrils.

"This is exactly how the patrol was killed." Cad informed Cyrus. "He has the same image and white powder on him."

"It looks like he was strangled by a thin cord." Cyrus pointed out the red crease circling the man's throat. He was killed some time ago; look how stiff his body is."

"Bloody ay!" Cad's eyes grew wide. "That means whoever did this intentionally waited to throw him from the roof. More then likely until we were in the bloomin' area. No doubt to send us another message."

Cyrus shook his head in disbelief. "What are we up against? And why kill this man? He's not with us; I don't even recognize him."

Cad didn't have any answers. "I wish I knew."

A figure came out of the shadows in the alley and startled Cyrus and Cad. Both men grabbed the hilt of their swords and started to pull their weapons, not about to end up like the man lying before them. To their relief they recognized the sudden visitor.

"Don't be doing that mate." Cad warned.

"Especially at a time like this." Cyrus agreed.

"What are you talking about?" Scorpyus grinned. "Don't tell me you didn't see me walk down the alley." Scorpyus was always the one for a little practical joke. When he saw his friends in the alley he couldn't pass up the opportunity to sneak up on them. Besides, it was good practice.

"You can't fool me Scorp. At any rate, you're just in time. Someone threw this poor bloke from the roof. Not before they strangled him though; and some time ago at that. From the looks of it, it's the same people who killed the patrol." Cad was back down to business.

Scorpyus looked the scene over. "This building is the closest. I'll search the roof."

Scorpyus shimmied up the stone building with incredible agility. Standing on the ledge of a first story window, he reached up grabbing the rail of a second story balcony and eased himself up. Standing on that rail, he maneuvered to get his fingers on a third story shutter and pulled himself up to a small decorative ledge. A jump of about a foot gave Scorpyus a finger-hold on the roof, and soon he was on top of the three-storied structure. Other than his scabbard banging against the wall on the last jump, he completed the task with relative quiet.

"That was fast." Cyrus was impressed with what he saw.

"For such a day as this was Scorpyus born." Cad explained.

"I agree." Cyrus saw that the crowd in the street was growing. "I don't think I could have climbed up there."

"That may be mate, but from what I've seen, you still have plenty of other skills." Cad placed a hand on Cyrus's shoulder. "Now let's get a couple of chaps to carry this poor bloke to the undertaker before the whole town turns up."

Scorpyus surveyed the roof. It felt a lot windier up there then at street level. The building was a fairly large building, one of the few structures in Xylor made of large cut stone blocks. The roof had a two-foot high decorative border around the outer edge, though not tall enough to give Scorpyus a sense of ease when standing next to the side. A strong gust of wind could very well topple a man over the small border. Several chimneys protruded from the roof, each in varying size, shape and height. There was a trap door not far from where Scorpyus had ascended the structure. A quick tug on the handle revealed that it was locked from the inside.

Scorpyus knelt down to get a better look at the roof in the starlight. Even in the dim light he could tell that the thick layer of soot and dust on the roof had been disturbed near the trap door. There was what looked like drag marks going to the wall at about the place where the corpse would have been thrown from the roof.

Scorpyus walked back and forth on the roof going from side to side taking four-foot sections at a time. There were five other trap doors going below, each locked from the inside. At least two of the other trap doors had been used to access the roof recently, one to repair a chimney judging from some new mortar and stones. Thanks to Scorpyus there were now footprints all over. Satisfied that there was nothing else to see, he headed back to where he had scaled up. As he neared the trap door he saw a movement on the roof near his feet. Something darted from left to right just in front of his toes. It startled Scorpyus causing him to hop and jump to one side. He scanned the area expecting to find a rodent. Instead he saw what looked like a piece of cloth that was blowing slightly in the wind.

Scorpyus picked it up and held it to the starlight. It was made of thin cotton fabric and appeared to be a handkerchief. Upon closer examination he realized there was a 'BM' monogrammed in one corner. Scorpyus smiled and tucked the handkerchief into a pouch on his belt. With the wind up here, the handkerchief could have blown over from the other side of the roof where the chimney repairs had taken place. Or maybe it belonged to the dead man or his killer. At least he would have some place to start. He hated going back to the others empty handed.

Scorpyus walked back to the edge of the roof. He could see Cad and Cyrus talking below. They had been joined by Novak and Zephyr. A man in a brown cloak with a gold sash stood with his friends. He seemed to be silently taking in the scene. No doubt the man was a witness, hopefully with some good information. The corpse had already been carried off, and the crowd was starting to thin a little.

Scorpyus paused a moment before descending from the roof to enjoy the cool salt breeze on his face. It felt good, and carried the vague scent of fresh bread. The ocean climate suited him well, and the view was beautiful from up there. Scorpyus could see to the docks, candlelight flickering in several windows. The fog was still off shore. The sound of the street was muffled below. Other then a few sea gulls squawking overhead, it was a tranquil night on the roof. Scorpyus was going to wring a few moments pleasure out of God's creation while he could. Life was too short not to pause and reflect once in a while.

Suddenly the man in the brown cloak with the gold sash turned around and looked up at the roof. He looked right at Scorpyus holding a constant gaze. Almost simultaneously a foot scraped on the roof; from a roof that was supposed to be void of any others. Instinctively Scorpyus ducked down and rolled to the side, springing to his feet several yards from where he once stood. He turned in time to see a black shadowy figure lurch forward to where he had been standing, a thin wire garrote stretched taught between its hands. A cloud of white powder enveloped the place where Scorpyus had been. The scent of lotus blossoms wafted in the breeze. Frenzied, Scorpyus put some distance between himself and the poisonous, powdery cloud, visions of the contorted faces of the lost patrol racing through his mind.

The dark figure was agile and recovered quickly, darting into the shadow of a chimney and disappearing. Before Scorpyus could react the faceless entity was gone. He spun and turned frantically searching for this mysterious foe, scanning the dark mercilessly. The entity dissolved in with the black of night, and was not to be seen. Scorpyus stood still and listened intently. He could hear nothing but his pulse racing through his ears, a bead of sweat trickled from his brow. Squinting into the night, his keen vision registered nothing. At that moment Scorpyus felt a presence close behind him. For a fraction of a second, he sensed hot breath on the back of his neck that caused his hair to stand on end. Immediately Scorpyus thrust up a hand in front of his throat, just as a garrote whipped over his head. The thin wire jerked back against the palm of his hand forcing his knuckles against his windpipe. The dark figure pulled back on the garrote with such force as to lift Scorpyus from the ground by his head. It yanked, twisted and pulled forcefully carrying out its vicious attack.

Scorpyus sputtered a choking cough as his hand was forced hard against his throat. He could feel the thin wire biting into his hand through his leather gauntlet. The shadowy figure repeatedly jerked hard on the garrote trying to sever its victim's head. With each jerk, Scorpyus feet were lifted off the ground. He could feel his face flush and his eyes were watering. Choking sounds gurgled forth with each jerk of the garrote.

Scorpyus was already starting to feel light headed. He had to act fast. With his free hand, he unsheathed his dagger and thrust it behind him with all his might; all the while being pulled up and backward by his neck. His blade hit something solid, and Scorpyus felt the tension release from his throat. He fell to his knees coughing and inhaled deeply a much needed breath of air. Pain throbbed in the palm of his left hand. He shook his head trying to clear away the dizziness. Still coughing, Scorpyus massaged his throat and forced himself to his feet. He turned, dagger still in hand, to face this formidable adversary. Letting the enemy out of his sight was an event that Scorpyus didn't care to repeat.

The dark figure was now languidly circling Scorpyus, moving its hands and arms in a peculiar motion. It moved with a smooth fluidity; like black smoke billowing and rolling, it changed positions continually. Scorpyus had never seen anything like this. The shadowy figure was in the form of a man. It clearly had arms, legs, a head, and torso, but was without any other detail. There was no face to speak of, but a slight bump where a nose should be. If a man's shadow could come to life this is what it would look like. There was blood on the blade of Scorpyus's dagger. The entity may look like a shadow and move like a ghost, but it bled like a human.

With a sudden lunge, the figure attacked again. Scorpyus ducked and spun, able to dodge a few punches, but felt a kick to his left thigh. He lashed back with his dagger, trying to slash across the figure's arms in an effort to disable an appendage. The figure avoided the blade with unprecedented speed. Scorpyus side stepped a few more blows and then landed a kick of his own to his adversary's ribs. The figure let out an agonized grunt. The shadowy being launched a series of swings and kicks in a blur of limbs. Scorpyus tucked and rolled barely staying one step ahead of the entity. Scorpyus connected with a right cross and took a kick to the side. Another kick sent his dagger sailing from his hand and over the roof. The entity then released a flurry of blows and kicks even faster then the previous ones. Crouching and retreating, Scorpyus was forced on the defensive. He couldn't avoid all of the blows taking several to the ribs.

Scorpyus was fast. In all of his life he had yet to meet anyone quicker then him. He always knew that someday he would meet one with superior speed. Today was that day. Prolonging this fight was not to his advantage. He thought about pulling his sword, but the entity was keeping so much pressure on him that he didn't even have the chance. Scorpyus didn't want to divert his attention to draw his sword and thereby run the risk of facing the garrote again.

When the shadow kicked Scorpyus in the side again, he grabbed its foot and lifted it up high sending the figure off balance backwards. As the shadow fell, it kicked out with its free foot and caught Scorpyus in the chin. Scorpyus went sprawling backwards and fell against the outer edge of the roof. The entity, feet up in the air, fell back on its hands. In an amazing feat, the entity pushed off the floor with its hands, springing to its feet again. Like a mad dog it was over Scorpyus and pummeling him with kicks, keeping him against the short ledge at the edge of the roof. Amidst the blows, Scorpyus forced himself to his knees and shot a jab at the shadowy figure catching him square in the solar plexus. The figure doubled over, and Scorpyus followed it up with a fist to the jaw. The figure lurched backwards and started to fall. Scorpyus started to stand finally seeing a chance for victory. Instead of falling backwards, the figure did a flip in the air landing on its feet. It sprang at Scorpyus and thrust out with a sidekick that caught him squarely in the chest. The move was so quick and spectacular that Scorpyus didn't have a chance to move much less counter the attack. Scorpyus stumbled back two steps until he felt the edge of the roof against the back of his calf. His eyes grew wide in panic as he started tilting over the side. He swung his arms forward in an attempt to regain his balance, but it was too late; his body was already committed to the fall. It would be a three-story drop.

In a last final effort; Scorpyus clasped his hands on the top of the ledge digging his fingers in trying to stop his fall. His feet shot skyward as his head thudded against the side of the building. For a brief second he hung upside down with his feet up in the air, his fingers griping the edge of the outer border near his thighs. Gritting his teeth he clung for dear life, but momentum overcame his valiant efforts. The dark entity watched with satisfaction as Scorpyus disappeared over the side.

Cad and Cyrus were speaking with Zephyr and Novak in the alley below. A massive clatter and the sound of shattering pottery exploded in the night. All eyes darted to a second story balcony where a ruckus was taking place. A wooden railing obscured most of what was happening. Ceramic shards and the leg of a chair rained to the ground below.

"Bloody ay man! What on earth was that?" Cad reflexively pulled his sword.

"Someone's moving on the balcony. I see an arm." Novak reported. Zephyr drew back her bow aiming for the balcony. At the first sign on an attack an arrow would be protruding from the person attached to the arm.

Groaning could be heard from the balcony, and there was some slight movement. A swath of cloth floated to the earth. Slowly the arm reached for the top of the rail and pulled a body to its knees. Grunting and groaning a man rose to his feet.

"Scorpyus?" Zephyr recognized the dazed figure.

"I think I found the thing that killed the patrol and the man in the alley." Scorpyus leaned against the rail for support.

"Are you alright?" Cyrus inquired.

"Yeah, I'll be fine…now. Zephyr and Novak get a rope and come up to the roof. I'm sure the thing is gone by now, but maybe we can track it. I wounded it, but it's fast and lethal. Stay alert and be careful." Scorpyus slicked his hair back then massaged his throat.

Novak ran to get some rope. Zephyr moved toward the balcony, scanning the alley for trouble.

"Cyrus, lets get out to the street. They can handle this. Maybe someone saw something." Cad took one last look around then left with Cyrus close behind.

Cad and Cyrus had scarcely stepped out to the street when a woman ran up to them beseeching them for help.

"Oh, thank God I found you so quickly. I think someone is trying to break into my room. I heard a loud noise on my balcony, and scraping sounds on my shutter." The woman clutched a shawl with one hand and Cyrus's arm with the other.

Cyrus smiled and gave Cad a knowing look. "We have that taken care of. One of our men was having a look around the roof and fell. There's no need for alarm."

The woman was visibly relieved that no one was breaking into her room. However, her look soon turned to one of being puzzled.

"What was your man doing on the roof?"

"You'll have to get that story from your neighbors in the morning. Not to worry though, we'll have our chap down and you can go back to sleep." Cad was polite but left no doubt that he and Cyrus had more pressing matters at hand.

The street was becoming a bustling corridor of foot traffic. A few more curious or perhaps nosy stragglers loitered in the area of the alley intent on watching Cad conduct the investigation. One was intent on finding out if this murder was going to be properly dealt with, covered up, or even condoned. The others were just fascinated with the gore of it all. The woman who had been awakened by Scorpyus's fall was now a member of the latter group.

Cyrus stood back a few steps as Cad inquired of those gathered if they had seen anything on the roof, or if anyone had run from the vicinity. It looked like no one had judging from the shrugging shoulders and blank expressions. Cyrus thought about that. How could several people who are in rapt, mouth agape attention, watch a murder investigation and not see anything? Any one of them could probably tell Cyrus what their neighbor had for dinner the night before, or report on the state of their neighbor's marriage, or lack there of. Gossip traveled fast in the port city.

Cyrus glanced down in contemplative thought. The clouds must have blown off shore allowing more starlight to shine. Cyrus could see his shadow cast dimly on the street. The buildings on either side of the alley cast their shadows as well, with Cyrus's dark image caught between the two. It was as if his shadow was in a box.

Cyrus caught a movement out of the corner of his eye on the ground. A shadow appeared from the side of one of the buildings, perhaps on a balcony. The shadow reached one hand behind its back and pulled a thin dark line out from behind its shoulder. The shadow proceeded to place the thin line across a thicker curved line, and pull it back. Cyrus eyes grew wide and he spun around to where the shadow was being cast. There on a balcony a man was notching an arrow in his bow. He was looking over Cyrus toward Cad's vicinity.

"Look out!" Cyrus shouted and ran toward the startled group. Cad instinctively dove to the ground on Cyrus's explicit recommendation. The citizens still stood in shocked wonder at the shouted warning.

"Get down!" Cyrus reiterated and grabbed two citizens pulling them to the ground as he himself dove to the street. His helmet clanked against Cad's greave. There was a dull thud followed by a woman's shriek. Cyrus raised his head to see the shaft of an arrow protruding from the right side of the woman's chest. It was the same woman who came to report a man breaking into her window. Her breathing was labored and pink foamy blood gurgled from her mouth. She clutched her chest in agony.

"Bloody ay mate, where'd that come from?" Cad scanned the alley from his supine position in the street.

"A second story balcony; the building across from the one Scorpyus was on." Cyrus reported. No one seemed to be on the balcony now.

Cad could see three-second story balconies on that building. "Cyrus, see what you can do for the woman, I'm going to try to get that bloke before he gets out of the building."

"What's all the yelling?" Novak yelled from the roof. Scorpyus and Zephyr stood next to him.

"Someone took a shot at us from over there!" Cyrus pointed to the now vacant balcony. Those gathered picked themselves up from the street and circled the wounded woman. Cyrus stopped a passing cart vender and volunteered one of the bystanders to help him carry the wounded woman to the cart. As he loaded her he noticed Scorpyus, Novak, and Zephyr repel down from the first building.

Scorpyus ran to the far end of the alley. A figure was running towards town, a door swinging ajar at the back of the building.

"There he goes! Let's go Zephyr!" Scorpyus motioned for his friend to follow and was off like a jackrabbit. Novak joined Cyrus at the front of the building. The wounded woman was moaning, clutching her chest and writhing on the cart. An elderly man placed a rolled up cloak beneath her head. Cyrus tore her dress away from the wound to get a better look.

The arrow penetrated the woman's side between two ribs just below her right breast. Pink frothy blood bubbled from around the shaft, and the flesh around the wound was deep purplish like a bruise.

"I can't breathe, I can't breathe…" The woman gasped, as she took short heaving breaths of air. Her face was pale and her lips blue. Blood oozed from her mouth and trickled from her nose.

Cyrus jumped on the cart and applied a cloth to the wound to curtail some of the bleeding and stabilize the arrow shaft. He didn't dare pull it out. That would only cause more damage.

Novak knew the woman was gravely injured. "Let's get her to see Doc." He grabbed the handles of the pushcart and started it rolling toward the compound. Several bystanders stepped quickly aside to clear a path. They stood transfixed in a mute awe at the tragedy. A sickly pallor graced their faces.

Cyrus gave Novak a somber look and nodded as he tried his best to comfort the woman. "Did we get the person who did this?"

Novak shrugged his shoulders as he muscled the cart down the road. "Scorpyus and Zephyr ran after someone. He won't get away." Novak was confident in his friends.

Cyrus started to say something but stopped short when the woman let out a moan and clutched his sleeve tightly. Each bump in the road flashed pain in her eyes.

"Help…me." The women pleaded through tear streaked eyes. She stared up at Cyrus, holding tight to his arm. Her breathing was rapidly growing weaker.

"Just hold on ma'am. We'll have you to the doctor soon." Blood had seeped through the bandage soaking Cyrus's hand.

The woman shook her head feebly side to side. "Too…late," she gasped.

"Don't talk like that." Cyrus felt the woman release his sleeve. He clasped her hand tightly as Novak picked up his pace.

Novak pushed the vending cart as fast as he could. Cyrus and the woman rocked and swayed as they traversed six blocks. Blood started to pool on the cart, and the woman was no longer groaning with every bump in the road. Novak knew she was slipping away fast.

The woman stared up at Cyrus blankly. She was ashen and her breathing was barely audible. Cyrus instructed Novak to stop the cart.

"She'll be gone soon," he said as he cradled the woman in his arms. "Someone should hold her as she dies." Novak removed his helmet and wiped the sweat from his brow.

Cyrus consoled the woman as best he could. He reassured her that she would be with God soon, and held her close. She managed a faint smile. Cyrus was there for the lady as her body went limp and grew cold. He felt her breathing grow fainter and fainter. He watched the color slowly bleed from her deep brown eyes until they were a waxen gray. Then she was gone. A woman died in his arms and he didn't even know her name.

"We did what we could." Novak offered.

Cyrus nodded and gently lowered the woman's body to the cart. He took the cloak from under her head and draped it over her face. He and Novak were speechless. Nothing could be said that would change the fact that they had witnessed another day, with another death, in a string of deaths that stretched back farther then either one of them cared to remember. Ironically, further loss of life was the only way to stop it all. Novak had grown well accustomed to it. In fact he even thrived on the fight. He didn't like seeing innocent people die, but it fueled his anger against those who caused it. In a way he was like an avenger of women, children, and the helpless. For whatever reason, his personality was built that way.

Cyrus on the other hand fought only when he had to. He took no pleasure in doing this part of his job, but unfortunately it was necessary and few others stepped forward to do it. His soul bled for each needless death he had to witness. This woman's death filled him with anguish. She was scarcely thirty and had plenty of life left to live. The cold blank eyes that stared up at him was once someone's little girl. Was there a mother, or a sister, or a husband somewhere who would be missing her? Was there a child somewhere who would never know his or her mother? The questions gnawed away at Cyrus.

Cyrus stared long and hard at the murdered woman. He removed the cloak from her face and wiped the blood from her mouth and nostrils. If anyone came to retrieve the body they didn't need to see that.

"She died like a dog in the street." Cyrus shook his head. "The poor lady was at the wrong place at the wrong time. The arrow was never meant for her."

"What are you saying? What did you see?" Novak furrowed his brow quizzically.

Cyrus took a deep breath. "I think the archer was trying to kill Cad. I'm fairly sure he was in the line of fire before he dove to the ground."

Rage replaced Novak's quizzical look. "Kill Cad? Did you see who it was?"

"It was a man…between thirty and forty, with a dark green cloak. It happened so fast…I can't be sure of much more than that."

"Well let's hope Scorpyus and Zephyr catch him." Novak pounded a fist down on the cart. "This won't be tolerated! After all we did! We risked our lives for these people, and to think some ungrateful…"

Cyrus placed a hand on Novak's shoulder. "Most of the people are with us. There are still some Reddland loyalists out there though."

"Ya, I know."

"And no matter how good things get, we will never please everyone." Cyrus continued.

Novak nodded. "Ya, I know that also. I have little patience for those who fight like a coward…from the shadows hiding like a frightened child. If someone has a problem, face us like a man. Why risk killing an innocent woman. Then again, we're not dealing with honorable people, are we?"

"No Novak, we're not. They view the death of civilians as furthering their cause. Reddland did it as a matter of practice. He kept the citizens in a state of terror to better control them."

"Do you know what really bothers me?" Novak wore a worried look. "The fact that we're up against more then just a dissatisfied citizen turned assassin."

"What did Scorpyus say about his fight on the roof?" Cyrus inquired.

"Not much. He couldn't say for sure what it was that attacked him."

Cyrus's eyes grew wide. "He didn't know what it was? How can that be?"

"He said it was a dark, featureless, figure." Novak searched for the words to describe what Scorpyus told him and Zephyr on the roof. "I guess you could call it a shadow assassin." Novak didn't like the sound of it any more then Cyrus liked hearing it.

"God help us." Cyrus went pale. The day just kept getting worse.

———◆◆◆———

The unidentified man glanced back at his pursuers as he rounded a corner to a different street. He was aghast to realize that half his lead had already vanished. He thought himself a swift fellow, but the man in the burgundy tabard and the woman in the green short cape had swiftly closed in on him. A few more direction changes should do the trick.

Scorpyus glared at his prey from beneath arched eyebrows with the deadly intent of a serious predator. This man, pumping his arms in a mad dash for escape had a lot of explaining to do. A little longer and he would be close enough behind the man so as not to lose him. Then Scorpyus would let the man tire himself out before catching him.

Zephyr was right behind Scorpyus running as fast as her legs could carry her. Scorpyus, with his longer strides was the only one she knew who could run faster than her. Both were clearly faster then the man they were chasing.

The unidentified man took an alley and pulled over a stack of empty crates to slow his pursuers. Scorpyus and Zephyr easily avoided them. They followed him through the alley and down the street. The man was running toward the docks; exactly the part of town where one would expect to find a would-be murderer.

Scorpyus and Zephyr closed to within twenty feet when the man turned away from the docks down a street in a wealthy area. He came to a six-foot high stonewall and scaled it like a cat. Immediately Scorpyus and Zephyr angled to a place on the wall about twenty feet from where the man climbed over. They had been doing this for a long time and weren't about to scale the wall in the same place as the man. If the man thought he was dealing with novices, he would have another thing coming.

Scorpyus clasped the top of the wall and was up and over in a flash, landing in someone's yard. Zephyr was right behind him. He looked to the right and saw the unidentified man with his dagger out, crouched by the wall waiting to slash whoever was fool enough to climb the wall in the same place he had. When Scorpyus and Zephyr landed twenty feet away, it took the man by surprise. He practically leapt out of his skin. Scorpyus couldn't help but grin as he rushed toward the guy.

His ambush having failed, the man bolted through the yard and exited an open gate. He proceeded down a tree-lined street in front of nice homes. Dogs barked in some of the yards anxious to join the chase. The man turned back toward the docks leaving the upscale neighborhood. A few residents appeared in their doorways to see what had riled up their dogs. Scorpyus and Zephyr gave the residents apologetic nods as they ran by.

Scorpyus and Zephyr maintained a safe distance behind the man, allowing him to tire himself out. For them, his meager pace was like a brisk jog. They had scarcely gone a mile when the man's pace began to slow. They could hear him panting hard. Each time he looked back his expression grew more and more frantic. Scorpyus signaled Zephyr that he was going to make his move.

With a burst of speed, Scorpyus rapidly caught up with the man and shoved him from behind as hard as he could. The shove pushed the man's torso faster then his legs could carry him. In a cloud of dust the man tripped forward and tumbled down the street, his dagger flinging to the side. He came to rest flat on his back and in a bit of a daze. He had an abrasion on his forehead and a cut on his left wrist; probably from his own dagger. A passerby fled the scene thinking a robbery was taking place.

The man sat upright and attempted to get to his feet. Scorpyus swept the man's chin with his knee knocking him back again. The unmistakable sound of a dagger being unsheathed could be heard, and the man felt a sharp stinging pain at the base of his throat. His right arm was being pinned down; the left was being stepped on by Zephyr. The man, out of breath panted heavily into the face of an olive skinned stranger with a moustache.

"Don't give me a reason to kill you." Scorpyus glared at the man with a piercing stare. The man froze motionless and gurgled his understanding.

"Nothing else." Zephyr reported, kneeling with her foot firmly on the man's left wrist. She confirmed the fact that the man had no other readily available weapons and started searching through his pockets.

"Now you're going to answer a few questions." Scorpyus stated through gritted teeth, his anger clearly displayed on his countenance. "Why were you trying to kill those men back there?"

The man's eyes grew wide with a bewildered look. "I didn't try to kill anyone." The man replied in a raspy voice as if he were choking. Scorpyus let some of the pressure off of his throat.

"Are you going to lie to my face?" Scorpyus twisted the man's right arm until he could read the discomfort on his countenance.

"I don't know what you are talking about. I didn't try to kill anyone. It had to be someone else." The man was in his early twenties and appeared to be genuinely afraid.

"The man has seven shillings and nothing more." Zephyr reported the findings of her search.

"Don't lie to me! I know you shot an arrow at someone from the balcony!" Scorpyus was loosing patience with the fellow.

"I didn't. It wasn't me. It had to be someone else. I don't know what you're talking about. I don't know the first thing about archery." The man pleaded for someone to believe him. His eyes went quickly from Scorpyus to Zephyr hoping to see some hope that they believed him.

It just dawned on Scorpyus that the man had neither a bow nor arrows on his person. In fact he couldn't remember the man throwing anything aside during the chase.

A doubt was raised in Scorpyus's mind. "Then why were you running from us."

"Because you were chasing me."

"We were chasing you because you were running from us!" Scorpyus raised his voice. "You better start making some sense. I've had enough with these games."

"I tell you this monsieur, Scorpyus almost decapitated the last man that lied to us." Zephyr fabricated a story that she felt would scare the man into talking. Scorpyus applied a little pressure to the dagger at the man's throat.

"Alright! Don't kill me! A man gave me five shillings to leave the building right away and run to the docks and deliver a message for him. He told me to tell the captain of a ship called the Orion that he would be late. The ship was going to set sail soon. This man was supposed to be on it and wanted to make sure the captain would wait for him. He told me not to tell anyone else. Then I realized you were chasing me. I didn't know who you were then. I didn't recognize you as the soldiers in charge of the rebel army. I'm for the new government. I thought you were going to rob me. Or maybe the man who sent me to the docks was a smuggler or something. I don't know anything else." The man was trembling as he looked pleadingly at his captors. Scorpyus's intense gaze sent the man a clear message that meant business.

"Who is the man that sent you? What's his name?" Scorpyus inquired.

"I don't know."

"Tell me!" Scorpyus growled.

"I swear I don't know his name."

"Why should I believe that? You would run to deliver a message for a man you don't know. Nobody, except maybe a seasoned swordsman, would go to the docks at night alone *for a friend* much less a stranger. Not in a port city like Xylor. Many men have been enslaved as sailors on some long voyage for doing that, and you would expect me to believe you would go for five shillings." Scorpyus was beyond angry. Someone had just tried to kill his friend and he wanted to get to the bottom of the mystery.

The man had a look of horror on his face. "I never considered that. All I know is that five shillings is more then I can make in two weeks, and I only had to deliver a message. I don't know anything else. You have to believe me." The man was near tears with his pleading.

Scorpyus looked the man over. He was dressed in very modest and well-worn apparel. Five shillings was a lot of money, about a week's wages for the average person. Scorpyus was still suspicious. The man could be dressing to look poor as a ruse.

"What is your name Monsieur?" Zephyr asked. She gave Scorpyus a look that let him know she believed the man's story.

"My name is Horatio," the man replied meekly.

"So you say," Scorpyus said sarcastically. "Well 'Horatio,' tell us, what did this mysterious man look like. Surely you got a look at the man as he gave you instructions about his message."

The man thought a moment. "I'd say he was around thirty-five years old with wavy brown hair and a small scar on his chin.

He was wearing a dark green cloak; you know…with a big hood. That's all I can tell you."

Scorpyus mulled the possibility over a while. Horatio described a good portion of the population. A brown haired man in his thirties wearing a cloak; that narrowed it down to practically everyone as far as Scorpyus was concerned. He knew Zephyr believed the man, and who knows, maybe she was right. This man didn't look the sort to be mixed up with an assassination attempt. Unless he was playing a part, he was too naïve to be a would-be assassin.

"Are you going to arrest me?" The man inquired anxious to have the dagger removed from his neck.

"We'll see." Scorpyus and Zephyr pulled the man to his feet and bound his hands behind his back with a leather cord.

"We're going to take you back to where our friends are. One of them saw the man who shot the arrow. Maybe he will recognize you, and maybe he will say it wasn't you. Either way, we better not catch you lying." Scorpyus grabbed one of the man's arms and led him down the street.

Zephyr retrieved the man's dagger and tucked it into her belt. "I am sure we will solve this mystery eventually."

Novak and Cyrus joined Cad back at the building where so much action had taken place. Cad had just finished convincing the gathered revelers that all was back to normal, and that they should go back about their business. After answering a slew of questions, the crowd was finally ready to move on.

"Scorpyus and Zephyr aren't back yet?" Novak walked up and stood next to Cad crossing his arms. Novak's imposing size encouraged the crowd to thin more rapidly.

"Not yet," Cad turned to greet his friends. He could tell by their faces that things hadn't gone well for them. "The lady didn't make it, I see."

Cyrus shook his head. "There was nothing we could do." The trio's conversation was interrupted.

"Fire!" A teenage boy was in hysterics, waiving his arms frantically by the livery stables. Orange flames could be seen dancing madly through the open stable doors. Inside the frenzied whinny of horses pierced the night.

"This night won't end." Novak stated bluntly.

The trio raced toward the stables at the end of the block. Flames were hungrily consuming the straw on the floor of one of the stalls, eagerly licking at the posts and wall. With all of the hay in the stables, things would soon get out of hand. The wooden structure would provide a sizable meal for a ravishing fire if it wasn't quenched soon.

Novak pulled the stable door all the way open. A burst of heat gushed out. Smoke was starting to seep from the cracks and crevices of the structure.

"Cad, look at this!" Novak pointed to the ground in the stall that was ablaze. The remains of a torch could be clearly seen in the flame.

"Bloody aye! Now we have an arsonist to contend with." Cad grabbed a bucket from the stables. "Novak you get the horses out. Cyrus and I will start on the fire."

Cyrus grabbed a saddle blanket and started beating down the flames. Cad ran to the watering trough with the bucket. He noticed that the crowd gathered at the livery stables now.

"Form up a line. There are a few more buckets inside. I'll get them, and then you chaps pass them back and forth from the trough to the stables…quickly." Cad pressed the bystanders into service. Most were glad to be of assistance. A few grumbled but complied.

Novak came out of the stables leading two horses. Both were wild eyed and in a panic, and reared up as Novak led them out. Once away from the fire they calmed down slightly, but continued to whinny and snort their displeasure at current events.

"There were only the two horses." Novak took them across the street and hitched them to a post.

Scorpyus and Zephyr walked up with their prisoner, surprised to see a fire in the stables.

"What happened?" Scorpyus asked.

"We don't know for sure yet. The fire was deliberately set though." Novak replied while eying the prisoner. "Is this the archer?"

Scorpyus shrugged a shoulder. "Hopefully Cyrus will help us out with that."

Thanks to one teenage boy who sounded the alarm, and quick thinking on the part of those in the area, the fire was brought under control. Most of the damage was limited to the one stall and to some tack and harness. Two saddles were lost in the blaze. Fortunately no one else was injured.

Cyrus and Cad joined their friends. Both wore sooty smudges, and were wiping the perspiration from their brows.

"There's a bloke among us who fancies himself an arsonist." Cad replied while eying the prisoner. Cad waved a finger at the youth. "You must be the archer from the balcony."

"I didn't do it. I tried to tell them that but they wouldn't listen." The young man motioned to Scorpyus and Zephyr.

"Let's settle this now," Scorpyus replied. "Does this look like the stranger from the balcony Cyrus?"

Cyrus had already been eying the man over carefully. "No, the archer was at least ten years older and wore a dark green cloak, but he does look familiar."

"Then who's this chap?" Cad looked bewildered. Why would his friends bring this man in if he wasn't the archer?

"Je ne sais pas. He was the one running from us though." Zephyr added.

"Why were you running if you are innocent?" Cad asked. Cyrus had been studying the man intently like he knew him from somewhere.

"He claims a man hired him to deliver an urgent message to the Orion." Scorpyus was still skeptical.

"It's true! I was just delivering a message." Now the man pleaded before Cad.

"I know who this man is. He's Horatio Larek. I knew I'd seen him about." Cyrus interrupted. Scorpyus confirmed that that was who the man claimed to be.

Cyrus continued. "I think you know him. His father owns Larek's stables. There's one in Sage and three here in Xylor. Thadus managed the one in Sage."

A look of revelation came over the four knights. They were well acquainted with the stable in Sage, and had spent a good deal of time there when they first arrived in Xylor.

"It is true," Horatio confirmed. "I have been grooming horses here in Xylor. My father won't let me manage one of his stables until I maintain a job for one full year. I haven't exactly been the ideal son previously. I'm trying to make a new start. I knew the man who hired me to deliver a message was a rough sort. He just paid me a lot more then I make grooming horses. I certainly didn't mean for all of this to happen. I'm sorry for any problem I've caused. Please don't tell my father. I'm just a few months away from proving to him I've changed."

Horatio sounded sincere, and besides, Cyrus had already said he wasn't the one who fired the arrow. There was no point in holding the youth any longer.

Scorpyus loosed Horatio's bonds. "Before you go, what did the man look like who hired you to deliver the message?"

"He was in his mid thirties, average height, wearing a dark green cloak. He was an ordinary looking guy." The youth rendered the same description he had given to Scorpyus a short while earlier.

"There was nothing else you noticed about him?" Cad asked.

Horatio thought a moment. "No, not really. He did have a tattoo of a woman on his forearm, but a lot of people have tattoo's; especially at the docks."

"Alright, if that's all you remember you're free to go." Cad replied.

V

⸺⸻◆⸻⸺

"SHALL WE GET started?" Thadus surveyed the grim faces gathered at the table. The last three days had been wearisome, and fraught with much trouble. The new government in Xylor was experiencing its first real trials and tribulations since its victory over Reddland's dictatorship. How they dealt with these tribulations would determine the success of that new government.

Sleep had been a scarce commodity for the nine gathered around the large wooden table. There was none of the usual chitchat and banter that normally went on at such meetings. Instead those gathered looked down at the table, or gazed out in the distance contemplating the difficulties facing them while they waited for Thadus to start the proceedings.

Abrams sat, hands clasped in front of his mouth with his elbows on the table, no doubt in prayer. Cad scribbled a few notes on parchment as he reviewed what had already been written. Cyrus held a cup of hot tea running his thumb along the rim, deep in solemn contemplation. Novak leaned back in his chair with his hands folded on his chest attempting to grab a quick catnap. The other three knights often jested about his ability to sleep anywhere. Emerald sat next to Novak with a worried look. It was the kind of look a woman has when she sees a loved one off to war. Bartus could barely sit still. He was as jittery as a mouse in a room full of hungry cats. News of recent events had cost Bartus his appetite, causing him a loss of sleep and a bout of indigestion. Scorpyus studied the others around the table. Dozens of different ideas, possibilities, and scenarios ricocheted around his mind as he waited for the meeting to begin. Zephyr bit her bottom lip, a sense of dread on her face, but yet a glimmer of hope could be seen in her deep green eyes. She was ever the optimist.

"Let's open with a word of prayer." Thadus continued. "Abrams, if you would please." Novak opened his eyes and leaned forward.

"Yes of course," Abrams replied and waited for the others to prepare. All bowed their heads and clasped their hands.

"Dear Lord, as you know dark days are upon this island. We ask for your guidance. All of our hope is in you. Give Thadus and those gathered here wisdom and knowledge to solve the problems before them. Protect them, and guide them, for their journey is wrought with much peril. Let us remember, as it is written: 'Yea, though I walk through the valley of the shadow of death, I will fear no evil; for thou art with me.' Thy will be done in all things, we pray in Jesus name, amen." Amens sounded around the table at the conclusion of Abram's prayer.

"Thank you Abrams." Thadus picked up the parchment before him. "First I would like to thank you all for your efforts over the last few days. I know it hasn't been easy as things have been chaotic. Your efforts have been appreciated."

Thadus continued. "Now about these 'shadow assassins,' what exactly do we know about them?"

"It's not good," Cad let out a heavy sigh. "In the last three days these shadow assassins, as Novak has labeled them, have killed fifty-three people. Most have been random citizens, men and women, old and young, even one child. All have been strangled to death with a garrote. Some have been mutilated. One tried to kill Scorpyus. It's been a blooming nightmare."

"Not to mention the dozen fires that have been deliberately set and the assassination attempt made on Cad." Novak added.

Thadus had a pained look on his face. "The attempt on Cad was not perpetrated by the same shadow assassin?"

"We can't bloody well say. He wasn't dressed in black when he tried to kill us."

Thadus grimaced. "So we may have more to worry about then these phantom-like rogues. There may be some citizens willing to kill to turn things back toward Tanuba."

"That's a good possibility." Cyrus stated.

Thadus bowed under the weight of the responsibility he was now carrying as Regent of Xylor. Leading an organized army had been out of his league three months earlier. Dealing with deadly apparitions was beyond comprehension.

"Is there any truth to the reports that these shadow assassins are actual ghost-like entities, who breathe fire, and vanish at will?" Thadus asked Cad.

Cad consulted his notes briefly. "I've questioned the chaps who reported those bizarre occurrences. I know they sound daft, but there is a bit of truth there. These things are indeed unlike anything we've ever heard of. There may be a spot of exaggeration clouding the testimony, but extreme fright has that effect. Scorpyus is the only one who saw one up close and is alive to tell about it." Cad motioned for his friend to continue the story.

All eyes were in rapt attention on Scorpyus. All could see the dark bruising on his throat, and the discoloration under his eyes. Knowledge about this ghoulish threat was meager, and fascination with the unknown guaranteed an audience. Even Bartus's curiosity outweighed his fear and forced him to listen to tales that he would rather not know of. If anyone was a credible witness it was Scorpyus. He had managed to survive what fifty-three others didn't.

Scorpyus thought back to the incident momentarily. "I understand why those who have witnessed one of the assassinations say such things.

They are dressed completely in black and difficult to see. They are fiendishly fast and agile. They use shadows and the dark like no other, and do indeed appear to vanish at will. In hand-to-hand combat they are experts. There is a lot about them we do not know, but this much I can say; they are human. They bleed like us, they have a solid form or body like us, and logically they must also be able to be killed like us."

Bartus let out a sigh of relief. "Well if they are human and can be killed then it will be only a matter of time before the threat is gone, right?"

Novak shook his head in disbelief. "Have you been listening Bartus? *Scorpyus* barely survived. He's one of the fastest fighters I've ever seen, and look at his throat. We may as well be up against ghosts."

"Oh dear!" Bartus squeaked.

"Cad and I found a white powder on the corpses of the missing patrol. Many who have been assassinated have had this powder on them. I believe the one that attacked me tried to throw some in my face. The powder has the smell of lotus blossoms. I believe it to be some type of poison. I don't know its effects yet, but I have collected some and I'm going to try to find out what it does. Until then, if you smell lotus blossoms move fast or it could very well be the last thing you ever smell." Scorpyus added.

Bartus's eyes grew wide. He didn't like the sound of that.

"You speak of 'them.' So we know there are more then one?" Thadus inquired.

"We've talked about it," Cad motioned to the other knights and Cyrus, "and think there could be more than one. The attacks have been too frequent, too much distance apart. These blokes may be quick but nobody is *that* bloody fast; we hope. If it is just one then it would indeed have the abilities of a supernatural being." The others nodded their concurrence.

"Dear God, this can't be happening!" Bartus voiced what the others felt inside.

Thadus furrowed his brow. "That's what I was afraid of. This shadow assassin has petrified the people. No one is safe. Emerald tells me she has heard murmurings against me, against all of you, even against God. They feel that life would be safer under the old system. How soon they forget. Reddland killed citizens randomly many times. Then again he had no phantasmagoric abilities attributed to him, now did he?"

"The shadow assassins prey on the people's superstition. That is why they must be stopped soon." Zephyr added.

"Those who said that are weak." Novak scoffed. He had a low tolerance for weakness, especially those who prepared for failure by searching for reasons to be afraid.

"Yes, but the people are looking to me to fix the problems; to obtain security." Thadus stressed.

"Government is not the only answer," Novak stated bluntly. "The people should take a stand and help themselves a little. The reason the shadow assassins have the effect they do is because too many people do nothing to help."

Novak looked to Cad and Cyrus. "Remember the other night? People are killed and no one sees anything. Too many don't want to get involved."

"Regarding the other night," Scorpyus interrupted, "What did that man in the brown cloak have to say? He may have seen the shadow assassin that attacked me."

"What man?" Cad asked quizzically.

"The one that was standing next to you and Novak about five minutes before the chaos broke loose."

"There was no man." Novak didn't know what Scorpyus was talking about. Cad nodded his agreement.

Scorpyus did a double take at his response. "You didn't see the man in the brown cloak, with the golden rope-like sash, sandals, and blonde hair? He was standing in your midst for several minutes."

"There was a lady; the one struck by an arrow…" Cad shrugged his shoulders.

"I don't remember any man in a brown cloak." Novak stated.

Scorpyus was a bit surprised his friends didn't see the man, but there was a lot of commotion. "Well he was probably just a reveler anyway."

Thadus brought the subject back to the matters at hand. "The question remains; where do we go from here? I have already issued a proclamation advising people to stay indoors during darkness, and to stay away from isolated areas at all times if possible. We must put this episode behind us if we are to have any hope of preparing for the four thousand troops Kelterland will eventually send. We have seen an increase in support, but it could diminish with these shadow assassins on the prowl."

Everyone knew that Thadus had worked hard to build trust with the citizens. Trials were open to the public, taxes were reduced to a third of what they had been, and Thadus was available to the community leaders. He did outlaw Tanuba worship, which angered a lot of the people, but he did nothing to stop anyone from worshiping the stone idol in their own homes. The oratory was reopened but no one was compelled to attend. In fact, all gathered insisted that a decision for God must be voluntary and not coerced in any way. Thadus was doing his best to appease everyone without compromising his morals. If the people were honest they would admit the quality of life was better now then it had been for many years; even with the current problems.

Cad leaned forward and put his elbows on the table. "I've talked it over with Novak, Scorpyus, Zephyr, and Cyrus, and we think we have a plan."

Thadus looked very interested. "Well, great, what would the plan be?" Abrams, Bartus, and Emerald looked on earnestly, their curiosity piqued also.

"We feel it would be better for Xylor if we stop these new troops from ever leaving Kelterland."

"I agree," Thadus stated. "But how on earth can we do that?"

"By taking the bloomin fight to them," Cad explained. "If we send an envoy to the mainland to organize some resistance, we could create enough problems that Kelterland would have no choice but to use those new troops to quell the uprising. With any luck we could organize a full-fledged rebellion. Once other chaps hear about our success here in Xylor, they will be more willing to take a chance and fight."

Thadus was visibly taken aback at the suggestion, but pondered it carefully. After several moments of thought he asked the obvious.

"Do you think that will be possible?"

"It will be the last thing Kelterland expects. We will have the element of surprise for quite awhile." Cad poured himself some more tea.

"I'll agree! Who in their right mind would predict that?" Thadus responded.

"S'il vous plait…um, that is to say please, Thadus. Trust us. I know it will take a leap of faith, but it could work." Zephyr encouraged.

Scorpyus nodded. "If God is for us, who can be against us?" Novak was in agreement with his friends.

Thadus stroked his beard in thought. "I don't know. It sounds far too risky."

"Look at it this way mate." Cad paused to take a sip of tea. "If we wait for the soldiers to come to Xylor it will be just as risky. We fought two thousand troops in the last battle…at a heavy cost to us. I know we've had some chaps come forward to help, but for the most part people are waiting to see what will happen.

They're waiting for assurance this new government will survive before they support it. We may not have the time to show this government is viable before troops arrive; especially with those shadow blokes about."

"The people have been through so much already. It will be good if we avoid another big battle so soon." Zephyr motioned for Cad to pass the tea. She warmed her hands on the outside of her cup after she poured herself some.

"I don't like this one bit," Thadus shook his head in dismay. "But unfortunately you may be right."

"If we can carry out a few attacks in Kelterland or the occupied territories, I think it will have a considerable impact on their moral. It should make them wonder how deep the rebellion goes, and how strong it is. The unknown possibilities should wear on their nerves like the shadow assassins do ours." Scorpyus tried to convince Thadus.

"I see your point, but won't that leave us unprotected here in Xylor?"

"Not if I can help it." Cad shifted in his chair. "The plan is to secretly send one of us with a few soldiers, make contact with the resistance, and organize some attacks. I pray enough blokes step forward to fight."

Thadus thought long and hard about it. "I suppose we can give it a try. We should know within months if the plan will work. At the very least it will delay Kelterland in sending troops. I assume Scorpyus will be going."

"Until recently that was the plan." Cad's voice became very serious. "However, Scorpyus is likely the only one who stands a chance against these nasty shadow blokes. It will take every bit of his skill in disguise and infiltration to find and destroy these assassins. The rest of us must stay on guard. We can best help by being ready to help anyone who comes under attack."

"Then who will go?" Thadus asked.

"Well mate, Zephyr is going to be needed to help Scorpyus. She will also be going to visit that hermit woman. If anyone has information about these shadow blokes it will be Hester. Zephyr will also be Scorpyus's replacement if that should become an unfortunate necessity."

Cad continued. "Cyrus and I will lead the troops here, and make preparations in case we can't stop those four thousand troops from coming."

Emerald's eyes widened at the sudden realization Novak would be the one going to carry out this new plan.

"I'm sorry Novak," Scorpyus was solemn and sincere. "I know infiltrating the underground is a job that I would normally do. There's really no other way." Scorpyus was afraid for his friend. Novak's first attempt at infiltration would be dangerous.

"If they are on the side of freedom there should be no danger in contacting the underground." Novak reasoned.

"It's finding them I'm worried about. If you contact the wrong people…it's an act of treason, and the three of us won't be able to help." Scorpyus was worried for his friend.

"Don't worry Scorp, I'm not going alone." Novak reassured. "Which reminds me, have we found someone to get me through the blockade?"

"I should think Dantes would be up to the task." Thadus was getting more comfortable with the idea. "I'll arrange for him to take you. When did you want to leave?"

"Tonight after dark. The less we do in the open from now on the better. The bloody enemy is mingled among us. That much is certain." Cad injected.

Thadus nodded his approval. "Tonight it is. Who besides Novak and Dantes is assigned to this mission? Or will it be just the two of them?" Thadus was more then happy to leave decisions about military matters to Cad.

"I have someone in mind…Novak will need help, and…" Cad stopped beating around the bush and got to the point. "How about Emerald, Thadus?"

"No! Absolutely not! It's much too dangerous."

"Now father! Wait a minute! I think I will be able to handle this. I'm not a child anymore." Emerald was adamant the she go now that the opportunity presented itself. Besides it would give her time with Novak.

"No Emerald, it's far too risky."

"It's as risky to stay here with the shadow assassins."

"How would it look if I let my daughter go into God knows what kind of situation?"

"You don't have a problem letting Zephyr go into harms way."

"But she knows how to use a sword."

"Now hold on here." Cad raised a hand. "No one said Emerald was going to fight. If the need arises Novak will do the fighting, hopefully with the assistance of many like-minded rebels. Emerald would go along to help. There are some risks mate, but no more than here; in fact maybe less."

Thadus sat quietly miffed. He didn't like that everyone else was making. It was true. He had no problem with Zephyr going. But Zephyr wasn't his daughter. That made it a lot easier. Ironically, it might even be safer to go. The daughter of the regent of Xylor would be a prime target for assassins.

Thadus realized Cad was right. He couldn't protect his daughter forever. She was twenty-five. Thadus felt confident Novak would protect her to the death if need be.

"Fine, Emerald can go, but I want you to take Bartus also." Thadus caved in with one request of his own.

Bartus's head snapped towards Thadus, and he went rigid in his chair. "But why? I would only slow Novak down. I would only hinder this mission."

Novak nodded vehemently in the affirmative. "Ya, for once Bartus, you are making sense."

"See, Novak agrees." Bartus pointed at Novak. "I've not fully recovered from my wounds either."

The others sat in silence waiting for Thadus's explanation. It had better be a good one as far as Novak was concerned. Cad stifled a grin thinking the episode amusing. Scorpyus eyed Thadus with suspicion. What could this request mean? Zephyr felt there would be a good reason though she couldn't think of one.

"Please hear me out, all of you." Thadus held up a hand. "Now I know what you're thinking Bartus, but you can be of use to this mission. For years you've kept an eye on the docks and let us know of activities that transpired there. The information you provided helped the rebellion immeasurably through the years. I know you saw yourself as a vagabond who lived under the pier, but whether you admit it or not, you were quite an effective spy. I'm not asking you to be a warrior. I do, however, think it a good idea to have an experienced observer along on this mission. Stay in the background, find out what you can, and assist Novak. There's a lot more to a mission then fighting. One thing I learned from the Clandestine Knights is for every man in the fight, two are needed in support."

Thadus knew Bartus didn't think he was worth much to the rebellion. After his family had been killed he became a shattered man. Bartus was just starting to take an active role again. Perhaps going on an assignment, even if only in a supporting role, would restore his confidence. Getting off the island might do him some good.

Bartus pondered everything Thadus said. Maybe he could be of help. After all, Bartus did keep close watch on the docks. He had never thought of himself as a spy before, but it had a nice ring to it.

Bartus cleared his throat and spoke softly. "If you really need me I suppose I can go." Bartus sort of looked forward to a little adventure. Of course he would leave all the fighting to Novak.

"Oh, uncle Bartus! It will be so nice having you along." Emerald squeaked with delight. She was so thrilled to see her uncle start to resemble the man she once knew. Novak rolled his eyes and promptly received an elbow to the ribs.

"Ya, why not." Novak replied without a hint of enthusiasm.

"Then it's settled," Thadus smiled. Novak, Bartus, and Emerald will go to the mainland to organize some resistance. Zephyr will seek out Hester and find out what she can about the shadow assassins. Scorpyus will gather what information he can. And Cad and Cyrus will lead the patrols and keep the peace. We have our next few days planned baring any unforeseen difficulty. Does anybody have anything to add?"

"I think I may," Abrams replied. "I was going through my father's personal effects and found something that may be of interest. I had no idea my father had been in periodic contact with anyone from the mainland. But after listening to all that has transpired, I now realize more then ever before that the Lord does indeed work in mysterious ways."

The others in the room were a little surprised because Abrams rarely commented on strategies. He preferred a role of prayer to that of military leader or politician. All ears waited for what he had to say.

"As you are all aware, when my father was killed I became heir to what few possessions he had. Much to my immediate surprise I found that he had been able to comprise a complete copy of the Gospel of John. This will in great measure further my ministry here in Xylor. With his personal effects I also found a letter from a Barrington Rathbone. The letter reported on the latest developments in the territory near the border of Kelterland and The Dales. For some reason the name Rathbone sounded familiar but I didn't know exactly why. Two months went by and I forgot all about it until I was reading through my father's papers again. I found a list of names of the men he went to seminary school with. One of those names was a Cyril Rathbone. It suddenly occurred to me that the Barrington Rathbone corresponding with my father was likely a relative to this Cyril Rathbone. The letter was vague and brief, but from the nature of its contents it seemed to be a report on Kelterland troop movements. Now I have no solid proof, but I believe that Barrington Rathbone is involved in rebel activities. Why else would one report on Kelterland troop movements? I know it's not a lot but I thought it might help."

Abrams words sunk into his listeners slowly. His conclusions made sense. If Isaac had a rebel contact established on the mainland it would make things a lot easier.

"How would we find this chap?" Cad inquired. "Does it say in the letter what town or village he is at?"

Abrams shook his head. "Unfortunately it does not. The letter reports on troop movements along the southern part of the border of Kelterland and The Dales. So I assume Barrington Rathbone can be located in that area somewhere. The letter mentions a Stonebridge, but I have never heard of such a place. It could be a code name for another town."

Cad looked at the others. Everyone gave an expression relating they had never heard of a place called Stonebridge.

"That's a pretty vast area to try to find a single man mate; several hundred square miles I'd say. There has to be some way to narrow it down a bit." Cad was open to suggestions.

Being familiar with spying methods, Scorpyus had an idea. "Who brought Isaac the letters? Was it Dantes? Maybe whoever smuggled them into Xylor would know how to find Rathbone?"

"No one smuggled them in. They came in legitimate shipments."

"Do you know what kind of shipments?" Novak asked.

"I'm sorry, I can't help you there." Abrams replied.

"Whoever put the letters in the shipping crates would know something that would help us find Rathbone." Scorpyus deduced.

"Is there anything else you can think of?" Zephyr asked.

Abrams thought a moment. "All of my father's papers were in a small wooden box with J&R Shipping written on it, but he could have gotten that box anywhere."

"J&R Shipping is a venture out of Astoria. They have a fleet of ten or twelve smaller vessels. Before the blockade they came to Xylor twice a week. I haven't seen one of their ships for over two months." If there was one thing Bartus knew, it was shipping and almost everything else that went on at the docks.

"It's some place to start." Scorpyus had his doubts. "Astoria is the biggest city in Kelterland. It won't be easy."

"Trust in the Lord and all shall go well." Abrams advised. Amen's sounded around the table.

"Novak has a difficult task before him, as do we all. Let us pray that we are met with success." Thadus responded. "I have one more thing."

Thadus pulled a small box from a sack he had next to his chair. "Since the victory against Reddland I've wanted to give you something to express Xylor's gratitude for all you have done. I wanted to give you these at the March Octave but they weren't ready in time. I was going to wait for another celebration, but now I don't know when that may be. I want you four to have these now."

Thadus reached into the box and retrieved four identical daggers with scabbards. Each dagger was a masterpiece of craftsmanship, the double-edged blade razor sharp. The handle was ornately carved with a swirling design, the hand guard made of two spike-like protrusions; one facing toward the point of the blade, the other facing the end of the hilt. At the tip of the hilt was mounted a large black gemstone, a jeweled Fleur De Lis etched on the gem. One petal of the Fleur De Lis was made of sapphire and the other of ruby. Each dagger had its own leather scabbard with a brass Fleur De Lis emblem trim. They were beautifully impressive displays of art as well as quite functional. Thadus handed each of the Clandestine Knights a dagger.

"Oh, monsieur, it is beautiful, merci." Zephyr unsheathed her dagger and noticed an inscription: *To our friends from Ravenshire, with gratitude-Beatus Es Dominus Deus En Aeternum.*

Scorpyus placed his on his belt, replacing his old dagger. "The banquet at the March Octave was thanks enough Thadus."

"I'll say mate, you didn't have to go and do this." Cad studied the ruby on the hilt. "This cost a few shillings."

I know the Fleur De Lis is the heraldry emblem for Ravenshire. That's why I chose it for the design." Thadus explained.

The four were humbly surprised by Thadus's grateful gesture on behalf of the new Xylorian government. None of them expected it. Especially after the huge celebration they already received at the March Octave.

"The Fleur De Lis is also our heraldry for the Clandestine Knights." Novak stated.

"What is the history of your heraldry?" Thadus gave a curious look.

Cad explained. "Well the standard Fleur De Lis has a three petal lily emblem, usually all of the same color. Ravenshire has a dagger blade for the center petal, and the two drooping petals on the side are colored; red on the right and blue on the left. Three rings bind the petals together."

Zephyr explained further. "That is because of the legend. It is said when Eve was banished from the Garden of Eden she shed many tears, and those tears fell on the petal of a lily. It is also said when Jesus was crucified a few drops of His blood fell on the petal of a lily growing at the foot of the cross. That is why we have one red petal; representing the one sprinkled with blood; and one blue petal; representing the one sprinkled with tears."

"The center petal is a blade representing strength, and the three rings binding the petals represent the Trinity." Scorpyus finished expounding the legend.

"That is a beautiful legend." Thadus replied. "And is a fitting symbol for our friends from Ravenshire. Thank you once again."

The four knights humbly accepted their gift and thanked Thadus many times over for his thoughtfulness. Emerald looked on proudly.

"You have all earned more then we could ever hope to pay." Abrams added. "Please accept the daggers as a lasting token of our appreciation as you are about to embark upon further peril for the sake of Xylor. I pray that they serve you well should you ever have to call upon them to defend your life."

VI

"CYRUS, I THOUGHT I was going to die." Iris tried to sit up slowly but a wave of nausea forced her to lie back down. Her illness had left her bedridden for the better part of two weeks. Many times, in a feverish state, Iris thought she wasn't going to make it. Her first attempts at serious prayer were pleas to God for deliverance from her sickness. She now felt much better then she had in days.

"I knew you'd survive." Cyrus had been pleasantly surprised to discover the boy he assisted earlier in the week was none other then Iris's son. He hadn't seen Iris, much to his dismay, since after the battle with Reddland's men. He was happy to have found her company again, though it wasn't in the manner he had envisioned. Cyrus had sent Doc by three days earlier to see what he could do for Iris. Doc started by immediately soaking Iris with water, for she was dangerously hot. He dispatched an assistant every few hours to check on her. Since that first day, Cyrus had been coming by to see that Iris and her son had food, and spent much of the night at her side. He kept a silent vigil, and tidied up a bit. When he first came, the small one room house stank of sickness. He made sure to air out the house. Now Iris's fever had finally broken, and she seemed to be on her way to better days.

"I can't thank you enough for all you've done. No one has ever cared…" Iris's voice started to crack and she cut herself short. A soft silence fell upon the room. Cyrus dabbed her forehead with a cool cloth.

Iris had lived a difficult and lonely life. Orphaned as a little girl, she had seen many sorrows and borne much grief. Her recent conversion to Christianity nearly cost her life. She underwent a long and arduous recuperation from the brutality she suffered at the hands of Reddland's men, only to be stricken by an illness as she was starting to truly enjoy life. In all the years she had spent in the temple of Tanuba she never felt that way. Now at thirty years old, she realized how good life could be. It was a rough blow to take ill just when she was getting a new start. Had it not been for Cyrus, she might not have recovered at all. Iris was so wracked with fever she had been unable to eat. Her young son was unable to help, and there was no money for a doctor. Having been raised in an orphanage, there were no relatives to provide assistance. Like a guardian angel Cyrus arrived. He arranged for medical aid, and stood by her side through the illness. No one else had ever done that. No one else had ever cared. In fact, until now men had despitefully used her. But not Cyrus; he was different. He did more then help, he paid for food and supplies to see Iris and her son through. He prayed for her recovery. Compassion was the hallmark of his creed. Forbearance in the presence of a lady was his habit. Cyrus was a man of honor, integrity and chivalry. Those had been foreign traits in the other men she had known.

Cyrus smiled as he gently caressed Iris's forehead with the cool damp cloth. A slight breeze cooled her feverish brow. Cyrus was confident that the worst of the illness was behind them. His gaze caught hers and he held it. Iris's sad brown eyes betrayed the smile she wore.

"I sometimes think you wouldn't be here now if you had known me before the rebellion." Iris said.

Cyrus set the damp cloth to the side. "You couldn't be more wrong. I know you went through a lot to take a stand for God. That day I saw you tied to that post…" Cyrus shook his head in disbelief.

"I thought you were dead. From that day I realized you were serious about your decision for a better life. I didn't know you before that day, and I didn't know what had become of you after the battle. One thing I can say is this Iris; I'm glad I found you now."

"No Cyrus, if you only knew…," Tears started to well up in Iris's eyes. She felt she had to be honest with Cyrus from the start. She didn't want rumors and gossip to be his first source of information.

Cyrus placed his hand softly on Iris's lips. "That's enough of that talk. We've all made our mistakes. Regardless of who you may have been, you're a new woman now."

Iris started crying. Kind words had been sprinkled sparsely in her direction in days past. Recently her life had changed so much, she wondered if anyone would recognize her. She certainly changed from her days of aspiring to be the temple priestess in the Tanuba cult. "Oh. Cyrus!"

"I think you're too hard on yourself. I have my regrets." Cyrus reassured.

"I can't imagine you doing anything so terrible." Iris replied.

"That's not entirely what I meant. Not all things past are necessarily bad." Cyrus mused a moment. "The past is such a vast tapestry, full of mystery and intrigue. Anguish, sometimes self-inflicted, is often wrought upon us. As people become acquainted, truth starts to come into light. None of us knows when a long kept secret may resurface. It is usually when we least expect it." Cyrus sighed deeply. "Sometimes the suspense is more then I can bear."

Iris looked puzzled. "What are you saying?" She dabbed tears with her bed sheet.

Cyrus changed the subject. "The main thing now is that you get well. The color has returned to your face. That's a good sign."

"Are you trying to tell me something?"

Cyrus smiled warmly. "I don't know…maybe I'm the lucky one here."

Iris was smiling and crying at the same time. "Who would've thought anything good would come from this war."

Cyrus propped Iris up on a few pillows, and went to the stove to ladle out a bowl of soup. "Let's see if you can hold some food down. It's lentil with chicken." Cyrus spoon-fed Iris, who was too weak to do it herself. Iris's appetite was back. It was another good sign that she was on the mend.

"I made plenty. There's enough for your son when he returns." Cyrus ladled out another spoonful of soup for Iris to eat. She ate hungrily. After several days without eating, mere soup had never tasted so good. Hunger is one of the best seasonings.

Iris looked into Cyrus's pale blue eyes wondering if all she was experiencing was too good to be true. She wondered out loud. "Why do you do it?"

"Why do I do what?" Cyrus asked.

"Why do you do the things you do?"

"Do you mean my job…or help you?"

"Both, now that you mentioned it."

Cyrus paused from spooning Iris the soup. "I suppose I'm a soldier because that's what I've been called to do. I never thought I would become one when I was a youth. I didn't even give it a thought. But as fate would have it, here I am. Being a soldier sort of just happened to me." Cyrus shrugged his shoulders unable to say exactly why or how he became a military man.

"I've been a soldier for quite a long time, and I likely will for some time to come."

"You don't sound too happy about that."

"I've resigned myself to my fate, albeit reluctantly. I wish I could be at peace about it like the others. They seem so confident in what they do. Don't get me wrong, they can get shaken, but it's as if they know things will work out eventually. Then again, if the worst that can happen is to die doing your best for God, then life was a tremendous success."

"Don't you believe that Cyrus?"

"Yes I do." Cyrus stirred the soup a moment, deep in contemplative thought. "It's just lately...the senseless killing wears on you after a while; seeing the innocent die, the citizens caught in the middle." His rough sounding voice betrayed the sentiment of his words.

"I can understand that."

Cyrus took a deep breath and sighed. "As a leader I've always felt a sense of responsibility to my men, but it's sometimes overwhelming to realize so many people are counting on me."

Iris placed her hand on Cyrus's. "Is that why you help me? Is it because you feel it's your duty as a soldier?" Her heart raced and she was afraid to hear the answer.

Cyrus set the soup aside and looked Iris in the eyes. "No, that's not why I'm here." There was a long pause before Cyrus continued.

"I know you don't remember this, but that day we brought you into the oratory a beaten mess, I visited you in the hospital frequently. You gave up a lot to join the rebellion. I was impressed with that. It's not often one walks away from everything they know and takes a step on faith. There are precious few women who would take such a stand."

"You gave up everything and I know how hard that can be. In a way we are kindred spirits. From the start I wanted to know you better but life became hectic and you disappeared. Now God has seen fit to cross our paths again. I'm grateful God gave me another opportunity. I don't aim to let it slip by."

Tears welled up in Iris's eyes. "You are like no other man I have ever known. I keep thinking this is too good to be true. I keep expecting to wake up any second."

"Well you are feverish." Cyrus joked.

"That's not funny." Both had a short laugh.

"Iris groaned. "Ohh, don't make me laugh. It hurts my head." She massaged her temple. "I heard the rebel soldiers were all wearing surcoats now. How come you aren't wearing yours?"

"We decided the top leaders shouldn't be readily identified as soldiers for the time being." Cyrus replied.

"Really, why is that?"

Cyrus hesitated, and chose his next words very carefully. Some things were better left unsaid. "I don't want to alarm you with the details now. Maybe after you are fully recovered I'll tell you. Getting well is all you need to worry about."

"Is everything alright Cyrus?"

Cyrus smiled calming his inner turmoil. "I'm sure all will work out fine."

———— ·•·•·• ————

Zephyr cinched the saddle of her horse down tight, and put her saddlebags in place. Her mount was beige with a black tail and mane. It was a fine specimen, lean, muscled, with a touch of a renegade spirit; just the way Zephyr liked her horses. Reddland's troops had amassed several hundred horses and Zephyr picked one of the best for herself. She had an eye for good horseflesh.

Zephyr grabbed the reigns and led her mount from the stable. At the doorway the horse balked slightly and whinnied with reluctance. She looked her horse's legs over carefully for signs of lameness. There was no swelling or tenderness that she noticed. A lesser handler wouldn't have picked up on the slight change in the horse's temperament, but Zephyr was an expert rider. He father had been a horse rancher; one of the best in Ravenshire, and she learned well from him.

"What is wrong?" Zephyr stroked her mounts cheek in reassurance. "You will be fine."

With a little coaxing Zephyr's horse exited the stable, and soon Zephyr was on her way out of the compound and heading toward the main road through Xylor. Billowing, puffy white clouds tumbled overhead, slowly contorting and changing shapes as they rolled across the sky. Birds chirped and fluttered about as a cool sea breeze tussled Zephyr's hair. It felt good on her face and carried the scents of Xylor's mild summer. Someone must have forgotten to tell nature that a war was going on.

As Zephyr was leaving town she happened upon a quaint little farmhouse with a fenced yard. It looked to be a small farm of perhaps ten acres. There was a man leading a cow into a weather beaten barn. She made a mental note to tell Novak where he might find some milk. Out front by the road was a young woman dangling a length of string from her outstretched arm, and laughing gleefully. As Zephyr rode closer she could see three tiny kittens scampering about, clawing at the string. She stopped her mount just outside the fence where the young woman stood.

"Bonjour Mademoiselle, how old are the kittens?" Zephyr asked.

The girl looked up and smiled. "They are seven weeks old." The girl was around eighteen years of age, with sandy brown hair, and modestly dressed in a faded green dress.

"They are very cute." Zephyr watched the kittens stalk up on the string, leap up at it, and tumble to the grass. Already they were little hunters intent on catching their prey.

"I raised them myself; fed them milk by hand through a piece of straw. A passing carriage killed their mother. One of the kittens's died, but these three are doing fine. They can eat small scraps of food now." The young girl happily reported.

"Oh I am sorry to hear that." Zephyr replied. "But it looks like you have done a fine job in raising them."

Zephyr watched the kittens play a minute longer. "I was wondering Mademoiselle, would you be interested in selling one of the kittens?"

The girl was interested. "I hadn't thought about that. What did you have in mind?"

Zephyr reached into her saddlebags and retrieved a bundle wrapped in cheesecloth. She unwrapped it and held it out for the young woman to see. "I will give you three dried fish for one kitten."

The girl eyed the fish hungrily. The fish looked tasty, and what was she going to do with three cats anyway?

"That is a good offer." The girl replied. "Which one did you want?"

"The black and white one is my favorite."

The young woman picked up the black and white kitten and handed it over the fence to Zephyr. Zephyr rewrapped the fish and handed it to the girl.

"Merci." Zephyr removed her short cape and folded it, placing it on her lap. She placed the kitten within its folds to keep it warm and safe for the journey.

"You're not from around here, are you?" The young woman asked.

"No, I am from Ravenshire."

"I would have guessed Montroix from your accent, not Raven..." The young woman's eyes widened. "Did you say Ravenshire?"

"Oui...you are familiar with my homeland?"

"No, but..." excitement rang in the woman's voice. "You must be one of the Clandestine Knights!"

"Oui Mademoiselle, but that..."

The young woman became giddy and squealed. "I can't believe I met you. We owe you so much. Do you know my Grandfather? He is working for the rebellion as a doctor."

"Merci," Zephyr was embarrassed by the adulation. "I am very fond of your grandfather. He has been a faithful asset to the people."

"You know him? That's wonderful! Oh where are my manners?" The young woman thrust up a hand. "My name is Katrina."

Zephyr shook hands with the damsel. "Pleased to meet you; it is a small island, no?"

The young lady nodded vigorously. "Yes. I still can't believe I met you. At the March Octave I couldn't get near your table."

Zephyr was blushing. She was uncomfortable with the situation, but grateful at the same time for people like Katrina. One Katrina made up for a dozen naysayers.

"Merci Mademoiselle, it is good to know someone is pleased; especially now."

Zephyr checked on the kitten. Its tiny head was poking up out of the short cape. For the time being the kitten was content.

"I must be going. Au revoir," Zephyr spurred her horse on and waved.

"Good bye!"

Zephyr took the main road out of Xylor and headed for Sage. From there she would take the trail north. The trail north would become narrower and more overgrown the farther she went. Eventually it would become non-existent. From there it would still be a couple of miles to Hester's cabin. Zephyr made the trip once before, and that was three months earlier. The last time the trip was a pleasant journey through lush greenery and verdant forests. This time it was eerie. Scarcely anyone was on the main road. The few that were remained quiet and moved swiftly not wanting to be out any longer then they had to. The solitude of a trail had never bothered Zephyr before. In fact she enjoyed being alone in nature. But now it was different. Every noise, every rustle of leaves sent a chill down her spine. Tree branches cast shadows across the trail as if they wanted to forbid passage. The sudden movement from a bird or squirrel sent a jolt of hesitation through Zephyr's bones. With the shadow assassins around, the mood was uneasy at best. The possibility that you could very well be hunted was frightening, and fear was evident in everyone's face. Whenever Zephyr did see someone on the trail, they would eye her with nervous suspicion. She eyed them back in the same manner.

Zephyr went through Sage. The fields that had contained so many workers on her last visit now lay deserted. The small village itself was scarcely better. A few brave souls briskly carried out their business. Most were already indoors even though it was still several hours before nightfall. A few businesses even had boarded up their windows. It looked as if the town was preparing for a siege.

Zephyr saw a man peek nervously from behind a ratty blanket he was using as a curtain to cover the jagged hole in a wall he used as a window. He watched her pass, steely eyed and apprehensive. Another man was nailing a plank across his shutters in front of his house while his wife fidgeted in the open doorway. She had a look of impending dread on her face, and seemed to be worried that her husband might be killed before he could make it back into their tiny cabin. The village was clearly on edge.

Zephyr had a suspicion what was bothering the town. "Monsieur, why is the village so frightened?"

The man paused from his work, hammer in hand, and eyed Zephyr nervously. Deciding she was not a threat he answered. "Some farmers found Seth dead. His face was all contorted and twisted, just like them folks that was killed in Xylor. Some say it's an evil specter that's been doing the killing. I didn't believe it till today. You best be finding yourself some shelter here soon before nightfall."

Zephyr reined her horse to a stop. "A specter?"

"Yes'um. These things have powers. They killed three of Seth's goats too; sucked every drop of blood right out of them by the looks of it. It's like nothing you've ever seen. As soon as I saw them carting the boy and them sheep in town I knew for sure that we were under a curse. We tried to tell Seth not to take his goats to the south and graze them, but he wouldn't hear of it. Now look where it got him." The man shook his head in disgust.

Zephyr was taken aback. This was a new development. So far there had been no reports of animals having their blood sucked out. "Where are the sheep now?" She wanted to see for herself. Perhaps the man was exaggerating.

"I don't know, and don't care. Hopefully nowhere near here anymore. Seeing those hideous carcasses unnerved more then a few of us. I say it's all Thadus's fault; him and those four trouble makers from Ravenshire. They blasphemed Tanuba and now she placed a curse on us. Tanuba had always done right by us. They took her statues away and closed the temple. Now Tanuba is angry. It's all their fault…stinking gypsies anyhow!" The man was infuriated. As far as he was concerned the Clandestine Knights had come to Xylor and stirred up a pot a trouble. He had never been an ardent Tanuba worshiper himself but it was a convenient way to explain what was happening. In the past he always wondered if there was really a goddess Tanuba that reigned sovereign over the island. He heard murmurings in the pub to that sort. And it made sense. Tanuba is stricken from the island; and now these specters are exacting her revenge. Reddland may have been a tyrant, but nothing bizarre and unexplainable was happening then as far as he knew.

Zephyr was grateful that the man didn't recognize her. "I am sorry Monsieur. I hope all goes well for your family."

The man cooled a little at Zephyr's genuine sincerity. "Thank you," he waived his hammer at her. "But if I were you I'd get myself somewhere safe. Don't be going and getting killed like Seth."

Zephyr smiled, waved goodbye, and heeled her horse on. It would do no good to try to reason with the man. He already had his mind made up. The cult of Tanuba had done more damage to the island then could be repaired in the three short months since Reddland's fall; or in three hours of reasoned discussion that neither Zephyr nor the man had time for.

Zephyr heeled her horse on out of the village. Almost immediately the trail started climbing up toward the not too distant mountains. It snaked its way north through a rolling valley along side a dry gulch that had once been a river in ages past. The late afternoon sun had yet to begin its descent below the western horizon, but already the air was noticeably cooler. Thick fog formed on the foothills like a puffy white cotton blanket. It brought a certain freshness to the air.

Zephyr was in awe. It was as if the first mists of creation hung new in the valley. No matter how many times she saw the wondrous glory of God's handiwork it filled her heart with reverence. The scene was amazing. How anyone could look at the magnificence of nature, the miracle of scores of complex life forms, the incredible vastness of the universe, and not believe in God was beyond her. Or worse yet credit it all to a stone mermaid in a jewel-incrusted temple.

The closer Zephyr drew to the mountains the more she was reminded of the eeriness of her journey. Several times she thought she heard a noise somewhere in the trees; like a foot scraping in the pine needles. It grew cooler and darker. She had her mount pick up the pace.

Zephyr listened intently as her horse started up the steep part of the trail. The tall pines grew denser blanketing the forest floor. Like a canopy they shielded the brightness of the sun. Zephyr thought about taking her short cape back from her guest. She glanced down and noticed the kitten's head was bobbing lazily in time with the horse's steps, its eyelids getting heavy. The feline's blinks were becoming longer. Zephyr smiled and scanned the trail.

The trail became fainter and fainter until it eventually disappeared. Zephyr knew she was getting close to Hester's cabin.

From here on she would have to rely on her skills to navigate the trees and boulders.

There was a sound off to the right. It clearly was the sound of a stick breaking. The kitten on Zephyr's lap flinched and jerked its head to face the sound. It stared, eyes peeled wide, its ears flicking, making fine adjustments to better pick up the sound. Zephyr froze in the saddle and halted her horse. She strained to hear further sounds but could only pick up the rustling of the wind through the branches.

Zephyr strained to see into the shadowy expanse of forest. Nothing seemed to be moving. The trees were capable of concealing a bear in this part of the woods.

The kitten was uneasy. It stood and pushed back away from the direction of the noise. Its wide eyes were intently fixed upon a point in the woods. Zephyr strained to see where the feline's gaze was transfixed.

The kitten meowed and a jolting spasm rocked it tiny body. It glared at some unseen entity that apparently only it could detect. A chill went down Zephyr's spine.

"What is it kitty?" Zephyr could see nothing, but something did make a noise. More then likely it was just an animal. On her last trip to Hester's she had a run in with a panther. She didn't see that coming until it was too late. Was the kitten acting that way because it was playing? It didn't seem likely. Worst of all, maybe it was a shadow assassin. Regardless, Zephyr wasn't going to stick around to find out. If the cat felt spooked that was good enough for her. Its sense of smell was superior; and as an instinctive hunter, it was made to detect the slightest of movements.

Zephyr spurred her mount on. "You will not mind if we leave now, will you Mademoiselle Kitty? We are almost to Hester's."

Zephyr brought her horse up to a full gallop, as fast as she could get it to go. Soon, whatever made the sound was long behind her. She crested a hill and came to a small verdant grassy plain. She avoided the open area and rode close to the tree line around it. The land took on a strangeness the closer she got to Hester's. Maybe it was the growing shadows brought on by the setting sun. The moss seemed to drip from the jagged tree branches like cold molasses from contorted fingers. The wind rustled through the grass sounding like a meandering serpent. Boulders crouched low to the ground trying to remain invisible. Then it dawned on Zephyr; there were no birds flying to roost in the trees as was their usual habit at dusk. There wasn't even the buzz if insects.

Just as the last rays of the sun were sinking below the horizon, she came to the familiar small cabin built into the side of a hill. It was the same frail looking log structure with a stone chimney she remembered. A well-tended garden flourished beside the cabin. The faint smell of smoke hung in the air, no doubt from a warm fire burning in Hester's fireplace.

The cabin was made from rough-hewn logs, and used the earth as one of its walls. Smaller logs covered with pine branches formed the roof. In the middle of the west wall was a stone and mortar fireplace. Shuttered squares cut into the walls served as windows. The door to the cabin was made from the lids of two packing crates, and looked like it had been reinforced since Zephyr's last visit. It was a reassuring discovery. A small pile of chopped wood was stacked on the porch next to the door. Another pile of wood was heaped in a mound a few yards from Hester's cherry tree.

Zephyr rode to the cherry tree and picketed her horse. She gathered the kitten in her short cape and looked around. There was no sign of the elderly woman who resided in the remote home. A tinkling sound flourished from a wind chime newly affixed to one of the branches. The tree had long since been harvested. Memories of delicious cherry cobbler from her last visit made Zephyr's mouth water.

Zephyr made her way to the porch. The last bastion of sunlight slipped below the horizon casting a cool darkness on the cabin. The temperature fell with the sun, and the mild days gave way to brisk nights. A bundled up kitten would soon be evicted from a short cape.

Zephyr padded closer. All was agonizingly quiet. Faint light peeped through the crack of Hester's closed shutter. An empty wooden crate sat under the window. Zephyr listened and watched for the unusual, her breath visible in the night air. The light peeping through the shutter flickered now and again. The weathered cabin released a tired creak from its aged joints. Before Zephyr could react, the cracking of a breaking twig sounded from behind her.

"Miss Zephyr, You're back!" A raspy old voice gleefully shouted.

Zephyr practically leapt from her skin and turned to greet Hester. "Madame, you frightened me nearly half to death!" Zephyr's heart pounded in her chest as she smiled at her old friend. How the elder woman could move so quietly was a mystery.

"Oh deary, what have we here?" Hester noticed the kitten poking out from the bundle Zephyr was now clutching tightly to herself.

"It is a gift for you Madame. The last time I was here you told me of the demise of your dear tabby. I thought you would perhaps like some company again." Zephyr held out the kitten for Hester.

Hester beamed and her eyes welled up with tears. "Oh Miss Zephyr thank you; you have warmed an old woman's heart in her last years."

Hester LaVecchia stood at just over five feet tall and was in her eighties, a ripe old age for Xylor. She wore a faded brown dress with a white apron. A tattered velvet hat covered her long, braided gray hair. She still had on the same pair of rabbit skin shoes as the last time Zephyr saw her. As usual, Hester wore a welcoming and warm smile.

"Well deary, it's lovely seeing you again. Though I see you are still foolhardy enough to brave the trip out here alone; this close to dark nonetheless! You're liable to kill me with worry, you are." Hester laughed and stroked the kitten in her arms.

"You are right Madame. I think I will take your advice and come with a friend next time." Zephyr neglected to tell Hester of the odd noises she encountered on the trail. "But Madame, do you not make the trip alone yourself at times?"

Hester erupted in laughter. "Oh yes deary, that's true. But I know the ways of the ancients." Hester grew suddenly serious and whispered, "The forest conceals many a mystery unfamiliar to most. Let's just say I've trod a course to ports unknown, and discerned a source, of sorts back home."

Zephyr was puzzled. "You have trod a course of sorts…"

"I've trod a course to ports unknown, and discerned a source of sorts back home. It's the way of the ancients." Hester repeated with a smile.

Zephyr was intrigued at the mysterious, lyrical saying and was not quite sure what it all meant. She repeated the phrase over and over in her head. "The ways of the ancients; is this another legend?"

Hester roared with laughter. "Oh Miss Zephyr, it's just a fancy way to say I'm as old as the forest and learned a few short cuts here and there. When you're older then the mountain you'll learn a few things deary."

Zephyr chuckled. "Pardon Madame, but I thought you were telling of another legend."

Zephyr had a feeling there was more to Hester then anyone really knew. The elder woman had surely seen many things in her long life, and was very intelligent though eccentric. No doubt she had a tremendous amount of wisdom to impart on those who would listen. Few realized the profundity that was deep in the mountains of Xylor.

Hester held the kitten up in front of her and looked it face to face, the kitten's tiny paws reaching for a firm footing no longer there. "I think I just found a name for you. I'll name you after me grandmum. How do you like Maggie?" The kitten looked nervously at the ground, which now seemed a long way off.

"One of us should have a proper cordial sounding name. Me mum saddled me with a stuffy name like Hester. I won't be doing that to a cute little bundle of fur like you Maggie." The kitten looked away uninterested.

"And I see you have the same devil may care attitude that me grandmum had." Hester chuckled and turned to Zephyr. "What say we go into me cabin and I put on a kettle? A thin lassie like you could use a hot cup of tea to warm your bones on this chilly night."

"Merci, that sounds good." Zephyr already had her short cape in place.

"Shall we then?" Hester motioned for the door to her home, but paused suddenly and looked into the now pitch black night. "You did say you came alone deary?"

Zephyr shot around and looked to where Hester was intently studying. "Oui, Madame. Do you see something?" That familiar dread Zephyr felt earlier on the trail was back. The kitten swatted at a tassel on Hester's shawl.

"Oh, it's probably nothing. Me old ears are not what they used to be." After taking one more look, Hester saw her guest into her cabin for a hot cup of tea.

———•◆•———

Muffled and dull sounds abounded at the docks of Xylor after sundown. Stifled laughs wafted from dimly lit barges anchored at port, and rough necked seamen settled in for an evening of drink. Hard working fishermen mended their nets in preparation for another day that would come before sunrise.

The smell of tobacco mingled with the salt air, and as usual, the strong odor of fish. A few seedy looking men and runaways drifted aimlessly along the vast docks with their intricately laced piers. Most were looking for a semblance of shelter for the evening. Others were looking for a victim.

Little shops and taverns littered the dock area scattered among large warehouses. Most catered to the seafaring clientele, and as such few regular townsfolk ventured to the piers. Novak, Emerald, and Bartus walked in silence as they made their way to their secret rendezvous. All three wore dark cloaks and tried to remain as anonymous and undetected as plausible in the circumstances. Remaining undetected as strangers to the docks would be miraculous. Remaining unrecognized however, was something the three were counting on.

Novak led the way with the other two in close tow. Their footsteps on the weather-beaten planks of the pier tapped out the rhythm of a brisk pace. The three turned out on a pier that stretched far over the water, over one hundred feet from the shore. It was suspended above the water by large wooden posts, and was about twenty feet wide. Several small boats were tied at stanchions. At the end of the pier across from a dilapidated one room shack was a small sailing boat docked at port. It was seven or eight yards long at best, and by the looks of things, it had seen better days. Its moniker, 'The Sea Urchin' was barely legible on its bow. The Sea Urchin's sails were down and it was deserted. Novak wondered if the vessel was even sea worthy.

The trio paused at the end of the pier. In front of the dilapidated shack sat an old man in a rocking chair. He wore well-worn brown pants and a gray cotton shirt. A tattered hat with a hole in it sat atop his head, and bare feet protruded from his raggedy edged pant legs. He rocked slowly smoking a pipe as he quietly watched the three newcomers to his pier. A lamp dimly flickered from a single window. A threadbare curtain hung in the opening.

"Do we wait?" Emerald whispered to Novak.

Novak shrugged a shoulder and looked at the old man. He still sat, slowly rocking in his chair, one hand on the armrest, the other holding a pipe to his lips. Every so often the tobacco would flare a cherry red as the old man took a drag from his pipe. Squinty eyes peered from a leathery weathered countenance. He had the face of an ancient fisherman, and a look in his eyes that spoke of far away places. No doubt the ancient man had seen far more unusual things in his time then three strangers on the docks. The man showed no emotion except for a peaceful contentment. If it wasn't for the slow rocking and occasional puff on the pipe one might mistake the old man for dead.

"Now what do we do?" Bartus asked while eying the old man nervously. "This man has surely recognized us by now."

Novak gave Bartus a scowl. How he got talked into bringing Bartus he didn't know, but he vowed he would never make that mistake again. "Don't get excited and stay calm. The way your eyes are bulging out of your head like a bullfrog has probably already made the old codger suspicious. Likely from the moment we started walking down the pier."

Novak saw the old man cock an ear towards his conversation with Bartus. He motioned for his friends to stay put. "I'll handle this."

Novak trod the short distance to the rickety shack. Not one to mince words he got right to the point. "Good evening. We're looking for someone and wondered if you had seen him."

The old man stopped rocking but said nothing. He continued to puff on his pipe.

Novak evaluated the man and his shack up close for a moment before deciding to continue. "His name is Dantes. Do you know him?" Novak was short and blunt.

"Excuse us a second." Bartus interrupted grabbing Novak's arm to pull him aside. He couldn't budge his large comrade, but

Novak turned aside of his own accord. Emerald stepped up to listen in.

"What do you want Bartus?" Novak growled.

"Do you think we should be giving this stranger so much information about our business; especially Dantes name? What if his loyalties are with the opposition? It could get Dantes killed." Bartus whispered forcefully.

"I considered that. I don't think we will have to worry about the old man." Novak exercised great restraint. Who was Bartus, an inexperienced adventurer, to question Novak who had done this hundreds of times?

Bartus's eyes bulged even farther. "Are you sure you're not just underestimating him because he's old and frail looking?"

"I underestimate no one. I assume everyone wants to try to kill me until proven otherwise. I've evaluated this man for combat based on the likely options he has available and planned a dozen different ways I could kill him should the need arise."

"All that in such a short time?" Bartus replied.

Novak let out an irritated sigh. "I'll explain once because you're inexperienced, and since you're Emerald's uncle. The *Sea Urchin*'s deck is deserted. The door to the cabin below deck was locked from the outside. If anyone is below deck they are locked in, and so we have no threat from the boat. The old man is unarmed. The door to his cabin opens outward towards the old man's rocking chair. That's why I stood off to the side and not in the doorway in case the person inside decides to come out. And *there is* someone inside since I saw a shadow pass behind the curtain when we first arrived here. The shadow moved down like the person inside was crouching below the window to eavesdrop on what was going on outside. Since the window is too small for a man to exit swiftly that leaves the door, which I anticipated and prepared for. Most importantly, there is a small metal cross above the door to the shack. It's starting to rust so it's been up for a while. If the cross is a ruse then the old man has been taking a

considerable risk for some time; especially out here isolated like
he is. Of course there are countless other smaller clues but we
don't have the time to get into now. All things considered, the
odds are we can take the chance to talk to this man. Doing what
we do you play the odds as best you can. If you live long enough
to get good at it then you have a chance to be successful."

Bartus was speechless. And once again, Bartus felt woefully
inadequate for the task before him. It reminded him of a sermon
Abrams once preached; 'even the fool, when he is silent, is counted
as wise.'

"I…hadn't looked at it that way, I guess you're right…once
you consider all the…things you mentioned," Bartus was
humbled and felt disgusted. He hated the fact that he looked bad
in front of his niece. She was his staunchest supporter. Emerald
on the other hand was enamored with Novak's expertise on the
matter.

Novak softened. "Just leave this to me." He gave Bartus a
few reassuring pats on the shoulder and what Novak felt caused
him to have a surge of pity for his jittery friend. Ribs and arm
bones could clearly be detected. Bartus was little more then skin
stretched tight over a skeleton. His arduous recovery had been
thus far miraculous, but was far from complete. Emerald smiled
at the display.

Novak turned back to the old man in the rocking chair.
He had been puffing his pipe patiently waiting for what ever
happened next.

"Do you know a man named Dantes?" Novak asked again.

The old man stopped rocking and pulled the pipe from his
lips. "That depends on whose asking," he replied in a raspy and
weak voice.

"Novak Reinhardt of Ravenshire."

The man's squinty eyes grew slightly wider. "So I meet you at
last. I've been an admirer of yours since the town square incident."

The old man laughed a wheezing coughing laugh that rattled him in his chair.

"I did what I had to. I wasn't going to bow down to a statue of a mermaid no matter who was around." Novak smiled slightly embarrassed. The event hadn't gone totally smooth. He did end up getting arrested.

"That was good work if I do say so myself." He wheezed a laugh that nearly shook him from the chair. Novak and the others looked at each other somewhat bewildered, not quite understanding what was so funny or how the old man came to know about the town square incident.

"I didn't realize it was common knowledge." Novak replied.

"Knowledge is one thing that is not common here in Xylor." The old man chuckled.

Novak grinned broadly but quickly redirected the conversation back to business. "You may be right, especially knowledge as to the whereabouts of this Dantes fellow. You wouldn't have any ideas would you?"

The old man sized up Novak through squinty eyes, and took a long drag from his pipe. "I figure a man like you already knows the answer to that. The way you walked down the pier, the way you move, where you stand. Yep, I figure you already have some ideas where Dantes is. I don't figure much gets by you."

"If he knew why would he ask?" Bartus interjected from a few feet behind Novak.

The old man craned his neck to see Bartus. "Now who might you be?"

Novak handled the introductions after giving Bartus a quick scowl. "This is Bartus Raistlin, and this is Emerald Raistlin, his niece." Novak pointed to the beautiful blonde woman that made up the third person in his group.

"Pleased to meet you both." The old man replied. Just as the old man said that the door to the shack opened with a loud groan. Out stepped a burly man around forty with curly black hair and a thick beard. He wore a long red coat with large cuffs, a black hat, and black pants tucked into knee high leather boots. He was stout and rough looking like one would expect of a seafaring sailor.

"Avast there matey, I've been expecting ya. I see ye had no trouble finding the place. Sorry for the brief deception but thar be nosey bilge rats crawling all over the docks. In me line of work ye can't be too careful."

"Ya, that's understandable," Novak replied. Bartus timidly took a step back.

"You must be Dantes." Emerald deduced with a warm smile.

"Aye, Lassie, and who might ye be? I wasn't expecting anyone but Novak." Dantes tipped his hat and bowed slightly.

"I'm Emerald, Thadus's daughter. I'll be traveling with you also." Emerald replied, her thirst for adventure evident in her voice.

"Don't tell me a dainty thing like you will be partaking in this dangerous voyage." Dantes said with some surprise. "Yer father said I would be approached by a big man, and I'd know him when I saw him. He was right. I do believe ye stand a full mast above other men, and yer as broad as a galleon. It's the other two's what made me wary."

"I apologize. Events are moving fast. We didn't even get a description of you." Novak's deep voice echoed in the still night. The old man sat taking it all in, puffs of smoke wafting up in regular intervals.

"And that thar be Marcesco. He keeps a keen eye out for scallywags on me dock." Dantes gave a nod toward the old man rocking in his chair then turned to Bartus. "And do ye plan on setting sail with us also, or do ye prefer to keep yer feet planted on firmer ground?"

Bartus was less then enthusiastic to make the trip to begin with. Now after meeting Dantes he was even less enthused. "I… guess I'm going."

"Ye don't sound too sure of yourself there Bartus, and I can't blame ya. The sea isn't for the tenderhearted. It can be an unforgiving lass, prone to swallow whole ships at her whim. Many a men have been lost to her mysterious ways." Dantes related in a growling foreboding tone, then leaned in close to Bartus and whispered while casting a glance skyward. A patch of dark clouds swallowed the moon momentarily inducing an eerie atmosphere.

"Let this be a warning says I, thar be squalors ahead. They have a tendency to stir up many a peculiarity, not to mention strange sea creatures. You'll be needing yer sea legs for this one."

"Sea creatures," Bartus's voice quivered. "What kind of sea creatures?"

"Thar be all kinds of rumors afloat on the sea; many too horrible to tell. Most sailors haven't lived to say exactly what sent them to a watery grave." Dantes drifted off in thought like he was searching his memory for lost friends.

"Have you seen any yourself?" Now Emerald's nervousness was piqued.

"Aye, thar be a squid so large it makes the *Sea Urchin* look like a wooden bowl." Dantes gave Novak a wink. Marcesco took it all in with a wry smile.

"Well let's be off. Maybe we'll see it before we put to port in Kelterland." Novak waved goodbye to Marcesco and stepped toward the *Sea Urchin*.

"What?" Bartus was aghast. Novak was crazy. Before he could protest Dantes was off with Novak and Emerald not far behind.

"Don't worry yourself Bartus." Marcesco said. "A little danger in a voyage is what turns landlubbers into old salts."

Bartus nodded unconvincingly in the affirmative. "Deep down I know all is in the Lord's hands. I just don't feel the need to test His resolve. God forbid it be His will I meet my end tonight. I should think I would rather pass while on land."

"Are ye coming aboard, or do I need to haul you along like a ton of cargo?" Dantes shouted from the deck of the Sea Urchin.

Bartus ran over and stepped gingerly into the vessel. Dantes and Novak drew in the lines that held the small boat to the pier. With the speed and proficiency of a seasoned expert, Dantes had the sails hoisted and the *Sea Urchin* creeping toward the harbor. There was a good wind and Novak settled into place next to the rudder where Dantes was maneuvering the vessel for open waters. The lights of Xylor faded in the distance. Once clear of port the wind picked up tremendously filling the sails with enough force to cause the mast to creak. The aged ship was full of groans as she headed bow first into modest breakers.

After a few hours, a solemn silence fell upon those gathered on the *Sea Urchin*. It was the kind of silence brought by a reverent awe of the sheer vastness of the seas. A chandelier of stars stretched overhead blinking like thousands of candles in a sea of black. The moon reflected off the water providing evidence of endless swells ahead. With no land in sight, and the lights of Xylor well behind them, each person realized their insignificance when compared to the Astorian Ocean. The *Sea Urchin* was but a speck in the ocean, in the world, in the universe.

Emerald scooted closer to Novak. "Don't you just love it? Here we are drifting on a wine dark moonlit sea. It's as if the war has stopped momentarily."

Novak nodded. "Ya, it is a benefit of our adventures. Tranquil times like this make up for the times of terror."

Dantes overheard Novak and Emerald's conversation. "Aye, out here on the sea is true freedom. Each man is his own master beholding to no one, excepting the sea herself of course. Jest place yer bow to follow the stars, and with the wind at yer back you'll find yer way."

Bartus was uncomfortable thinking about the immensity of the ocean. He pictured miles and miles of water beneath him, waters that held unknown dangers and many sea creatures. Even so, Bartus wasn't about to say anything that would betray his fears.

"This reminds me of something Isaac once said, and I've never forgotten it." Emerald thought a moment then continued.

"I think it was from Job. 'He stretcheth out the north over the empty place, and hangeth the earth upon nothing.'"

The other three contemplated what Emerald said. For a moment all thought of the chaos, killing, and of the war was forgotten. For the time being all thoughts were on questions eternal.

—•◦•—

Hester poured Zephyr another cup of tea. "So what brings you here deary? I can tell by your countenance that something is weighing heavily on your mind. A young lass like yourself eating like a bird; and you've scarcely been able to keep your eyes off the door since you've arrived. What is it Miss Zephyr? It never did a soul good to keep things all bottled in."

Zephyr caught herself glancing at the door twice as Hester was speaking. "You are right Madame; I do have need of some assistance. But I was enjoying our visit, and I tell you, I did not want you to think I only came…"

Hester interrupted Zephyr. "Nonsense deary, I know you regard me as a friend. I'm just happy you feel you can turn to me when you need help. Helping is what old people like me do best. It makes me feel useful, like I still have something to contribute to the world. It's when the young stop listening to sound counsel that they find themselves in a predicament."

"Oui, Madame, merci," Zephyr was relieved. "If you would not mind; I do not want to take up more of your time."

"Fiddlesticks!" Hester laughed. "I've got nothing but time. Now that I returned from me recent outing I had nothing pressing or more exciting planned then dusting around here and tilling my garden. Which reminds me; excuse the mess, I've been away for a spell."

"You have been gone?" Zephyr was amazed that the elderly woman would venture away for more then a short while.

"Oh deary, I'm as well traveled as I am old, and that's saying a lot." Hester laughed. "And don't pretend you didn't notice the dust."

"Madame, at your age? Is it safe?" Zephyr looked around again. Now that Hester mentioned it the shelves were rather dusty; around a few weeks worth of buildup.

"Miss Zephyr, I've got a few miles left on me legs. I get around more then one would think. The Lord moves in mysterious ways, and He's allowed me to roam this world longer then most."

"I tell you that is incredible!" Zephyr hoped to get around as good as Hester in her old age.

A long pause settled on the small one room cabin. Hester broke the silence.

"Now deary, I think we've beat a well worn path around the bush. What's troubling you lassie?"

Zephyr took time to phrase her response properly. "Well Madame...there is something dark...some entity or person preying upon people in Xylor. We were hopeful you held some answers."

A worried look came over Hester. "What do you mean deary; a dark entity?"

"Je ne sais pas," Zephyr shrugged her shoulders. "We call them shadow assassins. They appear from the darkness and kill. They usually strangle their victim with a wire. The victims often have a contorted expression on their face in death. On my way here a man told me the blood had been sucked out of animals. I tell you this Madame; we do not know what they are."

Hester went pale and became visibly shaken. A sense of dread filled the room, so thick you could cut it with a dagger. Hester fidgeted with the tassels along the edge of her shawl, and started rocking back and forth rhythmically in her chair, like a child trying to console herself.

Hester cleared her throat and swallowed hard. "Did anyone report smelling lotus blossoms?"

"Oui Madame, does that mean you know what they are?"

Hester bolted upright in her chair. "Oh no, deary! No, no, no." Hester went to the door and immediately bolted and bared it. She then went to her window and scanned the darkness. Hurriedly she secured the shutters and extinguished one of the candles on the table. The other candle she placed on the hearth by the fireplace and shielded much of its light by placing it into a cauldron. Between the shielded candle and the glowing embers in the fireplace, the small cabin took on a dim cave-like feel. Zephyr hadn't seen the old woman so flustered. Sensing the gravity in Hester's movements sent a chill down Zephyr's spine. The kitten lay uninterested curled up in a ball on the bed, barely able to crack open an eye at the sudden activity.

Hester retook her spot opposite Zephyr in her rocking chair. She pulled her shawl tight around her.

"Madame, what are they? You have me spooked."

"Oh Miss Zephyr, I'm so, so sorry. I didn't expect me ears to be hearing of such things again. My prayers are with you and the others. May God see you all through this dark time." Hester's lips quivered as she spoke.

"What are they Madame?"

Hester reflected with horror on something from the deepest reaches of her memory. Twice she started to speak but stopped herself short. Shaking her head she started to wring her hands and her eyes moistened with tears. Finally she forced herself to recall disturbing memories, and choked out the words in relating them to Zephyr.

"When I was a young lass meself, about your age deary, this thing of which you speak of happened to us. It must be over fifty years now back when Kelterland made their first attempt at conquering Xylor. Not on me life did I think it would happen again, but now that it has, it does stand to reason. Me grandmum always said Kelterland would resort to this devilry again if they felt the need. It seems with you and your friends defeating Reddland the Kelterlanders feel threatened enough to revive their dark ways."

Zephyr's brow furrowed. "So Madame, are you saying that soldiers from Kelterland are doing this?"

"Yes and no deary." Hester could see the puzzled look on Zephyr's face and explained further. "There is a sinister cadre of malefic fiends who have on occasion been employed by the Kelterlanders to do their bidding. To call them assassins, Miss Zephyr, would be a terrible understatement. For there is nary a group so wicked…so depraved as those who belong to the Order of the Valkyrie."

Zephyr's eyes grew wide. "I tell you it is a relief to see you have heard of them. What kind of humans are they that can vanish at will, and cause people to die with the most horrible expression on their face."

"Oh deary, don't get too hopeful yet. These may be 'people' in the physical sense, but they are far from human. No person so cold and callous, so embracing of evil should ever be considered human. They are without conscious, without feeling, and dead to the world though they live. They are empty shells housing only a demon's rage. Reddland was an evil man, but the Order of the Valkyrie are far worse." Hester warned.

"How do they seem to have powers beyond human capability," Zephyr asked.

Hester leaned forward in her chair and spoke just above a whisper. "They are practitioners of sorcery; well trained in the dark arts of assassination. They are known to enhance their skill with potions and trickery, and are very dangerous deary. You and your friends must be alert. They dress in black, moving in the shadows to better blend with the night. They patiently sneak into position close enough to their victims to throw a powdery substance in their face. That Miss Zephyr usually spells the end for an unsuspecting soul. The white powder when breathed causes hallucinations and paralysis. That makes for a helpless and easy kill. The powder is made with ground and dried lotus leaves. Me grandmum said that was more for the living; so they would know who did the killing. They have been known to tattoo some of their first victims. The swan is their emblem of choice. They are fast and sneaky. Few live to tell about an encounter."

Zephyr was sickened by what she heard. "But what about the ghastly expressions on the dead, and sucking an animal's blood?"

"Oh Miss Zephyr, that's just to confuse and frighten the people. Chaos is what they're after. An assassin operates better when things are topsy-turvy, and they have many a concoctions to do many a thing. Some make a person's face tighten up and contort. Others will dry up a carcass after it's been drained of blood. It's all to confuse and strike terror. It happened to me and me family fifty years ago."

Hester's voice took a serious tone. "But make no mistake about it deary, they're here for a reason. The Order of the Valkyrie is sent to kill people of importance. They will kill others but it's you and your friends who are in danger. Anyone who is a key member of the new government is in grave danger. You must be careful lassie." Hester placed a hand on Zephyr's arm, and had a look of deep concern in her eyes.   Zephyr placed her hand on Hester's. "Merci Madame for your concern. I pray I do not meet one of these assassins, or Valkyrie's as you tell me."

"The name 'Valkyrie' comes from the customs of a people who once lived beyond the ethereal region. There is an ancient cult who believed young maiden spirit beings hovered over battlefields to select those who would be slain. The Valkyrie is the chooser of the dead. The Order of the Valkyrie took that ancient cult and mingled it with sorcery. Now they fancy themselves as chooser's of the dead. I hoped me lips would never have to speak of them again. For your sake Miss Zephyr, I hope me ears hear word of their disappearance soon."

Zephyr released a heavy sigh. "Madame, what are we to do?"

"I wish I could say deary. I don't think anyone knows for sure. If me memory serves, last time they left after one of their own was killed. The Order is a superstitious lot. If they lose a man they regard it as a bad omen and fade into the night; as it was fifty years ago. But lassie, we weren't rid of them until we killed one. They are as tenacious as a rabid dog on a piece of meat. They are not known to give up until those they are here for are dead. Once they arrive, it's like a curse; a curse of the Valkyrie."

Zephyr contemplated what she heard and then her eyes lit up with an idea. "How were you able to kill the Valkyrie fifty years ago? Maybe we could employ the same method now."

Hester smiled. "Isaac killed the Valkyrie. We never knew how, what with Isaac not being a fighter. Oh that's back when he was a strapping young lad."

"How can that be?" Zephyr asked astonished. Scorpyus, one of the fastest and most experienced soldiers in Xylor, was lucky to survive an attack. The thought of an untrained man meeting success was surprising.

"Remember deary, the effectual fervent prayer of a righteous man availeth much. Me grandmum maintained that God helped Isaac in the task."

Hester saw the wind slowly go out of her friend's sails. "What is it deary?"

"Oh Madame, as you know Isaac died three months ago. In all honesty I doubt that there is anyone like him; especially in matters of fervent prayer."

"Yes Miss Zephyr, you are probably right," Hester nodded her head. "Isaac was indeed a man of constant prayer. Few ever maintain such a walk in this life. Isaac was an inspiration to us all. He will be sorely missed."

"Perhaps his son Abrams could do it." Zephyr was hopeful.

"Abrams is a good man like his father. Don't worry yourself deary. If it's God's will for that to happen, He will find a way. Me mum used to tell me, 'God doesn't need the strongest, or smartest, or fastest, or best. He just needs the willing.' So you see lassie, worrying won't help matters. God found David to fight Goliath. He can find someone to fight the Valkyrie's also."

Zephyr smiled warmly. Hester was so full of wisdom, and had a way of making one feel that everything would work out. "Merci, you are right as usual. I just pray that we can be rid of them before too many more die. They could kill many before one of them is finally killed."

Hester continued with her advice. "There are probably three or four Valkyrie's in Xylor. Rarely do they send their full strength."

"How do you know this Madame?"

"It's a guess Miss Zephyr. Last time they sent three. The Order is made up of only thirteen assassins; one leader who is always a female and twelve others."

"The leader is always a woman?"

"Yes deary, and a beautiful woman at that. It is keeping in tradition with the ancient cult. The Valkyrie was a female spirit who chose those who would die. Only a woman can ascend to the leadership position. The outgoing leader chooses her replacement from the other twelve. The odd thing is; some of the others are men."

Zephyr thought about all she learned. She and her friends were up against an Order of thirteen assassins who are led by a beautiful female. They employ sorcery and all manners of slight of hand to terrorize the people. Three or four of them were at work in Xylor. The last time they came they continued their reign of terror until one of them was killed. Was there any guarantee they would leave this time if by some chance she or her friends could kill one. What if these Valkyrie's were more dedicated, or perhaps better paid. Were they here to kill Thadus? Or were they after Zephyr and her friends. Maybe they were here to kill all the rebel troops. There were many variables that only time would tell. At least this was someplace to start.

"Merci Madame, for your assistance in this matter." Zephyr was overwhelmed by it all.

Hester smiled and clasped Zephyr's hand. "You're welcome deary. Just promise me you will be careful. As long as the Valkyrie are here, I fear you and your friends are in grave danger."

Zephyr placed her hand on Hester's. "We will Madame. And you be careful also. You have been a good friend."

Hester smiled then looked off into a corner deep in thought. "That's strange. I wonder why I didn't think of it earlier. It seems an ancient lyric is coming to me mind. Of course most things I remember are ancient." Hester laughed.

"I don't remember where I heard it. Me thinks it was from the apothecary me grandmum used to know. Now how did it go?" Hester searched for an obscure and distant memory. Zephyr sat in rapt anticipation.

Hester squinted like she was trying to read small print on the far wall. "I can almost see the old apothecary shop now. If me memory serves…" Hester recited the words as she recalled them.

'There upon a rocky crag
Appeared a weathered, leathered hag
Wood chips and leaves, at once she uttered
Other commands she hissed and sputtered
Unsavory words in undue season
Apparently for no rhyme nor reason
Screeching, spitting, muttering hag
Not far from her does evil lag'

"He was an avid reader, the apothecary was. Always had his nose buried in a book. He told me that many years ago when the Valkyrie's were at their worst. He said he found it written in some old manuscript that had origins in the ethereal region. He maintained it was about the Valkyrie leader." Hester related.

Zephyr looked slightly puzzled. "But Madame, I thought you said the leader was a beautiful woman. The lyric speaks of a weathered hag."

"Oh Miss Zephyr, beauty is manifest on the outside. One's deeds and thoughts cut clear to the bone. Though a Valkyrie may be fair to look upon; where at first glance stands a lovely maiden, is indeed but a weathered hag." Hester warned.

"And another thing deary; give this to your friend." Hester produced a small folded scrap of paper from a cloth handbag. The paper was intricately folded and sealed with wax. Its yellowed hue spoke of its age.

Zephyr reached for the paper. "Which friend Madame?"

"The dark one. I've seen him about a time or two. It's something me mum once wrote, God rest her soul. I'm led to feel he may find it of interest."

"Oui, I will deliver it."

"Now how about a little snack? I made some bread earlier, and I happen to have a spot of butter." Hester went to a shelf to fetch the items.

Zephyr nodded enthusiastically. The kitten was fast asleep on the cot.

———◆◆◆———

Cad snatched the young man by the nape of the neck and shoved him against the wall placing a hand high on his neck at the base of his jaw. Cyrus had a teenager in an arm hold close by. A man and woman in night cloths stood by horrified.

"You lads will not be doing any looting tonight." Cad growled.

"You people come here and ruin everything," the man spit. "At least I had a job under Reddland!"

"Cad squeezed the young man's jaw so tightly it pursed his lips like a fish. "Listen up matey, that doesn't give you the right to break into this man's house and steal his wife's jewelry."

Cad was angry. This was the third similar incident he and Cyrus handled that night. All he wanted was to get a bite to eat and some rest.

The citizens were enjoying liberty for the first time. Many proved they could not be trusted with their freedom. Instead of using their liberty to conduct themselves properly they abused it. This latest young man blamed it on a lack of a job. It might have been a viable excuse had Cyrus not known the man as one who never maintained regular work. The young man was nothing but a thief, an opportunist taking advantage of a little unrest.

Cad waved for a passing patrol. "Hey sergeant, take these lads to the jail. They tried to rob this man and his wife."

The sergeant instructed his squad to shackle the two men.

Cad watched them go and after the man and woman thanked him, he and Cyrus were on their way again.

"I'm starting to wonder if we will ever get to eat tonight." Cyrus stated.

Cad shrugged his shoulders. "These bloomin shadow assassins have got the island spooked. As long as they're around, there will be people who take advantage of it. Let's hope Zephyr has some answers for us tomorrow."

VII

---•·◆·•---

THE PATH STRETCHED into the dark abyss, winding its way from Xylor, wending away from the prying eyes of curious townsfolk. The path meandered several hundred yards from the pale glow flickering in the windows of dockside taverns, to a place of solitude. Out where the creatures hunted prey, far from the ears of nosy peasants, the path passed by a tree. It was a tall tree, wide in circumference; wide enough to hide a man. Moss dripped from the branches, clinging tight but threatening to fall to the ground if provoked by the slightest wind. Vines fought for an equal share of the tree, coiling its host like a malignant nuisance, slowly carrying out their plan to stretch higher then the uppermost branches. Down below leaves rustled in the breeze, lazily tumbling along the ground to nowhere in particular, unconcerned for the struggle for dominance going on above them. An owl hooted from the tree it had thought to claim as its own. Instead of a tasty field mouse, the owl would be witness to matters of utmost secrecy.

A foot appeared on the path next to the tree; a foot wearing a tight form fitting soft leather shoe. Attached was a black cotton pant leg that fit snuggly to the lower appendage it helped to hide in the darkness. The foot took a step closer to the tree crushing a leaf in the process.

"It's no wonder you failed. With a heavy step like that you sound like a pack horse," a voice whispered from the darkness. The voice was a mix of scratching cough and hissing breath, and it was full of overt hatred.

"Brynhild, is it you?" A hushed voice a few feet above the foot whispered . This voice sounded like that of a man.

"Fortunately for you it is. You would likely be dead otherwise." Condescension reeked from the scratchy whisper.

"Now hold on," the foot became angry. "I have always completed my mission. The dark one was lucky, nothing more. He has some speed and it bought him some time."

"Apparently. Needless to say Lady Valfreyja is displeased."

"Tell Lady Valfreyja it won't happen again." The foot vowed.

"You are right about that Sigurd. I will handle the dark one. You have been reassigned to the new Regent."

"The Regent! He is hardly a worthy challenge. Why not give the Regent to Hildr?" Sigurd asked.

"Hildr has the female. Besides, you allowed yourself to be wounded."

"This is only Hildr's second assignment. With all due respect Brynhild, I think I am more capable of handling the female." Sigurd tried to explain.

"After last night I'm not so sure."

Sigurd stomped. "That is unjust! You have known me for a long time Brynhild. We were selected together, we trained together, and we have been on several assignments together. I have never failed before. Why all of a sudden am I looked upon as incompetent?"

Brynhild let out a heavy sigh. "I know Sigurd, I know. When Lady Valfreyja gets angry I am the one to hear about it, and I assure you she was infuriated. This is an important assignment. The Kelterlanders are paying a king's ransom, and there is a lot at stake. We command a handsome fortune because we are the best. A failure here in Xylor will tarnish our record. Failure is not an option."

"You're right Brynhild. I'm as upset as Lady Valfreyja is. Does she think I like the fact that the dark one eluded me?"

Sigurd explained further, "Had we orders to kill them my skill would not be put into question now. We have never tried to take captives before. Were it not for that, my reputation would still be intact."

"That's all changed," Brynhild whispered impatiently. "I know Kelterland was going to pay triple for anyone we took captive. But after yesterday the plan has changed. Lady Valfreyja feels it is more important for us to maintain our reputation rather then gain the extra money. The four are more experienced then we were led to believe…"

Sigurd interrupted, "Only because Wallace was an imbecile. I always felt that Asgard relied far too heavily on his reports. Wait till he learns that Wallace was killed. It serves him right. How could anyone have so underestimated the four from Ravenshire? Was Wallace blind?"

"Asgard knew, as did we all that Wallace was a mere novice among professionals. He had no chance of performing like a Valkyrie, but he was all we had to work with," Brynhild recalled.

"A lot of good he did. We still had to identify our targets ourselves."

"As you so eloquently stated Sigurd; it is because Wallace was killed. We will overcome this minor obstacle and prevail. Lady Valfreyja has authorized the removal of our targets if we think it best. As I stated earlier, taking a captive isn't worth the extra money if killing them is easier and it saves our credibility. Hildr knows this as well."

Sigurd was relieved. "At last logic prevails."

"You have your orders. And remember, you are of the Order of the Valkyrie. Last night was theirs but the battle will be ours!" Brynhild encouraged.

Sigurd stepped away from the tree and faded into the blackness. He had a score to settle. He was a lethal assassin who would not be mocked. With a resolve that he felt in the pit of his stomach, he would succeed.

Up on its perch the owl sat unaware that it had seen the shifting shadows more clearly then any living human; shadow assassins with the voices on men. Few, living or dead had seen a Valkyrie as closely. As fate would have it, more Xylorians would be cursed with the opportunity.

⸺•◆•⸺

Zephyr pressed both hands around her cup of tea, absorbing the warmth in her fingers as she took a sip. Steam wafted from the hot beverage filling Zephyr's nostrils with its pleasant aroma. Hester pulled her shawl tightly around her shoulders. There was a lull in the conversation that provided the opportunity to soak up the ambiance of the small cabin. The glowing embers in the fireplace snapped and popped sporadically in a soothing crackle. The flicker of the candle cast its soft light causing the shadows to dance rhythmically. Even Hester looked younger in candle light, her chair creaking as she rocked. With the advancing chill, the kitten left its place on the cot for warmer comforts. It now napped, curled up in a ball on Hester's lap, purring softly as its ear was scratched.

"I could fall asleep Madame," Zephyr smiled. "It is so peaceful here."

Hester stroked the kitten's head with her fingers. "Yes deary, living here certainly has its advantages. And I'm so glad you decided to stay till morning. You'd have turned the rest of me hair gray had you went back tonight. With you out in that dark forest, and after all we discussed, I do believe you saved me an early grave Miss Zephyr."

"After what we discussed Madame, staying here till daybreak may have saved me some gray hair." Zephyr laughed.

"Sometimes when the wind is just right, and it's quiet like this, you can faintly hear laughter carried up here by the breeze. The port is a long way off, but me ears can still hear it at times. I sit and rock in me chair, and can almost picture happier days. It's as if a distant memory comes to life, being carried on the wind." Hester closed her eyes and smiled.

"What was it like Madame," Zephyr asked. "Before the war and before the realm grew apart from God?"

With her eyes closed and a smile on her face, Hester looked as if she was taking in the sweet fragrance of a rose. "Oh Deary, it was a golden season. It was a time of innocence. The children had time to be children, neighbors helped each other, and there was a lot less wickedness. Morals were much higher lassie. Why, when I was a girl we didn't have to bar our door at night. I could walk by the docks if it was in me head to do so."

Hester opened her eyes. "But the times have changed deary. Thank God for you and your friends; people who are willing to sacrifice and fight for what is right. The past is gone now Miss Zephyr. However, the history of the future is still ours for the writing. As long as there are those willing to take a stand, hope is not lost."

"Merci Madame, there is much wisdom in what you have…" Zephyr paused when the kitten's ears snapped up. With a sleepy look still in its eyes, the kitten cocked its head toward the door, its ears twitching to pick up the slightest sound.

"What is it Maggie?" Hester stroked the animals back as it stood on her lap.

A dead silence enveloped the room. Human ears strained in vain to hear but were met by nothing. Zephyr could hear her breath in her nose and her pulse in her temple but nothing more.

And yet the kitten stared at the door, remaining perfectly still, its ears twitching slightly.

Hester and Zephyr both strained for the slightest sound, each glancing from each other to the door. Their patience was not in vain. Out in the darkness, Zephyr's picketed horse let out a spine tingling whinny. Zephyr had heard that sound before, three months ago when her mount was being stalked by a panther.

The kitten arched its back and let out a nasty hiss. It dug its claws into Hester's legs causing her to jump. With its ears folded back and its lips curled into a growl, the kitten hissed and glared at the door.

"Something is out there Madame!" There was panic in Zephyr's voice as she bolted from the chair and went to a shutter. Slowly she unlatched the hook and cracked it open enough to take a peek outside.

"What is it deary?" A worried look creased Hester's her brow. The kitten jumped from her lap and continued to spit and hiss at the door.

Zephyr could scarcely see anything. She peered intently past the woodpile where her horse was picketed. She caught the glimpse of a dark figure between the shadows of two trees. It looked like it was moving towards the woodpile.

Suddenly a tremendous whooshing sound shattered the night and the woodpile erupted into an inferno of flames. The brightness of the fire caused Zephyr to squint. Twenty-foot high flames shot skyward from the blazing woodpile, and Hester's house was momentarily lit up like it was daytime. There, running for the door to Hester's cabin, was a shadowy figure with a garrote stretched taught between its hands.

"Madame, it is one of the Valkyrie's!" Zephyr shouted in terror and slammed the shutter closed and relocked it.

Hester sprang to her feet knocking her chair over. "Oh dear Lord I was afraid this might happen."

Zephyr overturned the table sending her cup of tea clattering to the ground. She placed it up against the shutter and braced it with her chair. Hester took the other chair and jammed it under the doorknob. No sooner was the chair in place when there came a loud slamming on the door. The kitten ran for cover underneath the cot.

The Valkyrie slammed repeatedly against the door. The bar started to groan and crack under the onslaught.

Zephyr's eyes welled with tears. "Oh Madame, forgive me. I must have led it straight to you. I can't…" Zephyr didn't have to go on. Her face said it all. She would never forgive herself for inadvertently causing the old woman's death. Hester didn't stand a chance against a Valkyrie. Zephyr wasn't sure she did either, but at least she had a chance of escaping if she ran. Few people, Valkyrie's or not, would be able to hold their own in tracking through the woods after Zephyr.

Hester put a hand on Zephyr's shoulder. "When the door comes down Miss Zephyr, you must run for your life. Flee, and don't look back!"

Tears flowed from Zephyr's eyes and her lip started to quiver. She decided on a course of action. "I can not leave you alone with that thing Madame. You are my friend and I will stay no matter what the outcome. You can not fight it alone." Zephyr drew her sword and prepared to fight it out. The Valkyrie continued to smash at the door like a frenzied animal after its prey.

"Now deary," Hester placed a loving hand on Zephyr's cheek and wiped one of her tears. She too now had tears trickling down her face. "Thank you for your kindness lassie. You don't know what it means to me to have a friend such as yourself. But you must save yourself. It is your only chance."

"I can not leave you here to be killed by that thing Madame. It is my fault you are in danger." Zephyr was moved by the old woman's compassion.

Hester clasped one of Zephyr's hands. "But deary, the Valkyrie is not here for me. Do you not remember what I've told you? It is you who it's after. They do not waste their time on unimportant people unless it will cause terror. Don't you see Miss Zephyr; you are the important one. You are one of the leaders of the rebellion. You must flee at once when the door comes down."

Hester picked up a large wooden stick used to stir her cauldron. "I'll distract it as long as I can. You run through the woods and save yourself. I'll be all right. The Valkyrie will follow you, so you must be swift."

Zephyr and Hester embraced briefly, each with tear streaked cheeks, each willing to sacrifice their lives for the other if need be.

A horrible clatter erupted on the other side of the door. It was mixed with grunts and groans, and the sound of bone hitting flesh. The banging moved from the door to the side of the cabin, and with such ferocity as to knock foodstuffs from the shelves. There was the sound of stomping and a metallic sound. After a muffled cry of agony the noise stopped. Hester and Zephyr looked at each other perplexed at the sudden change. Zephyr leaned down close by the door to listen. For a few seconds there was silence.

"Open up, it's me." Scorpyus's voice could be heard outside.

Zephyr's eyes grew wide, "Scorpyus?"

"Yes, it's me." He repeated.

Zephyr drew the bar back and cracked open the door. In the light of the burning woodpile she could see her friend, a stream of blood trickling from the outer corner of his left eye. His hair was disheveled and his tunic partially pulled up from under his belt.

Scorpyus stepped into the cabin. "Are you all right?" Immediately he and Zephyr engaged in a tight embrace. Scorpyus held Zephyr close, her face against his chest. Zephyr sobbed great heaves of relief. "How did you find me out here?" She clung to her friend, a familiar bastion of strength in a chaotic and frightful time.

The two embraced a few seconds more then Scorpyus pulled back and spoke with great urgency in his voice. "You have to get away from here Zephyr. It could be back at anytime."

"What about you? I know the thing wants to kill you also. I have been talking to Hester and she said…"

Scorpyus interrupted and grabbed Zephyr by the hand. He opened the door and looked outside. "We don't have much time. I followed it here and was able to take it by surprise. I gave it a small beating; enough to distract it for a spell, but it will be back."

"Deary your friend is right." Hester added.

Zephyr gave Hester a quick hug, and then Scorpyus pulled her out the door. He took her past the burning woodpile toward where her horse was picketed. Zephyr did a double take. She thought she saw a man, arms crossed, standing near the woodpile. He wore a brown cloak with a golden sash.

"Did you see that man?" Zephyr asked.

"Who?" Scorpyus turned to where Zephyr was pointing but saw nothing.

"I thought…" Zephyr saw nothing but a burning pile of wood now. Scorpyus forced her along not wanting to waste any more time. The two moved swiftly and silently, all the while scanning from side to side. Weaving through the trees they came to Zephyr's horse.

"What kind of madness are we in now?" Zephyr looked to her friend, the left side of his face wet with blood.

"I don't know but you have to go. It will be back. It's on foot. It won't be able to keep up with your horse." Scorpyus looked Zephyr in the eye, worried concern evident on his face.

"What about you Scorpyus? You will be alone with it."

"I'll be fine." Scorpyus placed his hands on Zephyr's shoulders. "I survived one encounter, and I can do it again."

"No, come with me. Do not take the chance. My horse can carry us both." Zephyr pleaded.

"The horse won't get far with all that weight on it; especially down hill. It will stumble and become lame or break a leg." Scorpyus could see the tears well up again in Zephyr's eyes.

"Then you take the horse. Maybe it will think you are me." Zephyr offered. "You're fast Zephyr, but I stand the best chance against it. If not, I am quite good at hiding." Scorpyus brought Zephyr's horse around and held the reigns so she could mount. "Please hurry." Scorpyus begged.

"It's by the cherry tree!" Hester shouted from the darkness.

"Quick get on!" Scorpyus practically lifted Zephyr into the saddle himself.

Zephyr mounted the horse and took the reins in her hands. Tears were streaming down her face. "You better return," she choked out.

Scorpyus eyes welled with tears. Would this be the last time he would see Zephyr? He reached into the pouch on his belt and pulled out a ring. It belonged to the man he knew as a father. He pressed it into Zephyr's hand.

"Take this just in case."

Zephyr started to sob uncontrollably. If Scorpyus parted with that ring then she knew he must not be sure he was going to live. "No Scorpyus, no." Her lips trembled as she looked at her friend. How much more of this could she take in her life?

"And Zephyr, I …" Scorpyus's voice trailed off and became inaudible.

"What is it?" Zephyr leaned down to hear.

"I, uh," Scorpyus coughed, choked up and unable to talk. He could see the sadness in Zephyr's deep green eyes. The two had been through so much together. There was little left to say. No words could describe the feelings going through the two scared and lonely souls. The two held each other's gaze for what seemed like days, each reading the bitter grief, the sullen longing on the others face. The urgency of the time wouldn't allow a proper goodbye. They were forced to say it all with a glance.

Scorpyus reached up, placing a hand behind Zephyr's head and pulled her down to him. Footsteps echoed in the forest a short distance away, now coming from two distinct directions.

"Goodbye," Scorpyus choked out. He drew Zephyr close and placed his lips fleetingly on hers. A flood of emotion swept over the two. For a brief second life in a war torn hell was worth living. And then it was over.

The Valkyrie was yards away. Scorpyus slapped Zephyr's horse smartly on the rump, sending it onward. Zephyr heeled the horse, coaxing it to a full run. She looked back as Scorpyus disappeared into a thicket of brush. She didn't wait to see the Valkyrie. She raced toward the trail dodging trees and rocks. Somewhere behind her was death. She prayed that it wouldn't find Scorpyus. Not now, it couldn't end like this.

The snorting of a horse snapped Zephyr back to her task at hand. Was there someone else out here? She didn't want to wait around to find out. Instincts took over, and Zephyr leaned down low on her mount. She exited the thicket and hit the main trail at a full gallop. Right now nothing would look better then the lights of Xylor.

The *Sea Urchin*'s sails strained in the fierce wind, its ropes groaning to keep the main sail set. Dantes steered into the waves, the sea crashing into the bow of the small vessel sending a spray of salt water on deck. The four on board were drenched. Bartus sat shivering in the biting wind as he manned a bucket. In the bilge, Novak passed buckets of seawater as fast as Bartus and Emerald could empty them overboard. It now took a concerted effort by all to keep the Sea Urchin sailing.

"Avast there Novak, if this squalor be getting much worse we'll have to strike the sails." Dantes shouted over the din of the storm.

Novak poked his head up from below deck. "Ya, hopefully the Kelterland navy will decide to stay in dock. It will make getting through the blockade easier," he replied while handing Emerald a full bucket.

"The last thing we need is to run across an enemy ship. This storm is bad enough," Bartus lamented.

"We'll know soon enough Bartus. It'll be light soon." Dantes fought the rudder fiercely. The storm was worse then he expected. As usual it came up swiftly, but it had been ages since he saw a storm grow so fierce so quick. He didn't want to alarm the others, but he wanted to put to port as soon as possible. By his calculations the *Sea Urchin* was still two hours from shore. Land should be visible at dawn. With any luck, no enemy vessels will be out.

The first rays of light betrayed all hopes. There off the starboard side was a war ship; a large one at that, and it flew the colors of Kelterland. It would only be a matter of time before they spotted the *Sea Urchin*.

"Oh dear God, a ship! Is it one from Kelterland?" Bartus froze in horror.

Emerald looked to where Bartus was pointing, and Novak came up on deck.

"Ya, it is," Novak shot a look at Dantes. "What do we do next Dantes?"

"Angle away towards port and hope for the best. They'll not be able to board us in this weather. But ye can bet yer last shilling they'll try to stop us from putting ashore."

The sun continued to rise over the horizon. Land became visible and so did the *Sea Urchin*. The Kelterland war ship cut a course to intercept the little vessel.

A flash of lightning sent a crash of thunder rolling across the stormy sea. Gray clouds that at first loomed large on the horizon, moved in oppressively, casting a familiar air of foreboding dread on those experienced with sailing the seas. A torrential downpour followed; big drops of biting rain pelted the two ships. It was like being attacked by a swarm of angry hornets.

The *Sea Urchin* tossed violently as Novak and Dantes struck the sails. They struggled valiantly in the fierce wind and rain, but the storm took a violent, menacing turn, and became bent on destroying all things in its grasp. Untying the ropes became impossible. The force of the wind kept them pulled taut to the point of breaking. Novak drew his dagger and cut the ropes. Instead of falling to deck, the main sail whipped violently like a flag, its rigging beating rhythmically against the windlass.

The sail swallowed Dantes, his muffled shouts coming from a bulge under the sailcloth. Novak clawed at the main fabric, bringing it towards him fist full at a time, trying to free Dantes. His thick fingers dug into the sailcloth drawing it in, the wind diligently trying to suck the sail out to sea. It was a battle of brawn versus storm.

Rain fell in an endless cascade drenching the four occupants of the *Sea Urchin*, drops pinging as they pelted Novak's cuirass. The small vessel quickly took on water. Emerald, white knuckled, took the rudder and held on for dear life. The rudder jerked her from side to side as if she were trying to tame a wild horse. Bartus clung to the tiller, visibly shaken, offering his assistance in keeping the vessel on course.

A loud ripping noise sounded and Novak looked to see the greater portion of the main sail tear away and shoot out into the sea. Part of the rigging hit Dantes in the head on its way overboard, opening a gash on his forehead. He staggered forward a few steps then fell to his knees clutching his head.

"Dantes!" Emerald's screech was barely audible above the wind. Her concern didn't pull her from her duties at the tiller, which was becoming more and more impossible by the second. Already the rudder groaned out in protest against the strain of the rough seas, as was the whole ship.

"It feels like the boat is going to fall apart!" Bartus yelled his face wet and ashen.

Novak hurriedly secured the remains of the sail. "Look at it this way Bartus, the Kelterlanders are facing the same storm. By the looks of it they've turned their attention from running the blockade to saving themselves."

The crew of the Kelterland war ship was busy striking their sails. They looked to be trying to set their ship aground near shore. Apparently the sudden fury of the storm took them by surprise as well.

The groaning, splintering crack of wood shook the *Sea Urchin*, and Emerald and Dantes fell to the deck.

"Oh dear God, we've lost the rudder! Now we're adrift heading for who knows where." Bartus bellowed while rubbing his freshly bruised elbow.

"Relax Bartus!" Novak roared. "Panic won't fix any problem. I'll take my chances with the sea rather then a dungeon in Kelterland, which is where we were headed not long ago." Novak stripped his armor and placed it into a burlap sack, tying it firmly closed.

"What are you doing?" Bartus didn't like the look of Novak's actions.

"Preparing for a shipwreck. This stuff will only serve me now as a way to see the bottom of the ocean." Novak stated flatly.

"What are you talking about, a shipwreck?" Bartus exclaimed.

"Use your head and look around." Novak grew impatient with what he perceived as cowardice. Oh, how he wished he made this journey with Cad or one of the others.

"The wind is taking us right for those rocks." Novak pointed to a point on the mainland that had a rocky shore and jagged bluffs. "And without a rudder, it doesn't look like we're steering around them."

Novak stayed calm in the face of danger. It was one of the traits that kept him alive and well thus far into his career as a Clandestine Knight. He had an ability to quickly survey his predicament, and adapt to the situation in order to come up with a new course of action. Deep down, Bartus was envious of Novak's ability to forge ahead unfretted. He wasn't as experienced as Novak, nor as brave; but few could be? What did Bartus have? He wondered why he agreed to get involved again. Was it to please his brother? Perhaps it was just to regain some shred of self-respect after years as a homeless vagabond. Novak said it was never over as long as you still had the breath of life. He survived many times in combat at the last possible second, and he intended to fight till the end. Maybe Bartus could learn something from that attitude. It was time to stand up and be counted.

Bartus felt a firm resolve building within. He was determined to stay focused and perform usefully. No longer would he be indecisive and visibly frightened. He may not be a warrior like Novak, but he had something worthwhile to contribute.

Bartus surveyed his surroundings and then stormed across the deck. "Here, let me help you," he placed a hand on Dantes shoulder, leading him to a seat. He set to work bandaging the gash on Dantes forehead as best he could in the downpour.

"Thank you matey. I am feeling a might dizzy, but I suppose we have more important things to be worrying about." Dantes tucked his hat into his coat.

"Novak thinks we'll shipwreck into those rocks," Bartus explained as he dressed the wound.

Dantes squinted into the horizon, his head throbbing with pain. "Aye, that we will matey, that we will; unless we sink first. The way the *Sea Urchin* is listing to port it'll be close."

Novak came up from below deck and threw a chest overboard. "That's it. We're as light as we're going to get."

"What's our plan?" Bartus asked with a tone that spoke of confidence in being able to handle what would come next, rather then fear of the unknown.

Novak nodded approvingly in his friend's new mood. "Dantes, you're the sailor. What do you suggest?"

Dantes thought a second. "I've had the misfortune of being in two other shipwrecks matey, and I've witnessed several other ships go down to a watery grave. If there's one thing I learned it's that we don't stand a chance to make it to shore if we sink out here. Thar be currents far too contrary out this far. If we make it to those rocks we'll be standing a chance."

Dantes took on seriousness in his voice. "Those who are still able to swim after we run aground should grab onto a plank or a handy piece of debris and swim for shore. Those who are injured in the process…well let's just be saying it's not good. We lost a third of the crew on me last ship. When the waves are beating all about like a galleons flag in a gale, it's hard to find those who can't stay afloat a while on their own. In most cases the uninjured will be lucky to make it to shore alone, much less with the weight of an injured man weighing ye down like an anchor."

The sobering thought didn't have long to sink into those aboard the *Sea Urchin*. Wave upon wave smashed into the tiny boat as a rip current propelled it toward a rocky shoreline. Freezing rain bit at exposed flesh causing a grimacing squint on the four passengers. Dantes forced his eyes open against the onslaught of raindrops. The shoreline was growing fast.

"Aye, it won't be long now. Brace yerself." Dantes sat flat on the deck and wrapped an arm around the tiller. Bartus followed suit and clung tightly to the deck rail. Novak led Emerald to the mast and held her tight against it. He would do his best to protect her. He could feel her trembling with fear and cold.

"It will be alright." Novak reassured with absolute confidence in his voice. The thought of failure rarely entered his mind. Somehow, Novak felt he would always prevail. It was a trait that inspired calm in others. Emerald smiled and nodded to Novak, her white knuckled grip on the mast relaxing a little.

With a jolt, the *Sea Urchin* shuddered to a halt. The sound of splintering wood cracked and groaned above the din of the storm. A rocky crag just below the water surface, punched through the Sea Urchin's hull near the bow. Seawater immediately started flooding into the bilge.

The collision was tremendous. Dantes flew forward landing facedown on the deck and slid into Novak's legs. The force of the impact tore Bartus from the deck rail and sent him tumbling down the stairs below deck. Novak and Emerald were thrown from the mast and sent sprawling across the deck in a tangle of arms and legs.

Novak was first on his feet and assessed the damage. The *Sea Urchin* was listing to port terribly, and standing on deck was tricky. The little ship sat impaled on a jagged protrusion one hundred yards from shore. Shore bound waves crashed against the hull, irritated at the ship's attempt to impede their progress. Novak grabbed the burlap sack that contained his armor, and after spinning it around a few times hurled the bundle as far as he could toward shore. He watched carefully where it landed fully intent on recovering it if possible after the storm passed.

Dantes struggled to his feet rubbing his aching head. Twice now it had met with a hard surface. "Thar be a nasty galleon waging war in me skull. Me brains will be coming out me ears before long."

Bartus scampered from below deck. "We don't have much time; it's flooding quickly down there!"

Dantes ran below deck and was back seconds later. "Aye, Bartus is right. We have less time then I thought. We best be swimming for shore now."

The quartet scurried to the port side deck rail, which due to the listing ship was near water. Bartus jumped into the turbulent sea, Dantes close behind.

"Let's swim to shore together." Bartus replied as Novak helped Emerald over the deck rail. Dantes clung to a piece of floating debris. Lightning flashed and a boom of thunder rumbled across the waters. Rain mercilessly pelted the shipwrecked crew. Emerald looked up to Novak who waited for Dantes to Help Bartus to a piece of floating debris.

A sizzling flash followed by an explosive crack caused Emerald to momentarily become flash blinded. When her vision returned Novak lay slumped over the deck rail, lifeless and flaccid. *The Sea Urchin*'s shattered mast laid splintered on deck.

Novak!" Emerald screamed and swam near the ship. Blood was dripping from the left side of Novak's head.

Dantes swam over and pulled Novak into the water. Novak let out a groan. "He's still alive, but he won't be swimming for a spell." Dantes took Novak to the piece of debris and placed him on it. Immediately it started to sink into the water, so Bartus released his hold on the plank.

"It's not going to float with all of us on it." Bartus replied.

"Aye, you and Emerald swim in with Novak. I'll chance it alone." Dantes fought to hold Novak from being washed off the plank.

Bartus deliberated the predicament. He knew he wasn't strong enough to keep Novak afloat on the plank in this treacherous storm. Dantes, a thick and burly man was having a difficult time doing it. Dantes would have to be the one to get Novak to shore. Novak had to be saved. He was the party's best chance for surviving through this dangerous mission. Bartus was not going to accept a place on the debris if it meant displacing Emerald. Even though he was frightened beyond belief and wanted so desperately to cling to that plank, he was also tired of being a coward. He could see it in the others eyes every time a tense situation presented itself and he saw it in the eyes of the citizens who knew him. They all thought he was a cowardly nobody. The others went out of their way to help him through trying times, like Dantes was doing now by offering to let him get Novak to shore when he knew that wasn't the best idea. As far as

Bartus was concerned, that was all going to stop. He might not get another chance to prove himself. It was time to take a stand and become the man he once was. Bartus felt a surge of courage; a feeling he hadn't felt since before the war. A grin appeared on his face with his new found confidence.

"You'll have to get Novak to shore Dantes. I couldn't possibly keep him afloat and swim in this storm simultaneously. You're the only one strong enough."

Dantes was relieved to hear Bartus decision. He reluctantly agreed, as there was no other choice.

"Aye," Dantes nodded his approval. "But stick close and we'll be ashore in no time."

The party left the meager shelter provided by the listing Sea Urchin and swam into the storm tossed waters that beat against a foreign shoreline. Dantes, the experienced sailor, knew all too well the danger the party was in. Emerald and Bartus were blissfully unaware of the true danger of the situation. There could be rip currents, cross currents, or dangerous eddies; any of which could slam the party into the rocks, or carry them hopelessly out to sea where they would eventually drown. Dantes squinted in the beating rain as he fought to keep Novak afloat on the plank. He carried the knowledge alone

Wave after wave cascaded down on the four sending them spinning and tumbling under the salty sea. Each time Dantes would resurface with Novak and wrestle him back onto the plank. Each time he would search nervously around and let out a sigh when he saw Emerald and Bartus resurface also. Dantes coached them through a cross current. It was swift and it shot them one hundred feet west of their previous location in a matter of seconds. Progress toward shore was slow and difficult. The party fought to keep their heads above water in the tumultuous waves. Dantes encouraged the others, reassuring them all would be fine. The shore beckoned in the early morning light. The one hundred yards of sea separating them from land stretched on achingly ahead. It was a short expanse for their eyes, but an eternity for their pounding hearts. The four pressed on, wet and windswept; each wondering if their fate lay in the bottom of the sea.

VIII

─────◆◆◆─────

"LOVELY MORNING AY, Cyrus." Cad stretched in the saddle and inhaled a deep breath of the crisp cool air. The faint aroma of baked bread wafted in the breeze, and Cad's stomach rumbled in approval.

"It sure is." Cyrus surveyed the street. After a fearful and hunkered down night, Xylor was fast becoming a bustle of activity. Everyone hurried to finish with what they needed to do so they could get back indoors. Pushcart venders rolled their goods into place, and shops were opening. The blacksmith pounded horseshoes on an anvil as sea gulls circled overhead scavenging what they could find.

The main street through Xylor reflected the population of the small island. Well-dressed businessmen smoked pipes in front of a ritzy restaurant. Prim and proper ladies shopped while their buggy driver waited patiently for their return. Two blocks away poor pheasants in tattered clothes begged for alms from those passing. Others awakened from alleys where they had spent the night after a wild evening of cards and rum. Many of these people were homeless and in a perpetual cycle of imbibing too much, recovering, and then imbibing too much again. But these were the extremes. Most owned or worked at the many shops, inns, stables, and other businesses. Without them nothing would get done in Xylor. They were the backbone of the island community.

Cad and Cyrus patrolled looking for the unusual. Both decided to take horses this morning. Maybe that would make it easier to get from incident to incident should the new day be as busy as the previous one.

"How about a bit of breakfast Cyrus?" Cad asked cheerfully contemplating the scent of many fine foods in the air. Before Cyrus could answer a shout came from the alley signifying breakfast would once again be delayed.

"Hey!" A man shouted at Cad and Cyrus as they passed his alley. When they stopped their horses he continued. "Someone stole my shoes last night!"

Cad looked at the slight and grizzled man right into his bloodshot eyes. "Someone took your shoes mate?" Cad looked the man over. He was indeed barefoot, dirty lesion covered feet stuck out from the tattered legs of gray soiled pants. The pants had a tear in one knee and what looked to be a bloodstain around the tear. The man was unkempt, unarmed, and smelled of rum. Cad filled in the rest of the story on his own. The guy must have been rolled when he passed out in the alley. Why anyone would have wanted this man's shoes was a mystery.

"What's your name, mate?" Cad asked. Cyrus looked on somberly; feeling sad for the state of being the man unwittingly placed himself in.

"I'm Artois," the man replied hesitantly.

"Well Artois," Cad released a heavy sigh. "Go to the warehouse at the end of Torchlight Street. It's near the compound. Thadus has set up a charity. The warehouse is filled with bloomin stuff that people have donated. I know the chaps down there have plenty of shoes, or even boots. That is if you don't mind wearing boots once belonging to the Royal Guard. Not to worry though, the lads did a good job cleaning them up."

Artois looked at Cad in disbelief. "Nobody is going to give away free shoes. Are you jesting with me mister?"

Cad shook his head. "No, ask Cyrus here."

Cyrus confirmed Cad's statement. "Thadus set up the warehouse on Torchlight Street as a charity. It's to help through the tough times brought on by the blockade. The cloths and other items there are free to those who have a need and are willing to clean a horse stall or two."

"All I have to do is clean a horse stall and they'll give me a free pair of boots?" Artois's eyes lit up. He had never heard of such a thing.

Cad shook his head. "All you have to do is show you are a straight bloke who is willing to do a little something to help himself. You might even want Doc to check out your feet mate."

"I just might," Artois smiled. "Thanks a lot." He tipped his tattered cap and gingerly walked off toward Torchlight Street.

"Now for that breakfast," Cad motioned to Cyrus and both took their patrol toward the source of the savory aroma.

The events of the last few days served as a reminder that Xylor still had a way to go before a comfortable order would be restored. Of course, the vagrant poor would always be a consequence of any society no matter how good. Cad figured Artois to be one of those unfortunate souls who just started out having a couple of steins now and again, then a few more, and as time passed was unable to stop.

Cyrus was caught off guard when Cad suddenly stopped his mount. Cad peered far down the street, mouth slightly agape, at something apparently of great importance. Cyrus scanned the street ahead for anything unusual. There was no scuffle, noise, or suspicious movement. Everything seemed as it should.

"What is it?" Cyrus asked.

"That horse plodding toward us on the north side of the street; it looks like Zephyr's." Cad motioned to a rider less strawberry roan.

Cad and Cyrus heeled their mounts forward to investigate. As they got closer, Cad confirmed the horse did indeed belong to Zephyr. The reins hung down to the ground, and a sweaty lather bathed the steed's neck and hindquarters. The saddle hung askew angled off to one side, the horse's mane an unkempt tangle. Something was wrong. The horse looked exhausted. It paused to drink greedily from a trough.

"Bloody ay Cyrus, something's not right." Cad spurred his mount and galloped to Zephyr's horse. He immediately dismounted and inspected for clues. Cad's face went ashen with a grave look of despair. He ripped off a gauntlet and touched a stain on the saddle with his fingertip. Rubbing his fingers together, he inspected it closely in the sunlight.

"It's blood." Cad's brow furrowed in worried anger. All sorts of scenarios played through his mind, all of which caused his head to swim with a dizzying rage. He tried to reason some logic into the situation, but couldn't. Zephyr was his friend. If harm befell her, he would personally kill the person responsible.

More blood stained Zephyr's saddlebags, and some spotted the horse's left flank. The mount seemed to be uninjured. Cad searched through the saddlebags. Nothing was missing so Zephyr didn't appear to have been jumped by highwaymen. Then Cad found it. There tucked into the folds of Zephyr's bedroll was the familiar white square swath of cloth with a black swan emblazoned on it.

Cad turned purple with rage and slammed his helmet to the ground. "Those bloody pigs! I'll hunt them down to the very gates of hell! They'll rue the day the…"

Cyrus placed a hand firmly griping Cad's shoulder. He whispered and signaled with his eyes for Cad to look around. A few people had gathered at the angry outburst, and more were milling about to see what was the matter. It wouldn't do for Cad to cause a scene.

"We don't know what happened to Zephyr. She could be alive and has escaped her attacker. This might not even be her blood." Cyrus reassured.

Cad softened. Cyrus was right. They didn't know for sure what happened to Zephyr yet. "Alright Cyrus, you get a squad and track Zephyr's horse back as far as the trail will allow. Find out what you can. I'll have the rest of the men organize aggressive patrols. We have to defend this city at all costs. The shadow assassins may be planning an attack against us today. If they did get Zephyr it would surely serve to embolden those daft lunatics. Scorpyus should be back soon. He played a hunch last night. I'll need to talk to him before I finalize our next plan of action."

In an amazing show of self-discipline, Cad put aside his extreme anger and resumed complete command of the situation. In seconds he formulated a new plan based upon the new changes. Cad was a born leader, and carried a presence that spoke of confident authority

"Consider it done," Cyrus's curiosity was piqued. "What hunch was Scorpyus playing out last night?"

Cad clasped Cyrus's hand in a handshake. "Trust me Cyrus, you don't want to know."

Cyrus nodded his understanding. "I don't know when I'll get back, but I promise I won't come back without something."

"Thank you Cyrus. You're a good chap. I have to know what happened to Zephyr." Cad watched Cyrus mount up and ride off. He placed his hand in his pocket and felt for the letter he received from Ingrid. It was still there. Knowing he had Ingrid provided Cad with some semblance of sanity in a world of chaos and morbidity.

From under the stairs and behind a crate in an alley, Brynhild took in the scene before her. It had been challenging trying to keep up with Cad and Cyrus as they were on horseback. She learned a lot already by just watching. Cad had been visibly upset by what he saw. That was a good sign. Lady Valfreyja and Hildr must have been successful. Lady Valfreyja insisted on going herself after Sigurd's earlier failure. Brynhild would find out the details in due time. By nightfall she would have the full story. Lady Valfreyja suggested the Order move against the dark one, but plans changed when the sprite-like woman was seen riding out of town. Now it looked as if one obstacle to success had been removed. The four were intriguing to watch. They were clearly masters of their craft, and worthy adversaries. The dark one may have even stood a chance of becoming a Valkyrie. The thought had been voiced, but Hildr assured the Order the dark one wouldn't be swayed from his God and beliefs. It was stubborn fanaticism that made the four so dangerous. They were unyielding in their moral code. In a way, Brynhild admired that trait. For it was unyielding loyalty to the Order that made the Valkyrie's so powerful. Even though Brynhild could admire her enemies, she still held them as inferior.

Brynhild knew Kelterland could not afford to let this attitude spread. It filled her with a sense of pride to think Kelterland chose the Order to ensure this attitude end before it spread from Xylor. That was a compliment indeed.

* • * • *

The Wisteria River flowed from high up in the mountains on Xylor's northeast corner until it met with the Xylorian River. From there the cool mountain waters flowed through town and emptied at Xylor's port. A few miles north of the main road the Wisteria curved westward cutting a deep gouge in the surrounding hillside. It was also here that the river slowed from its turbulent white water course and widened into a large vernal pool before continuing to the Xylorian. Normally this pool was a favorite fishing spot for the locals. However, with the current state of terror, the pool was all but deserted; for had any fisherman been here this day they would have been privy to an unusual sight.

Movement in the nearby reeds startled a bathing sparrow. It fluttered off to the branch of a fir tree unwilling to investigate. A disturbance in the water just below the surface slowly moved from the reeds to shore. It started as a ripple, but left a clear wake as the submerged entity moved toward shore. The sparrow fluttered nervously from the safety of its perch.

The ripple came to a halt at the edge of the pool. Fingertips emerged above the water surface, first from one hand and then the other, moving slowly so as to ensure the dripping water would make a minimal splash. The fingertips reached for a hold on the shore a few feet from the bank. Then like the moon rising on the horizon, a head rose from below the surface, a length of reed pursed between its lips. The head paused a moment to let its eyes scan the surroundings. When all appeared safe, the neck and upper torso came forth from the chest deep waters of the Wisteria. The hands removed the reed and cast it aside.

Scorpyus slicked back his raven hair and took another good look around. He looked haggard and exhausted. The air hitting his drenched clothing sent a chill throughout his body. Scorpyus climbed ashore, removed his tabard and wrung it out, all the while glancing around nervously. He held the cool damp tabard to the black and swollen bump at the corner of his eye. He winced with pain, but the coolness felt good, and he dabbed some of the oozing blood away. After another scan of the area he padded to a wild blackberry bush and hungrily ate the delicious berries. They were the best berries he had ever eaten.

It had been a long night. Scorpyus estimated he had run at least ten miles during the night through a rough and steep forest. He felt confident he had led the shadow assassin away from Zephyr. Scorpyus was taken by surprise and came close to death once again. After a violent but short battle, Scorpyus was able to escape. The determined Valkyrie persistently tracked him for over a mile. Scorpyus was finally able to loose his enemy by jumping in the swift flowing river. It was a risky undertaking that proved successful three months earlier when he and Novak were being run down by attack dogs. Drowning was a better alternative then being strangled by a thin wire.

For a brief moment Scorpyus thought he might have accomplished the seemingly impossible. He surprised the Valkyrie once near the trail from Hester's, but when he moved in for the kill, it vanished into the night. Before it disappeared he got a good look at it in the pale moonlight. The Valkyrie had the distinct form of a human with arms, legs, head, and torso. He already knew they wore black clothing wrapped tightly to fit the contours of the body. What he didn't notice before was the scarlet sash they wore around their waist. One more interesting discovery was perhaps an answer to reports of the Valkyrie's fire breathing ability. At first Scorpyus was stunned when he saw the white smoky billows coming from the Valkyrie. He already decided the fire breathing report to be nonsense. But there before his now wide-eyed stare were regular puffs of white emitting from the Valkyrie's head only to disappear in a vapor. For a split second Scorpyus teetered on the brink of superstition, but in the end logic prevailed: For he noticed the same smoky cloud coming from his own mouth; his panting breath in the cold night air. So much mystery and fear surrounded the Valkyrie it bread superstition. Scorpyus shook his head a little disappointed in himself for almost falling victim to outlandish rumors. As he maneuvered in closer he could vaguely make out the form of a face under the Valkyrie's black cheesecloth style mask. There were dark circular spots where the eyes and mouth would be, and a slight mound at the nose. The mesh cloth concealing any further features of its wearer. When Scorpyus took a few more steps closer, the Valkyrie jerked its head toward him and then slipped into the shadows. By the time Scorpyus closed the last ten yards there was no sign of the dark entity except for an unusual footprint. Scorpyus studied the footprint intently. It was made with a flat-soled soft leather shoe. No lines or striations were present indicating a smooth sole. The heel and ball of the foot of the print sunk farther into the dirt then the arch which again was consistent with a human foot. One peculiarity did stand out. Like a mitten that has a place for the thumb with all the other fingers in a common compartment, so did the shoe of the Valkyrie. The big toe had its own compartment separate from the other toes. Scorpyus had never seen anything like that and wondered what purpose it served. It was then Scorpyus heard a noise behind him and realized the Valkyrie circled around in an attempt to flank him. Scorpyus bolted to the left and then ran in a wide arc to the rear attempting to come up behind his attacker. Again the Valkyrie proved to be a formidable opponent and was gone by the time Scorpyus completed his move.

Thus the murderous cat and mouse game dragged on through the night leaving both parties exhausted. Through the course of the night Scorpyus was able to give the dreaded thing a few good punches, and a heavy stomp to the arch that elicited a loud yelp. That was combined with the pummeling he gave it at the door to Hester's cabin. Scorpyus was sure the Valkyrie would be nursing an aching body. Hopefully it was feeling as battered as he did.

Scorpyus decided to start back to Xylor. A warm bed would feel good right about now. He walked south for the main road. Cold and miserable in his wet clothes, Scorpyus couldn't wait to dry off and wolf down a hot meal. Even Astorian black tea would be a welcome antidote to his chilled body.

Scorpyus trod west on the main road. It was deserted. Scorpyus hadn't been on the road long when he noticed a Valkyrie footprint on the north side of the trail. He followed the track north at an excited jog. One hundred yards from the road Scorpyus lost the track. The trail had been heading north so he continued hoping to pick up some sign again. Then a disturbing thought occurred to him. What if the Valkyrie was intentionally leaving tracks in order to lead Scorpyus into a trap? They were certainly intelligent enough. Was it coincidence he found the trail of the Valkyrie after searching all night to no avail? It was daylight now, and the Valkyrie tired and more apt to make mistakes. Scorpyus slowed to a cautious walk, listening intently. He stalked northward holding his sword to stop it from clanging against his hip. If he could find where these things were staying, perhaps he could come back with Cad and some men to attack the Valkyrie's and be rid of them once and for all. Scorpyus shook his head. He could only hope it would be that easy.

Scorpyus froze when he heard a noise. It sounded like a splash of water. Slowly he crept closer to the noise, every sense on alert, his heart pounding in his chest. He inched agonizingly silent toward the sound. As he got closer he heard another splash, and then another. After a few more yards he heard a voice. It was a woman's voice. Scorpyus paused to listen. There was the sound of water dripping on water, and what sounded like a woman softly humming. Scorpyus oriented himself to his surroundings. He estimated he was between the main road and Granite. Why on earth would anyone be out here? He inched closer to the sound until he came to a clump of bushes. He heard a woman humming a tune on the other side. From the splashing and dripping noises it sounded like she was doing laundry in a basin. Who would be out here doing laundry?

All of a sudden a loud splash sounded and the humming stopped. Then he heard something like scratching. Did the woman hear him? Scorpyus couldn't wait to find out. He bolted around the bushes to take whoever it was by surprise.

When Scorpyus rounded the bushes he froze in his tracks, eyes wide and mouth agape. A woman stood facing him wearing nothing but a towel. She stood next to a wooden tub, and was working another towel through her wet hair. A small cabin stood forty of fifty feet away.

A loud scream erupted from the woman, loud enough to send birds fleeing from all of the nearby trees.

"How dare you sneak upon a bathing woman! Do you know no decency? One could expect to meet with such perversion at the docks, but at one's home it could only be the work of a mongrel such as you!" The woman stopped drying her hair and clutched that towel in front of her.

"I'm sorry my lady," Scorpyus sputtered. "I thought you were…I mean I was looking for…"

The woman cut Scorpyus short. "A degenerate reprobate such as you is always looking for trouble. Have you no honor? You are the type for which a woman must always guard her virtue."

"I'm sorry my lady," Scorpyus knew the situation looked bad and there would be no explaining. He tried to backtrack and get himself out of the jam. "I assure you my lady, I mean you no harm. I'm looking for…"

Again the woman cut Scorpyus off. "I know what you are looking for as you have yet to avert your eyes from me. If you have even a shred of honor you would leave at once, or shall I scream for help. My husband is not far off. I'm sure he would not approve of you being here." She glowered at Scorpyus with a look that suggested she meant what she was saying.

Scorpyus turned away at once. The woman was a dark haired beauty in her thirties. She had soft features, red pouting lips, and dark brown eyes that glared at Scorpyus with a deep-seated hatred. There would be no explanation adequate enough to console her. All she knew was that a wet, unkempt and battered stranger with a bloody bruise near his eye appeared out of nowhere while she was taking a morning bath. Scorpyus looked like a suspicious character in his present condition. Even cleaned up, most people thought gypsies as the unsavory sort. Realizing there was no point in continuing the contact Scorpyus decided it best to leave.

"I'm truly sorry my lady. It won't happen again." Scorpyus turned and left. A short distance from the woman he ran for the main road wanting to put the incident behind him as quickly as possible. If the Valkyrie had indeed come through the area Scorpyus would in all likelihood have found the woman dead.

"I should hope it never happens again!" The woman yelled after Scorpyus. When he was long gone a wry smile crept on her lips. She threw the towels aside and limped to a nearby tree, her right foot swollen and tender. Reaching down she retrieved a bundle of black clothing. Valfreyja quickly got dressed again. She was confident of her deception, but took nothing for granted. Had Scorpyus looked inside the cabin he would have found the freshly dead corpse of a middle aged farmer, his throat slit from ear to ear. Normally a Valkyrie didn't kill the unimportant, or those whose corpse would remain undiscovered. But Valfreyja made an exception this time. She was getting tired and had a busy day ahead. She wanted to sleep and get something to eat; things she couldn't do with Scorpyus around. The dark one was tenacious. He would be a challenge to kill. Valfreyja wanted to be rested before that confrontation. This time she was sure of victory. She helped herself to the dead farmer's food then vanished into forest.

———•◦•———

Novak felt the presence of someone hovering overhead, someone who appeared to be radiating a tremendously bright light. He squinted, his eyelids tight slits against the brilliant white luster surrounding the dark figure. The aura was so intense it caused his head to throb painfully. He couldn't make out the figure's face, but did see a hand protruding from an elongated robe-like sleeve. Novak tried to move but couldn't. It hurt too much. The firm and lumpy surface he was laying on did little to provide comfort. He could move his fingers. They dug into a gritty substance, and he could wiggle his toes.

The figure just stood over Novak, patiently waiting for a response. It was speaking something in a voice that sounded garbled and muffled. Novak pondered the situation while enjoying a cool breeze across his face.

Judging from the pain throbbing in his head, Novak ruled out the possibility he had died. In heaven there would be no pain. Perhaps he was about to die and the figure was an angel that would escort him to the other side. Novak could remember the shipwreck, but then everything went blank. He could very well be dying. The thought didn't scare Novak, as he was a saved believer. He knew his final destiny and realized death was always a breath away. He thought hard. He must have been seriously injured in the shipwreck. What would the others do? They were counting on him. He couldn't die yet.

Novak closed his eyes against the glare. He felt a hand clasp his shoulder and shake him gently. The angel was getting impatient.

"Novak, we have to go soon." A soft voice whispered. Novak was too tired to move.

Novak felt meaty hands grab him by the collar and pull him to a seated position. They had to hold him up to keep him from falling back to a laying position. Boy, when it's your time to go there's no delaying it.

"We needs to be moving on thar matey." A gruff voice with garlic breath stated.

Novak forced his eyes open. An angel wouldn't have garlic breath, would it? Novak found himself looking into Dante's face.

"Aye, yer back with us. And just in time too."

"What happened? How did we get to shore? The last thing I remember is helping Emerald into the water." Novak looked around groggily for Emerald. She stood nearby sullen and morose.

"The wind sheared off part of the mast. She came down on yer head. Thank God it was a glancing blow lest ye would have sailed yer last voyage." Dantes handed Novak a burlap sack. "I retrieved yer armor when the storm died down."

Novak glanced toward the sky. It was still overcast, but the gusty wind had died down to a breeze. "How long have I been laying here?"

"You've been out the better part of the day matey," Dantes replied. "But we needs to be going. Thar could be patrols from the king's brigade searching for us. It'll be dark in a few hours, and we'll need to find a safer place to camp."

Novak forced himself to his feet and stood wobbly for a moment while he regained his orientation. Emerald rushed over to help steady him.

"I was worried about you. You were mumbling something about an angel." Emerald said. She looked like she had been crying. Her clothes were still damp and sandy from the ordeal, and had her now frazzled hair pulled back into a bun.

"How are you doing?" Novak asked. Emerald reassured him unconvincingly she was fine. Novak didn't see any obviously serious injury on her so was satisfied for the time being.

Novak looked up and down the coastline. He could see no sign of the Kelterlander's warship that had been pursuing them. He pointed northeast along the shoreline. "Astoria is that way. I guess J&R Shipping is where we are going."

Dantes knew what Novak was thinking. "The sea was unforgiving to the Kelterlanders as well. I hiked a ways while ye were in yer slumber. Their ship is run aground a mile or two north of us. They were unloading by row boat."

Novak was glad to hear that. "That's good to know. We'll avoid the beach on our way to Astoria. I would hate to interrupt their party." Novak laughed. Emerald and Dantes offered weak smiles. It was uncharacteristic of them. Novak didn't know for sure about Dantes, but something was definitely bothering Emerald. His head hurt too much to contemplate it.

"Well let's get going." Novak grabbed the burlap sack containing his armor. He would put it on later. Dantes gathered up the few possessions he managed to salvage from the *Sea Urchin*.

It only amounted to a dagger, sword and a few baubles he fit in the pouch on his belt. Emerald had only her clothes and a sword. The party had no food.

Emerald and Dantes were ready to leave. Novak glanced around. "Where is Bartus?" No sooner had he asked when the somber mood of Emerald and Dantes suddenly made sense to him. Emerald broke into tears.

"He never made it ashore," Dantes replied gravely. "I searched up and down the coast, but found no trace of him. I fear he is lost at sea."

Novak felt a lump in his throat. He felt terrible for Emerald. Emerald released the heaving sobs she had been holding back. Novak placed an arm around her shoulder to comfort her. She wept uncontrollably. Emerald had always been fond of her uncle. They had grown even closer during the last few months. Emerald had high hopes for what this mission would do for her uncle. He had even begun to find his courageous spirit once more. To die now just as it looked like he would recover was more than Emerald could bear. For the moment she would not be consoled.

Though Novak had only known the man a short time, Bartus had grown on him despite the frustration he sometimes caused. Novak had more respect for Bartus then the average man who did nothing. Bartus at least did something. He had integrity and character, even if bravery sometimes eluded him. Novak regretted not having more patience with Bartus, and would actually miss the slight fellow.

Emerald pulled away from Novak's arms and wiped her eyes. "Thank you. I'll be all right…eventually. I'll see my uncle again someday."

Novak nodded in the affirmative. "Bartus is in a better place."

Dantes stared at the ground in awkward silence. He had just met Bartus and didn't really know him. "Aye, in some ways he may be fairing better than us. Our future is a might less certain."

"I know. Thank you both." Emerald removed a kerchief from her bodice. "We should be on our way."

Novak motioned for the others to follow him. He would lead the way. Emerald had an inner strength. It was a trait that endeared her to Novak. Emerald, like Zephyr, was a strong woman who didn't lose her feminine side. Novak was a fearless warrior who respected strength and courage in others. As a result Emerald was one of the few women who could impress Novak on every level. Few men could even boast of that.

The somber trio trudged on by foot arching away from the beach so as not to be spotted by sailors from the Kelterland war ship. They kept well in the tree line and out of sight. The party traversed the two miles northeast to where they could eye the Kelterlander sailors making camp on the beach below. The sailors were preoccupied salvaging as much as they could from their ship. Others were building a fire. It looked as if they were going to camp for the night.

"Do you think they'll be looking for us?" Emerald peered from behind a tree.

Novak saw several of the sailors lined up in front of a keg, each taking turns filling their goblets. Several more kegs were being unloaded from a rowboat. There were four rowboats in all, each with a crew busy ferrying goods from the war ship to shore.

"No," Novak studied the activity on the beach. "We won't have to worry about this bunch. But just in case…" Novak opened the burlap sack he was carrying and proceeded to put on his armor and weapons. When he was done he tucked the empty sack under his belt.

"Aye Novak, this band of scurvy bilge rats will be sponging up rum till the wee hours of the morning. It'll be mid-afternoon before they'll be up and about their merry way."

"Ya, that's one less problem," Novak started walking. The others followed suit. "It'll be dark soon and we don't have any food or water. If we come upon a farm house maybe we'll be able to buy something to eat."

"Food sounds so good," Emerald replied hungrily.

"Then let's hurry," Novak smiled. "Somewhere out there, food waits."

The other two responded with a halfhearted chuckle. The trio set off northeast towards Astoria. They didn't know exactly where they were, or exactly how far they had to go. But those answers, and hopefully food, lay somewhere ahead.

IX

---◆◆◆---

CAD COULD SCARCELY see twenty feet ahead in the thick
fog. The vaporous mist overtook the island rather quickly,
and now clung thick like a heavy wet quilt. Cad thought he was
walking through clouds, his face and armor moist with tiny drops
of water. The fog brought a cold chill to the air, one that seeped
through his clothing like icy fingers groping for heat, pilfering all
the warmth they could find.

The fog all but obliterated the sun bathing everything in a
pale shadow-less light. A certain eeriness swept the docks. Sound
seemed muffled and all was abnormally quiet and still. Cad could
hear sea gulls overhead but couldn't see them. Water splashed
against the risers that supported the dock, but it too was lost
beneath a cloudy veil. Muffled voices and the clanking of goblets
drifted through the mist, coming from no particular location.
Creaking wood from the many plank ways sounded all around
Cad. It made for a lonely, uneasy walk as Cad continued out the
pier, his footsteps on the damp wood being his only company.

Cad stopped when he came to the end of the pier. He stared
out into the vast white expanse that concealed an even more vast
sea. The fog had no beginning or end. It just drifted endlessly all

around. Except for twenty feet of pier, nothing else seemed to exist.

Cad relished his first moment of solitude in an otherwise hectic and problem filled day. The wooden pier creaked in unison with the ebb and flow of the sea. The rhythmic creaking was reminiscent of a rocking cradle or chair. It became a serene sound that made for a comforting prelude to thought.

Cad pulled out his letter from Ingrid. It still held the scent of her perfume. His mind swirled with joyous memories of times spent in Ravenshire. It was hard to believe. Just over three months ago he and the others were home; a cobalt blue lake in the mountains. Novak's sister got married and for a day all was merry and blissful. It was also the last time all of the family and friends had been gathered together; for it was two days after the wedding that Cad and the other three set off for Xylor. At the time, Cad told Ingrid he would see her in a week or two at the most. A lot changed since that time. Cad wondered if it was worth it. Novak had nearly been killed and now Zephyr was missing.

Cad didn't like to second-guess. If the Clandestine Knights didn't take a stand for what was right, who would? That's why the four joined forces in the first place. They wanted to make a difference in the world, and were definitely blessed with the skills to carry out their calling. Everything seemed to come together in Xylor all at once. It was more than coincidence. God had a hand in it. Still Cad couldn't help but feel doubt. His longing to see Ingrid and Ravenshire would always be in conflict with his sense of duty. Did the others feel that way?

The thought of settling into a life with Ingrid was quite tempting. It definitely sounded better then dealing with shadow assassins. Was it really Cad's responsibility to save Xylor? At the moment Xylor was rather bleak and depressing. There was no light at the end of the tunnel. But one never knew. If you never give up you may be surprised what could happen.

Cad envied the others. The bulk of the organization and planning fell to him. Novak lived for the battle. The tedious politics in between skirmishes was the only thing that annoyed Novak. Cad wondered if his friend had thoughts of settling down. He seemed get along fine with Emerald, but one never knew with Novak. His mind was not changed easily. He would never want to risk making a young lady a widow; not a lady he truly cared about.

Scorpyus was not acting himself lately. Cad knew it was because of bad news from home. The situation was complicated. Cad wondered about his friend. Did he ever feel like calling it enough and going back to Ravenshire? Scorpyus spent a lot of time alone on his assignments. Surely he had plenty of time to think. Yet, they all continually found themselves in positions for which they were best suited. If this wasn't their calling, what was? No matter how much the four tried to plan their course, they found themselves being carried along by circumstance. It was like paddling a boat on a river. Sure you could change your course with the oars, but in the long run you were still going to end up where the river took you.

And what about Zephyr? Cad refused to believe she was dead without proof. His logic wouldn't allow it. Zephyr could very well have eluded the shadow assassin. After all she allowed a pursuer to track her rider less horse on many occasions. What about the blood on her saddle? Zephyr survived other wounds. Did she ever get tired of the risks? Did she ever want to settle down? Many men tried to court her, and many men failed to keep her interest. Cad surmised few men would be strong enough to meet the task. Zephyr was a skilled warrior. Any prospective man would have to be confident in his own abilities, and not intimidated by her. Most men couldn't take being bested by a woman. Plenty of egocentric men assumed they were fit for the part, and those were exactly the type that annoyed Zephyr. Cad wondered if she fancied slowing the pace down, maybe only an adventure a year.

Cad closed his eyes and took a deep breath of his perfumed letter. Oh how he longed for simpler times. Cad contemplated that statement long and hard; simpler times. Was there ever really such a thing as simpler times? Maybe the reason things looked so good in the past, was that things were so bad right now. Deep down, Cad knew it was perfectly normal to long for Ravenshire. But now duty called, and Cad always answered. He placed his letter back in his pocket.

The future was as clear as the fog. The only way was to move was forward, even if the view was obscured. Abrams preached once 'faith was the substance of things hoped for, and the evidence of things not seen.' That now took on a deeper meaning for Cad.

A footstep sounded on the pier from somewhere behind Cad. It was the soft step of someone trying to be quiet. Cad turned quietly and grasped the hilt of his sword. He wasn't in the mood for trouble. If whoever materialized from the fog was looking for trouble, may God have mercy on them because Cad wouldn't.

"Blooming ay Scorp, do you always have to sneak up on a chap?" Cad was relieved to see his friend and released the tension that had built up in his body.

"Sorry I'm late. I needed to get a little sleep. I must have overslept. Besides, with this fog you can't really tell when it's midday." Scorpyus explained.

"Don't worry; it gave me a bit of time to think." Cad's eyes grew wide when his friend drew closer. "Well, it looks like you tangled with a nasty bloke."

Scorpyus did look battered, but took the time to shave and wash up. "You should have seen me before."

"Was it a shadow assassin?"

"Yes, but it got away. I lost its trail. They're good. I'm lucky to be back. The Valkyrie had other plans for me."

Cad raised an eyebrow. "Did you say Valkyrie?"

Scorpyus filled Cad in on everything Zephyr learned about their formidable adversaries. Cad hung on every word shocked and amazed; yet relieved to know they had some answers. He never heard of such an order of people. Zephyr came through once again. Cad would have to meet this hermit friend of hers someday.

"That's bloody incredible! The reports were sounding daft. But now I can see why." Cad shook his head in amazement.

"They are to be reckoned with." Scorpyus agreed.

"What about Novak, did he leave safely?" Cad inquired.

"He left last night from this very dock as scheduled. After that I trailed Zephyr just as we had decided, and it was a good thing too." Scorpyus filled in Cad on all that transpired the night before at Hester's.

"It sounded like you had a full night."

Scorpyus rolled his eyes. "You don't even know the half of it. It was brutal. After Zephyr got away all…"

Scorpyus could tell something was wrong by the look on Cad's face. "What is it?"

Cad swallowed hard. "Zephyr didn't make it back."

"That's impossible! I made sure she got away."

Cad shrugged his shoulders. "I don't know what to tell you Scorpyus. Her horse came back but she didn't."

"So she's just missing? We don't know for sure what happened yet."

"Not yet. I have Cyrus looking for her." Cad took a deep breath. "And one more thing; Zephyr may have been hurt. There was blood on her saddle."

Scorpyus went pale. His mind swirled with all the possibilities. How could that have happened? He was sure he kept the Valkyrie busy most of the night. There should have been enough time for Zephyr to escape

Scorpyus pounded his fist into his palm. This was impossible. "Cad, I know I kept the Valkyrie occupied all night. I have the bruises to prove it."

Cad shrugged his shoulders. What could he say? Something happened to Zephyr. "I don't think it was a robber. With those blasted Valkyrie's about, all the crime has been pushed into the city. At any rate, Zephyr could hold handle a thief."

Scorpyus thought about it. "There has to be an explanation. Unless there was…" A light went on.

"Unless there was more then one Valkyrie last night." A sick feeling welled in the pit of Scorpyus's stomach. How could he have missed that? Was he so intent on tracking the one Valkyrie he failed to notice the other?

Cad could see the anguished look on his friends face. "Now I know what you're thinking Scorp, but…"

"No," Scorpyus interrupted raising a hand, "It's my fault. At some point I should have realized there were two of them. It's my fault she's gone." Tears welled up in his eyes. Scorpyus turned away so as not to look Cad in the face.

"Now wait a minute. You did what you could. Maybe the other Valkyrie was tracking you. There would be no way to know that…"

"Cad," Scorpyus interrupted again while staring blankly into the fog, "That's an obvious possibility I should have considered. We *both* knew there was a good chance that Novak and Zephyr would be attacked. You came to me and said 'I suspect there is a bloody informant keeping the shadow assassins briefed on our actions.' Those were your exact words. We decided I would secretly follow them just in case. Novak and Zephyr didn't even know about our plan! And you were right. Novak made it all right, but as sure as the sunrise there was a Valkyrie tracking Zephyr. We foresaw this. We planned a solution, and I failed. It's as simple as that."

Cad knew Scorpyus long enough to know there was nothing he could say to change his friend's mind. His brooding comrade would work through it on his own. As was his custom, Scorpyus would wander off alone to deal with his emotions. Cad had seen it many times. He kept it all buried under a dark and mysterious persona. If he wasn't playing the joker, he would be lost under that dark stare, eyes penetrating outer oblivion just like they were now.

As far as Cad was concerned, he was the only logical one when it came to emotions. It wouldn't do to wear your emotions so obviously like Zephyr. But it also wouldn't do to keep them buried like Scorpyus or act like nothing bothered you like Novak. When Cad was angry he never lost control. When he was happy he didn't over do it and become giddy. When Cad was sorrowful, people thought he was angry. Each method seemed to work.

"Well, let's not put the blooming cart before the horse," Cad advised sympathetically. "We don't know if Zephyr is dead. Hopefully we'll know more when Cyrus gets back. In the mean time, we have a job to do. I know you may not feel like it, and I can't say I don't feel like abandoning this mess at times myself. But Novak is out there counting on us, as are several hundred rebel troops. Our best chance of coming through this bloody mess is to forge ahead. We are serving something bigger than all of us. It is the Lord's fight. The next generation deserves a life rid of oppression. If we quit now Scorpyus, we condemn the next generation to a worse life then we've had. Things will only get worse. Fight the fight so all the little boys we see don't end up like us. Fight the fight so little girls don't end up like Zephyr and Isabella." Cad put a hand on Scorpyus's shoulder. "It has to end Scorp. Somehow we find ourselves in the middle of this daft whirlwind."

Cad even managed to convince himself of the need to push on. If Scorpyus only knew what Cad had been thinking a few minutes earlier.

What could Scorpyus say? Of course Cad was right. Kelterland's rule did have to end, but that was unforeseeable at this dark time on the miserable little island that had become Xylor. Scorpyus had no intent of quitting the fight now. Now it was more personal.

Scorpyus thought back to the last time he saw Zephyr. Each was convinced it would be the last time they would see the other. And maybe they were somehow right. Scorpyus didn't know what to make of what transpired. That had never happened before. He wondered if the finality of the exchange allowed them both to express innermost feelings that had always been brewing below the surface. Was it the desperation of the moment? Now Scorpyus felt he might never know. He didn't share in Cad's optimism. Zephyr was more then likely dead and the Valkyrie's would pay.

A surge of hatred pulsed through Scorpyus's body. The thought of killing a Valkyrie filled him with euphoria. Oh how good it would feel to slice one of the damnable things to pieces. They killed several citizens and deserved it Scorpyus reasoned. They killed Zephyr, and would pay with the blood of their own. Scorpyus couldn't wait for his next encounter.

"Don't worry Cad," Scorpyus managed a meager smile. "I'm not going anywhere. So what's next?"

Cad let out a sigh of relief. It was good to know he could always count on his friend. "Well, we could start with the rest of your report. Did you find out anything about that blooming kerchief?" And just like that the two were down to business. No matter what the ordeal, and the four knights had seen their fair share, they knew they could always count on each other. Outside of God, each one knew deep down that at least three other people in the world would give that last full measure of devotion. It had become instinct. It was the bond that only people who faced death together could have, and it was stronger then blood ties.

"Cyrus and I had a tough time last night. Tensions are running high. Thadus is really worried. He doesn't know how long he can keep the influential businessmen pacified. The blockade was hurting them before. Now with the Valkyrie's…I told him we're doing our blooming best. But now with this fog…"

Cad shook his head in frustration, a grave look in his eyes. "The daylight had always been a reprieve from the blasted Valkyrie's. Now the fog is so thick it could conceal a ship. After last night I could sure use a spot of good news…if you have any."

"I did find out a few interesting things yesterday afternoon." Scorpyus looked around instinctively for eavesdroppers but it was all but futile; the fog obscured all visual traces of possible threats.

Cad's eyes popped open in mild surprise. "Really, say on mate."

"Well the cloth was monogrammed so finding out who it belonged to was the easy part. I went to the local laundries and tailor's until I found someone who knew what '*BM*' stood for." Scorpyus smiled recounting his success. "It turns out it belonged to a Braydon Mendax."

Cad furrowed his brow. "Never heard of the chap."

"Well as it turns out he heard of us; and hated us with a passion."

"Is he the bloke who plunged from the roof?"

Scorpyus nodded his head yes. "He also was a liar who liked to stir up discontent."

"What do you mean?"

"Braydon Mendax liked to frequent local taverns where he would find a ready group of listeners; especially if he bought a round of ale." Scorpyus looked around once more for eavesdroppers then continued. "In my down trodden peasant disguise I went to the taverns to see what I could find out. It didn't take long because Braydon was the talk of the taverns. It seems he was stirring up wrath against Thadus and us the night he turned up dead. He said we mistreated some child, or something, and had half the place ready to mutiny."

"The bloke was obviously daft. What did we do to him? Did he have relations in Reddland's royal guard?"

"No," Scorpyus shrugged his shoulders. "From what I gathered he wanted notoriety. He liked to stand up before a crowd of drunken patrons and go on one of his diatribes. He always had something so important to tell he felt everyone should know about it. His friends in the taverns were the only ones who would listen. With us he was always critical of our activities. But he wasn't stupid. He never criticized Reddland's government. When Reddland was around his talk was about the latest sea monster story, or gossip from the main land. Now it's about how inept Thadus is, and how we are ruthless mercenaries."

"What advantage did all this get him? It sounds like he was a typical talebearer." Cad had anger in his voice. He didn't like to hear someone spreading lies. "Or did he fancy himself to be someone?"

"He liked the attention." Scorpyus stated. "He wanted to be important."

Cad knew the sort, always wanting recognition but unwilling to do the work, or take the risks to legitimately gain it. The world was full of them. The problem was they often resorted to criticizing others as a means of making themselves look better. "How did this chap come into his money? No one has monogrammed clothes unless they have money."

"I don't know exactly. No one could say," Scorpyus glanced down the pier. "It looks like he lived a moderately well to do life. I can't say for sure, but I got the impression he took a few ignorant men in minor confidence games. He was a schemer. He did have dealings with the black market. The bartender said 'Braydon was a weasel who never made an honest shilling in his life.' They didn't have flattering things to say about him, and yet they were mourning his untimely death."

Cad thought the information through. It just didn't make sense. So Braydon Mendax was a shady fellow. It sounded like he was a small time swindler. What did he do to warrant being thrown from the roof? Why was he up there in the first place? Was he just some unfortunate chap who unwittingly happened upon a Valkyrie?

"Do we have any idea why this bloke wound up dead?" Cad asked, a puzzled look on his face.

Scorpyus shrugged. "No, I was hoping to find out more by going through his personal belongings. He rented a room at the Regent Inn; the tower room to be exact."

The Regent Inn was once an illustrious place situated near the port of Xylor. It boasted of a five-story tower overlooking the bay. In its prime, it was the epitome of luxurious accommodations. Some of the most influential businessmen from the surrounding regions stayed in the famous tower. But that was before Reddland's regime. After Reddland assumed power, all sorts of unsavory sorts were attracted to the port city. The docks became a haven of crime and immorality. Respectable people moved away from the area. As a result, the Regent Inn and much of the surrounding area became a den for highwaymen and the like. Now ten years later and badly in need of maintenance, the Regent was little more luxurious then a barn. Ladies of the evening and their clients utilized the rooms. It was said the kitchen was infested with roaches, and more then one patron claimed to have found a little extra something with their meal. Those who frequented the Regent now were down on their luck, or inebriated sailors and their purchased companionship. The tower room provided a little better accommodation then the lower floors. It afforded more privacy and still provided a breathtaking view of the bay.

"The Regent Inn," Cad exclaimed. "That place is a bloody rat trap! I thought this bloke had money."

"He did," Scorpyus threw up his hands. "I know it doesn't make sense but that's where he was staying. I think we need to search the tower room before someone loots it. That is if it hasn't been done already. I was planning on going at sundown. I could help for this one if you aren't busy."

"And one more thing," Scorpyus added. "Braydon was seen talking to a woman the night he died."

"What woman? What did she look like?"

"No one seems to know. She wore a hooded cloak." Scorpyus replied with more then a hint of sarcasm in his voice.

"You don't believe them?"

"It's possible they're telling the truth," Scorpyus relented reluctantly. "But I met so many people who were there when it happened and yet were not in a position to hear or see anything. I couldn't press them on the matter without seeming unnaturally interested and running the risk of exposing my disguise."

Cad mulled it over for a moment. "Perhaps the woman was a tart, one that he met at the Regent."

Scorpyus didn't have the answer. For all he knew the woman was his sister. The people Braydon associated with didn't know who she was or didn't care. If they did they weren't saying. The mystery woman's identity would have to be solved later.

Cad shot Scorpyus a strategizing smile. "Let's bloody well find out. Sundown it is. I've got a few things to do before then, but I'll meet you at dusk. The people need for us to solve this problem. Having assassins running amuck isn't exactly good for moral. We need to find…" Cad stopped short when he heard footsteps approaching.

Footsteps echoed from somewhere in the mist. The distinctive clank of armor and weaponry could also be heard. Scorpyus and Cad moved to the sides of the pier and drew their swords, ready for whoever was blundering upon them. Slowly the figure of a man materialized in the vapor.

"Cad, is that you?" Cyrus's gravely voice asked.

"Yeah mate, we're down here." Cad relaxed and sheathed his weapon.

Cyrus walked to his friends. "Sorry I took so long. I wanted to be thorough." Cyrus looked haggard and saddle sore. The strain of the situation was clearly evident on his face.

"Did you find Zephyr?" Scorpyus asked anxiously.

Cyrus looked down. "No, I didn't…sorry." Scorpyus turned away.

"Thanks for trying mate. It's not your fault," Cad reassured. "Did you find out anything about what may have happened?"

"Not a lot," Cyrus voice sounded tired. He noticed Scorpyus's interest pique and saw him glance over through the corner of his eye. "The trail abruptly ended a mile west of Sage. There was definitely another horse besides Zephyr's, and a little bit of blood on the ground. I also saw a few strange footprints."

Scorpyus eyes snapped to Cyrus. "Did the footprints have a separate compartment for the big toe at the front of the shoe print?"

"Well yes, how did you know?" Cyrus was surprised.

"So there was another Valkyrie! I can't believe I was…" Scorpyus's irate outburst soon turned sullen. Anguish washed over his face.

"I told Zephyr I would take care of the Valkyrie. She trusted me. She wasn't expecting two of them. It's my fault. Had she known…?" Scorpyus's voice trailed down to a whisper. He didn't wait for the others to reply. Instead he stormed to the end of the pier, staring into oblivion, and rethinking his last moments with Zephyr.

Cyrus stood shocked. He didn't have any idea what Scorpyus was talking about. "What's this 'val-ker tree'? Was he with Zephyr when she vanished?"

"Valkyrie," Cad clarified. "That's what the assassins are called. No he wasn't with her when she vanished. He thought he was keeping the Valkyrie occupied so she could escape. We found out the hard way there were two of the blasted things in the woods. Scorpyus feels he should have known. But who could have predicted that. A short while ago we had no bloody idea what these things were, much less how to predict their tactics."

Cad decided to find something good in the bad news. "If you didn't find her body she could still be alive."

"That's true," Cyrus agreed. "There wasn't a lot of blood; not enough to suggest a mortal wound. It didn't look like there had been much of a struggle. The footprints went into the thicket. We lost them a short distance from the road."

Cad listened intently. "Was there any other clues; anything at all?"

Cyrus thought about it. "I don't know if this is a clue, but I didn't notice the other horse's tracks leaving the area of the confrontation. Zephyr's horse left sign all the way back to Xylor. The other horse's sign ended right there."

"Could the Valkyrie have erased the horse tracks?" Cad inquired.

"That's possible, but why didn't it erase its own footprints if it was going to go through the trouble. Besides, it didn't look like anyone tried to cover them up. If they did they were done so well I couldn't tell."

Cad stroked his goatee. "That is a bit odd. Was there anything else?"

"Well there was this…no it couldn't mean anything."

"What is it Cyrus? It could be important."

"There was this small pile of leaves," Cyrus pictured it in his mind. "It wasn't unusual in and of itself, but…" Cyrus paused.

"But what?" Cad asked.

"It was just a small pile of wood chips and leaves. The leaves weren't from any nearby plants. How could that mean anything?" Cyrus asked bewildered.

"I don't really know." Silence fell upon the duo momentarily while Cad mulled it over in his mind. "But it has to mean something. Scorpyus and I found saw dust and leaves at the place where the patrol was killed."

Cad turned toward Scorpyus and asked in his direction. "Hey Scorp. Cyrus found a pile of wood chips in the area where Zephyr was abducted."

Scorpyus looked back from the end of the pier. A flashing hint of recollection expressed itself on his face. Scorpyus searched his memory of the previous night with Zephyr. "Yeah, Zephyr rattled off a lyrical legend about a weathered hag. I can't remember how it goes. We didn't have a lot of time. The lyric mentioned something about wood chips and leaves."

"A lyric about the Valkyrie?" Cad's interest was piqued. "What did it say about the wood chips?"

"It's at the tip of my tongue," Scorpyus said with frustration. "I can't remember! It was something like 'wood chips and leaves the hag commanded.' It was an order she gave to get wood chips and leaves."

"Did it say why the hag gave the order? What do they use them for?" Cad inquired.

"The lyric didn't say why they wanted the wood chips or leaves. That much I do remember." Scorpyus was certain. "I'll try to find out."

"There's a lot to learn about these buggers. It will drive a man daft figuring it all out." Cad was perplexed. "And another thing…"

Cad, Scorpyus, and Cyrus froze when a plank creaked in the fog. Each held their breath with the realization they were no longer alone. In unison they turned to face down the pier where the noise had come from.

"Did that sound like a footstep to you?" Cad whispered.

Scorpyus nodded. "I think so. You two keep talking. I'll see if I can flank who ever it is."

Cad strained to listen. The slosh of the tide against the pier, and distant voices was all he heard. Whoever was out there was silent now. Cad could feel his pulse race in anticipation for a figure to materialize from the murky mists. He and Cyrus clutched the hilt of their swords for comfort, and squinted into the white veil of fog. The hair on the back of their neck stood up.

Scorpyus silently eased himself away from the others. Cad and Cyrus made small talk about nothing of importance, being careful to use the same tone of voice they had previously been using. Scorpyus continued to the side of the pier and lowered himself into a small rowboat. He untied it from the hitch gently laying the rope at the bow, and paddled it quietly along towards shore. He crouched low in the boat keeping his head below the side of the pier.

Scorpyus slowly slipped the oar into the water and gently moved the boat shoreward, being careful to keep it from scraping against the barnacle encrusted pier supports. The boat drifted towards where he heard the noise. He listened intently for any other sound. All was silent. Before he could seriously contemplate the possibility his ears were playing tricks on him, Scorpyus heard another sound. It was a metallic noise and sounded similar to a weapon being removed from a sheath. Scorpyus rowed a little farther and then peeked above the side of the dock. He could scarcely make out a shadowy figure. It stood still.

Scorpyus dark glare fixated on the figure. He could feel his senses pique and his vision tunnel. Experience and instinct caused him to take a quick glance around whenever he felt his vision tunnel in. The figure appeared to be alone.

Scorpyus placed his fingers on the edge of the pier and pulled himself onto the dock. He froze when the figure cocked its head as if it heard a noise. Cad and Cyrus were making indiscernible conversation in the distance. Was the figure trying to eavesdrop?

Scorpyus pulled himself fully onto the pier. The figure continued to stand with its back toward him, motionless except for an occasional slight movement.

Scorpyus's heart pounded in his chest as he slid his dagger from its sheath, and tip toed towards the shadowy figure. As he approached, the figure steadily materialized through the fog.

Whoever it was wore a dark hooded cloak. Scorpyus couldn't see the person's hands but could tell that he was manipulating something with its fingers near its left side. Whoever it was appeared to be skulking around suspiciously.

Scorpyus methodically and painstakingly crept up on the individual. He debated weather or not to thrust his blade into the person as soon as he was within range. It this was a Valkyrie he could scarcely afford not to.

Scorpyus decided to identify the individual first. He approached behind the cloaked figure as it eavesdropped. With one hand Scorpyus prepared to grab the individual around the neck. He would pull the person off balance and quickly put his dagger to their throat. If the person surrendered, fine. If not and they chose to attack, with his dagger to their throat he should be able to maintain the upper hand.

In a flash, Scorpyus pulled the intruder off balance, his dagger pressing against the hooded individual's throat. Simultaneously a shrill piercing scream echoed from the dock. It was the shriek of a woman.

"Don't hurt me!" A woman's voice sobbed. The voice sounded strangely familiar.

"Identify yourself," Scorpyus demanded. Cad and Cyrus came running to his location. The woman didn't respond and sobbed uncontrollably.

Impatient, Scorpyus ripped the hood from the woman's head to see who he was dealing with. He froze in disbelief when he uncovered a familiar face.

"Natasha," Scorpyus was stunned and lowered his dagger. "What are you doing here?"

"Scorpyus, thank God it's you. I was so scared." Natasha replied amid tears. Cad and Cyrus burst on the scene, swords drawn. They lowered their weapons when they realized what was transpiring.

Natasha spoke at a frenzied pace, staring at the ground, running on uncontrollably. "Thank God I found you. I didn't know what to do. I came looking for you then I heard a noise and I didn't know who it was, and I was so scared I couldn't move. I didn't know who was up there but I was too afraid to turn back, and I just couldn't go on, oh Scorpyus it was terrible. I didn't…"

"Slow down. Everything will be alright now." Scorpyus placed his hands on Natasha's shoulders. "Start from the beginning. You were…"

Scorpyus stopped talking when Natasha looked up to meet his eyes. "What happened Natasha? Who did this to you?"

Natasha's face was battered. She had a black eye and her lips were swollen. A series of bruises and abrasions were scattered throughout her countenance. "It's nothing. I don't want you to worry." Natasha looked away.

Scorpyus filled with rage. He placed his hand under Natasha's chin and raised her head to meet his gaze. "Tell me who did this."

"Scorpyus, I don't want to bother you with my problems. You are too busy to worry about me." Natasha gestured to Cad and Cyrus. "I obviously interrupted something. Maybe we can talk later when we can be alone."

Scorpyus had that look in his eyes that could penetrate iron. "Any man that does this to a woman deserves what he has coming. Tell me what happened. You're not interrupting. We were finished anyway."

Cad nodded in the affirmative. "We were done. We'll find the bloke who did this. We'll not tolerate his sort." Cad had no sympathy for any man that beat a woman.

Natasha softened and relented almost ashamed to tell the story. "I was attacked last night. I don't know who it was. It's my fault. I should never have left the compound alone especially at night. It's just that, well, I was getting tired of being holed up in the compound working all day. I wanted to go for a walk and have a little time to think. I have a lot to think about." Natasha gave Scorpyus a smile.

"Anyway, I didn't get far when this hairy, smelly man came from out of nowhere. He tried to pull me into the forest. When I resisted he started to hit me. It was horrible Scorpyus. I was too afraid to scream. I didn't know what to do, I was…" Natasha broke down again with sobs.

Scorpyus gave her a minute to sob. "It's alright now," he replied in a soft understanding voice. Natasha managed a meager smile.

"He didn't…uh," Scorpyus started to inquire.

"No, no, thank God for that," Natasha said, relief evident in her voice. "I bit him on the arm and he let me go. When he did, I ran as fast as I could.

"And you didn't get a good look at him?"

Natasha shook her head. "It was dark and it happened so fast."

"Which arm did you bite him on?" Scorpyus was relieved that Natasha was able to escape before things went further.

"I'm sure it was the right arm."

"Well Natasha," Cad interjected. "If we see a chap with bite marks on his right arm he's going to bloody well have some explaining to do."

"Thank you all." Natasha wiped tears from her eyes.

"Let's get you back to the compound." Scorpyus motioned back toward shore. He noticed Natasha was now carrying a dagger on her waist. It was a modest weapon of sturdy but plain workmanship.

"I see you are carrying a dagger."

Natasha placed an unsure hand on her new weapon. "Yes, I got it this morning so I would feel safer. A lot of good it did me though. I was as petrified as ever when I heard you on the docks. My head started to spin. The voices I heard didn't sound like you. All I could hear was that man…I just froze…"

Scorpyus interrupted not wanting her to think about the unpleasant experience any more. "Let's get you back to the compound, and get you something warm to drink."

Scorpyus gave Cad a look that let him know he would meet up at their appointed time and escorted Natasha back to the compound. He would make sure she made it safely. Natasha was deeply troubled by the experience and it looked like it would be several days before she would feel comfortable leaving the compound alone again.

Natasha would flinch, startled at any loud noise as she and Scorpyus walked through town. Scorpyus felt sorry for her. She was so jittery she practically shook in her boots. Any man who would try to rape a woman deserved to die as far as he was concerned. Natasha escaped and yet she would be affected for the rest of her life. Zephyr wasn't as lucky. She carried the scars that no woman should have to bear.

As Scorpyus walked with Natasha, he caught his mind drifting off to Zephyr. It was troubling and confusing. Here he was enjoying the company of Natasha, but not fully focused on the moment. A lot of troubling emotions were racing through his head. He had been through a lot recently, what with the letter from Zenith, the goodbye with Zephyr, and the stroll with Natasha. And he was exhausted with no rest in sight. It made his stomach tie itself in knots. Natasha said she needed time to think. Scorpyus could sympathize with that sentiment. A span of quiet to pray would go a long way in soothing a troubled soul.

———— ◆ ————

With a muscled arm Novak hacked with his sword cleanly severing the limb. He tossed the small branch aside and cut a few more sprigs from the tree. He now had a clear view of a peculiarity he noticed up ahead in a clearing. Emerald and Dantes crouched behind a prickly bush waiting for his report. The three trodded several miles from the beach, and darkness was descending quickly. A suitable campsite would be a welcome relief.

"I don't see anyone." Novak studied what appeared to be a cave in the side of a hill. It wasn't your usual cave though. This one bore evidence of a man made stonework archway around the entrance. Writing and symbols were carved into the stones, but Novak couldn't discern their meaning from his vantage point. Stairs led to the archway, about ten in all. They were cut from the rocky face of the hill. Wide block banisters were at the sides of the stairs, more for decoration then function, as they were too low to provide support while ascending the steps. A lot of time was put into beautifying what would otherwise be a hole in the side of the mountain. The stonework did show signs of age and little recent activity. Even so, whatever lay inside must have been of some importance at one time.

"What is it?" Emerald inquired.

"It's some sort of a tunnel. Someone built a decorative entry. It doesn't look like its being used much anymore. The path leading to it is overgrown. It's practically unrecognizable." Novak appraised the others.

Dantes stood next to Novak and took a look for himself. "Thar be a mystery for sure. It be looking like no structure I've seen before. In all me life I can't figure why a landlubber would fix up a cave entrance so proper."

The trio scanned the entrance and surrounding forest for a good while. There was no one to be seen and nothing to be heard except for wind rustling through trees. Novak motioned for the others to follow him and led the way to the cave.

Up close, the stone archway bore the signs of time even more. Though it was masterfully crafted with each stone being precisely cut for a perfect fit, the stonework was now moss covered and discolored. Years of exposure to the elements were evident, and cracks were starting to appear. Several pictographs were carved into stones, each now faded due to years of wind and rain. Many were symbols of unknown meaning to the trio, but Novak recognized the two-headed serpent on the top of the archway.

"This must be a temple of Balar. It doesn't look like it's being used much anymore." Novak peered into the black tunnel. "I'll prepare a torch. We'll need one if we're going in."

"Why would we go in?" Emerald didn't like the look of the entrance. It was dark and spooky. Spider webs clung to the top of the arch, and she was sure there would be many insects and rodents lurking inside. She saw no reason to ever enter a temple of Balar. She would just as soon take her chances outside.

"Are you hungry?" Novak asked her.

"Yes I'm famished. We haven't eaten since we left Xylor."

"Unless one of you has a better idea then, we'll need to go in," Novak said while tying some cloth to a stick. "These temples usually have food inside. They use it for offerings. Unless they have completely abandoned this temple, there should be something to eat."

Emerald's hunger outweighed her fear of the unknown. Her stomach growled its agreement with Novak, and Emerald acquiesced. "Alright," she thought a moment. "Then you've been in a temple of Balar before?"

"Novak shook his head. "No, but they have these all over Ravenshire. Xylor got stuck with Tanuba; we got stuck with the Kelterland snake god. In Saltwater they were always hauling food inside. It's worth checking."

The others hoped Novak was right. It had been a long strenuous day, and another hard day appeared ahead. Food would be a welcome blessing.

In a matter of minutes Novak had a spark kindled in some dry grass, and soon a rudimentary torch was glowing. He smiled and shrugged his shoulders then led the way inside. Nervously they crept down the dimly lit corridor.

The ceiling stood about seven feet high and the passage sloped uphill. Novak noticed the cobwebs were high up towards the corners of the tunnel giving indication somebody used the temple often enough to keep the cobwebs from growing across the whole corridor. The tunnel appeared natural for the most part, but there was evidence of tool marks where builders modified and expanded the tunnel. The air was thick and musty. The farther the party walked into the tunnel the fowler the air became. Soon the putrid smell of something rotten overpowered all else.

"Briny barnacles, the stench would gag a vulture!" Dantes exclaimed. He drew a laugh from his friends.

"Ya, you may be right." Novak tried to breathe as little as possible. He picked up his pace anxious to be out of the fetid air.

After one hundred yards of hiking up a moderate incline, the tunnel opened up into a wide cavern. Here the ceiling was twenty feet overhead. Directly across the cavern stood a large stone statue of a dual headed serpent on a raised platform. A wooden altar was before it. From what Novak could see of the walls, someone spent a lot of time and energy in making this room. Wood paneling covered the walls, and decorative tapestries hung in place. Ornately carved wooden chairs with lush scarlet upholstery lined the perimeter in neatly spaced intervals. A large shelf was to the side of the platform near the altar. Scores of gold and silver vessels graced the shelves, each decoratively etched. Other than a thin layer of dust everywhere, the interior had been maintained. This was definitely the main temple room. A cool breeze came from somewhere, helping to rid the room of some of the stench.

Novak noticed torch filled sconces around the room. "I'll light a few more torches. Then let's look for food and get out of here."

The others were in complete agreement. There was just something about being in a pagan temple that made one's skin crawl. The very idea didn't sit well with Novak. He experienced the Balar invasion of his homeland all too personally.

As Novak went from sconce to sconce, a yellow flickering light slowly filled the cavern. Dantes watched the door while

Novak completed his task. Emerald waited by the altar. The visibility of the cavern was much improved. Much to her regret it allowed her to experience the room more thoroughly; most notably the rotted corpse lying on the altar. No doubt it caused the stench. Emerald held her hand to her mouth and gagged at the sight.

"Oh my, what is that?" Emerald's eyes filled with horror at the sight. There, with his hands and ankles bound to the corners of the altar, was a pale, dehydrated, partially clothed corpse. It appeared to be human but Emerald couldn't say for sure. She refused to get a closer look.

Novak reeled around. By the tone in Emerald's voice he knew something was the matter. He rushed to her side and stepped up for a closer look.

The corpse was pale and gaunt, smaller then the average person, perhaps four and a half feet tall. Its mouth was agape and its beady eyes open in narrow slits. It had a small under-developed chin and a long thin nose. Even though the body was in no doubt human, there was something unusually bizarre about its features. It was no race of human Novak had ever seen or heard of. Novak likened the look to that of a weasel or ferret, and felt sorry for a man that went through life like that. In fact he had to admit the person looked a little non-human.

The corpse wore ratty brown cloth pants and nothing more. A deep open gash was cut into the upper left quadrant at the heart; no doubt the cause of the poor soul's demise. The wood of the altar was stained crimson. By the looks of it, more than one person met their end in the same manner as the individual now there. Cords cut deep into the wrists and ankles of the body.

The sight sickened Novak. "It looks like he was sacrificed...I would say two or three weeks ago."

Emerald had to turn away. "But what did they do to the poor fellow to make him look like that?"

Novak studied the body again. "I think that's just because he's been dead so long." He had no other explanation for why the corpse didn't look quite human. Maybe whoever killed the man mutilated him also. It was hard to tell this long after death, and Novak didn't care to study it in any great detail.

Novak knew Dantes was a well-traveled person. Maybe he would know. "Dantes, have you seen anything like this before?"

Dantes turned from looking down the corridor and saw Novak gesture to a lump on the altar. "Did ye find some food?"

"Not yet." Novak waived Dantes over.

Dantes took the stone stairs to the altar with the others. His eyes widened and he froze. "Briny barnacles, me ears have heard tales of such things, but never did I think those old salts would be telling the truth."

"The corpse is familiar," Novak asked as a question more then a statement.

"Aye, it has to be." Dantes shook his head in wonder. "It's just like they be telling me when I was a youngster."

Dantes explained. "On me first voyage I sailed with a crew of old salts who were on a voyage to the ethereal region; Marcesco himself be on that voyage."

"The old man we met at the docks," Emerald asked, disbelief in her tone.

"Aye, when Marcesco was a young lad he and a crew of adventurous salts set sail to explore the Ethereal region. It be the first voyage attempted of its kind, and it also be the last. Out of sixty sailors that went on the venture, only Marcesco and seven others lived to return six months later. They brought back tales of horror and bewilderment. They told of a misty land with strange and dangerous people, where nothing is as it should be." Dantes shuddered at his recollections.

"What did they say?" Novak hung rapt on Dante's story.

"Thar be a strange gloomy land, shrouded in a thick mist where water flows uphill and balls of fire thunder abound like hoards of listless cattle. It be a land full of swamps, and the ground is liable to disappear from under yer feet. The trees tower high and choke out the sun, vines and moss dangle everywhere. Thar be all sorts of unsavory creatures lurking about for a meal."

Dantes put his hands up in a halting motion. "Aye Novak, it be a land ye never want to find yerself; that I can say for sure."

Novak was visibly shocked. The Ethereal region was stranger then he imagined. "Is this man from the Ethereal region?"

Dantes looked at the shriveled corpse once more. "If me memory serves, that thar be a Trepanite. They be the scourge of the human race; worse then a galleon full of scurvy bilge rats, they be."

"A Trepanite; I've think I've heard of them. Are they dangerous?" Novak could scarcely believe such small frail looking people were worth being afraid of. What could they possibly do? Were they great warriors?

Dantes placed a hand on Novak's shoulder, and spoke with absolute authority. "Aye Novak, they be dangerous…and wicked. They roam the Ethereal region like locusts, pillaging and devouring. Like a scavenger bird, they seek out the weak, preferring to attack from advantage and superior numbers. Marcesco said ye must always be wary around them. A good number of his crew lost their lives to the nasty scalawags."

Novak looked puzzled. "How are they any worse then the Kelterlanders?" Dantes shook his head in understanding. "I be knowing what ye think Novak. But the part that makes a Trepanite the scourge of the Ethereal region is, how shall I be saying it…" Dantes saw that Emerald was terrified and didn't want to say his piece so harshly as to frighten her further.

"What is it?" Novak asked.

"What makes them worse," Dantes whispered, "Is their culinary habits."

Dantes took a deep breath. "Ye see matey, those unfortunate to be killed by a Trepanite are soon to become part of their dinner. And may God have mercy on those captured alive."

"They eat those they kill!" Emerald felt nauseated, and so horror-stricken she wanted to leave the temple immediately. She regretted ever agreeing to go on this mission.

"Aye lassie, worse then that," Dantes replied. "For ye see, they don't eat the whole body. They be using a thin bladed dagger to bore into their victims skull in order to eat the brains. They be known to get frenzied like a shark feeding on a school of fish. And some of them be frothing at the mouth, insane with madness even before hand. I tell ye two; they be the bilge rats of humanity."

The Ethereal region had always been a place of fear and trepidation for those who lived within the Astorian Realms. Legends, myths, and even outright fantasies had been told of the place since Novak could remember, and he heard his share of tales. Everywhere the knights traveled, they encountered the murmurings of this mysterious land. But this was the first time he heard anything about Trepanites. The fact the information came from Dantes lent credibility to it. The fact a tribe of people would eat human brains wasn't that shocking. After all he had witnessed the temple of Balar sacrifice babies. It was how his niece died. There was however one consistency throughout all he had heard about the Ethereal region; all who spoke of the place did so with nervous trembling.

"Well this one is dead," Novak stated as a matter of fact, sounding not the least bit worried.

"Shouldn't we leave? There may be more." Emerald looked horrified. She may very well die on the spot should she ever see a live one.

"We still have to finish our mission." Novak could tell Emerald was petrified. "And besides, Dantes said the Trepanites live in the Ethereal region. We're in the south of Kelterland, far from their domain."

Emerald wasn't consoled by the thought. "But this one is here," she pointed once again to the corpse.

Novak's brow furrowed. Emerald had a point. "Well if we see a Trepanite I can guarantee you I'm not going to let it live long enough to eat our brains."

"Aye Novak, I be with ye on that." Dantes chimed in. "And I wouldn't be worrying about seeing another one. This here Trepanite was no doubt taken captive near the northern border. The temple of Balar be known to buy slaves for their sacrifices."

Dantes glanced at the dead Trepanite. "I be willing to bet he unwisely ventured into Kelterland to do a little scavenging and was taken by the King's Brigades. They be patrolling their borders vigorously."

Emerald wanted to believe her friends, and what they said made sense. She just couldn't shake the fear knotting up in the pit of her stomach. She was in a pagan temple, a dead Trepanite lay withered before her eyes. Emerald could no longer remember why she wanted to go on an adventure. If this was what it was like she could live without it. How did Novak cope with this? How did he walk through a wicked and hideous world, risking his life daily, and remain sane?

Emerald's eyes welled up with tears. What was wrong with the world? How could people so evil exist? Something had to be done to reclaim the realm for good. Then it dawned on her; that's what Novak, her father, and her friends were trying to do.

Emerald's father told stories of his youth when things weren't like they were now, when the realm was Godly and wickedness was the exception, not the rule. A lot of her generation didn't recognize the wickedness around them. They grew accustomed to it, deadened to it. What once was scandalous was now the norm. It reminded Emerald of something her father said: 'Wide is the gate and broad is the way that leadeth to destruction, and many there be which go in threat; and straight is the gate and narrow is the way which leadeth unto life, and few there be that find it.' Her father instructed to take the straight and narrow way. It made her sad to realize it had become the road less traveled.

"Emerald," Novak placed massive hands on Emerald's shoulders and waited for her teary gaze to meet his. "Over my dead body will I let anyone hurt you."

Novak spoke with absolute confidence. He was so confident it had a soothing effect. It is what Emerald wanted and needed.

Emerald never felt safer then at that very moment. Any doubts were put to rest right then and there. For from that moment on, she knew Novak was the one she had been waiting for all her life. She couldn't imagine feeling safer with or loving anyone else more than him. She could only pray he would feel the same.

"I be hearing bells, I be." Dantes had a big grin plastered on his face. Novak turned beet red.

"Let's look for that food." Novak changed the subject. Emerald wiped her tears.

"We'll be fine," Novak whispered and smiled reassuringly. He wondered how he could convince Emerald of that in light of the fact Bartus had died. Deep down he knew the next battle could be his last. If Novak suddenly found himself in heaven then it meant he must have died. And it was a good thing he would have to die before going to heaven. Because if he wasn't dead when he arrived, the shock of realizing he had been beat in combat would most certainly have killed him otherwise.

"I'm sorry; it's just that this is all so crazy." Emerald smiled weakly. She didn't want to be a burden.

"Don't worry," Novak replied. "We all get discouraged sometimes."

"Do you?" Emerald inquired. Novak seemed to always stand like an oak.

Novak thought of the time he thought Scorpyus died. It was a devastating moment for him. "No, not really," he lied. He wasn't ready to reveal that detail yet.

"Avast there matey," Dantes exclaimed. "I found something here."

Novak and Emerald turned to their friend. He stood next to a small table at the bottom of the steps. The table was inlaid with gold designs and ornately carved with several caricatures of Balar. Atop the table was an earthen vessel painted elaborately. It was shaped like a large bowl, and Dantes lifted the lid. Both table and bowl were of great value.

"It not be in the best condition, but I've ate worse on a long voyage." Dantes reported.

The bowl contained fruit, most of it soft and turning bad. No doubt it had been there a while.

"It's better then nothing." Novak riffled through the bowl with Dantes and salvaged what they could. It amounted to two questionable pieces of fruit apiece. The three wouldn't be eating like kings, but it was better then going hungry. They all had eaten worse.

The three hungrily ate what they found. A golden engraved platter with a lid lay on the table also. Inside was several dried fish. The trio wolfed the fish down hungrily. "Well, thank God we found something." Emerald sighed.

"I knew they offered food to their idol," Novak stated. "I didn't know they sacrificed people."

The three sat in the ornate chairs and rested their weary feet. It was decided the party would not spend the night in the temple. Anyplace else would be better. They would follow the scant trail from the temple to a main road. If they reached the main road and there was no sign of a town being, the party would find a safe spot for a few hours sleep.

"Are you two ready to move on?" Novak asked. Emerald was more then ready to leave the temple. Dantes stood up reluctantly, but forced himself to continue. The time off his feet felt good, too good. It was hard to get going again.

"What was that?" Emerald tilted her head toward the corridor. Novak and Dantes glanced at each other skeptically. They hadn't heard anything. Emerald was already spooked. Could it be her imagination?

Novak moved closer to the corridor. The torches in the temple lit it up for several yards. Nothing could be seen. And then he heard it. It was a soft pattering scamper; the sound a dog's toenails make when they run across a smooth hard surface. Dantes heard it this time also.

Emerald's eyes grew wide and she backed away from the corridor. "What is it?" Novak darted his eyes around the temple, formulating a strategy. "Let's go up the steps near the altar. We'll claim the high ground."

The three took the steps two at a time and waited. The noise got louder and shadows flickered in the corridor.

"Whatever they be I'm prepared for a fight," Dantes said through gritted teeth. "I didn't survive a shipwreck to have it end in this cursed temple."

In short time they had the answer as to what was making noise in the corridor. Much to their horror, eight short, ghastly pale figures entered the temple. The eight were as surprised to see the room already occupied as Novak and the others were to see them. It was their worst fears come to haunt them.

"Oh God no, it can't be!" Emerald drew her sword, and went as pale as the eight intruders who scampered in, their beady eyes darting all around. "Trepanites," her voice quivered.

At first the Trepanites faces registered shock. Then they saw the corpse on the altar. One of them, a female with long natty black hair, pierced the temple with a mournful guttural wailing sound and ran sobbing toward the altar. Since she did not have her weapon drawn, and none of the Trepanites made any aggressive movements yet, Novak moved away from the altar towards the statue of Balar where Dantes and Emerald were. The female clasped the hand of the dead Trepanite and sobbed uncontrollably. When some of the flesh separated from the rotting fingers she collapsed to her knees, a look of abject horror etched in her features. She muttered something in an unknown language. Novak heard a variety of languages; but nothing like this. The Trepanite tongue consisted of harsh throaty syllables punctuated by growling sounds and grunts. Occasionally the female would shriek, but Novak wasn't sure if it was because she was upset or that was their language.

Another Trepanite, one who appeared to be the leader, listened to what the female said and then looked to Novak and the others with hatred burning in his eyes. The other Trepanites glanced back and forth from the corpse on the altar to Novak and his friends. Each was now filled with wrath, their beady eyes aglow under furrowed brows.

"What you does? You kills Gorgon!" The leader spit vehemently in the common tongue of the realms.

Novak drew his two handed sword. He knew he had little chance of talking reason to these Trepanites. He felt that hate filled, blinded gaze upon him many times before. It was the look of revenge. The Trepanites assumed Novak and his friends were responsible for the death of their comrade.

Even Emerald, a battlefield novice, realized the grave position she was in. "Tell them we didn't kill their friend."

The leader grunted something and the other Trepanites circled the steps to the altar.

Novak was worried, a rare occurrence for him. Not for himself, but for Emerald's safety. He knew Dantes could take care of himself. Emerald never wielded a weapon against another. Could Emerald bring herself to kill? If she hesitated for but an instant it would mean her death. This would be a trial by fire for a green fighter. The Trepanites moved like a well trained squad. The stress of having Emerald there weighed heavily on Novak. It was worse then he anticipated. He realized how he had taken Zephyr for granted.

"You must die for this!" The Trepanite leader shouted and then barked orders to the others. They were taking their time, taking full advantage of their numerical superiority, and allocating their resources. By the way they were positioning themselves, four would attack Novak, two for Dantes, and one for Emerald. What the grieving Trepanite would do, Novak didn't know yet.

The Trepanites chanted maniacally in unison, each stomping their feet and pounding the hilt of their weapons against their small wooden shields in a pounding rhythm. Perhaps they were making supplications to their god. Maybe the tactic was meant to induce fear. Whatever the reason, Novak wondered what was taking so long.

The monotonous thud of the stomping echoed through the temple. The dull pounding seemed to resonate within the Trepanites bringing them into a trance like state. Their eyes rolled up into their skulls, their nostrils flared; clearly they were experiencing some deep inner sense of fulfillment. Slowly the mood of the Trepanites transformed. Wrath gave way to a lusty look. They started licking their lips like a starving dog before dinner; salivating at the thought of food. One fingered a long thin bladed dagger on his belt. Others started yelping gleefully like hyenas.

"Oh God!" Emerald turned a fleshy white pallor.

"Emerald," Novak said without taking his eyes from the Trepanites. "I will see you through."

Before Emerald could respond the Trepanites launched their frenzied attack. Salivating and slobbering, they scampered up the steps intent on revenge, and then later would enjoy their favorite delicacy.

Novak squared off to meet the four Trepanites attacking him. Like a pack of rabid dogs they leapt and lunged at Novak, thrusting their spears ferociously. He side stepped the point of one spear, and blocked another with his buckler. The four were swift and kept jabbing at him. It was difficult and far too risky to continue allowing a four-pronged attack. The Trepanites would have to be dispersed.

With a deep booming yell, Novak swung his sword mightily in an arcing swath at his short attackers, intent on harvesting Trepanite heads like a farmer with a scythe harvests grain. His blade caught the first one on his left temple cleanly severing the top of his skull in a strawberry mist. A second Trepanite managed to get his wooden shield up in time to save himself, but the force sent him sprawling down the steps. A spear point caught Novak in the cuirass, as he heard Emerald scream behind him. Off to his right rang the sound of metal against metal and Dante's voice cursing the Trepanites as bilge rats.

Novak refocused his concentration on his attackers. The best way to help his friends was to win his battle. Now two Trepanites thrust at him vigorously but with more caution, keeping their distance from his sword. They were experienced fighters, fast and dexterous, and planned well, or so they thought. Knowing Novak had greater reach, the four Trepanites utilizing spears attacked him. The swordsmen and mace wielder were assigned to the others.

The Trepanites took turns stabbing at Novak; first one then the other. He was quick to pick up the pattern. Though they varied their technique and target area, the Trepanites consistently attacked one at a time, back and forth. It gave one Trepanite time to reposition for his next attempt to skewer Novak while the other kept him occupied with defense. It was a method that begged to be exploited.

Novak waited for the right moment to make his move. He swung and caught one of the spears as it was thrust at him knocking it to the side. Charging in with the full force of his two hundred and forty pounds, he shoved his blade through a Trepanite chest for a second kill, then planted his foot squarely in the center of the others groin. The attacker went tumbling down the stairs. With a jerk he dislodged his weapon from the impaled rib cage. Before he could pursue the two remaining Trepanites, he saw movement from the corner of his eye. The grieving Trepanite entered the fracas. She held a club in a white knuckled grasp. A few feet away a slumped corpse lay in front of Dantes. He locked swords with a stocky bearded foe.

"Ye be fighting dirty ye filthy cockroach." Dantes bellowed, slashing with his sword. A crimson line appeared across his attacker's midriff.

A stabbing pain in Novak's shoulder redirected his attention to his two remaining foes. How did they ascend the stairs so fast? Novak knocked them down hard. They couldn't have possibly made it back up.

Novak turned to face an empty space. A spear lay at the top of the stairs. At the bottom of the stairs a Trepanite rolled in pain cradling his groin. Another stared up at Novak wide eyed and spear-less having taken a chance by throwing his weapon. The risk didn't work. Seeing Novak's massive form barreling down the steps sent him in a full sprint for the exit.

Novak bounded after the fleeing Trepanite. Were more waiting outside? The last thing he wanted was for any others to be alerted and drawn into the fight.

As Novak passed the injured and writhing Trepanite, the man reached for his spear. It was a bad move. Novak stepped hard on the reaching appendage. The crackling on bones could be heard. The Trepanite let out a bellowing cry and reached for his spear with his good hand. Novak had enough and slammed the point of his blade into the Trepanites throat. A third attacker succumbed to a highly skilled warrior. Not wasting any time, Novak ran down the corridor in pursuit of the last Trepanite.

The Trepanite attacking Emerald was quick and agile. She swung her sword frantically trying to keep him at bay. The Trepanite blocked and dodged her attempts, swinging his mace at her. Soon Emerald was on the defensive, concentrating only on avoiding the mace.

Emerald's attacker became giddy with the realization he was the better fighter. It emboldened him and he unleashed a barrage of blows that forced her up against the statue of Balar. With a hissing growl the Trepanite swung for Emerald's legs. She tried to step aside but the handle of the mace caught her mid-calf dropping her to the ground and sending her sword clattering down the steps. Emerald maintained the presence of mind to draw her dagger. The Trepanite immediately pounced on her, pinning her arm with the weapon to the floor, and holding firmly onto her hair. The Trepanite dug his fingers into her thick locks and banged her head against the ground. Emerald struggled to free her hand with the dagger but couldn't. With her other she pushed the face of her attacker trying to gouge his beady eyes. He screamed and gnashed at her hand catching one of her fingers. Pain shot through Emerald's hand, and she could feel the trickle of blood. The banging of her head against the stone altar was causing her to feel faint. Panic started to grip her body. The stench of her attackers panting breath stung her nostrils.

"On dear God help me!" Emerald pleaded.

With her free hand she reached for her attacker's throat. Once again teeth bit into the flesh of her hand. Desperation filled her heart. Mustering up her last bit of reserve she lashed at the Trepanite. When he pulled her head up in order to slam it down, she sat up and thrust her forehead against the bridge of the Trepanites nose. Large drops of blood fell on her face.

The Trepanite let out a painful cry and paused momentarily. Emerald seized the opportunity reaching for the Trepanite's face with her free hand. This time she found his eyes and drove her fingers deep into his eye sockets. Another painful cry came from the Trepanite and she started to writhe and wiggle from his grasp.

In excruciating pain, the Trepanite reached for Emerald's hand. He twisted the appendage from his face and slammed it to the ground, maintaining his position astride Emerald. Beet red and watering eyes tried to focus on his victim. Emerald met his gaze with a knee to the groin. With a groan the Trepanite lurched forward so his head was over Emerald's left shoulder. She quickly turned her head to the side and sunk her teeth into something fleshy. The thought of biting someone would normally have never occurred to Emerald had the Trepanite not bit her twice already. Now confronted with the possibility of imminent death, biting became a viable tactic; a tactic she recently learned the hard way.

The Trepanite let out a blood-curdling scream and tried to pull away. Emerald bit down for all she was worth. The taste of blood was revolting to her tongue. The more the Trepanite struggled, the closer a sizable chunk of his cheek came to being dislodged. Finally the Trepanite would do anything to alleviate the burning pain in his face. He reached up with one hand trying to pry Emerald's mouth open. The attempt was futile. Both combatants struggled against the other, a tangled squirming twist of limbs. The Trepanite heaved and pulled attempting to break free from Emerald's bite. She held tight like a starving dog on juicy piece of meat. The two squirmed and writhed, soon finding themselves at the edge of the stairs; Emerald's head hanging off the first step. The Trepanite reached up and clasped a hand around Emeralds throat. No matter how much pain his face was in, he relentlessly kept his firm grip on the hand with the dagger.

Emerald gagged, a stubby thumb pressing into her windpipe. Her vision started turning black around the edges. With a grunt she rolled to the side over the edge of the top stair. Both combatants cascaded down the steps, becoming separated and crashing to the floor some ten stairs below. The Trepanite, temporarily blinded, struggled to his feet. His gouged eyes searched frantically through blurry tears for Emerald. Emerald sprang to her feet and spit a chunk of flesh from her teeth. Blood ran down her chin. She moved on the Trepanite, dagger in hand.

The Trepanite saw her blurred form and lunged for the arm he believed held the dagger. He came close grasping her shoulder, partially tearing the sleeve from her dress. Emerald thrust her blade into her attacker's side. A flood of sticky warm liquid washed over her hand. The Trepanites face went expressionless, a long gasp escaping his lips. Slowly he sank to the floor. Emerald stood over her fallen attacker, trembling uncontrollably. Stifled sobs rattled her torso. She killed a man for the first time. The thought was crippling. A flood of nausea filled the pit of her stomach. She looked at her blood soaked blade and then to the dead Trepanite in shocked disbelief. The feeling was far worse then she ever imagined. Yet a part of her was glad; glad she had survived; glad she had won. She turned toward the stairs searching for her friends, wondering if they might need any help. Dantes was lying still sprawled at the top, and Novak was nowhere to be seen. Terror struck, she took the steps two at a time.

Reaching the top of the stairs Emerald was confronted by a gruesome sight. Four dead Trepanites lay sprawled about, one with the top portion of his head missing, and Dantes lay tangled in their midst.

Emerald ran to her friend. "Dantes, are you alright?" His hair was blood soaked and he let out a groan.

Dantes opened one eye. "Aye, me head can't be taken much more of this."

Emerald helped him to a seated position. "What happened?" She noticed a fresh gash on the back of his head.

"I can't rightly say," Dantes groaned and rubbed his head. "I just finished off me second Trepanite when I felt a crack on the back of me skull. Everything went black until just before you got here. That thar be a spell of bad luck; having yer head keel hauled twice in one day."

Emerald was relieved to see her friend wasn't hurt seriously. She looked frantically for Novak. He was nowhere to be seen.

"Do you know what happened to Novak?" Emerald was worried.

Before Dantes could answer a familiar form entered the temple from the corridor. Novak's had his sword in hand, the blade dripping with blood.

"There you are!" Emerald sighed with relief.

Novak surveyed the room to make sure all Trepanites were dead and accounted for. Then he turned to Emerald. The sleeve of her dress was torn; she had blood droplets on her face and running down her chin, and the disheveled look of having been through one of the worst experiences of her life.

"You're not hurt, are you?"

Emerald erupted with a flood of pent up emotion, tears running down her face. "Oh Novak it was terrible. I thought I was going to die. He pinned me to the ground, I was so afraid. Look, he even bit me!" She held up her left hand. Teeth marks were evident on the blade of her hand, and her index finger had been bit clear to the bone.

Novak inspected the wound. "Put some of Scorpyus's medicine on it." He retrieved medicine from the pouch on his belt and started dressing the wound with bits of cloth torn from the scarlet curtains behind the statue of Balar.

Novak wrapped Emerald's hand snugly. "It looks like you don't need me after all. I wish I could have spared you this experience."

Novak felt bad for not being able to protect Emerald. It complicated the fight. The Clandestine Knights had an unwritten policy of not working closely with those they were romantically involved with; mainly for times like this.

"You don't approve," Emerald asked. The conflict written plainly on Novak's pained expression.

"I don't think…I don't know what I think." Novak replied. "You survived your first battle. I'm grateful for that. How do *you* feel about it?" He changed the subject.

"Honestly, I feel sick. I mean…" Emerald's voice trembled. "My God Novak, I killed a man! And when I think you do this all the time…how do you do it? You poor soul; the burden you must carry. I thought my life prepared me to go with you. Lord knows I've seen my share of carnage. And don't misunderstand; if anyone deserved to die it was this grotesque, cannibalistic man. He lapped up my blood after he bit me! But to be responsible for taking a life; I just don't think…"

Emerald grew pale. "I can still feel my dagger entering his body, the hollow sound, the feel of the blade grind against bone. And the look on his face, the blood curling off his lips, his gasping for breath, and the look of terror in his eyes as they slowly glassed over. I think I shall never be the same." Emerald swiftly turned aside as a flood of nausea wreaked her body.

"Let's get you some fresh air." Novak helped Emerald up and started her down the corridor. Dantes, who remained quiet throughout the previous exchange, brought up the rear.

As the trio exited the tunnel they had to step over a dead Trepanite. It was now the dark of night, a half moon providing some luminance.

"I got him before he escaped." Novak motioned to the corpse. He felt no remorse for killing such a vile one. He knew full well the dead Trepanite would have gladly killed him instead. There would be no feast of brains tonight. It filled Novak with a sense he had undeniably furthered the cause of good.

Dantes nodded his approval. "Aye, where shall we be off to now?"

"Let's go this way." Novak pointed to the north. "We'll camp at the first suitable place we find."

"What about down that way?" Dantes pointed to a nearby clump of trees.

Novak shook his head in disagreement. "No, I searched the area quickly when I chased the Trepanite out just in case there were more. There is a dead man down there, a cleric of Balar. He had a hole bored in his skull. No doubt the Trepanites got him before they came in and found us."

Emerald's felt ill. "Let's just get out of here."

The trio left wanting nothing more then to leave the whole episode behind them. Each hoped to never again meet up with a Trepanite, and had a new found resolve to never visit the ethereal region.

X

SCORPYUS SHOULDERED HIS way down the busy street, his
gloved hands clasping his tabard snuggly around his shoulders
to keep out the growing chill. The fog had been thick all day, and
the evening was shaping up to be more of the same. He glanced
away, keeping his head down, not looking anyone in the eyes,
and swiftly meandered through the crowd. In less than an hour
it would be dark and the townsfolk were in a hurry to buy what
supplies they needed. The Valkyrie's were still about, though
all afternoon there had been no further reports of their bizarre
killing.

Scorpyus passed through the busy people like a phantom in
the shadows, unnoticed and drawing little attention. A few people
shot him a cursory glance, but went swiftly back to their business.
Scorpyus, however, was able to catch the snippets of assorted
conversations as he trod his way to the Regent Inn.

Fear hung in the crowd like a corpse from a tree. Many
citizens spoke of the mysterious killings and their growing
dissatisfaction with the government for not putting an end to it.
None knew the details behind the killings. It was an intentional
omission decided upon by Thadus on the advice of Cad. Telling

the citizens that professional assassins were lurking about in the shadows would send the island into utter chaos. Telling them the Order of the Valkyrie, a cultic, poison using cadre of highly skilled and mysterious assassins were running lose would send the island over the edge. Thadus shuddered at the thought. At least right now the people enjoyed an illusion of safety in their homes.

Others held plenty of criticism for the way Thadus was running things, and the way Scorpyus and his friends were handling keeping the peace. The fact that crime still occurred irked many craftsmen who were being shoplifted of their wares.

The talk kindled anger within Scorpyus as he angled down the street. Everyone had plenty of ideas on how they could do better, and yet few came forward to join forces with the new government. Most of the complainers were satisfied to let others do their fighting. They wanted peace and prosperity but didn't want to do anything to earn it themselves. They wanted the new government to hurry up and earn it.

Scorpyus thought about it all the way to the Regent Inn. The cause of good and freedom had always been bought with blood. And it needed to be maintained in the same manner. Many spilled their blood in times past to buy and keep the society that once was the Astorian Realms. Growing complacent and taking it all for granted was the beginning of the end. Scorpyus shook his head. Some things never change. That's why history repeats itself.

Scorpyus slipped down an alley and found himself a nook behind a crate and under stairs where he could keep an eye on the Regent Inn. He liked to survey a place for a time before going in. Cad would show up not long after dark.

Scorpyus curled up with his back against the building. He peered through a space between the crate and the bottom of the stairs. A few seedy sorts were loitering around the entrance to the Regent Inn. Candles were flickering from behind a few shutters. A lady of the evening assumed her place at the hitching post out front. A lone scraggly horse was hitched to the rail and waited patiently for his owner.

Scorpyus shifted his position and heard the crinkle of paper. He remembered the note Zephyr's friend Hester had given him. He slipped it out of his tunic and unfolded it. There was still enough light to make out the writing.

Through flame and anvil, metals embrace
Refined till they be pure
A touch that leaves its velvet trace
How long can one endure
Where one shall be, the other goes
A reason for the day
If one should find a winter rose
Don't let it slip away

A shudder ran down Scorpyus's spine. The writing on the parchment cut through his soul like a jagged blade. 'Winter rose' lashed out like a whip. The coincidence was overwhelming. Who was Hester anyway? Why would she give Scorpyus this note at such a time?

Broken images of memories danced before Scorpyus. They were thoughts that he was scarcely able to bear. He was exhausted, yet his mind was a cyclone of activity. What was happening to him? He thought of his last moment with Zephyr. That wasn't supposed to happen, was it? The knights had an agreement. And now the parchment from Hester, it was all too much. It had to be a mistake. Death loomed on the horizon. Powerfully emotional times caused frantic grasps for something more, something sacred. A tortured soul will long for one moment of life in an otherwise bleak existence. That's all it was, and nothing more.

Scorpyus remembered the words of the aged alchemist he knew in Ravenshire. After his grandmother died he often turned to the wise old sage for advice. He once told him "Purest truth can only be bourn when death is near. Trying times strip all lives down to what really matters. How many on their death bed state they wished to have been able to finish plowing the north forty? Most wish for more time spent with the wife and children or perhaps taking their travels. Wish though they might, when death is knocking it will be too late for regrets. This warning serves for the living as well. I've seen many a broken soul bury their dear departed, having never made amends before their loved one slipped into eternity. There is no way to assuage that grief. Once words are spoken, they can never be recanted. Once someone is dead, you can never speak the words that should have been said while they yet lived. Heed me well Scorpyus, avoid that mistake; seize the moment, for none know how long they have."

It was too much to think about. Scorpyus rubbed his tired eyes and peered out toward the Regent Inn. There was nothing of interest to see. He rested his head back against the wall and stifled a yawn. Just a little while longer and he would be catch a few winks. Searching the room shouldn't take long.

When Scorpyus was a boy of thirteen he remembered an incident that happened in Ravenshire. A street vendor, a tall thin man, had a pushcart of fish. The man was waving a fish with one hand and shouting out what sounded like "poison" to all who passed. At first Scorpyus thought he was warning people about tainted food. He looked on bewildered, as one person actually reached into their pockets and paid for what Scorpyus believed was poisoned fish. Why did a few people buy it? The vendor clearly cried "poison, poison" and waved a fish. Maybe the person had a rat problem and poisoned fish was the answer.

Just then a young girl walked up to the fish vendor. Dressed in a green tunic, black boots and a gray cloak, she appeared quite the outdoor type. Her boots were mud caked as though she came from the forest. Judging from the bow and quiver of arrows on her back, perhaps she was returning from a hunting trip. She was a fair skinned beauty with pouting red lips, and sure to attract the attention of the boys of Ravenshire. She glanced at Scorpyus, then to the dagger on his belt, and then back up to his eyes. The two locked glances momentarily. Though she had a carefree nature about her, there was certain sullenness in her deep green eyes. The girl smiled warily then turned and spoke to the vendor. Scorpyus was intrigued. Here was a young girl, around his age who carried herself with confidence, and seemed to be streetwise. Right away he could tell that there was something different about her.

Much to Scorpyus's horror the girl bought a fish from the vendor. She patted her stomach and smiled as she spoke with the man. She obviously intended on eating the fish. The tall thin man nodded with a grin and wrapped the fish in a piece of cheesecloth. He then collected a few coins in payment. Didn't the girl hear the man say "poison"? Scorpyus had to warn her before it was too late.

The girl was fast and made it well down the block before Scorpyus knew it. He ran to catch up.

"Excuse me." Scorpyus tapped the girl's shoulder. She jerked around warily to face him and assumed a balanced fighting posture. She shifted her package of fish to her left hand thereby freeing her right to draw the dagger she wore if need be. Scorpyus was clearly impressed. This girl could take care of herself.

"Bonjour," the girl replied hesitantly. "What is it you want?"

"I mean you no harm. I just wanted to warn you about the fish."

A skeptical look came to the girls face. "What is it about the fish that requires warning?"

"Didn't you hear the man," Scorpyus asked quizzically. "He said the fish was poisoned."

"Poisoned?" The girl exclaimed. "Why would he say that?"

Scorpyus shrugged his shoulders. "I don't know. But before you got there he was waiving a fish and saying "poison, poison."

The girl furrowed her brow in thought. After a few seconds she burst with laughter.

"What? What's so funny?" Scorpyus asked, irritation in his voice. He was trying to save the girl's life and she thought it was hilarious.

"Oh, Je regrette," the girl said between laughs. "The man wasn't saying poison." A huge laugh shook her petit frame.

This was rude as far as Scorpyus was concerned. He still didn't see what was so funny. "Then what was he saying?"

The girl finally was able to stifle her laughing. "Oh, Je regrette…I am sorry. I do not mean to be laughing but he was not saying 'poison,' he was saying 'poisson.'" The girl showed Scorpyus how the word was enunciated "pwah-son".

"In Montroix poisson means fish. The man was letting people know he had fresh fish for sale." The girl smiled broadly. "Merci, I know you were trying to help."

Scorpyus never heard of such a thing, and now felt embarrassed. Pride wouldn't let him stay around. "Sorry for wasting your time." He turned and started to walk away.

The girl placed a hand on Scorpyus's shoulder. "No, do not be mad. A lot of people do not know the language of Montroix. My family comes from there. That is why I know. I am sorry if I offended you by laughing. Merci…I mean thank you for being concerned." She saw Scorpyus's dark brooding glare soften.

"I had to be sure…I guess," Scorpyus replied sheepishly, and feeling rather foolish. He held out his hand. "By the way, my name is Scorpyus."

The girl shook his hand. "My name is Zephyr," she replied cheerily.

After a few minutes of conversation the two parted ways, each promising to say hello to one other should they see each other about Saltwater. Over the following weeks they held true to their promise and would greet each other in passing, and even take a few minutes to catch up on the latest news. Scorpyus soon realized he and Zephyr had a lot in common, most importantly a common faith and the desire to see Ravenshire return from its present decline. Zephyr was also a knowledgeable tracker who knew the woods well. He thought about introducing Zephyr to Novak and Cad; two others of like mind who recently become his closest friends. But it wasn't until two months later that circumstance would forge a binding friendship between the two.

Scorpyus walked along a seldom used trail that ran along Lake Caeruleus. It snaked along the north shore of the lake and came near the northern Isle called Jade Inish, nearer then any other trail. Few ventured down the trail because it was believed that Jade Inish was haunted. Jade Inish along with the Isle of Myst was situated in the northern part of Lake Caerulcus. Scorpyus was not a respecter of superstitions and had started using the forbidden trail because it was the closest point to the islands from which to launch a small boat. He, Cad and Novak were currently occupied in exploring the two islands; a venture which would terrorize the average citizen. Many legends and rumors circulated about the two islands; most of which involved haunting spirits or evil apparitions. A few of the stories involved strange creatures or highwaymen. The most popular legend held a mysterious race of people called the Aeolians used to inhabit the islands in ages past. The Aeolian's were rumored to be a mysterious people who were at one with the water. They always lived near the sea or a lake. It was said late at night one could still hear the whispering voice of the Aeolians on the wind; the sound resembling the haunting notes of a bagpipe. Scorpyus heard the distant sounds a few times. It was always on that rare occasion when the wind came from the east. The legend served to dissuade the general population from venturing there. It was a legend the Clandestine Knights fueled through the years in order to maintain the solitude of Ravensclaw.

So far Scorpyus saw no problem with using the trail. It was overgrown and steep in places, but other then that it was quite a beautiful walk that provided a breathtaking view of the lake. There was some indication that at least a few others used the trail as a shortcut on their way around Lake Caeruleus. Most were willing to travel the extra ten miles in order to stay clear of the north shore, but apparently not all were swayed by the haunting legends. So far there had been no sign anyone else actually ventured to the islands. It was a fact that made Scorpyus, Cad, and Novak feel quite brave in their teenage adventures.

On this particular day, Scorpyus was alone and on his way to repair a leak in the boat. He, Cad and Novak barely made it back to shore the previous day for the small wooden vessel took on so much water it listed and capsized thirty yards from shore. Cad and Scorpyus pulled the dilapidated vessel to land and hid it in the bushes, resolving to repair the craft in the morning. In reality the trio needed a newer boat. Their present vessel would best be put to service as firewood, but it was all they could afford. All was not lost for it was on that day Novak learned how to swim the hard way; in much the same manner the trio learned all the skills they acquired.

Scorpyus pulled the battered boat from the bushes and started to examine it. Water seeped through the cracks in the boards. Hopefully a fresh coat of pitch inside and out would cure the problem, but Scorpyus wasn't exactly sure. He was no expert boat builder, but something told him if you can see light through one of the cracks, pitch wouldn't be enough.

A shriek echoed from somewhere down shore. It was a full throated cry of horror, and then all was silent. Scorpyus whipped around and squinted in the direction of the cry. He kneeled and scanned the tree line one hundred yards away, but saw nothing to explain what he heard. He started towards the tree line at a moderate jog, compelled on by a nagging feeling. The shriek was so chilling, so mournful, that investigating the source was the only option. If some lady was in that much terror, someone had to do something.

Reaching the tree line Scorpyus heard a moan up ahead. Slowing his pace he pulled his dagger and padded towards the sound. Heart pounding in his chest he eased his way nearer the moaning sounds. Coming to a thicket of brush, he paused to listen. He was close now. The moaning quickly faded to labored breathing. Scorpyus was confused. The shriek he heard was of a woman, but the moaning sounded like a man. Mustering all of the courage his thirteen years would provide, Scorpyus forced himself to creep around the bushes to whatever may be on the other side.

Scorpyus rounded the brush and saw the opening of a small clearing. He could no longer hear the breathing. Fear closed tight on his chest. Did the person hear him? Was an ambush waiting on the other side? Trembling, with dagger at the ready, Scorpyus moved forward and stepped into the clearing not knowing what lie ahead.

At first he thought the clearing was empty, but then he noticed a seedy looking man laying on his back, sword in hand, staring right at him. He could see the man's gritted teeth through his bushy beard.

"Drop the sword or I'll cripple you!" Scorpyus demanded forcefully and swallowed hard. The man didn't move a muscle. He just stared unblinking. Scorpyus glared at the man and braced himself for the inevitable attack he felt was coming. But the man didn't attack, or even move for that matter. He just stared blankly straight ahead. After a tense two seconds it dawned on Scorpyus the man was dead. He moved closer and saw a deep crimson stain on the man's left side high on his ribs. Upon closer inspection, the man's eyes were dull and lifeless, his skin ashen. A deep slash could be seen on his side equal in size to the gash in his crusty leather tunic. Scorpyus felt for breathing. There was none; the man was definitely dead having recently been killed.

Scorpyus surveyed the clearing. The short grass was ripped up in several spots, and a torn cloak lay crumpled nearby. A struggle had taken place here. Heavy footprints were all over the soft grassy soil of the clearing. The footprints circled and hopped around the middle and then moved toward the east growing farther apart in spacing as they got closer to the edge of the clearing. Judging from the size and depth of the footprints, they were made by two large men who decided to run east after their friend got killed. Scorpyus studied the area closer and noticed a smaller, lighter set of footprints running in the same direction. So he had heard a woman screaming after all. In a flash, Scorpyus ran east, following the trail as fast as the sign would allow. Afraid of what lay ahead he said a quick prayer, the whole while a nagging feeling eating at the pit of his stomach.

Scorpyus followed the tracks east, hopping rocks and fallen logs, and meandering around bushy saplings. The tracks then curved southward through the forest and circled back until it met with the trail along the eastern shore of Lake Caeruleus. Now on a proper trail, Scorpyus was able to sprint at a brisk pace.

Scorpyus may not have been the biggest thirteen-year-old boy in Ravenshire, but he was probably one of the fastest. He bolted along the trail like a jackrabbit, and soon heard voices. The voices grew louder and louder until finally he reached what appeared to be a makeshift campsite on the eastern shore of the lake. A campfire was burning, a kettle suspended above the fire. A tired looking pack mule grazed nearby, tethered to a wooden stake. Just a few feet from the waters edge was the source of the voices.

Scorpyus's mouth fell agape in horrified disbelief. A girl cried, lying on her back, a large muscled man crouched above her pinning her wrists to the ground. The girl kicked a second man who approached from her feet.

"Hold her down for me Rufus." A man with long stringy hair bellowed. Both men roared with laughter.

"Do not touch me you filthy pig!" The girl yelled tearfully and kicked the man with the stringy hair.

The man threw his head back in laughter. "You may have got Demus, but now you will pay. You might even enjoy yourself." Again both men roared with laughter.

"I will kill you if you touch me!" The girl screamed through gritted teeth, tears running down her face. She could not break free from Rufus, who held her hands above her head in his steal grip.

"You'll stay still unless you like the feel of a hot iron." The stringy haired man grinned. He held a poker from the campfire, the tip glowing red hot. He moved toward the girl licking his lips and dodging her kicks.

"No, God No!" The girl cried and shook her head back and forth. The man crept closer.

"Stay away!" The girl yelled, as both men cackled joyously at her futile attempts to free herself.

Scorpyus was sickened by what he saw. It reminded him of what happened to Isabella. Memories of what he had been trying to forget came flooding painfully back. His sister was forced before his eyes just two years earlier and he was powerless to stop it. Scorpyus never forgave himself for not being able to spare his sister from the horror of wicked men. Now he looked on as it was about to happen again. This time things would be different.

Scorpyus padded toward the men his dagger at the ready. The men were bigger and stronger then he was but that didn't matter. He would gut the first one like a fish and then try for the second one. It was all they deserved.

The man with the poker hovered over his victim. This time the girl didn't kick at him. Instead, in a remarkable feat of agility, she rolled up on her shoulders and threw her feet hard above her head planting a foot squarely in Rufus's face.

"Argh!" Rufus bellowed, blood dripping from his crooked nose. He proceeded to cuss the girl vehemently. Before he could recover a foot smashed him in the face again, this time splitting his lip.

The girl on the ground planted a few more kicks to Rufus's face before the man with the hot poker decided he better lend his friend a hand. The man lunged on top of the girl's legs to bring them under control. Flailing appendages knocked the iron from his hand. A piercing shriek shattered the air.

Scorpyus charged forward and leapt through the air landing on the stringy haired man's back. Quickly he reached his arm around to bring his blade to the man's neck. Fingers gripped tightly around his wrist as he brought his blade to bear. The man faltered off the girl, coming to his knees grabbing Scorpyus's arm with his free hand. With a jerk he ripped Scorpyus from his back and slammed him to the ground in a tumbling roll. The girl continued to scream in agony. A sizzling sound could be heard, and there was the distinct smell of burning flesh.

"S'il vous plait God, help me!" The girl cried.

The voice sounded familiar to Scorpyus. "Zephyr?" he jumped to his feet in a flash. He glanced at the girl and saw it indeed was Zephyr. Still being held down, she arched her back violently throwing the hot poker from her midriff, a wisp of smoke coming from a hole burned in the fabric of her torn tunic.

Relief swept Zephyr's face when she saw Scorpyus. Thank God someone was there to help. She was no longer alone.

The stringy haired man pulled his short sword and lunged at the Scorpyus.

"You should have minded your own business boy." He growled and swung his sword.

Scorpyus dodged and ducked the man's attacks. He knew there was little he could do armed with a dagger, but even at that age he was fast and dexterous. The man chopped and hacked at him desperately. It was like trying to catch smoke in a net. Though Scorpyus was quick, with only a dagger he could do little more then keep one step ahead of the blade.

Knowing someone was there to help filled Zephyr with a renewed confidence. She mustered her strength and threw her feet above her head for all she was worth. This time instead of kicking Rufus in the face, she laced her legs around his neck in a scissor lock. Nearly upside down, Zephyr squeezed her legs so tightly together they started to tremble. Rufus turned beet red and started coughing. He released his grip on Zephyr's wrists and tried to pry her legs from his neck. When that didn't work he started beating Zephyr's thighs with his fists. She gritted down and took the pain, refusing to release her grip. She squeezed Rufus in her scissor lock hoping to pop his eyes from his skull. Hatred coursed through her body; hatred for Rufus, and the men who would do such a thing. She fell victim to men like Rufus before, and she would die before it happened again.

Rufus coughed and wheezed and fell to his side. Zephyr saw him place a hand on the hilt of his sword. She reached over and held his sword in its sheath. The two struggled for the weapon; he trying to draw it, and she trying to keep it sheathed. The two writhed on the ground in their struggle.

The stringy haired man grew angry with Scorpyus. The gangly youth proved to be too fast to lay a blade on, so he tried a new tactic. He ran to his campsite and retrieved a small wooden cask, pulling a large cork from it. In the mean time Scorpyus picked up a sizeable rock. When the man returned with the cask, Scorpyus let loose the rock, launching it at his attacker. The man's head snapped back and he let out a string of profanity that called into question the marital status of Scorpyus's parents at the time of his birth.

The man came at Scorpyus, blood oozing from his mouth, and a fresh gap in his teeth. Since his attacker was armed with only a cask, Scorpyus rushed in and planted a fist in the man's belly. The man let out a grunt and then sloshed Scorpyus with liquid from his cask.

The liquid hit Scorpyus on the left shoulder, some of it splashing in his eyes and face. Tears welled from between tightened eyelids, a deep stinging sensation blinding him with pain. Drops of the liquid ran down his cheeks. It was the most powerful rum Scorpyus had ever smelled. It was tremendously effervescent and vaporous. Scorpyus forced his eyes open in time to see the man step in close. He kicked the man in the back of the knee just as a hand snatched him by a lock of hair. The two tumbled to the ground in a heap with Scorpyus on top. Cool vaporous liquid poured from the cask onto the stringy haired man thoroughly drenching his clothes. A fist caught Scorpyus in the chin sending sparks through his blurred vision. He was knocked to his back but quickly rolled to his knees, frantically rubbing the burning liquid from his face trying to clear his eyes. His hair was soaked.

The man seized his blinded foe in a headlock and dragged him to the campfire, rolling with laughter. "Now for a lesson maggoty gypsy trash like you won't soon forget."

Scorpyus forced his stinging eyes open. He saw he was being drug to a campfire, feeling the heat when he got near. A kettle was suspended above the fire, flames licking the bottom. The sound of boiling liquid came from the kettle, the scent of rabbit soup wafted thick in the air.

The man gripped Scorpyus by the nape of the neck and tried to force his face into the flames. Panic tore through the boy's lithe frame. He wrapped his arms around the stringy haired man's waist and clung like a leach in desperation. The man's fingers bore down into the boy's neck as he tried to pry off the unwelcome parasite and cast him into the fire. Scorpyus braced his legs against the rocks circling the campfire. It was futile. The rocks gave way and Scorpyus's foot slid into hot ash beneath the flame. He howled in pain and jerked his foot from the intense heat. His heel caught one of the supports for the kettle, knocking it from its place. The kettle cascaded to the ground sending a wave of boiling rabbit stew onto the left shin of the stringy haired man. Now it was his turn to yelp in agony.

The man released a collage of profanity in a violent rage. He hopped on his good leg, the other burning immensely and blistering from the scalding soup. He started beating on Scorpyus, cursing and screaming outrageously, crazed with pain and anger.

Repeatedly he brought his fists down on Scorpyus, trying to beat him off while struggling to balance on just one foot.

The man worked Scorpyus toward the fire with his fists. He then tried vehemently to shove him into the flames again. He leaned into the boy, shoving and putting his weight into the task, swearing and cussing continually. The man cursed the very God that Scorpyus was petitioning for assistance.

Scorpyus started to collapse under the man's explosive tirade. The heat was uncomfortably hot on his body. Unfortunately he was getting tired and the stringy haired man was stronger. An intense fear of burning alive wracked Scorpyus's mind as he begged God for deliverance. He was only thirteen, far too young to die. Sobs heaved in the boy's chest. He fought till he was ready to collapse, his legs trembling. Scorpyus begged God for a quick death if death had to come. God answered his prayer. A sense of peace washed over him. He wasn't afraid anymore. This time when the man shoved at Scorpyus, instead of resisting he leapt toward the flames. The determined force of his attacker shoved him incredibly hard; so hard that the force carried Scorpyus over the campfire, tumbling him out the other side.

Scorpyus fell face down in soft dirt, taking in a mouthful of the gritty soil. Instinctively he scrambled to his knees and fled running, tripping and crawling his way away from his attacker. He stumbled blindly until he came to his knees with a splash. He realized he found the edge of the lake. Instantly he held his breath and plunged his face into the water. He rubbed his eyes and forced his eyelids open to get the burning liquid out. The cool waters of Lake Caeruleus felt good.

Panic shot through Scorpyus's heart when he felt a hand on his shoulder. He shot up from the lake, his wet hair flinging streams of water arching backward.

"Do not be afraid. It is me." Zephyr reassured her friend. Scorpyus slicked his wet hair back. Through bloodshot and watery eyes he saw a familiar out of focus face. Before the two could enjoy their brief reunion, a ranting shrieking came from behind them. Scorpyus and Zephyr snapped around toward the sound. Both of their jaws dropped in ultimate horror. They saw an image that had to have been vomited from the depths of hell. It was the most horrible, frightening, and ghastly sight the two had ever seen.

Staggering towards Scorpyus and Zephyr was the stringy haired man. Only now he no longer had any hair, or much skin for that matter. Were their eyes deceiving them? No, there he was in monstrous form. Faltering toward them was the horribly burned smoldering remains of a human being. There was little skin left on the man's face, his sinews and tendons exposed. His lips were burned away revealing skeleton-like toothy jawbones. One lidless eye stared out from its hole, the other a running blob of clear jelly. His ears were burned off, as was his nose; a hideous black pit in his head where it once was. The man's clothing had been incinerated exposing his red, raw, and blistered flesh, some of which dripped from his arms like bloody moss from contorted tree branches. Bones stuck out from flesh-striped fingers. Flesh dripped from his torso like grotesque wax from a twisted candle. Blood oozed up from somewhere deep within his chest cavity, and the stench of charred flesh was nauseating. How the man could live through such severe burns was unknown. Scorpyus and Zephyr froze in abject horror, unable to move a muscle. The man spit garbled curses and plodded toward the two young people. The man fell victim to his own scheme.

The man came toward Scorpyus and Zephyr in erratic, staggering steps, jerking as if he were a demon possessed tree. Perhaps it was rage that propelled the man onward. Or perhaps it was some evil force. The two teens didn't care.

Clasping hands, Scorpyus and Zephyr held onto each other and stepped slowly backward farther into the lake. The burned man kept coming. The two retreated until they were waist deep in the cool water. Sputtering unintelligible curses the beastly sight drew nearer and nearer. At the edge of the water the man paused, glancing down. For a second the ranting profanity stopped. He studied the thing in the water, wondering what it was. The man realized his reflection upon the water's surface. Instead of his usual features, staring up at him was a ghoul from hell. An awakening realization appeared in his eye, as he became aware of what transpired. He vaguely recalled falling in the fire. He was the horribly disfigured image in the water!

The man emitted a piercing shrill, and flailed about madly, his good eye rolling wildly. He fell into the lake and thrashed in the shallows. The man gripped his head as if he were trying to silence daunting voices. He moaned a low-pitched gurgling sound reminiscent of tortured cattle, and wept bitterly, gnashing on his swollen blistered tongue. There was no turning back; no second chances now. He had gone too far. This nightmare was forever. He crossed the point of no return. All the regrets in the world couldn't stop the torment now. His hell was here to stay and it crippled his mind. He was reduced to a frothing animal, lost within the horrors of the underworld.

Zephyr and Scorpyus looked at each other horrified beyond human comprehension. Surely they just witnessed a man cross into complete and utter insanity. It was a glimpse of hell from earth.

The man eventually stopped flailing about, and lay still face down in the shallow water. In shock, Scorpyus and Zephyr waded back to shore. Minutes passed before the two regained their composure.

"We can tell no one of this." Zephyr never wanted to relive this event, not even to tell what happened.

Scorpyus nodded numbly. His eyes were sore, but his vision was returning to normal. He pulled off his boot to inspect his foot. It was red and tender but not badly burned. He would recover.

"How are you?" Scorpyus inquired. Zephyr looked a mess. Her tunic was torn, her shoulder exposed. Over in a clump of grass lay the crumpled form of her attacker. His face was blue from asphyxiation, a victim of Zephyr's frantic scissor lock.

"I tell you this, I am too afraid to look, but I was burned with the hot iron." Not long after leaving the cool waters of the lake pain became evident in Zephyr's grimaced features.

"Maybe I can help," Scorpyus offered. "My grandmother taught me about medicinal remedies. Where is the burn?"

"Merci, but I better sit down first." Zephyr was feeling considerable discomfort and a little faint. She sat and leaned against a log. She slowly and painfully peeled her wet tunic away from her skin pulling it up to expose her abdomen. Three inches below her ribs on the right side was a terrible burn shaped like the tip of the poker. The burn was blistered and red around the edges.

Tears came to Zephyr's eyes when she saw the wound. "S'il vous plaît God, no!"

"You'll be alright," Scorpyus encouraged. "I have something for the pain."

"It will leave a terrible scar." Zephyr lamented. She had been through so much. The thought of having a sizable scar was disheartening.

"It's not that bad." Scorpyus offered with a smile.

Zephyr smiled and wiped a tear. "Merci, you are a good friend. Thank you for helping me."

From that day Scorpyus and Zephyr became close friends. He would introduce her to Cad and Novak, and together the four formed what would become the Clandestine Knights.

A boot scraped on rock startling Scorpyus awake. How long had he been asleep? His heart pounded at the possibility. Peering from his position under the stairs, he saw a large figure looming a few feet away.

"Psst Scorp, are you alright?" Cad's voice came from the shadowy form. "That is you under the stairs isn't it?"

Scorpyus chastened himself for allowing himself to fall asleep. No doubt had he been discovered by someone else, they would have thought him nothing but a derelict passed out from an over indulgence of ale. Just the same it was a foolish risk.

"Yeah, it's me. Are you ready?" Scorpyus got up from his cramped position and stretched. It was now dark. He guessed he must have been asleep for close to an hour.

"That's not like you mate. I thought you were planning on sleeping earlier." Cad replied.

"That's a long story." Scorpyus yawned and rubbed his eyes.

Scorpyus and Cad walked to the tower of the Regent Inn, going to the seldom used backside near the shoreline. The two glanced warily around. If there was a boat off the coast it was obscured by fog. The tower had no doors to the back, but five windows, one for each floor, faced out to sea. A rotted rag and a length of tangled twine bore evidence the shore side of the tower saw at least a few visitors.

The tower was built on a rocky crag. The hewn stones were discolored with black mold and patches of green moss. Red ceramic tiles made up the roof. Unlike the four lower floors that had shuttered slots for windows, the top floor had a wide and broad glass window fitted into an iron framework. A long hall connected the bottom floor of the tower to the rest of the Regent Inn some thirty yards away. This was the first time the pair had seen the structure up close.

"I bet this used to be a light house of sorts; before the Inn was built onto it." Cad observed with a keen eye for architecture.

"You could be right. This north side of the port is rocky." Scorpyus fingered the cracks between the towers stones. "We'll need the rope. There's not enough space to get a finger hold."

Cad placed his shield and helmet on the ground then removed a coil of rope from over his shoulder. Tied to one end of the rope was a grappling hook. He scanned the roof. "There's not much to hook the blooming hook on, is there."

Scorpyus agreed. "There's part of the wooden roof support jutting out every few feet around the top. That's all I can see."

"I don't know mate," Cad replied shaking his head. "Do you really think you can throw this hook onto one of those? Its fifty feet straight up! Maybe we should go through the Inn."

"If we do that we have to get by the Innkeeper and several patrons. Even if they have a room available in the tower how will we be able to go to the rooms without arousing suspicion? The place is crawling with seedy characters that are always looking for trouble, and we could be recognized. This is an important job that doesn't need to be noticed if we can help it. The longer we keep our actions from our enemies the better, and the rebellion has a few including the man who stayed in the room we are going to." Scorpyus didn't see any other way.

"And this is too important to send one of the rebel chaps." Cad grimaced. "We're daft either way. But slim odds are what we're all about mate! Let's do it."

Scorpyus smiled and took the rope. He stepped a few feet from the tower, grabbed the rope a few feet from the hook and started swinging it in a circular motion. With a mighty heave he swung the hook up towards one of the jutting roof supports. A second later there was the sound of shattering glass. Scorpyus and Cad looked at each other wide eyed as a few shards sprinkled over them. The two quickly pressed themselves flat against the tower, holding their breath, and listening intently.

Two minutes went by before the pair moved. No one poked a head out one of the windows. No one gave the alarm. If anyone heard the window shatter they didn't come to investigate. It was a fortunate break. The accident was without witness.

"Missed the wooden support ay Scorp?" Cad chuckled.

Scorpyus laughed as he pulled the rope taught. "Not by much."

It reminded them of when they were scruffy teens and just formed the Clandestine Knights. Fortunately the pair's skills increased sufficiently to keep incidents like this to a minimum.

Scorpyus climbed the rope first. He carefully removed the jagged slivers of glass that remained in the iron framework and placed them on a table inside the room. By the time Cad ascended the rope, he had already entered the tower room through the unplanned, yet welcome breech. Cad handed Scorpyus his shield and then squeezed into the room, barely able to fit his armored frame through. He pulled the rope up after he entered.

The room was near total darkness except for a light flickering under the door. Scorpyus felt around the table and found a candle. Cad's dark form was scarcely visible as he drew the windows curtains closed. He shoved the drapery into the window box trying to seal as much of the window as possible.

"We're going to need some light. It looks like the Inn has a lamp in the hall. I'll be right back." Scorpyus went to the door and pressed his ear against it. Satisfied no one was there he cracked open the door. After a cautious glance he slipped out of the room and lit the candle on the lamp in the hall, returning quickly thereafter. He locked the door behind him. The candle cast a pale light basking the room in an eerie flickering silence. It always felt strange to be in unfamiliar territory.

The room, for offering a stately view, was mediocre at best. A large bed with plain butternut quilting was in one corner next to a nightstand. It did have an ornately carved headboard. Upon closer inspection, Cad realized the bed's quilting had at one time been white but was now terribly soiled.

A wooden dresser with a basin and pitcher stood against a wall. In the center of the room were a table and four chairs. And a sizable desk with a fancy embroidered chair stood near the doorway. The stone walls were stained with age and deferred maintenance. The walls were bare save for a lone painting of a dapple-gray horse in a meadow. Clean patterns on the walls marked where other paintings and tapestries once were.

"I'll start with the desk." Scorpyus whispered and started his search for information. Cad nodded and moved to the dresser.

Cad rifled through the dresser drawers. Braydon Mendax may have not stayed in the most luxurious quarters, but he did own the nicest clothes available in Xylor. Rich silks and fine linens filled the dresser. The clothing, though fancy, was well worn. Perhaps Braydon fell on hard times before his death. In the top right hand drawer Cad found a black velvet bag. Inside were forty shillings and a small silver ring worth about the same. Cad took the ring nearer the candle to examine it more closely. It bore no inscription and held no significant features. He replaced it in the bag and finished searching the clothing in the dresser. There was nothing more to find. The basin on the dresser was empty, and the pitcher was half filled with water.

"Did you find anything?" Cad inquired.

"I know why the walls are bare." Scorpyus read a thin book next to the candle. "It looks as if Mendax was selling the furnishings of this room. This ledger documents the sale of various tapestries and paintings. The entries go back six or seven months."

"I wonder if the Innkeeper knew this bloke was thieving away with the furnishings." Cad chuckled.

"Did you find anything in the dresser?"

"Yeah, forty shillings and a ring worth about the same. It's not a king's fortune, but it is a lot of money when you consider most of the poor chaps here make one shilling a day. Many make less." Cad added. It was certainly enough wealth so as not to have to resort to selling off the decorations.

Cad went to the table and started sifting through the items there. There was a quill pen, some blank parchment, wax and a seal, and a stein. The stein was part ways filled with warm ale. Cad turned his attention elsewhere.

"Hey Cad," Scorpyus called in a loud whisper. "I think this is a diary, or something. This Mendax made meticulous notes on everything."

"Really?" Cad went to the other side of the table and peered over Scorpyus's shoulder.

"It's actually notes for a book, I think." Scorpyus thumbed through a few pages. "He writes about exploring uncharted territory, finding gold, and citizens asking him to lead Xylor."

"It's obviously a bunch of rubbish. The bloke fancied himself to be somebody." Cad scoffed.

"That may be," Scorpyus furrowed his brow. "But some of it sounds true also. It says here he sold the mirror that hung above the dresser for five shillings. Why would he make that up?"

"Maybe he only sold it for two." Cad looked to the dresser and sure enough there was a clean square empty place on the wall. "What's his last entry?"

Scorpyus flipped to the last entry and held it in the candlelight to read.

> June 13—I've just met with Lydia, though I feel that is not her real name. She thinks she can fool me easily, but I am much too clever for her. Last night we met at the tavern, where she obviously saw that I was a man of considerable influence and knowledge. She came to me and inquired if she could meet me later, where there were less people. She said she had a few questions that she felt a person of my intuition would be able to answer. She even stated she would make it worth my while. Lydia came to my room under the guise that she was new to town and wanted to know a little of Xylor; namely who was leading the new government. But I know it was just a ruse to meet in private. The poor woman is obviously smitten with me. Oh, she tried to be a proper lady and hide her attraction; even to the point of offering me forty shillings to tell her the name of the strangers who were helping Xylor. Now I'm nobody's fool. If someone wants to be rid of forty shillings that easily, maybe they will be willing to part with sixty. The poor dear's intelligence apparently doesn't match her ravishing beauty; her long dark locks and exotic features betraying her origins of somewhere far

from Xylor. Though she posses beauty, she does not possess all. Who but a dim one would pay for information they could readily obtain simply by walking down to Thadus's compound? And Lydia agreed to pay sixty shillings! She gave me forty up front and is going to pay the twenty later. I told her I would provide her with the names after I received the other twenty shillings. I am to meet her on the roof of a building; supposedly for nothing more than to give her the information and collect the debt. Does she take me for an idiot? I know what she's really up to. She is going to great lengths to ensure I meet her on the roof of one of Xylor's tallest buildings. And she thinks I don't know why, the poor misguided woman. She must think she's dealing with an amateur. It is not uncommon for young paramour's to meet me on the roof, look out over the city, and see the lights flickering in the night, quite the romantic setting. I must admit, Lydia is quite attractive, and it will be my pleasure becoming more acquainted with the woman. If she wants to act like she's going to pay me for some worthless information just to swoon me, so much the better. A fool and her money are about to part company. Though I do feel a little guilty taking advantage of the poor naive dear, she will one day look back on this incident having learned a valuable lesson. However, I do know something about Lydia she had little intention of revealing. My keen observations spied a parchment in her handbag when she retrieved the forty shillings. And this was no ordinary letter mind you. It bore a seal of regal proportions; fancy and elaborate. It was obviously the seal of someone of great wealth and importance. I decided that I must examine that parchment further. Perhaps Lydia can afford to be purchasing many more of my services; services that I shall convince her she desperately needs. Seeing as she is quite taken with me, the task shouldn't be too difficult.

Immediately I sent for Algernon and put him to the task. Algernon may be a dull blade, but he is quite handy at relieving a person of the contents of their pockets. And the insipid lad agreed to the task for a paltry three shillings. I told Algernon I would pay upon delivery. Why pay in advance and waste three shillings should the lad get caught? Besides that, I have always paid for his services in a timely manner. He agreed and stated he would slip the letter under the door should I not be in my room, and collect his pay on the morrow. It is well to keep such handy fellows on good terms. At any rate, by morning I shall be embarking upon a new chapter in my life; one that is of substantial wealth should all go as I plan.

Cad and Scorpyus digested the last entry in what turned out to be a volume of diary entries mixed with short stories and notes.

"The bloke fancied himself in high regard," Cad shook his head in amazement. "His days of swindling drunken sailors apparently bolstered his pride and made him feel overconfident. This Lydia played him like a harp."

Scorpyus agreed. "He made the mistake of underestimating his foes. It cost him his life."

"There's a bit of a lesson there for all of us." Cad added. "The chap was taken at his own game. You reap what you sow."

"And it looks like Mendax provided Lydia with information about us. Why is that information worth sixty shillings?"

Cad stroked his goatee in thought. "I don't know mate. And why kill the bloke after he provides the information?" A thoughtful pause enveloped the room.

Finally Scorpyus spoke. "Because he could identify a Valkyrie; unfortunately for Mendax, he found himself in a position he couldn't foresee. He may have been beaten at his own game, but he wasn't so stupid as to not be able to figure it out eventually. Once news of us being killed by the Valkyrie's started circulating, it would only be a matter of time before Mendax pieced it together; the people he identified turned up dead. Lydia knew this." Scorpyus's voice trailed off, a disturbing thought crossed his mind.

Cad was impressed with the thoroughness of the Valkyrie's planning. They came to town, spied it out, obtained information in a rapid manner, and set their plan into action. In most circumstances, the Valkyrie's would be long gone before the town or village knew what hit them. "I'll be glad when we're rid of the Valkyrie's for good."

Scorpyus looked to Cad with a look of angst. "I don't think we ever will be rid of them."

Cad could tell that Scorpyus was troubled immeasurably. Even in the candlelight his friends face looked ashen. "What do you mean?"

"Be it now or later, eventually they will kill us all or we will kill all of them. This will never end for us…or at least for me."

"What are you talking about Scorp?" Cad asked, a bewildered look on his face. Scorpyus remained silent. And then it dawned on Cad, "You've seen one, haven't you?"

"I think so." Scorpyus related the incident where he happened upon the bathing woman. "Looking back, there can be no other explanation. I tracked the Valkyrie in that direction. Now that I think about it, she had to be this Lydia. She fits the description in Mendax's journal."

"Are you sure?" Cad asked even though he knew it was true. Scorpyus's instincts were usually correct. Who else would pay two months wages for information? The Valkyrie's had wealthy financial backing from Kelterland. Cad rolled it over and over in his head. It was two months salary. The more he thought about it, the more something just didn't make sense.

"I keep asking myself one blooming question." Cad announced. "Why would I pay so much for information that I could obtain eventually through time?

"You didn't want to wait; you want the information now." Scorpyus answered.

"Exactly, and that doesn't fit with the way these blokes do things. They seem more the type to have their plan in place before making their first move. They must have already had us and Thadus identified. The Valkyries are too bloody well experienced to do otherwise. They wouldn't slip into town and unleash the chaos without first knowing who they were here for. People were already dead by the time Mendax was killed." Cad shook his head. "No, they already knew who we were before they paid Mendax for the information."

Scorpyus thought about it and it made perfect sense. "So the question is, why pay for information you already have?"

"Because we didn't trust our first information and wanted to confirm it." Cad replied, and Scorpyus closed Mendax's journal.

Cad smiled. "For some reason this Lydia wanted to confirm our identities. If we find out why, we will have moved closer to solving this crisis."

Scorpyus's eyes lit up. "Are you thinking the Valkyrie's have a traitor in their midst?"

"Some chap must be suspected of providing false information. It could be one of their own. God forbid it's someone close to us. More then likely the Kelterlanders have a sympathizer here in Xylor. My guess is this Lydia is the leader since she's the one tracing down the confirmation."

Cad and Scorpyus felt comfortable with the conclusions they had drawn from their venture in the Regent tower. Yet, there was still an impending sense of doom hanging over their heads. Their exhilaration at solving some of the mystery could not outweigh their sense of urgency. Time was running out, for them and for Xylor. The feeling that they were on the verge of success or collapse could not be shaken.

The troubled look was back on Scorpyus's brow. "We don't have much time. If Zephyr is still alive she won't be for long, especially if she can identify her attacker. They would only have kept her alive to torture her for information anyway."

"And our suspicions are confirmed; there's a bloody spy working against us," the gravity of the situation evident in Cad's voice.

The two friends, brothers in battle, looked at each other. Each one was reading what the other was thinking. Years of tribulation and lives risked together had forged an understanding that transcended mere words. In that darkened room, in that dark hour, with Zephyr and Novak absent, the two friends could count on nothing but each other. Nothing else mattered. They each had the undying loyalty of one friend, and that was more then most could boast of. They didn't know if the traitor was inside the rebellion or outside of it, and they didn't have the luxury of time in order to find out.

"It's down to us, isn't it Cad." Scorpyus wore a grave look in his dark eyes.

Cad nodded, his bleak countenance showing a hint of fear. "We can't leave this room without a plan. We have to work it alone. At least until we find out who the Valkyrie agent is. Hopefully this whole blooming episode will be over by that time."

The two tired friends set to work on a plan they hoped would see them return to Ravenshire alive. There was no direction to go but forward. Had it not been for the possibility of finding Zephyr alive, Cad and Scorpyus may have quit. But abandoning the task now was tantamount to abandoning Zephyr. They also gave Thadus their word. Novak was doing his part, and a Knight doesn't abandon a fellow knight. Without loyalty, integrity, and honor, a person is worth nothing. They are a bag of bones taking up space. The Clandestine Knights decided long ago to amount to being more then a bag of bones.

XI

CYRUS WALKED BRISKLY down the street pausing only to step around a rotund patron that burst from a tavern doorway into his path. The inebriated fellow eyed Cyrus on jittering legs, squinting to focus. Cyrus smiled weakly and tried to be about his business, but unfortunately he would be exposed to the rotund gent's mannerisms. The man patted his protruding gullet with both hands, his cotton shirt stretched tightly around his considerable girth. The overtaxed garment could not conceal all it was employed to cover. Cyrus was privy to observe a midsection as hairy as that of a bear. Deplorably, the man issued forth a belch that would have been combustible had it been near an open flame. The violent fume assaulted Cyrus's nostrils and left a bitter taste on his tongue. Cyrus had enough. With a disgruntled look he shoved the miserable beast aside and continued on. The man stumbled against the tavern door, cackling raucously at his complete lack of etiquette.

Soon, Cyrus was at the door to Iris's home. He paused before knocking, something weighing heavily on his mind. The fog cast a pallor on the small home, and put a pained look in Cyrus's eyes. He hated the fog, and was fast growing tired of its suffocating numbness. Like the other rebel soldiers he had not been getting much sleep. The fog only added to the general depression of the time.

War was wearing Cyrus thin, like the soles of aged shoes or the worn knees of linen breeches; he felt he would give out at any moment. As far back as he could remember war encompassed his life. It was war he fled when he came to Xylor in the first place. But as circumstance would have it, much to his dismay, he found himself a member of Reddland's Royal Guard. Cyrus never bought into the ideology of Reddland's regime, but it was the perfect solace from suspicious and prying eyes. He left the guard after several years and thought he was done with the soldiering business. Then for the right reasons he agreed to secretly train the rebel soldiers for an eventual revolution. For years it looked like that revolution would never come.

Then out of nowhere four strangers appeared in Xylor, and it changed everything. Cyrus was thrust once again to the forefront of battle. He had known from birth his destiny would hold conflict and struggle. His own mother told him he was bound for great things, and destined for leadership. He never put much stock in her words until the untimely death of his two older siblings. It was then the mantle of his mother's expectations passed to him. For a time he bore the mantle diligently. Then war came, spreading from Ravenshire like a consuming disease. And like in Ravenshire, the lives of Cyrus and his fellow citizens were turned upside down. Cyrus and his younger brother fled what was sure to be an abrupt end, each going in opposite directions on the advice of a trusted friend. Cyrus came to Xylor; his brother was headed to Gyptus. He had no contact with his brother ever since, not even knowing if he survived the journey.

So yes, Cyrus was tired of war. He was tired of the devastation it wrought upon families. There was little good to be found in the practice as far as he was concerned, and yet he knew it would always be with him. He searched for a way out but found none. Like his mother said, it was his destiny. And so with a heavy heart, he carried on, begging God for strength to see him through. Perhaps some day there would be peace in the realm again. Cyrus prayed he could endure to that day. Lately he had been reduced to taking it one minute at a time, trudging slowly toward his duty. There in front of Iris's door was a torn man; a part wanting to forget the past and reach for one moment of happiness, and another part knowing his future was sealed by blood; a fate he couldn't escape. It was also a fate honor and duty bound Cyrus to fulfill.

Cyrus reached to knock on Iris's door, his arms feeling as heavy as stone. Oh how he dreaded the days to come. The dreary midnight was an appropriate backdrop for his weary soul. The sound of footsteps preceded the creaking open of a wooden door. Iris's beaming face smiled from beneath the cloak wrapped tightly about her to fend off the night chill.

"Cyrus, come in!" Iris stepped aside to let Cyrus pass. "When you didn't show up after dinner, I didn't think you were coming today."

"I'm sorry for coming so late. I can't stay long. We had a late meeting and this was as soon as I could make it." Cyrus removed his helmet. Iris closed the door and motioned to take a seat.

Cyrus pulled a chair from the table and seated Iris and then took a seat opposite her. He placed his helmet on the table. "How are you feeling? It's good to see you up and about."

"I'm doing much better. My strength is returning, but I still have a ways to go." Iris's eyes misted up. "And I can't thank you enough for all you have done for me Cyrus."

"I'm glad I could help." Cyrus smiled weakly, and looked down at his helmet preoccupied.

"What's wrong Cyrus? Is something the matter?" Worry vibrated in Iris's voice.

Cyrus said nothing but swallowed hard and stared into the distance. The silence settled in the pit of Iris's stomach.

Something was troubling Cyrus and she dreaded what it might be. She tried to read Cyrus's face; some clue as to what was going on.

Cyrus cleared his throat. "There's no easy way to say this."

"What is it Cyrus?" Iris pulled her shawl tight with trembling hands.

"How do I say this?" Cyrus took a deep breath sighing deeply. "There's something I must do. I've put it off as long as I could. Now I must start on my course. It is the only path before me, and I must walk it."

"What are you saying Cyrus? What are you telling me?" Tears welled up and ran from Iris's eyes.

"I can't really say. I've lost my direction, and I no longer know what the future holds. All I know is I must do this alone. I can't involve you in this. It wouldn't be right."

"No Cyrus, tell me. I have to know. I'll do this with you. What ever you say, wherever you go, I'll do it. Just let me help you." Iris pleaded.

Cyrus stood and turned away. "I can't Iris. I'm sorry."

Iris jumped from her seat and went to Cyrus, trying to look him in the eye. "What's happening Cyrus? I thought I meant something to you."

Cyrus placed his hands on Iris's shoulders. "You do Iris. More then you'll ever know. There's just so much you don't know about me. If you really knew me…I'm sorry for not being more honest with you. I should never have let us get this far without you knowing. Now I've hurt you, and for that I am deeply sorry."

"Well tell me now Cyrus." Iris erupted in a flood of emotion. "I love you Cyrus, just as you are. There is nothing you can tell me that will ever change that. Don't you see?"

Tears welled in Cyrus's eyes, and he embraced Iris. "I love you too Iris and that's why I can't tell you. Maybe some day I will. But for now there is something I must do. What I'm about to do, I have to do alone. It is very dangerous. Involving you could cost you your life. I care for you too much to let that happen."

"No, Cyrus no," Iris sobbed. "Tell me, I'll die with you if I have to."

Iris's last statement tore Cyrus's heart from his chest. Iris was willing to die with him. It made him love her all the more. He reached into his tunic and withdrew a letter. It was sealed with wax, and he handed it to Iris.

"Here, take this," Cyrus choked back the tears. "Read it only if I never return."

Iris looked up, her face contorted into the most anguished heartbreaking sorrowful look. "You're not coming back are you?"

"I don't know." Cyrus wiped a tear. "But this I promise you. If I have but one breath left in me when this is over, I will return."

"There must be another way. I don't like the sound of it. Can't one of the Clandestine Knights undertake this task?" Iris pleaded.

Cyrus shook his head. "They've done enough already, besides there are only two here in Xylor; and that not for long."

"What, are they deserting us when we need them most?" Iris asked shock evident in her voice.

"I've said too much already. Please don't inquire any further." Cyrus looked into Iris's sad brown eyes. "If you want to help, pray that I may someday return. Do that and remain inconspicuous. Things may get worse before they get better."

Iris was deeply troubled. Cyrus was acting so uncharacteristically. She saw a side of him she hadn't before. Perhaps she really didn't know the man as well as she thought.

"What's happening Cyrus?" Iris wiped her tears.

"I've told you all that I can. Your son needs you. Pray for us all." Cyrus stepped toward the door.

Iris squeezed Cyrus's hand. "Alright, do what you must. But I swear before God I will be waiting for your return. And if that day should never come, then alone I shall remain, for my heart will go to no other."

Cyrus chest tightened and he choked back the tears. He placed a hand under Iris's chin and raised her eyes to meet his. "Even a king is not worthy of such a lady," he whispered.

Iris stood at her doorway and watched Cyrus disappear into the fog. She clutched the letter close, tears streaming down her cheeks, staring into the nothingness. A poem she heard once came to mind:

> *One day I knew what love was for*
> *Was caught within its vice*
> *If it be true forever more*
> *One first must pay a price*
> *Limitless undying love*
> *Abides yet patiently*
> *What young and old have visions of*
> *So few will chose to see*

—•◆•—

Astoria was a bustling city with a large population. Its buildings displayed the latest in architectural advances, and stood proudly, the epitome of wealth and splendor. Engraved stone work in marble and alabaster graced many of the structures. Statuary and ornamentation abounded. It was an ancient city, once belonging to The Dales, a people known for their construction prowess. Now in the possession of the Kelterlanders and their incredible wealth generated from the nearby mines at Kronshtadt, the city took on an even more regal appearance. People from all walks of life passed through Astoria's illustrious streets, many of which were paved in cobblestone. Its merchants were esteemed throughout the realm for offering the finest of wares. Anything imaginable could be bought in Astoria; "if it is worth asking for, then it is worth paying for" seemed to be the merchant's motto. If an item or service was illegal or hard to acquire, then it only added to its value. For the right amount, it was yours.

On this bright morning the merchants were out, anticipating their profits eagerly. Many prepared for the day long before the sun, which had just surfaced above the horizon. Few took notice of the large hulking man and his two weary companions as they made their way down the street. All three were in awe of the sheer grandiose of Astoria. No other city in the realm could compare with Astoria, even the jeweled cities of Gyptus. As first time visitors, Novak, Dantes, and Emerald beheld wonders the likes of which they had never seen.

"It is more spectacular then I imagined." Emerald was excited. Now this is what she thought an adventure should be like, not what happened at the temple.

"Ya, it is bigger then I heard." Novak looked around taking it all in. "Where do we start? There must be a hundred streets. J&R Shipping could be anywhere."

"Aye," Dantes agreed. "Maybe thar be a scallywag willing to provide directions, no doubt for the cost of a pint."

Dantes walked to a man who set up a cart of fresh baked bread in the alley between two buildings. "Avast thar matey, how much ye be asking for a loaf."

The man smiled and quoted a price twice what Dantes expected. "Briny Barnacles, ye be asking a steep price."

The merchant furrowed his brow, puzzled. "You must be new to Astoria sir. A quarter shilling is the going price. This isn't a peasant village you know."

It made sense to Dantes. "Ye drive a hard bargain. I'll take a loaf; and perhaps you can provide me with directions to another Astorian establishment."

The merchant handed Dantes a loaf of bread and collected his payment. "What place are you looking for?"

"J&R Shipping."

Recognition showed on the merchant's face. "Yes, I know where that place is." The man smiled coyly and added, "What's information like that worth to a gentleman such as you?"

Dantes turned red. "Ye charge me for directions after I bought bread from you. Ye be nothing but a filthy bilge rat." He expected as much from the citizens of Kelterland, but wanted to voice his displeasure on the matter anyway.

The merchant feigned shock. Now sir, there's no need for harsh language. The bread is of the highest quality, and you'll find it to be well worth what you paid. I perceive you are indeed new to Astoria. Here everything has a price. If its worth asking for its worth a shilling."

"Does thar be any honor in this city? Or do ye all take advantage of strangers? Have ye no fear of God?" Dantes was enraged. If this was indicative of the whole city, it was clearly overcome with greed.

"Who is this God, that I should fear him?" The merchant asked sarcastically while rolling his eyes. "You're in Astoria now. The shilling, the coin of the realm rules here."

"I be sorry to hear that. Ye be misplacing your faith, says I." Dantes paid the merchant who greedily snatched up the coins. He provided the directions with a cheery smile, reveling in the thought of his effortless income.

"Is everything alright?" Emerald asked when Dantes returned. "It looked like an argument was starting."

"Aye, the scallywag charged a shilling for directions. Judging from him, I fear thar be many here in need of a keel hauling." Dantes related.

"Ya, that is what I heard about this place. The sooner we leave the better." Novak scowled. Fortunately for the merchant, he conducted his dealings with Dantes rather then Novak.

The trio walked the cobblestone streets, following the directions provided by the bread merchant. It was a long journey to the other side of town. Upon orienting themselves to the city, they realized they had entered from the northeast. The storm blew them farther off course then they imagined.

The trio passed several taverns, inns, stables, shops, cobblers, fletchers, blacksmiths and anything else you could think of. Everything was for sale. As they made their way toward the outskirts of town, the buildings became less elaborate. The tall stone structures became smaller, and then eventually wooden. Stately buildings became less decorative, and faded into structures in need of repair.

By the time the trio made it to the docks, the streets were a bustle of activity. Dantes and Emerald shouldered their way through the growing crowds. For the most part, people got out of Novak's way, eying him nervously as they passed. Standing a head and shoulders taller them most, Novak had a clear line of sight down the street and was the first to spot J&R Shipping. It was a large wooden warehouse that stood dockside. A woman entered the small office nearby. The building was in better condition then those nearby. Several piers stretched out into the water, one with a ship anchored along side. Men were busy unloading cargo from the ship and stacking it on the docks. Others loaded up the goods in carts and were wheeling them toward the large warehouse.

Dantes and Emerald followed Novak into the office. A dark haired man with a mustache stood behind the counter. He was a thin man of around forty years of age, and wore a leather apron. His shirtsleeves were rolled up above the elbows. The man was nodding as he listened patiently to the woman at the counter.

The office was small, about ten feet by twenty feet. A waist high counter ran the length of the room; a quill pen, inkbottle, and parchment on top. Behind the counter were shelves that went from the floor to the ceiling. Wooden boxes of all shapes and sizes were squeezed onto the shelves. Most had names written on them, and some had cities of the realm identifying their points of origin.

"I cry all night just to give me something to do." The woman proclaimed. She was a large lady, far less then five feet tall with long black hair, and spoke in a loud voice. Novak and the others waited for her to finish.

"I see," the man behind the counter nodded and shot a glance at the trio who entered his office. "I don't know how I can help you."

The loud woman continued. "I think I scare people away. They're not used to someone who speaks their mind. I thought maybe you would know what to do. It's not easy when you have a twelve year old son."

The man behind the counter had a bewildered look in his eye. "I don't know how to explain this any better. I run a shipping business. I can't cut your son's hair. I'm sorry you spend your nights upset, but I can't help you. There are places you can get your son's hair cut, but not here." The man was being as polite as he could. The woman was bizarre. She obviously suffered from a condition that couldn't be explained solely by the odor of rum on her breath.

"Your sign says 'All business welcome, no job is too small.'" The woman complained.

The man was beside himself. "Lady…that means I'll haul a ship full of cargo, or just one package. I didn't think I had to specify it referred to shipping business."

"Well you should be clearer. " The woman spit vehemently and stormed from the office.

The man's jaw dropped. He watched her leave and shook his head. After a moment he turned his attention toward his potential customers. "How may I help you?"

"Hello, we are looking for the owner of J&R Shipping." Novak walked up to the counter.

"That would be me," the man held out his hand. "I'm Rex Baculum, one of the owners of this business. My brother Justin and I run things around here."

Novak shook hands with Rex. "I'm Novak Reinhardt, this is Emerald, and this is Dantes."

"Pleased to meet you all. How can I be of assistance?"

"Where do I start?" Novak thought a while. "I hope you are able to be of assistance to us in finding someone. A mutual friend thought you could help."

"What friend is that?" Rex inquired.

"Isaac Abrams."

Rex's eyes grew wide, and he came from behind the counter. He opened the door to his office and glanced around. He then locked the door and closed the shutters.

"How do you know Isaac?" Rex replied nervously, fumbling with the papers on the counter.

"Actually I don't," Novak admitted. "But I helped his friends in Xylor. They said Isaac was a friend of yours, and you would help us find someone." Novak wasn't one for beating around the bush, or speaking in delicate phrases and innuendos.

Fear and suspicion swept Rex's visage. "Uh, we may have corresponded a time or two, but, ah…I haven't been in contact recently." Rex was petrified. Sweat started to bead on his brow. People were killed for their association with Isaac. He eyed the door and regretted locking it. Surely he was finished. He had been linked to Isaac, and now the King's brigade sent the biggest goon they could find to kill him. But not before the looming gargantuan wrung all the information he could out of him. Rex clasped his hands on the counter, feeling his legs would soon buckle.

Novak scowled, knowing Rex was being less then fully truthful. But then he softened realizing Rex had gone pale. "I am here as a friend. I understand your apprehension. You do not know me, and yet I know about you. But you must believe me; I am not with the Kelterlanders or Reddland. We fight the same enemy. I know you and Isaac were very good friends, and you aided the rebellion by smuggling goods."

Dantes could tell Rex was having a hard time with the episode. "It be true matey. Novak and his friends be the ones who led the rebellion to victory in Xylor."

"Novak is a Clandestine Knight," Emerald added with pride.

"I never heard of the Clandestine Knights." Rex was unsure about the whole exchange. The good thing was no one threatened his safety yet.

"Well ye'll be hearing of them soon." Dantes replied.

Rex took some time to compose himself. "Assuming you are right, and I'm not saying that you are; how can I know you are not trying to trick me into trusting you?"

"Because if I was working for the Kelterlanders I would have already killed you."

Emerald elbowed Novak in the arm. "I'm sorry, what he meant to say was rather then taking time to explain who we are, if we were with Kelterland we would have just confirmed your identity and moved to the next stage of the interrogation. You must believe us. Thadus Raistlin is my father. Novak and his friends did lead the Xylorian rebellion to victory. Reddland is dead and no longer in power. Isaac was killed also. His son found letters from you among Isaac's possessions. My father didn't know there were others outside of Xylor who were interested in our cause, which as it turns out Novak, his friends, Dantes, and even you have in common. However, Isaac knew, and I now thank you on behalf of my father for your help through the years."

Emerald had Rex's attention and continued. "And now that is why we are before you here today; to further the cause we all have in common. It was decided Novak would come here to try and thwart the Kelterlanders before they have a chance to retaliate against Xylor. Isaac knew of a cadre of soldiers near Astoria who believed as we do. We thought if we found them we could organize some local resistance that would force the King's Brigades to stay here rather then sail for Xylor. For some reason, Isaac felt you would be able to direct us to the local resistance."

Emerald explained the situation tactfully. Now she too had committed a great taboo and spoke of rebellion against Kelterland, a crime punishable by death. She hoped it would put Rex at ease.

Rex took a moment to evaluate all he was hearing. "Well, you certainly seem to know a lot about Xylor. Few others would know the details of what you told me. You must be careful; talk of organizing resistance to Kelterland is enough to get you executed. I admit it is quite convincing. Nevertheless, there is one question I must ask before I will trust you. It is a question I am very sure that a Kelterlander agent would never be able to answer. For the blind can not answer what they do not see."

Novak looked to Dantes and Emerald. They both nodded for him to continue. "Alright, what is your question?" He didn't know where Rex was going with this, but didn't see much choice in the matter.

"Who is it you say the Lord is?" Rex asked.

Was this a trick question? The answer seemed too simple for Novak. There were several possible responses, all of which were correct.

"He is the only begotten Son of God, the Messiah, Immanuel; He is God among us." Novak stated with absolute conviction and certainty.

Rex smiled broadly and shook hands with his visitors again. "Welcome to Astoria. It is good to see others of the faith. Unfortunately we are few and far between in these parts."

Novak nodded his agreement. "Ya, but I hope that will change someday."

"And it is a pleasure to meet you," Rex added. "I heard about the victory in Xylor. It has sent a bolt of excitement and hope for the future through the circle of believers here in Astoria. We heard about the four strangers who appeared to assist the rebellion. It is an honor indeed to meet one of the four. You say you are called the Clandestine Knights; well it is a name I shall never forget."

"And someday the whole realm will be rid of the Reddland's," Novak vowed. "Today you can help us further that cause."

"Certainly," Rex was only too happy to be of assistance. "How can I help? Do you need something smuggled into Xylor?"

"No, we are looking for Barrington Rathbone. Isaac's letters led us to believe you might know how to contact him."

"Barrington is a good man. You will find him to be a valuable ally. But," a coy grin spread on Rex's lips, "Barrington is not one to be found. He will be the one who finds you."

"What do you mean?" Novak inquired.

"Barrington has been eluding capture now for several years. He and his men are known by the Kelterlanders as the 'phantom soldiers'. They are known for their ability to vanish into the woods. The king's brigades have been unable to find him; try though they might, it has all been in vain." Rex explained. "No Novak, your task will be getting Barrington to find you."

Novak furrowed his brow, puzzled. "Isn't Barrington at Stonebridge?"

"Sometimes," Rex replied. "But Stonebridge isn't on any map. Few know it even exists."

"Barrington sends one of his men here every few days or so to pick up supplies. One of his men is due to arrive later today in fact. I'll have him tell Barrington to be expecting you. In the mean time I'll give you directions to the general location of Stonebridge, but Barrington keeps the pass well guarded. I'm sure he will find you first." Rex drew a crude map on a parchment and handed it to Novak.

"Stonebridge is exactly that; an old stone bridge. Years ago there was a meandering trail from Astoria to Port Suffolk. It wound far north in order to cross the river at a narrow spot. A more efficient road that runs along the coast replaced it. The old trail became overgrown and forgotten, and has been reclaimed by the forest. The old stone bridge that crossed the river still stands to this day. So there, out in the middle of the woods for no reason, is this bridge. It is what is now known as Stonebridge. Barrington stages his men near there." Rex pointed out a detail on his crude map. "It is near here between where the river forks and then comes back together. If you find this place, I assure you Barrington will find you."

Novak studied the map. "Thank you. You have been a good help."

"No, no, no," Rex held up his hands. "Thank you. Few would risk their lives to help strangers. You are welcome anytime."

Novak, Emerald, and Dantes bid Rex farewell and started for the door. Novak turned one last time to Rex.

"Maybe we will see you again sometime."

"I'm sure you will Novak," Rex laughed. "I'm sure you will."

XII

MUFFLED SOBS ECHOED from behind the wooden door. Abrams paused before knocking, realizing this was a bad time to pay Iris a visit. She would probably want to be alone and he started to turn away.

And then Abrams heard it; that still small voice. You want me to talk to Iris now? At a time like this, Abrams thought to himself.

Abrams turned back to Iris's door. He was a man of prayer, and had been for many years now. He was very much aware of the leading of the Spirit. It was the same small voice, the unspoken feeling deep within that let all people know the difference between right and wrong. Most would hear the voice at least some of the time. Some ignored or rebelled against it for so long that for all practical purposes they were now deaf and without direction. Abrams regarded the Spirit as an old friend; one who was always there when he needed it. For that reason, Abrams knocked on the wooden door before him.

"Cyrus," Iris asked hopefully as she cracked the door ajar. Her eyes were bloodshot and tears streaked her face. She clutched a lacey white kerchief in her hand.

"Hello Iris, I'm sorry to disturb you, but it sounds like you could use a friend." Abrams spoke with the most soothing voice he could muster and smiled warmly.

Iris nodded in the affirmative and erupted with a sob. "Actually I could use a friendly ear right now Abrams, you have perfect timing."

God has perfect timing, Abrams thought to himself.

"Do you want to come in?" Iris opened the door and motioned to the chairs around her table.

Abrams spied the rustic bench on the small porch. "Let's have a seat out here. A little fresh air might do you a bit of good, even if it is moist with fog." Abrams also wanted to avoid the perceived impropriety of entering the residence of a single woman, especially one who was being courted by another man.

The two took a seat on the rustic bench. Abrams said nothing as Iris regained some composure and wiped her eyes. Her kerchief was damp with tears. She had been crying for some time. Abrams waited patiently for Iris to begin the conversation.

"Thank you Abrams, for coming by. I haven't known you long, but you really seem to care about people. I always see you at the orphanage, or visiting the soldiers, helping others out. It seems to keep you quite busy."

"It is my privilege Iris." Abrams smiled. "It is the least I can do for my fellow citizens; especially after many have done so much for me. The soldiers fought for my freedom as well as their own. The children are not to blame for being in a position of need. Many of them lost their parents; some even sacrificed their fathers in the rebel army. It is an honor to be in the ministry doing the Lord's work."

Abrams's words reassured Iris who didn't want to be a burden. She knew others had their own problems, many much worse then hers.

"So what seems to be on your mind?" Abrams realized he would have to coax her gently. "I may be able to help."

This was all Iris needed to hear. A flood of pent up troubles came pouring out.

"Oh Abrams, I just feel so terrible. Cyrus left…he didn't tell me where he was going, and I don't know if I'll ever see him again. I can't help feeling he doesn't want to see me anymore…that he regrets he started courting me in the first place. I know he's a good man…I think he thinks I'm not be good enough for him. I know I have a sordid past, and only recently became a Christian… I mean I have a son already and I've never been married. I just know I'm not good enough for Cyrus. Why he even stayed around this long is anybody's guess. I suppose I knew it would end some day, but I wasn't prepared for how bad I would feel. I tried to be the kind of woman Cyrus would want, but he deserves so much more. In fact I know I'm falling far short of what God expects of me also. I'll never be good enough to get into heaven. I've just done too many things in my past. I don't even know why I bothered in…" Iris began sobbing uncontrollably. She spoke so rapidly and on so many subjects that Abrams had a hard time keeping up with her. It took him a few seconds to sort through what she said to make sense of it all.

"Now let's take this one question at a time." Abrams spoke in a calm and caring tone. "Did Cyrus say he would return?"

"Yes, but…"

Abrams cut Iris off. "Did Cyrus say he no longer wanted to see you socially?"

"Well, no," Iris sobbed.

"Then let's not assume anything. I've known Cyrus for some time, and he has always been a man of his word. If he says he will return, then nothing short of death will keep him from his word." Abrams reassured Iris.

"If he never said he no longer wanted to see you socially, then let's not assume that. If he wanted to end the courtship he would have told you. In fact, it is my belief he cares for you deeply. Your past has nothing to do with who you are now. We have all done things in the past we wish we hadn't. We are humans. It is what you do from now on that's important. I see no reason why Cyrus would not want to see you anymore." Abrams counseled and waited for his words to sink in. It made sense to Iris. In fact Cyrus told her as much before he left. She was so overcome with grief she let her sorrow get away from her. Before she knew it she was wallowing in misery.

Iris wiped her eyes and again regained some composure. "Thank you, I guess I just needed to hear that from someone else."

Abrams smiled warmly. "I'm glad to be of help. There is just one thing that bothers me though."

"What?" Wonder shone in Iris's eyes.

"It's what you said at the end; the part about not being good enough to get into heaven." Abrams had a concerned tone in his voice.

Iris heart beat forcefully in her chest and a look of fear come to her face. "There's no hope for me to go to heaven is there?"

"On the contrary," Abrams was taken aback. It became painfully apparent that while Iris now believed very much in God, she still had no knowledge on how one can know they will some day go to heaven. "You do indeed have hope. We are all sinners. We have all fallen short of the glory of God. None of us really deserve to go to heaven. There is no good deed we can perform to earn our way there."

"Then how can we be saved?" Iris asked with great interest.

"That's the good news." Abrams continued. "God offers us all a gift. A gift is not earned, it is given freely."

Iris had a puzzled look on her face. "I don't understand."

Abrams explained further. "We are all sinners, Iris. Now don't get me wrong, those sins have to be paid for. We can pay for them ourselves; that means when we die we end up in hell. These Tanuba clerics won't tell you that. They want to hide the truth, but I'm your friend. I will tell you the truth." Iris didn't like the sound of that.

"Or," Abrams eyes lit up. "We can accept God's free gift and ask Jesus to pay for our sins. That is why he came. And that is how to go to heaven."

Abrams told Iris the greatest story ever told. "Paying for our sins wasn't easy. In fact it was bloody and painful. But that's what it took, for without the shedding of blood there is no remission of sins."

Abrams now held Iris's undivided attention. "Jesus was kidnapped in the middle of the night and beaten mercilessly. A sack was placed over His head and He was buffeted, punched, and beat terribly. When they took the sack off, His hair was matted with blood, His lips split, His eyes swollen almost shut, His nose flattened, His face completely disfigured; the Bible says 'His visage was so marred, more than any man.' And it gets worse."

"They whipped Him endlessly with a cat-o'-nine tails, over and over until they had reduced Jesus to raw meat, flogging the flesh from His bones. The Bible states 'I may tell all my bones, they look and stare upon me.' They beat Him with staves, they pulled His beard out, and they rammed needle sharp thorns down on His head. It still gets worse."

Abrams had a deep reverence in his voice as he related the story. "They forced Him to carry a heavy wooden cross to the place of his execution. The people scorned, and spat, and mocked him all the way. He had been beaten so badly that He fell down several times as He made His way through town. Each time He fell He would be beat and whipped back to his feet. Finally, even those carrying out the execution realized He couldn't go on. They forced a bystander to carry the cross the rest of the way. Eventually they came to a hill outside of town. They robbed Him of His clothes. Large iron spikes were hammered through His hands and feet. They lifted up the cross and slipped it into its mount. It landed with a thud and the force caused His shoulder's to dislocate; 'I am poured out like water, and all my bones are out of joint.' Hour after hour He suffered on the cross, pulling Himself up with his hands and pushing up with his feet in order to gasp a breath. All the while the mob cursed Him and laughed, enjoying their handiwork. Finally He died for us. 'Greater love hath no man then to lay down his life for his friends.' Why did Jesus do all of this?"

Abrams explained, tears now streaming from his cheeks. "To pay for our sins; the Bible says 'He was wounded for our transgressions, He was bruised for our iniquities: the chastisement of our peace was upon Him, and with His stripes we are healed.' So you see Iris, your sins have already been paid for; all you have to do is ask. 'For whosoever shall call on the name of the Lord shall be saved.' How do you get to heaven? Jesus said, 'I am the way, the truth, and the life: no man cometh unto the father but by me.' God loves you Iris. So much so that he gave his only begotten Son so that you may have eternal life in heaven. It is a gift. And like any other gift it is free. All you have to do is accept it. If I held out a gift right now, you would have to take it from my hand in order to receive it. In order to receive God's gift all you have to do is ask. Pray to God and ask. It's as simple as that Iris. That is the foundation of the Christian faith. The reason we try to be good or obey the rules as it were is out of gratitude for what has already been done for us, not to earn our way to heaven. That is why I do what I do. How can I not do something for God after what he has done for me?"

A light went on in Iris's eyes. For the first time it all made sense to her. She wasted no time in accepting God's offer. She was humble enough to know she needed it. She prayed the best she knew how. "Dear God, I know I have done a lot of things in the past that were wrong, and I ask for Jesus to pay for my sins. If he went through all that for me, accepting it is the least I can do. Amen."

Iris opened her eyes and looked at Abrams. She was crying again, this time out of joy. "Did I do alright? I'm not really used to praying."

Abrams nodded and wiped his tears. "Any sincere prayer from the heart is a good one."

"Thank you Abrams." Iris smiled for the first time that day. Then a disturbing thought occurred to her. "My son will be back this evening. Cyrus got him a job working in the stables. Promise me you will come back and tell him what you just told me."

"I would be more then happy to." Abrams rose from his seat and turned toward Iris. "And remember; don't assume the worst with Cyrus. All things will come to light in due season. There is a time and a purpose for all things. Though it is sometimes hard, we must all be patient as the Lord unfolds our future. He is trying to direct our path. We must follow His leading even if it seams unclear to us. That is the beginning of your faith Iris. Discerning the right path gets easier the more you grow. I'm here to help."

"Thank you once again." Iris smiled as Abrams took the path back to the road. She felt as if a huge weight had been lifted from her shoulders. She couldn't explain it. Though she was still upset about Cyrus's departure, she now had an inner joy and peace about it. For the first time she felt she would survive should she never see Cyrus again. It would break her heart, but she would recover somehow. This sure beat the emptiness that accompanied her with the Tanuba cult. Iris was truly embarking upon a new life. And after all that had happened over the last ten years; it sure felt good."

<hr />

The day passed uneventfully for Cad and Scorpyus. There had been no new attacks from the Valkyrie's, and no major troubles from disgruntled citizens. It had been almost too quiet. Cad couldn't escape the nagging feeling something was brewing, that this was nothing but the calm before the storm. To make matters worse, Scorpyus turned up no new intelligence as to the identity of the Valkyrie's. Somewhere in Xylor was the enemy. As far a Cad knew he had seen one unawares.

Cad went over the information in his head. He felt there was an informant within the rebel ranks. He and Scorpyus agreed to no longer share information, not even with Thadus. They didn't suspect Thadus, but didn't know if the possible informant would have contact with him. For now it had to be only between them. It was a burden of immeasurable consequence.

"Ay Scorp, anything new?" Cad waived his friend a few feet into the alley.

Scorpyus gave a pensive look. "I found out nothing that will end this nightmare, if that's what you mean. The day wasn't all in vain though."

Cad's interest was piqued. "Say on."

"Well, I went back to the cabin in the woods where I saw the woman bathing. I found a man dead in side. His throat was slit. There was no odor of lotus blossoms, and there was no marking of a swan, but it was definitely the work of a Valkyrie."

"It's like we expected then. The lady you saw has to be Lydia." Cad let out a whistle. "She has to be the leader of the bloody Valkyrie's mate. We know what she looks like! Of course finding her is another matter; especially since the blokes have been lying low all day."

"Really?" Scorpyus was amazed. The Valkyrie's hadn't paused in their subversive efforts since they started.

"They're blooming well on to us Scorp. What else can it be?" Cad shook his head, a look of futility in his eyes. "I know they're up to something. I think the blokes realize we know something and have decided to take it slower. I shall feel better when this is all behind us."

"Are we going ahead with your plan?" Scorpyus inquired. It sounded to him like Cad already made his decision.

Cad nodded in the affirmative. "I see no other choice."

"Very well." Scorpyus released a heavy sigh. He was ready to back Cad's plan all the way. "I also was able to find out more about this substance the Valkyrie's use; the white powdery stuff. It took half the day, but thank God it was not all in vain."

"Well done mate," Cad exclaimed. "What are we up against?" Scorpyus's knowledge of herbal remedies and alchemy had come through for the knights time and again. It reinforced that no matter how bleak things looked, the knights could always count on each other

"With the assistance of the local alchemist I was able to identify three individual ingredients in the Valkyrie poison. Each one could kill on its own. I guess they want to be sure." Scorpyus smirked and continued.

"Belladonna and Wolfsbane are the main ingredients. It is an old sorcerer's brew thought to make one able to fly if it is rubbed on the skin in ointment form. Taken internally, or inhaled as the Valkyrie's employ it, the stuff is highly poisonous, and produces an effect on people's mind. They may see things that aren't there, or think they are animals, or as in the case of the sorcerer's it could make one think they are flying like a bird. The alchemist knew of an old legend where it was believed that the Belladonna plant would actually transform into a beautiful lady in order to kill men. Wolfsbane has been used to poison arrow tips throughout the years."

Cad had a horrified look on his face.

"Just wait, it gets better." Scorpyus replied sarcastically. "The third ingredient is Bloodroot. It is one of the few plants that have a red bloodlike sap. The alchemist said it doesn't grow anywhere in the realm. He's only seen it twice before. This stuff will make you drool and foam at the mouth. It has also been known to distort a person's vision."

Scorpyus let out a deep sigh. "The poison starts working within seconds, and is very lethal. The odd thing is the Valkyrie's are poisoning people they intend to kill anyway. Other then the potential vision problems and delirium, the stuff really offers no advantage to the assassination. I'm telling you Cad, they probably only use this stuff to get a grotesque effect on the corpse."

"They're bloody freaks mate! This stuff is right out of the pit of hell." Cad was disgusted to think anyone would go to such lengths. The Valkyries were indeed a terrifying organization; one that had shown themselves exceptionally well versed in their trade.

"What do these daft blokes use the lotus blossoms for?" Cad asked.

"It serves no purpose other then to add scent to the concoction. I think it is their way of leaving their signature on their handiwork. Lotus is rumored to flourish in the Ethereal Region, usually in ponds or pools."

"What say we go deal with Algernon and be done with this day?" Cad was anxious to get some sleep. Before Scorpyus could answer, a voice called out.

"Scorpyus, Scorpyus, oh there you are." Natasha called from across the street. Her eyes lit up when she saw him standing with Cad.

"Natasha, what are you doing out after dark?" Scorpyus didn't want to see her fall to any harm.

"My word Natasha, the bruising around yours eyes is much worse today?" Cad was shocked to see her battered features again.

"She suffered a brutal beating most assuredly." Scorpyus answered for Natasha. "That is why I thought you were going to stay at the compound."

"I know Scorpyus, but I wanted to talk with you." Natasha smiled coyly. "I haven't seen you all day."

"I apologize, I know I said I would meet you today but honestly, it's been hectic and busy." Scorpyus replied sincerely and Cad nodded in concurrence.

"Do you have time now?" Natasha related bashfully not wanting to seem overbearing.

"I wish I could, but Cad and I are in the middle of something, and we have a meeting with Thadus later." Scorpyus was apologetic.

Disappointment resonated in Natasha's eyes. "Oh all right, I suppose I can wait. Isn't it late to be having a meeting with Thadus? I just came from the compound and the council chambers were all locked up and dark. Usually the staff will light some candles and prepare a fire in the fireplace."

"We're meeting in the compound stables, just us and Thadus. It a private meeting, informal… to discuss a personal matter."

"I suppose I can wait a little longer." Natasha's deep brown eyes gleamed with the hint of a smile. "But don't take too long. I must rise early to report to the kitchen to assist with the morning meal."

"I'll do what I can." Scorpyus didn't make any promises. "Now you get back to the compound where it's safe." Even though Natasha was carrying a dagger it provided little solace. Natasha was not a warrior, and the Valkyrie's were very skilled. She would stand no chance against one of the elusive assassins.

Cad watched Natasha walk back toward the compound. "I do believe the lass is taken with you Scorp. Any chance you may be feeling the same."

"I don't know what to think right now Cad. A lot has happened recently. I honestly don't know how I feel about much. I'm going along on instinct, and concentrating on our mission. That's part of the reason why I haven't had time to meet with Natasha. Truthfully, I'm avoiding it." Scorpyus stared out into the distance void of emotion.

Cad wasn't going to pry any further. "Well, let's see what this Algernon chap has to say."

Scorpyus and Cad made their way to the dilapidated wooden structure that passed for an inn. It was on the east side of Xylor away from the port. Residents of the inn were some of the poorest in Xylor. Algernon was even further down on his luck then them.

He was allowed to stay in a small tool shed on the property in exchange for laboring at menial tasks for the owner. Judging from the look of the place, none of his labor was used to maintain the premises.

"Candle light is flickering in the tool shed." Cad surveyed the surroundings. The shed was forty yards from the inn. A stone fence lay in a shambles around the property.

"He must be here. Let's see what he has to say."

Cad and Scorpyus went to the door of the shed and listened. Nothing could be heard save muffled laughter coming from the inn. Light flickered from underneath the poorly fitting door of the shed.

"Ready," Cad whispered. When Scorpyus nodded yes, he rammed the door open with his shoulder.

Cad and Scorpyus burst into the shed with weapons drawn, the door slamming against the wall with an enormous bang. Algernon had been sound sleep. He leapt from his cot, eyes bulging, and a confused look of fear on his face. Immediately he made a run for the door, not waiting to find out what was going on. Cad snatched him by the collar and forced the spindly youth back toward his cot. With a flick of his wrist, Cad shoved the lad into his cot with enough force to tip the cot over. Algernon tumbled across the floor in a heap.

"Sorry about that mate. We just want to ask a few questions."

"What do you want from me? I done nothing to you." Algernon was petrified. He was a painfully thin youth of about eighteen. He wore tattered brown pants and a burlap shirt. It looked like he made the shirt out of an old sack. The lad trembled so violently that his knees knocked together.

"We're not here to hurt you. We just have a few questions and then we'll leave. You have my word on that." Cad tried to reassure the youth.

"Please, I done nothing to any of you." Algernon proclaimed his innocence. He knew better then to get two well armed men angry with him.

"Relax, like my friend said we are not going to hurt you. We just want to talk to you about a meeting you had with a Braydon Mendax." Scorpyus replied.

Algernon shrank away from his interrogators and started to whimper. "I swear I didn't kill him. Please believe me. I never kilt anyone." The lad broke down sobbing, feeling certain he would be blamed for Braydon's death.

Algernon was a pitiful sight. The poor youth was buck toothed, and his left eye was crossed. His Adam's apple bobbed up and down in his spindly neck. He was in need of a bath, his dark brown hair was unkempt. He evoked a strong sense of mercy and compassion in Cad and Scorpyus.

Cad sheathed his weapon. "We know you didn't kill Braydon. I apologize for the way we barged in here, but we didn't know what kind of a bloke you were. Now we see you're a fine chap, a little misdirected, but not a killer. We just have a few questions." Cad extended his hand to Algernon and helped him up from the floor. Scorpyus sheathed his weapon as well, confident that Algernon was no threat.

Algernon calmed down a little, righted his cot, and wiped his eyes. He lips were barely able to close over his overbite.

"Why do you want to ask me questions?" The youth was still scared and leery.

"Because we know that you and Braydon knew each other mate."

"I'm not going to lie. I knew him." Algernon stared at Cad with his right eye, his left staring at his own nose.

"Did you 'retrieve' a letter for him?" Cad asked a delicately as possible.

Algernon flushed white. "I'm sorry mister. I didn't want to steal it. Braydon said he would pay me if I got it from this lady. I was hungry and didn't know what else to do."

"Well I can't condone stealing, not from any bloke, but that's not why we are here." Cad kneeled down to be at eye level with Algernon. "We want to have a look at that letter, that's all. Then we'll leave."

It sounded too good to be true to Algernon. Surely these armed men would kill him once they obtained the letter. Still Cad's statement seemed to be laced with hope for survival, and hope was the one thing Algernon had little of. Like a starving man, he found himself irresistibly drawn to the offer; even if it was only the hope of living another hopeless day.

"Do you mean it? You'll leave after looking at the letter?" Algernon's voice trembled.

Cad nodded. "You have my word."

The boy managed a faint smile and shoved two fingers into the top of his well-worn boots. He pulled out a rolled up piece of parchment and handed it to Cad.

Cad unrolled the letter. After being in Algernon's boot for some time, the parchment was very crumpled and damp with sweat. All that was left of the wax seal was a small red stain along one edge.

"Did you read it mate?" Cad asked curiously.

Algernon shook his head in the negative. "I done never learned how to read."

Pity welled up within Cad. Did this poor lad have anything going for him? "Where are your parents?"

"My ma died five years ago", Algernon recalled solemnly. "And I never knew my pa." He replied then looked at his feet ashamed.

Scorpyus placed a hand on Algernon's shoulder. "You have nothing to feel bad about. It's not your fault. My father abandoned my sister and me also. Just keep going. Don't give up. It'll get better." Scorpyus offered encouragement he wasn't quite sure he believed in at the moment. But he felt sympathy for Algernon's plight and wanted to help. Algernon smiled appreciatively.

Cad held the letter so Scorpyus could read it also.

My dearest Hugo,

I hope this letter finds you well, as it has been some time since I last saw you. All is well with me, though I miss you terribly. I long for the day of my return when I can once again feel your arms around me. This dreary detail should soon be over, and I should hope to find myself at our estate none too soon.

The peasants on this quaint little island have posed little trouble for us. I liken their intelligence to be just above that of a dog. Even the Trepanites pose a greater threat than these unfortunate dirges. The majority of the populace is content to sit on their nether portions and let a foolhardy few contend with the chaos we have visited upon them. It is a wonder that the Kelterlanders lost control of this island in the first place. There are few here who stand to fight, and those that do are no match for us. That is not to say our efforts have not been met with some difficulty. There is a quartet from Ravenshire who seem to have led the few victories this island has seen. If not for them we should have been on our way home. Though they are a credible force, it is nothing we can't overcome.

Sigurd and Hildr have learned rough lessons about overconfidence and underestimating a foe. And in all honesty, I must admit that one of their number is exceptional. I myself had a time eluding him, but in the end superior intellect ruled the day.

At any rate, thanks to my personal involvement, we were able to reduce their quartet to a trio. The female of the four proved to be more formidable then anticipated but never the less we were successful. And it is reported that another of the four has fled the island. I have been able to confirm his departure, but not his motives. He does not strike me as a coward so I must assume he has plans to return, possibly with additional forces. We shall have long vacated this island by the time he returns.

The remaining two from Ravenshire and the nefarious new leader should be dispatched with utmost certainty in the near future. The one fancies himself a strategist, but like his dark friend will fall short of the task. It is very fortunate that circumstance placed us to deal with this quartet now. I have little doubt that left unchecked; the four from Ravenshire would have amassed a formidable following. They and their friends allow a remarkable amount of freedom, and have managed to turn the island away from their native god. They may lack some support, but I see their popularity growing daily. Had we not eliminated this situation in Xylor now, I fear it would have grown until it was at our doorstep. And as you have always maintained Hugo, freedom in the wrong hands is dangerous. Combine that with a God who demands allegiance above kings, and disaster is afoot.

And now my dear I must bid thee well. My work here is nearing an end and I shall see you soon. I have one last 'interesting' development to look in to. It should not keep me here much longer. If all goes as planed, I should be home not long after this letter. Until I see you again my love, I will be counting the days.

Love always, Helga Vaagner

The letter was signed in a flourishing penmanship, a personnel signet stamp underneath. Cad turned the letter over. It was addressed to a Hugo Hellbourne. The day in Algernon's sweaty boot rendered the address illegible. The few letters in the city's name that were readable corresponded to no city Cad ever heard of before anyway. He slowly refolded the letter and glanced at Scorpyus.

Scorpyus's face twisted into an awkward grin, and Cad swallowed hard. The letter was an interesting intelligence find. Its contents left Cad and Scorpyus feeling uneasy; the same sort of feeling one would get upon returning home to find out they'd been burglarized. It was an eerie vulnerability to know someone had been watching that closely and become privy to some intimate details about your life. What else did Helga know and observe? The letter answered some questions, but raised many others.

"What do you think Scorp?" Cad asked.

"We know this Lydia's real name is Helga Vaagner. I don't know how that will help us now, but it certainly will at some point. It's good to hear we are worrying her a little, even though she still feels certain of victory. And that superior intellect bit…" Scorpyus laughed and shook his head.

Cad stroked his goatee. "She does sound a tad confident. Of course, that may very well work to our advantage. It raises more blooming questions then it answers. She appears to have a good take on the island, and on our activities. But most importantly; we know that it's us and Thadus the Valkyrie's came for."

Cad turned to Algernon. "Do you mind if we keep this letter mate?"

"Uh…" Algernon was hesitant.

"We'll pay you the three shillings Mendax promised you." Scorpyus retrieved the coins from the pouch on his belt and held them out to Algernon.

Disbelief washed over the young man's face. "How did you know…"

Cad cut him off. "We're trained professionals mate. Do we have a deal?"

Algernon snatched the money quickly, just in case the offer was repealed.

"And listen," Cad continued. "You seem like a decent bloke; stealing isn't the answer. You may find yourself in a spot of trouble if you keep doing it."

"You are associating with the wrong people." Scorpyus warned; "People who would kill you for little reason."

Algernon shrugged admittedly. "I know. I can't get a job. People just laugh at me because of the way I look. Sometimes I clean a stable or something, and the guy will cheat me out of my pay. The last guy said I was too stupid looking to handle money and just threw me a piece of bread. I can't see good enough to fight him."

Scorpyus turned beet red. He suffered the same treatment because of his gypsy heritage. "If you want a job, go to the compound tomorrow. If we're not there, tell them Scorpyus and Cad said to give you a job."

"That's right mate. Cad agreed. "We need the help. If you're willing to work, we can use you."

Algernon beamed. "Thank you. I promise you won't regret it."

Cad and Scorpyus stood and moved toward the door.

"There are empty beds in the barracks if you don't want to stay here anymore." Scorpyus shook Algernon's hand as he exited the shed.

"Thank you both," Algernon shook Cad's hand excitedly. "I won't forget what you done for me."

———— ·•·•· ————

"I think we'll be a bit late." Cad glanced up in a vain effort to find the moon. The fog continued to obscure all traces of things beyond twenty feet. Without the moon at night, gauging the passage of time was quite difficult.

"Yeah, the moon must have peaked by now." Scorpyus kept surveillance on the street ahead for anything unusual. There were a few more people milling about then there had been. There hadn't been a new killing all day, and already a few people were feeling bolder. Scorpyus shook his head in disbelief; how soon some people forget.

Cad and Scorpyus took long hurried strides toward the compound. They didn't want to keep Thadus waiting. They paused briefly to speak with the sentries at the portcullis. All had been quiet. There was nothing unusual to report. A patrol arrived a while ago, and a fresh one departed. A few brawls near the docks were all they encountered. There seemed to be far less happening now then on the typical night.

The lack of news didn't sit well with Cad. "It's too blooming quiet Scorp. Has the island gone daft as well? We know the Valkyrie's are planning something. Why are the rabble rousers behaving?"

"Are you complaining there isn't more trouble?" Scorpyus asked.

"It's been nonstop for the last…" Cad was cut short by shouting at the perimeter wall. "Let's go."

Scorpyus and Cad sprinted to the wall. They climbed the ladder to the parapet and found a sentry hunched over another who was sprawled on his back. Two more guards ran along the parapet to the same location.

"What happened?" Cad inquired.

"I came to relieve Franz from post and found him dead!" The sentry spoke in a fast shrill panicked tone.

Scorpyus knelt beside the fallen sentry. His throat had been slit nearly severing his head. He lay in a large pool of dark blood. "He hasn't been dead long; probably only a few minutes. His body is still warm, and the blood is very fluid."

"And nobody bloody well saw or heard anything? How can that be?" Anger resonated in Cad's voice.

Scorpyus inspected the area. There was no sign of someone using a rope or ladder to scale the wall. Both would be near impossible to utilize quietly, and undetected.

Scorpyus inspected the outer wall. The stones were precisely cut and fitted together tightly providing little in the way of finger holds. No one he knew could scale such a wall.

Cad questioned the two sentries that responded from nearby posts. Both looked to be in their late teens. "You two chaps didn't see a thing?"

"No sir, nothing," they replied in unison.

"Did you hear anything?"

"No sir."

"Did you come on duty at the same time as…Franz?"

"Yes sir we did," one sentry replied tearfully. "I'm sorry, we didn't see a thing. I don't know what happened. Franz was our friend. I can't believe he was killed and we didn't even know it."

Cad softened. The guards were young, but dependable. He knew they would second-guess themselves about this night forever. He didn't want to add to that burden.

"It's one of those shadow assassins, I just know it." The other guard trembled. "What else could it be?"

The guard voiced what Cad had been avoiding. "Now stay focused lads. Remember, these assassins are flesh and bone like you and me. We'll get them eventually."

Cad spoke with calm assurance and absolute confidence in what he was saying. The young guards held reservations about the matter, but nodded in agreement somewhat reassured.

"Hey Cad let's go!" Scorpyus exclaimed.

Cad looked over the parapet back inside the compound. Scorpyus climbed down from the wall and was waiving him down urgently. A soldier stood near by with an ashen face. "What is it?"

Scorpyus pointed to the soldier. "This man says he saw a shadowy figure running toward the stables."

Cad was horrified, his mouth agape. "Thadus!"

Cad scaled down from the parapet like a man on fire. Both he and Scorpyus ran towards the stables, their arms pumping frantically. Nearing the stables they drew their weapons and ripped the doors open with such force they slammed against the side of the building. Dim lantern light flickered inside. The two shot through the doorway, swords at the ready, and scanned the area. Thadus lay on the ground bleeding profusely, and moaning. A shadowy figure, barely visible in the dim light, sprinted for the back door to the corral.

Scorpyus bolted, anger burning across his face, hot on the heels of the fleeing Valkyrie. Cad ran to Thadus who cradled his midsection.

"Hang in their mate." Cad encouraged and tore open Thadus's shirt, and forced his arms out of the way. He had deep lacerations across his abdomen, his innards eviscerated. Thadus's intestines were bisected in several places, and a sizable chunk was cut from his liver. For all intensive purposes, he had been drawn and quartered. Cad knew there was nothing he could do for his friend.

Thadus clutched the sleeve of Cad's shirt with a blood soaked hand. His head trembled as he raised it from the sod floor, and his lips moved like he wanted to say something. Cad clasped Thadus's other hand and leaned down close to his face.

"I'm sorry mate. We failed you." Cad's face contorted in abject sorrow. His friend was dying; a friend that trusted him for protection. Tears forced their way from the corner of Cad's eyes against his will.

"Not…your…fault." Thadus words were throaty and labored. He swallowed hard. "You are…good friend." Thadus coughed. It caused him to grimace in pain and grip his midsection.

Cad's lips started to quiver. "I'm so sorry. If only we had been here earlier…" He took it hard. Cad was the leader, and the leader was always responsible. He wondered if there was anything he could have done differently that would have prevented the travesty.

The color left Thadus and his lips turned blue. "You freed… my people."

Cad looked on a friend he had been through a war with; a brother in the faith he had grown to respect; one that took a stand along side him for what was right. Friends like that don't come around too often. Especially ones that are willing to make the ultimate sacrifice.

"You freed your people Thadus." Cad's throat tightened in anguish. "You held onto the dream for all these years. Had you not done that; Reddland would still be in power. All of our help would have been blooming lost had it not been for your vision."

Thadus managed a faint smile, and then coughed up a blotch of blood. He gritted his bloodstained teeth and closed his eyes tight. Taking a deep breath he squeezed Cad's hand.

"Tell…Emerald I…love her." Thadus let out a terrible wheeze and wretched up a crimson froth.

"I will mate. You have my word. And we'll see to your island as well." Cad knew it wouldn't be long now. He had watched a few people die, and it never got any easier. A few hours ago all was fine. Neither one knew this would be the last day. Life was indeed a vapor; and you never knew when that vapor would vanish.

Thadus's breathing became more and more shallow. His face and lips were a sickly white. His body went limp, and he didn't seem to be feeling pain anymore. His arms fell from his midsection, cold and lifeless. Thadus stared at Cad, a peaceful look in his eyes.

Cad looked at his friend, tears streaming down his cheeks. He waved off the soldiers who appeared in the doorway. He didn't want a crowd gathered to watch their leader die; especially the new recruits.

Thadus would not slip off into eternity alone. Cad would stay with him. He tried to comfort Thadus as best he could, and lifted his head from the cold hard ground. But Cad felt so helpless. He could do nothing more but wait and watch his friend die. Cad looked Thadus in the eyes. "You'll be with God soon. Say hello to my father for me when you get there."

A gleam twinkled in Thadus's eyes, and then he took his last breath. A second later his brown eyes flushed a glassy gray, and stared up lifelessly. Cad removed a gauntlet, reached out, and closed Thadus's eyes. The next time he would see his friend, he would be walking streets of gold.

———◦—◦—◦———

Hatred boiled in her veins. It was hatred so strong she could almost taste the bile in her mouth. Her brow furrowed with so much disdain it felt her eyes would explode. She glared at the lone figure at the end of the alley; evil flashing in her eyes like bayonets. The figure was a man. She could tell he was apprehensive and unsure by his tired and shuffling posture. The man glanced nervously up and down the street before slipping into the alley and walking toward her location. He didn't even know she was there. He just walked, somehow forcing himself onward. She despised the man and everything he stood for. She knew the man placed his trust in a God she cared little for, a fantasy as far as she was concerned. Men like this made her sick; always on some self righteous and fanatical bent. And his kind didn't approve of her kind. As far as he was concerned, she was an abomination. It was that way of thought, that judgmental posturing that fueled her hate. She would show him who needed to be saved. His kind knew nothing about real power. Real power was in the here and now, not floating on a cloud. His kind was weak and deserved to be eradicated from the world.

As he walked toward her she entertained the thought of ripping his spine from the base of his skull. Or perhaps sinking her garrote deep into the flesh of his neck would be more suitable. His tongue would protrude out, vainly gulping for air that was not to come. He would have time to think about death as he watched it slowly close in around him like a dark ominous cloud. She smiled at the thought. She sighed. It was not to be. She would have to wait, for the moment anyway, and let him live.

The man was with the rebel occupational forces. She knew he was among the leaders of the rebellion. Her every instinct wanted to assassinate this man, but she contained her rage. She would hear him out before deciding his fate.

She silently watched the man approach to within three yards. "Step no further lest you die," a sultry whisper commanded unapologetically.

The man stopped. He glanced to the shadowy stairwell from which he heard the voice. He squinted into the dark chasm, unable to see the source of the voice.

"I came as agreed." A gravely voice belonging to Cyrus responded.

"So I see." The sultry whisper reeked of sarcasm.

"Are you going to meet me face to face, or am I going to talk to a stairwell." Cyrus peered into the shadows. The Valkyrie had to be close but he could see nothing.

"Speak your piece from where you now stand. My patience is waning."

"Not until I know who I am speaking with." Cyrus took a chance by standing firm. But he had to know for sure he was talking to a Valkyrie.

"Call me Lydia." The sultry voice spit, anger evident in her tone. "Your message better be good or you shall die where you stand. You are in no position to make demands of me. It is by my grace that you yet live."

Cyrus saw a shadowy head and shoulders momentarily appear in the stairwell and then vanish. He knew he had the Valkyrie's curiosity piqued. The Valkyrie would not have entertained his request otherwise.

"I want this to end; the killing; it's gone to far." Cyrus swallowed hard.

"You waste my time with a stupid request?"

Cyrus heard a dagger be drawn from its sheath. "Now hold on, hear me out. I believe you are here to kill only the leaders of the rebellion. I can help you with that. I just want the chaos to stop. I don't have the stomach for it anymore."

"Continue," Lydia sounded intrigued.

Though it was a cool night, Cyrus was sweating profusely. He was sickened by this whole episode, and yet felt he had no choice but to continue. "I can hand the remaining knight over to you."

"How will you do that?"

Cyrus continued. "That's my problem. I'll lead him to the northern most pier tomorrow at midnight. You have an ambush waiting. All I want is your word that you will leave Xylor once you have him."

"You will lead the three remaining mercenaries to the northern Pier?" Lydia questioned. She didn't bother requesting Thadus to be brought along also. If all went well with her colleague there would be no need for such a request.

"Only one remains," Cyrus furrowed his brow puzzled. "One has fled the island, the other left for a mission. He will have no need to return with his friends gone."

Lydia knew about Novak. She wanted to test Cyrus. "Are you claiming the dark one fled?"

"Yes, he was seriously wounded and went for treatment." Cyrus lied.

"Very well; you come alone with the remaining mercenary. If you come with any others, or I suspect a trap, the deal is off and you will be the first one killed."

"Agreed," Cyrus replied with a heavy heart. He took no pleasure in what he was doing, but felt it was in Xylor's best interests. "Just promise me you will leave Xylor never to return once this is done."

"You have my word. My order shall leave once the remaining rebel leader is dealt with. I make no promises in regard to reprisals from Kelterland. I do not relish the thought of staying on this island for one moment longer then I must. But I will warn you; for some reason the Kelterlanders treasure this island. The future of your people is far from secure. I can not speak of what may transpire in the years to come."

Cyrus remained silent in thought. He knew he had little reason to trust a Valkyrie. They were little more then reprobates, and without honor as far as he was concerned. Still he believed this action would buy Xylor the needed time to strengthen its forces. As long as the Valkyrie's remained, the island was in danger of anarchy. It was a gamble for sure. And for some reason he allowed himself to be talked into taking the chance.

"Very well," Cyrus released a deep breath, surrendered to this course of action. The idea gnawed at the pit of his gut. "Is there anything else?"

There was no answer from the stairwell. Cyrus inquired of Lydia two more times, and twice more he was met with no reply. Finally he carefully crept to the stairwell, and glanced down it. He could make out the stairs in the dim light cast from a nearby window. The stairwell was empty. A shudder ran down Cyrus's spine. The Valkyrie slipped off undetected. It was impossible. Cyrus shook his head and rubbed his eyes. The stairwell was still empty. Gloom filled his heart. He was stuck in a nightmare from which he could not awake. It was a nightmare for which dying might be the only way out.

XIII

DEATH WAS IMMINENT; either for Scorpyus or for the Valkyrie he was chasing. He could feel it deep in his bones. It was a familiar feeling, like wearing a pair of well-worn shoes. He had known it since he was a child and had long become accustomed to it. He could feel his pulse in his chest, and all his senses were piqued. A surge of energy coursed through his veins. That same sick feeling weighed like a stone in the pit of his stomach. The loss of appetite, the tinge of fear, the deadened sense of pain and exhaustion; they were present once again. Scorpyus's dark eyes locked on his enemy from beneath arched eyebrows. His jaw clenched tight with determination. As far as he knew, this Valkyrie killed Thadus. The Valkyrie represented all that had gone wrong in the last few weeks. The disappearance of Zephyr, the attempts on his life, the killing of several fellow soldiers, all of his current misery was placed on the Valkyrie. And one way or another it would end tonight.

The Valkyrie ran for the northern trail, which would take it straight into the thick woods. The shadowy assassin pumped its arms furiously, trying to put some distance between itself and its pursuer. And it tried everything; tearing through bushes, and weaving around trees and over rocks like a deer. But each time it looked back its dark pursuer was still there.

Scorpyus hung back on purpose hoping to tire out his prey. It was becoming apparent the Valkyrie had as much stamina and endurance as he did; maybe even more. He pondered starting the inevitable battle.

Scorpyus said a quick prayer and prepared to let loose with a burst of speed he hoped would close the distance between him and his enemy. Before he could do so the Valkyrie darted around the trunk of a huge tree. Fortunately for him, Scorpyus instinctively swung wide around the same tree. Waiting around the trunk was the Valkyrie, crouched with a dagger in its hand. It lashed at Scorpyus as he rounded the tree missing him by inches. Scorpyus pulled his sword. The Valkyrie dove at him. Scorpyus side stepped and brought his sword down hard towards the hand holding the dagger.

With incredible speed, the Valkyrie danced out of the way and delivered a kick to Scorpyus's ribs. He doubled over, pain radiating through his whole side. Shadowy feet moved to his right. Quickly he swung his sword at waist level in the direction of the feet. The Valkyrie dodged the blade by falling to the ground. Scorpyus's sword cut swiftly through the air where the shadow once stood. The Valkyrie flipped to its side and swung a leg swiftly at the back of Scorpyus ankles. The move swept him from his feet. He landed flat on his back, his sword clattering out of reach.

The Valkyrie lunged atop Scorpyus with its dagger at the ready. It thrust the blade toward Scorpyus's throat. Scorpyus jerked to the side and the dagger sunk deep into the earth. He latched onto the wrist that held the dagger and twisted it away from his head. Instead of resisting, the Valkyrie gripped Scorpyus by the tabard with its free hand and rolled. The two combatants toppled in a tangle of limbs, locked in a duel to the death. The two rolled against a tree and stopped, the Valkyrie on top. Scorpyus brought his forearm up hard against the Valkyrie's chin. He heard teeth crack together like a dog snapping for a bone.

The Valkyrie released Scorpyus's tabard and clawed at his face. Dull fingernails dug shallow trenches along his right cheek. He brought his forearm up against the Valkyrie's chin again. There was another snapping of teeth, this time with a grunt of pain. Scorpyus felt a small drop on his lip, then another on the bridge of his nose. A few more drops sprinkled on his face. The Valkyrie must have had the tip of its tongue between its teeth before that last blow.

The Valkyrie brought its head down hard. Scorpyus saw the black veiled face coming down and tried to move out of the way. He jerked his head toward the tree hitting an exposed root. The Valkyrie's forehead smashed against his left eyebrow. A warm trickle flowed down Scorpyus's head into his hair. The black veiled face came down again. He reached his hand up to block the blow gripping at the mesh mask that the Valkyrie wore. It felt like cheesecloth to the touch, and he could feel the features of a face; nose, eyes, mouth, and chin. Blood oozed from the mouth. Scorpyus deflected the blow, but felt a sharp pain to the palm of his hand near his thumb. Agonizing pain shot through his hand. He wanted to pry the Valkyrie's teeth from his right hand with his left, but didn't dare release his hold on the wrist with the dagger.

The Valkyrie tried to twist its dagger free of Scorpyus grasp, and continued to bite down with all its might. Gnarled tree roots pressed into Scorpyus's back. With the heel of his thumb firmly between the Valkyrie's teeth, Scorpyus curled his fingers down and felt for eye sockets through the black cheesecloth mask. He drove his fingers into the Valkyrie's eyes. He didn't have a lot of leverage, but could tell he was inflicting pain.

Scorpyus's hand was throbbing tremendously. Putting the pain aside, he mustered all of his strength, gripped tightly his opponent's eye sockets, and whipped the Valkyrie's head toward the tree with everything he had. There was a sound like an axe handle hitting a log. Suddenly, Scorpyus's hand was free from the Valkyrie's jaws.

The Valkyrie froze, momentarily dazed. It had bit a hole through its mask the size of its mouth. Scorpyus could vaguely see part of a bottom lip and bloody teeth through the hole. He took advantage of the brief lull in the fighting, and threw the Valkyrie from off him. He sprang to his feet and drew his own dagger. Though somewhat dazed, the Valkyrie leapt to its feet before Scorpyus could go in for the kill. The two crouched facing each other, daggers at the ready.

Scorpyus wiped his sweaty hair back and circled his opponent looking for an opening. The Valkyrie tried to shake its daze and circled defensively. Scorpyus lunged swiping his blade at the shadowy figure. It wasn't moving as fast as it did before. Though it took a step back, Scorpyus caught the Valkyrie across the left shoulder. A slit appeared in his opponent's sleeve. The Valkyrie let out a gasp. The wound seemed to help it refocus on the battle.

In a flurry of swings and swipes, the Valkyrie attacked with a vengeance. Nothing encouraged a fight more then the desperation of death knocking on your door.

Scorpyus hopped, stepped and dodged the flurry with a speed fueled by sheer terror. It was as if the Valkyrie got a second wind. It relentlessly attacked forcing Scorpyus to retreat. All of Scorpyus's concentration was now focused on avoiding the swiping blade that came at him from all angles.

The Valkyrie felt a surge of confidence as Scorpyus backed up further and further. It slashed its blade for Scorpyus's throat. Slash after slash of the blade searched for flesh, as the Valkyrie pressed on with lightning speed, urgent to end this exchange once and for all. Scorpyus dodged and ducked as he yielded ground a step at a time.

Scorpyus groped with one hand behind him, blindly feeling his way while keeping his attention on the blurred implement of death flashing about his body. He backed into a bush, momentarily trapped. He sidestepped several angry swipes of the Valkyrie dagger, bits of severed twigs and foliage flying through the air from every spot he had just been. Fear was starting to take hold and the Valkyrie sensed it. Like a dog frothing at the mouth with excitement over an impending kill, the Valkyrie was in an euphoric frenzy.

Scorpyus grew weary trying to stay focused on the lightning blade. It took every ounce of his concentration. He felt several violent tugs through his tabard and knew the blade was getting dangerously close. One of the tugs was accompanied by a burning stinging sensation across his abdomen. Anger started to build in Scorpyus. Was there no way around or through this stupid bush? He couldn't believe one God forsaken shrub would be the end of him.

The Valkyrie blade continued to hack away bits and pieces of foliage all around Scorpyus like a demented barber. And it made him angrier. He was angry he allowed himself to be put so hopelessly on the defensive. He was angry he couldn't come up with a plan. All he could do was shimmy back and forth along a hedge, clutching a dagger that at the moment was doing him little good.

Scorpyus felt a sharp pain on his left shoulder. The Valkyrie blade kept slicing away. Scorpyus had enough. The Valkyrie slashed to his left, and he ran to his right for all he was worth. It meant running blind without knowing what obstacles lay ahead. If Scorpyus tripped and fell it would be over.

Scorpyus kept a hand along the hedge for some guidance. He had only gone ten yards when he felt the roots of a tree underfoot. Suddenly an idea came to mind. Quickly he ran a few more steps until he felt a tree trunk. The Valkyrie was right behind him. Scorpyus put his back to the tree and waited clearly tired, panting with his heart racing. He deliberately waited too long and knew an attacking blow was imminent. Without hesitation the Valkyrie stabbed for Scorpyus, thrusting its dagger into his abdomen. Mustering one final burst of energy, Scorpyus snapped sideways and threw his hips backward. The enemy dagger shot right by his abdomen slashing through his tabard. Like the bolt of a crossbow it struck the tree with a dull thud, sinking several inches into it. It bought Scorpyus the two seconds he needed.

The Valkyrie jerked on its dagger in order to dislodge it from the tree. Only the dagger didn't budge. The dagger would have to be worked up and down in order to dislodge it from the tree, and that would take valuable seconds.

A gasp escaped the Valkyrie realized the situation, but it was too late. With a roar, Scorpyus thrust his dagger into the solar plexus of the Valkyrie. A grunt escaped his shadowy opponent. Scorpyus was overcome with anger and revenge. He twisted his blade and thrust it in two more times. The Valkyrie groaned and reached falteringly toward Scorpyus to push him away.

In a frenzy of hatred, Scorpyus stabbed repeatedly at his opponent, the opponent that caused him so much grief. He thought only of Zephyr, the lost patrol, and the countless others who had been butchered by the damnable assassin. It would be a pleasure to rid the world of a Valkyrie.

The Valkyrie slipped to the ground, but Scorpyus wasn't through. He dropped hammering his dagger down into his fallen opponent. With each thrust he let out an anguished cry, the Valkyrie bearing the brunt of all that had gone wrong in his life. The shadowy assassin would pay for all the wrongs done to a small boy many years ago. The Valkyrie didn't abandon Scorpyus as a child, nor did it kill his family, but it would pay for those atrocities nonetheless.

Finally, dripping with the Valkyrie's blood and near exhaustion, Scorpyus stopped ramming his dagger into his opponent's body. The Valkyrie wasn't moving but was making a faint gurgling sound. Scorpyus stared on its limp shadowy form, satisfied in his work. He paused as he knelt near his beaten opponent to reflect on the conflict. What started as the thrill of victory turned strangely odd. The victory took on a sour hue. Scorpyus stared at his blood soaked hand and dagger; the dagger he had been awarded for being a hero. For some reason he didn't feel like a hero. Killing the Valkyrie was a good thing wasn't it? Scorpyus rationalized logically that indeed it was. Then why did he feel strange?

He looked at the Valkyrie as it wallowed in a pool of blood. Maybe stabbing it so many times was excessive. But it deserved it right? Scorpyus thought back to all the killings that happened in Xylor, and to Zephyr. Surely he didn't do anything wrong.

Scorpyus wiped his dagger on the Valkyrie's pant leg and sheathed it. The slumped figure made a sound like it was trying to talk. It took Scorpyus by surprise. How could the assassin be alive still?

"*Let's see what a Valkyrie looks like underneath the hood.*" Scorpyus reached for his opponent's mask. With a jerk he removed it from the mortally wounded Valkyrie.

All the blood drained from Scorpyus's face, and his throat closed tight stifling a shocking gasp. His lips started to quiver, and tears welled up and spilled down his cheeks. Nausea washed over his body. Deep agonizing sobs built up deep within his chest like the rumblings of a volcano. This was a nightmare he knew he could not wake from.

Scorpyus stared at the unveiled Valkyrie through teary eyes. He shook his head in disbelief. "Why Natasha, why?"

Natasha could only stare up at him through fading eyes. Her lips moved but no sound came forth. She lingered a few seconds and then passed to her chosen destiny.

Scorpyus sobbed uncontrollably. All this time Natasha was a Valkyrie and he didn't even suspect it. How could he have been so blind? His mind raced through a series of brief recollections. Like a cloud morphing into an image, the puzzle started coming together. Cad was right; someone was leaking information to the Valkyrie's.

Scorpyus recalled Natasha's tale of how she was roughed by dockside miscreants. That was the day after he fought a Valkyrie at Hester's cabin. The whole episode began to make more sense. He was closer to the truth then he realized. Natasha turned up at all the right moments almost as if she had been watching his every move. He had been responsible for the beating Natasha wore on her face. She was the Valkyrie outside the cabin door. It was Natasha he chased into the woods. But it was the other Valkyrie, Lydia that he ended up following.

"Noooo!" Scorpyus's voice echoed through the trees bringing all the chattering birds to a momentary silence. How could he not have seen it?

Sorrow and anger swirled in a dizzying, stifling agony he could feel to the pits of his soul. The undetected espionage and betrayal of Natasha, the vanishing of Zephyr, and the stress and fatigue of the battle all combined to bring Scorpyus to a place he had not been since his family was brutalized before his eyes.

Scorpyus had let feelings for Natasha cloud his judgment; feelings that he knew would pass like they always did before. He would never let personal feeling interfere again.

Then he remembered the letter Hester gave him, and thought of Zephyr. "*If one should find a winter rose, don't let it slip away.*"

A stabbing pain shot through Scorpyus's chest. Mixed emotions tore at each other. Personal relations did not mix with war. Decisions made during turmoil often later proved to be mistakes. Then again, some things could feel so right.

Scorpyus was in no condition to make decisions, and life as a knight looked to be a hard journey that wasn't soon to be over. He wanted to quit but knew he wouldn't. If nothing else, the Clandestine Knights had loyalty.

'And we know that all things work together for good to them that love God, to them who are called according to His purpose.'

Scorpyus believed that scripture even though he could see no light at the end of this tunnel. He collapsed to the ground, gritting his teeth and digging his fingers into the pine needle blanketed earth. War had already robbed his childhood, and it was still poised to rob his whole life. Agony spilled from Scorpyus like a kettle on the boil. Why was he born in this miserable time? Why was he involved in this miserable conflict? Were there no others to fight against evil? Why ask four that had already been through so much? The cost was more than any one, or four could bear.

Scorpyus raised his head from the cold damp dirt and glanced over at Natasha's corpse. She was a bloody mutilated mess. He had already won the fight. The extra twenty or thirty stabs of the blade were nothing more then bitter revenge rearing its wicked head. The Clandestine Knights were supposed to be better then the Reddland's of the world. And Scorpyus acted just like one. That's not how it was supposed to be, not for a knight anyway.

Scorpyus pulled himself from the ground, burdened and heavyhearted. The last five minutes numbed him so much he now felt nothing. Mechanically he set about the task of returning to town. He would take Natasha's body back for burial. Emotionally drained, and in a zombie like stupor he completed the grizzly task, feeling like a stranger in his own life.

———•◦•———

Cad starred into the distance and studied the figure straggling into town. The man led a horse up the street, a sizable bundle on its back. He was in no particular hurry.

Cad released a deep sigh when he recognized the figure as Scorpyus. He had been nervously waiting his friends return with stomach churning anticipation. Immediately he set off to meet his cohort.

As Cad drew near he could tell the bundle on the horse's back was a corpse wrapped in a blanket. The blanket, as well as the mount was soaked with blood. Heavy crimson drops dripped to the street periodically as the horse plugged along.

Scorpyus saw Cad approach, and couldn't even manage a half-hearted smile. He was feeling peculiar, like he was observing himself from a parallax view. A hand grasped the rein of the horse near the bridle, and led it along the street. Scorpyus recognize it as his hand, but felt separated from it somehow. Breath appeared in the cool air in his field of vision coming from the horse's nostrils. It was both close and distant simultaneously. He felt like he was drifting through the air toward Cad though his feet were actually propelling him. He heard his heartbeat in his ears. All else was strangely silent. Cad walked toward him, his metal greaves and boots making no sound. Scorpyus stopped. He felt a tug at his shoulder as the hand on the horses bridle brought the mount to a halt.

"Bloody ay mate! You're a welcome sight. You were starting to get me worried." Cad glanced at the bundle tied over the mounts back. "I take it this chap is the Valkyrie?"

Scorpyus nodded in the affirmative as three soldiers rushed over curiously to get the news on what happened. "I brought her back for burial."

Cad could tell something was bothering his fried tremendously. He looked to the three soldiers. "Give the Valkyrie a proper burial." The three soldiers started untying the corpse from the horse immediately.

"Are you alright mate?" Cad had a concerned tone.

Scorpyus shrugged his shoulders. "I just want to take a bath...and get this blood off of me." His voice cracked as he spoke.

"Good job Scorpyus! You hacked this Valkyrie to pieces!" One of the soldiers proclaimed after he unraveled the corpse from the blanket.

"That's all they deserve." Another soldier added. "It's better then they gave others."

Scorpyus turned away at the comments, a pained look in his face.

"What is it Scorp?" Cad placed a hand on his friends shoulder.

"You were right Cad." Scorpyus swallowed hard. "There was a traitor among us. This Valkyrie is Natasha."

Cad's jaw dropped, and he looked over to where the soldiers unwrapped the body. The lifeless eyes of Natasha starred blankly back at him.

Cad was rendered speechless. "I…uh, well…the…" The prospect was utterly dumbfounding, but given thought made unfortunate and bitter sense. Harsh realities stepped from the shadows to full illumination.

"So, Natasha killed Thadus?" Cad knew he was speaking truth but still couldn't believe it. Maybe if he said it over and over in his head it would sink in.

Scorpyus grunted. "Uh, huh; and I'm the one who told her Thadus was waiting in the stables, and she knew we would be late for our meeting. She knew Thadus would be alone."

"Bloody ay!" Cad pounded his fist into his palm. "We've been played for daft blokes." Cad rehashed the previous week's events. Was there anything else he missed?

Cad stroked his beard in thought. One traitor had already infiltrated the rebel government. There could very well be another. Various faces scrolled through Cad's mind. Each was evaluated as a potential threat. Though he had a few suspicions, there was nothing firm enough to act upon.

"Until this is behind us, you are the only one I can trust Scorp." Cad had a defeated tone in his voice.

"The way I feel right now," Scorpyus let out a deep sigh. "I don't know if I can even trust myself. Let's just pray your plan will work."

Cad wasn't comforted. "If I'm wrong, it could mean the blooming end."

"We've all placed our lives in the fate of your strategies before Cad. And you haven't let us down yet. It is your gift. We trust you. If it means the end; so be it." If anyone could think of a way out of this mess, it was Cad.

Cad knew his plan was tremendously risky. Now it was too late to turn back. "It's in God's hands now. I guess it's always been."

Both would have to have faith that everything would work out according to a higher purpose. Perhaps it was God's way to keep the Clandestine Knights humble and faithful. For only by facing the impossible would it strengthen their faith. It had seen them through many dark times already.

There was noting to do now but wait. The two friends parted ways for the time being. Scorpyus went to get a bath. Cad watched his comrade walk into the gates of the compound. He knew his friend was going through a very difficult time. He couldn't even imagine how the betrayal by Natasha was affecting him.

Cad motioned to one of the three soldiers. "Do me a favor. Let the other two handle the burial. Go find Abrams. Ask if he could drop by the baths."

The soldier nodded and set off on his orders, relieved to be excused from the burial detail. It was a gruesome task for which he had little enthusiasm.

Scorpyus sat submerged in a large wooden tub that looked more like an oversize barrel then a proper bath. He rested his head against the rim, a rolled up towel draped as a makeshift pillow. On a nearby shelf were a weathered brush, rag, soap and a dagger. His sword hung from a nearby hook. The tub was filled with hot water. It felt good on Scorpyus's aching body, and filled the tiny room with a humid thick-aired vapor. Moisture clung to the stone walls giving them a sweaty appearance. A hot bath was a rare luxury for Scorpyus, and sure beat the frigid waters of the creek. He had just settled back and closed his eyes when he heard a knock at the door.

"Who is it?" Scorpyus opened his eyes, looking toward the heavy wooden door.

"It's me, Abrams," a muffled voice responded.

"Enter."

The door creaked open and Abrams's peeked inside. He saw Scorpyus's head sticking above the water, his wet hair slicked back. A burst of hot moist air filled Abrams's nostrils.

"It is quite hot in here." Abrams walked the few feet to the tub.

Scorpyus readily nodded in agreement. "The attendant must have boiled the water. It took me half an hour before I could even get in." Scorpyus hand emerged from the water, his dagger in his grasp. He placed it back into its sheath.

"You can't be too careful." He explained.

Abrams smiled in understanding and took a seat on a rickety stool. He noticed that Scorpyus's water was tinged pink. A puzzled look graced his brow.

Scorpyus held up his hands and inspected them. "I've washed all the blood off, but I still don't feel clean."

Abrams smiled empathically. He heard about Natasha, and all that transpired. He dropped everything and came as soon as he heard. He made no reply, waiting for Scorpyus to continue when he felt up to it.

Scorpyus looked closely at his fingers. By now the blood had even been washed out of the fine lines of his fingertips. He took in a deep breath and exhaled slowly. The whole ordeal sunk in. War and death invaded Scorpyus's life when he was eleven, and never had the courtesy to leave. Though he was used to it, this time was different. He couldn't shake the feeling eating away at him. It forced him into some rather difficult soul searching. Questions were raised for which he had no answers.

After a long silence Scorpyus spoke again. "I don't think I should be a knight anymore."

The bluntness of the statement hit Abrams like a charging steed. It was the last thing he expected to hear. He masked his shock as best he could.

"Why do you feel that way?"

Scorpyus looked Abrams directly in the eye. "Do you know what happened?"

"I think so."

"Let me ask you a question then," Scorpyus had a serious tone in his voice. "Do you think God would feel I went too far?"

Abrams chose his words carefully. "Do you mean in regards to the Valkyrie?" When Scorpyus nodded in the affirmative Abrams continued.

"In that case no; no I don't think you went too far. The Valkyrie's have shed much blood in the short time they have been terrorizing the island. Most of their victims have been innocent civilians. They are the worst kind of villains; they are ones who kill indiscriminately. Nearly one hundred people lost their lives to the Valkyrie's, most in a brutal and gruesome manner. While the assassination of Thadus was a reprehensible and cowardly act, at least it was directed at the rebellion. But most were killed for no other reason than to induce terror. No Scorpyus, be not deceived; the Valkyrie's are murderers. 'He who sheds a man's blood; by man shall his blood be shed.' Sometimes evil goes unpunished. This time it didn't."

Scorpyus listened intently to Abrams's explanation, unblinking and taking it in like a soul starved for wisdom. His silence begged further response.

Abrams continued. "And that's the difference between evil and good. Sometimes it is necessary for good people to take a life. For the liberation of a brutalized and forlorn people, for defense against an aggressor, or for the protection of those who can't protect themselves. Good people sometimes must kill in order to bring about and maintain the common good. This war is a good example. Of course God never intended for man to kill each other. But in His foreknowledge He knew that mankind had a propensity for wickedness and planned accordingly. Once someone has transgressed another to the point of bloodshed, God has endorsed retribution. He even endorsed wars in millennia past. That's because God can see the end of days and knows what a nation will do in the future. At times even mankind can see that. We all know that if left unchecked, Kelterland will subjugate the entire realm and impose a brutal and harsh government on all. We know that many lives will be lost, that justice will be perverted, and that the rule of law will not be applied equally. We have had a taste of that already. Our children have been murdered, our women have been raped, and our freedoms have been stripped. Torture and killing are a way to maintain power. All of this is reason enough for war. And without the reasons I have said, as soon as the Kelterlanders forbade us to follow God, we were then obligated to disobey. Sometimes, that alone will constitute a war; especially when the powers that be choose to kill those who do not follow the directive."

Scorpyus took it all in, but still maintained a troubled countenance. "I can agree with what you said, but…I just…"

Abrams thought he knew where Scorpyus was headed. "Don't be deceived. There are those who would have the audacity to compare us to the Kelterlanders or the Valkyrie's, citing the killing the rebel army has done as evidence that we are no better. They would blur the lines between good and evil, if not reverse the two all together. Some may naively think if you treat an evil man with goodness he will eventually feel bad and return your kindness. We both know some men are so evil; the only thing they will understand is a sword. But let me tell you this Scorpyus, there is a difference between them and us. We are fighting for the cause of good. It is they who fight for the furtherance of evil. In an ideal world there would be perpetual peace. Sometimes peace is only found after searching through war. But as long as mankind has a sin nature, we will never have a lasting peace, and history repeats itself. Remember, it is they who have chosen war as a way to advance themselves. We were left with no choice. It is they who revel in the bloodshed and misery, and profit of war. We take no pleasure in any of that. You did what you had to do to survive. You didn't enjoy it."

Abrams waxed eloquently, his dialogue logical and filled with Biblical truth. He fully expected Scorpyus's composure to improve, but instead upon hearing the end of the dialogue, sorrow filled Scorpyus's eyes and he turned away from Abrams.

"That's the problem," emotion was thick in Scorpyus's voice. "What if I did enjoy it…killing the Valkyrie."

Scorpyus voice cracked and he splashed water on his face. "It turned out to be Natasha. I wish I had…" His voice trailed off, and he mumbled something about soap in his eye.

A sickly silence hung in the thick dank air. Scorpyus leaned back in the bath and closed his eyes. Abrams watched a bead of water trickle down the slick stone wall. It streaked a jagged path through other droplets, gaining in size as it weaved to the floor. It slipped into the crack where the wall and floor came together, and began its long journey toward the sea.

"I didn't know." Abrams wondered what else he didn't know.

Scorpyus opened his eyes but kept his head rested on the folded towel.

Abrams thoroughly searched for the right words before speaking again. "I understand how you may feel terrible. I also understand how one could feel incredible wrath against another. Watching Malvagio mistreat our wounded at the Oratory taught me about the depths of my own wrath. I'm not here to tell you how you should feel about this, or to judge what you did as right or wrong. Only those who have been faced with such life and death situations can make such a judgment. I have, however, made one observation. You obviously feel remorse. And that Scorpyus is what separates you from them. True repentance is the key to true faith. We are mere mortals, and we will make mistakes.

How we deal with them marks us as Christians. God forgave you at the moment of your salvation. Whether or not you forgive yourself will dictate how you feel tomorrow. And that my friend is the hardest part."

Scorpyus managed a very faint and brief grin. "After all that's happened, a part of me wonders why God didn't let me die long ago. There have been many opportunities."

"Scorpyus, you and your friends have been called to do what you do. Few people can boast of such a plain and stark realization of what their destiny should be. You and your friends have been prepared from birth for such a time as this. You are in service to the King of kings, and you still have work to do; work that only you can accomplish. Thadus's work here on earth must have been done. I don't understand why he had to go, but it was for a reason. I just know that God has it all figured out, and will not forsake us now, no matter how bleak it may look. Everything happens for a purpose according to His will. If we are still here, then there is a purpose for it. Your purpose is clearer then most. Generally, the greater the calling, the greater the difficulty."

Scorpyus shrugged his shoulders. "After today, I wonder if it matters."

Abrams contemplated Scorpyus's last statement deeply. A part of him had to agree. Life was but a vapor in the grand expanse of eternity. In that regard all was vanity. But on the other hand, everything mattered. Each action or omission to act held its own consequence. Not one sparrow fell to the ground without God's knowledge. He even had every hair on Abrams's head numbered. Unfortunately with his receding hairline, Abrams had been making it a lot easier for God to keep track. He smiled at the thought, and then remembered a story.

"There was a father who took his only son and his son's best friend fishing. The father was a faithful Christian as was his son. The son's friend was not. On the day they went fishing everything started out fine. The weather was beautiful, not too hot and not too cold. They rowed their small boat far out to sea and were enjoying the beauty of the water, and some of the best fishing the three ever experienced. The day had been filled with laughter, conversation, and the bond between father and son was stronger then ever. Both were happy to share the experience with the son's friend who recently lost his mother. Suddenly all this changed. The first hint something was wrong was a noticeable drop in the air temperature. It soon grew cold, and the wind started picking up. Before long, the three realized they would be caught in a terrible storm. Immediately the father decided to head the small boat toward shore. All three rowed furiously. But the storm grew swiftly and before long the wind raged furiously. Waves tossed the small boat, and rain pelted the three frightened occupants of the vessel. Still with the shore in sight, the three paddled valiantly, desperate to make it to solid ground. They realized it was now a fight for their lives."

Abrams held Scorpyus in rapt attention. "Then the situation took another turn. The storm capsized the small vessel. All three were tossed into the angry sea. The father found himself close to the capsized boat and clung on for his life. Frantically he searched for his son and his son's friend. Through the din of the storm he heard the cry of the two boys. Squinting through the blinding rain he located the two boys. They were several yards from each other but still within range of the boat's docking rope. Each was barely able to keep afloat and struggling against the waves that carried them farther and farther away from their only hope for rescue. The father grabbed the docking rope and prepared to rescue the two boys. In the short time it took to prepare the rope the boys had been washed even further away from the small boat. It became agonizingly apparent the father would only be able to rescue one of the boys; for in the time it took to throw out the rope and pull in one of the boys, the other would be carried far out of range to be rescued.

The decision tormented the father mercilessly. Each painful second was a knife in his heart. What should he do? He could rescue his son, his only son whom he loved dearly, and let the other boy die in the turbulent waves. Or he could rescue the friend and let his son die a watery death. Both cried out for help without ceasing, the pleas echoing through his skull. The thought of losing his son crippled the father, but letting the other boy die wasn't a pleasant prospect either. Then another thought came to mind. His son was saved. His son's friend was not. If the father saved his son, the friend would die only to end up spending an eternity in hell. If he saved the friend, he knew beyond a shadow of a doubt his son would be soon ushered into the gates of heaven. But the thought of sacrificing his son was incomprehensible! The friend made his choice and would have to live with the consequences. But no matter how hard the father tried, images of wailing and gnashing of teeth; a place of torment where the worm dieth not, and the flames are never quenched; a place of eternal suffering; all swirled into a haunting nightmare making his decision unbearable. Could he allow his son's friend befall such an eternity? What if the sacrifice of his son was in vain?"

Abrams paused and took a deep breath. "So you see, the situation was grim. The ordeal reduced the father to tears, his mind melting like sugar in the ferocious rain. Both boys cried for him to pull them out of the salty brine. The father knew he would have to act fast. He did the only thing he felt he could in that dire moment. 'I love you son,' he sobbed as he tossed the line to the friend. 'Father,' the boy cried as he was swept farther and farther away. By the time the father pulled the friend to safety, his son was no longer visible above the waves."

Abrams swallowed hard. "The father never saw his son again. The decision cost him his health for several years, and not a day went by he didn't think of his beloved son. It was the hardest thing he ever had to do. It still affects him to this day."

Scorpyus pondered the incredible story. It was an amazing testament to one man's faith and courage to do what he believed to be right. He knew of no one who would have made the same choice. To sacrifice one's own son to save another just didn't make sense.

"It may have been a courageous decision, but it sounds like he chose poorly." Scorpyus was blunt. The story was almost too incredible to believe.

Abrams smiled warmly. "Lord knows there were days when I agreed with you. But in the end, I can see it was meant to be."

Scorpyus furrowed his brow with suspicion. "Are you saying *you* are the father?"

"Oh, heavens no," Abrams chuckled. "I don't feel I have the moral fiber to make such a sacrifice. No Scorpyus, I was not the father in the story. I was the son's friend."

Astonishment swept Scorpyus's features. "But I thought the friend wasn't Christian?"

A certain somberness was in Abrams voice. "I am sad to say you understood correctly. Though my father was a pastor, I had no desire to follow in the faith. It was a fact that caused my father much grief. It took the selfless act of my friend's father to make a believer out of me. Not a day goes by that I don't think of my friend, and how he lost his life because of my hardness of heart. For I believe if I had been saved at the time of the storm, my friend's father would have chose to save him rather then me."

"Incredible," Scorpyus whispered.

"My life has never been the same." Abrams continued. "I vowed to make my life count from that day forth. I didn't want my friend's death to be in vain. I immediately turned my life around. A few years later, when I was contemplating starting a business, the most startling realization dawned on me. Our Father in heaven sacrificed His Son so that others could have life. It was then I decided to enter the seminary and follow in my earthly father's footsteps into the ministry."

"You are certainly full of surprises Abrams."

"You know what else; because of my friend's father's sacrifice, I ended up in the ministry. He sacrificed his son, but in the end his act saved countless others."

Abrams smiled broadly. So you never know Scorpyus, all things happen for a reason. What first seems tragic, may, in the end be a glorious occasion. You and your friends have freed a people. The fruit of that event will not fully be felt for years to come."

The wisdom of Abrams's words rang true. Everything he said made sense. To say he was a gifted and eloquent pastor was an understatement. To say he was a caring and compassionate friend was closer to the mark. Scorpyus felt better. For the first time in several days he felt hope for the future.

"Thank you, thank you for coming by. It means more then you know." Gratitude and relief welled up within Scorpyus.

Abrams smiled and stood. "It was the least I could do."

XIV

NOVAK STOPPED ABRUPTLY and held up a fist signaling for Dantes and Emerald to stop also. While staring through the trees, he held a finger to his lips.

"Shh," Novak's whisper was barely audible. "Something is out there."

Emerald's eyes grew wide. She didn't see anything, but froze where she stood. Dantes scanned for movement, his fingers nervously feeling for the hilt of his sword. All was quiet except for the faint sound of a babbling brook somewhere far in the distance. He could see no movement in the jumble of trees, limbs and bushes that lay ahead.

"What ye be seeing." Dantes kept deathly still, not even wanting to breathe too loudly.

"I don't see anything, but I know there is something there." Novak slowly and quietly slipped his sword from its sheath. Dantes followed suit and drew his weapon.

Novak's eyes scanned from side to side under a furrowed brow. A faint breeze dislodged dry pine needles from their branches sending them gently to the forest floor like light drops of rain. A few towering trees groaned under the stress of weighty limbs. An anonymous pinecone plunged to a pine nettle bed with a soft thud. It was the ancient, tranquil whisper of the forest. It had been a while since Novak had taken the time to hear it. Yet this time, it was different.

"How do you know so assuredly something is wrong?" Emerald asked in a whisper that was dangerously.

"Do you hear that?" Novak grimaced, uneasiness riling deep within.

Emerald strained to listen. "No."

"Exactly," Novak replied. "The birds quit making noise."

Now that Novak mentioned it, the usual animal sounds associated with the forest were eerily absent. All in the party shot a nervous glance at the other, remembering the chirping of birds moments earlier.

An immense thrashing erupted suddenly. It was the loud flutter of dozens of bird wings. The frantic flapping echoed through the dense coniferous branches. Scores of birds took flight from a cluster of trees one hundred feet from Novak. The sudden flight caused the trio to instinctively duck down, out of nervousness rather then necessity.

"Thar be something amiss, that much be certain." Dantes peered out from behind a tree. Let's pray it not be a Valkyrie."

Novak didn't want to wait to find out. Sitting and waiting for what would come next was not his style. He met problems head on.

"Let's spread out. Dantes; you walk to the left of those trees and I'll come up on the right. Emerald; stay behind me, about ten yards or so." Novak pointed the route for Dantes to take.

The three stepped ever so lightly onward, maintaining as much stealth as possible. Novak continually scanned the trees. Every instinct was screaming a warning. He had no doubt something was out there. If it was an animal, the problem should resolve itself swiftly. If highwaymen; bring them on. Novak would be happy to teach some hard lessons. But God forbid it should be a Trepanite.

Novak felt something brush against his shoulder. He spun around raising his sword. Emerald flinched in horror at the move.

"You scared me," Emerald whispered and strained to catch her breath. Her face drained of color.

"I scared you? You came up behind me. You were supposed to stay back a distance." Novak lowered his sword relieved.

"I know, but I saw something move. I wanted to tell you."

"Where?" Novak's eyes darted from place to place. Dantes stood only fifty feet away. He wondered what was wrong. Novak motioned for him to stay put.

"Was it in front of us?" Novak whispered.

"No, over there," Emerald pointed to a place twenty yards to Dantes right.

"Did you see it?"

"Not really. I thought I saw something green." Emerald squinted into the distance, apprehensive and afraid.

Before Novak could respond a loud crack sounding like a bullwhip shattered the air. It was quickly followed by the sound of something tearing through tree branches and Dantes distinct growling yell.

Novak caught movement in the corner of his eye. It was rapid and the size of a man. Dantes disappeared from where he stood, and something shot skyward from the same general location. The object hurtled upward and forward towards a tall thin tree. To Novak's amazement it was Dantes, upside down with his legs in the air, being propelled upward by an unknown force. Dantes stopped his upward ascent fifty feet from the ground, but continued swinging wildly like a crazed pendulum, his arms flailing about.

Deep worry creased Novak's brow. A length of rope went from Dantes ankles to someplace up in the tree. Movement rattled in the nearby brush, both in front of Novak and behind.

Activity erupted all around. Footsteps pounded against the earth everywhere. At first they were far off, but quickly grew closer.

"They're everywhere!" Emerald shrieked and pulled her dagger.

Novak knew he was outnumbered, but he wasn't going down without a fight. Several would die before they got him. He readied himself for the coming onslaught.

Soon enough his enemy became visible. Several men in dark green surcoats sprang from behind bushes, rocks and trees. Coming from all directions, they circled Novak in a large perimeter then started closing in. They were armed and meant business. They ignored Dantes coming straight at Novak and Emerald.

Anger flushed Novak's countenance. "I'll cut a hole through them, and then you run for your life." He instructed Emerald who stood trembling, yet poised to defend herself.

A man with a mace and shield made the mistake of being the first one within range of Novak. Without mercy, Novak's muscled arms hurled his sword down onto his opponent. The blade crashed into the man's shield with enough explosive power to send him tumbling to his side. Three more green surcoats replaced the one Novak knocked out of the way.

The three men flanked and centered Novak like experienced soldiers. At once the three parried keeping him on the defensive. Novak slapped their blades away with his sword, and made several slashes for his opponent's necks. They dodged and blocked then came at him again. Novak heard Emerald shriek behind him. It was accompanied by the sounds of a struggle and it angered him further. He tore at his three opponents with a vengeance.

His sword slammed into his opponents to no avail. The three coordinated their attacks, keeping him mostly on the defensive and preventing him from getting much more then cursory blows in. Yet he kept the three at bay and unable to land a good blow themselves. Before he could contemplate the fight any further, more green surcoats appeared. These new ones held crossbows, and leveled them at Novak.

"Hold it right there mate," one ordered in a thick accent of The Dales. The man had short-cropped brown hair and a ruddy complexion. He was stout and sturdy, very rugged looking. The expression on his face was grave.

The three men fighting Novak ceased their attack but kept their swords at the ready. Novak looked at the man with the crossbow. He had it trained right on him. Four or five others did as well. Novak looked back at the three men he had been combating. If he moved fast he could probably kill two of them before they knew what hit them.

It was as if the man with the crossbow could read his mind. "Don't do it mate. You'd be as daft as a jam buttie to try it. Just drop the sword."

Novak looked at the man puzzled. What in the world is a jam buttie? Whatever the man said, he was serious. He kept the crossbow trained and ready.

"Show me the girl first." Novak demanded.

The man with the crossbow motioned behind Novak. A young blonde man in his late teens brought Emerald to where he could see her. She had been stripped of her dagger, but wasn't bound or harmed in any way. She looked at Novak, fright in her eyes.

Novak took one more look at the man with the crossbow. The man wore chain mail under his surcoat, and a helmet much like the one Cad wore. His surcoat had a distinctive emblem on it; crossed falchions. Though clean, the surcoat was faded and well worn. It was an emblem Novak had not seen for a long time. A green surcoat with crossed falchions was worn by those belonging to the army of the Dales. Since Kelterland's occupation of the Dales, wearing the surcoat or emblem was considered treason and punishable by death. The army of the Dales was no longer supposed to exist.

Novak decided to take a chance and comply. The Army of the Dales had a reputation for being sharp and polished. These men's equipment and clothing was worn and fading. Several surcoats also bore the scares of having been mended. The men obviously took care of their uniforms, but nothing could be done to overcome aging equipment except replacing it. These men had not been presented with that opportunity in a long time. Novak pondered the situation. It made perfect sense. The Dales fell to Kelterland five years ago. Remnants of the army would find re-supply difficult if not impossible. The Kelterland presence was heavy in The Dales. Novak took a calculated risk. He dropped his sword and raised his hands. "So the rumors are true. The army of the Dales does still exist."

"Never mind me mate. Who are you?" The man with the crossbow motioned for a colleague to pick up Novak's sword.

"I'm Novak. This is Emerald. My friend Dantes is hanging around somewhere."

"And what brings three Kelterlanders to our forest?"

"I'm from Ravenshire, not Kelterland." Novak took great offense to being called a Kelterlander.

"Really, now we're a long way from home aren't we?" The man with the crossbow replied sarcastically. "So what's a chap from Ravenshire doing in our forest?"

"We are looking for someone." Novak stated.

"And who might that be?"

Novak contemplated weather or not to tell the man with the crossbow. He deduced that if the man wore the surcoat of the army of the Dales, he was no friend of Kelterland. He also carried a crossbow; a favorite weapon of the Dales. Then again maybe he was some sort of a spy.

"I can't tell you." Novak stated bluntly.

"You can when you're trespassing in our forest." The man with the crossbow grew impatient.

Novak wasn't to be bullied. He had to be sure of where the loyalties of the man with the crossbow lay. An idea came to mind. "That is the third time you called this your forest. Kelterland claims it is theirs."

The man turned beet red. "I don't care what they claim. They're dafter then a jam buttie. This is our forest. It rightfully belongs to the Dales!"

A shout of approval erupted from all the men who wore a green surcoat.

"We have something in common then." Novak responded.

"And what might that be?"

"A lack of fondness for Kelterlanders for starters. They occupy my country too." Novak decided he could trust the man with more information. "I'm looking for Barrington Rathbone. I was told I could find him around here."

When Novak mentioned Barrington's name the men grew quiet. The man with the crossbow looked suspiciously at Novak. "Who sent you?"

"A shop owner in Astoria said we could find him here."

"Why do you want to find him?"

Novak was tired of answering questions, but he didn't have a whole lot of choice at the moment. Besides, he felt this man knew where Barrington Rathbone was.

"A friend of mine in Xylor knows him and wants me to deliver a message to him." Novak knew he struck a nerve of interest.

"Xylor you say." The man's eyebrows rose. "We've heard about Xylor. The blokes there defeated and overthrew their dictator. They've set up a new government. Kelterland is planning a reprisal though. We're hoping they can maintain. If these Clandestine Knights are as good as the rumors claim, they just might stand a chance. It gives us hope to think it can be done." All the other men nodded their approval.

"Novak is one of the Clandestine Knights. He helped lead us to victory in Xylor." Emerald blurted, bragging. No longer terrified, she beamed with pride.

"Well I'll be a cheeky butter pie!" The man exclaimed. "Your legend precedes you mister Novak. So why come all this way to deliver a message? Surely your talents could be better spent in Xylor."

Novak was embarrassed and shot Emerald a look that said 'I'll get you for this.' "The fight is far from over in Xylor. In fact the peace is very fragile. It is being threatened by a group of assassins, and could use some help. That is why I am here. I was told Barrington Rathbone could be of assistance."

"I say there sergeant Greystoke, well done." A lean man with dark hair graying at the temples stepped forward from the squad of green surcoats. He was quite distinguished and wore a goatee. His walk and posture were that of a nobleman, and his speech bore the evidence of education. A falchion was strapped to his left hip, and he carried a shield. He walked up to Novak and handed him back his sword.

"I do apologize for the inconvenience. Rex relayed to expect you, but one can't be too sure. Better safe then sorry I always say." The man extended a hand to Novak.

"Allow me to introduce myself. I am Barrington Rathbone, Major, Her Majesty's Army of The Dales. It is an honor to meet one of the Clandestine Knights. We have heard much about you, and your work against Kelterland. How can I be of service?"

Novak accepted Barrington's hospitality. He noticed the falchion on his hip. "It is my honor to meet you Major. I notice you carry the fabled weapon of the Knights of Astor. My father told me great things about the Knights of Astor. Their courage and loyalty are legendary. I didn't think there were any more around."

Barrington was impressed. "I dare say you have a good eye. Few now remember such things. But yes, there are still a few of us left."

"It would be a crime to forget. Forgetting is what brought the realm to our current state of trouble."

The history of the Astorian realms was one of forgetting. One generation forgot the sacrifice and faith that forged the land and gave it its miraculous beginning. In the span of one generation, all was lost. Novak's generation suffered the brunt of that forgetfulness. And they were also the ones left with the daunting task of reclaiming the realm from the clutches of evil men. It was a tremendous burden. For Novak knew full well that he, his friends, and men like Barrington were the only hope for the land. They held knowledge, now precious memories of the way things were. They were the vital link between the generation that forgot and the generations yet to come. There were those who never knew life before the invasions; those who knew not what they were missing. And Novak owed a lot to Barrington and others like him. It was men like Barrington, those solemn few from the forgetful generation, those that saw the danger and tried to stop it. They were the ones that taught Novak and made sure the fires of faith, honor, and freedom were not quenched. Novak was a child during the invasions. Had it not been for a few diligent patriarchs like Barrington Rathbone all may have been lost. Novak was determined not to forget. And he would die trying to reclaim the realm for the next generation.

"Unfortunately many of my countrymen realized their error only after Kelterland was on the march; and then only after the fall of Ravenshire. Too little too late seems to be the predominant reflex for the naïve and wistful dreamers who clung to Kelterland's peace proposals. Deep down they knew full well King Phinehas Faust was a madman, and yet chose denial. Even after the fall of Ravenshire there were those in Her Majesty's court who still believed peace was possible. Now they know how preposterous their assumptions were. From the stockade reality is all too clear." Major Rathbone lamented the unfortunate events that culminated in the meeting of two warriors estranged from their homelands.

"You are right. But now is the time to take the fight to Kelterland; one territory at a time if we have to." Novak was ready to act.

"I say Novak; it is not often we entertain visitors. Your words are as cool water to a parched and weary traveler. Indeed the time is quite ripe, and Kelterland appears to have overextended themselves. The main force of their army invaded Montroix forcing them to assemble conscripts to recover their losses in Xylor. And yet many who would be for us are as of yet too afraid to act. Perhaps after a few more victories like Xylor we will persuade them to lend assistance." Barrington let out a deep sigh.

"Unfortunately the propensity of many is for self-indulgence and self service. Standing alone has always been a failing proposition. That was the first lesson taught at Her Majesties Military Academy." Barrington stated firmly.

Novak grimaced. "That is why we're here."

Barrington was curios. "Say on Novak."

Novak hated to admit it. He couldn't even look Barrington in the eye. "The victory in Xylor is far from certain. We did overthrow Reddland, but now face an even worse problem; an assassination squad called the Order of the Valkyrie."

Novak saw the countenances on Rathbone's men change. Some looked puzzled, and others looked afraid. Barrington's face became grave and serious.

"Have you heard of them?" Novak asked.

The Major nodded solemnly. "Indeed I have. They are an ancient cult. The Knights of Astor were nearly annihilated by them several hundred years ago. Little is known of the treacherous assemblage as few survive an encounter with them. They hail from the Ethereal Region and are assassins for hire. Few can afford their fee though. They are reputed to be among the elite ruling class but that is without confirmation. They are an extremely secretive lot, and few in number. At any rate they are a force to be reckoned with."

Novak was impressed. "Then I guess you know what we are up against; which brings me to why I am here. My friends are fighting for their lives. The Valkyries have killed dozens of people, and Xylor has become more and more unstable. We knew about the troops Kelterland was massing for another invasion. Right now would be a bad time for them to arrive. I was sent to find you and ask if you would help divert those troops. We think if we start an insurrection here, Kelterland will send the soldiers meant for Xylor to deal with the uprisings. We hope it will buy Xylor time to get strong." Novak knew he struck a nerve with Barrington and his men. A tinge of excitement seemed to sweep the ranks.

The Major mulled the proposition over. "And your friends, the Clandestine Knights will lend your services to us?"

"I am here now. The others will eventually come."

"And what of the Valkyrie's? Certainly Xylor can not go it alone against such an insidious clan; or can they?"

Novak shrugged his shoulders. "My friend Cad will handle that. He won't leave Xylor until they are safe."

"The Valkyrie will not go easily into the night. Are your friends confident they are up to the task? I know of no one who has defeated the Valkyrie. Few even survive crossing their path."

"It will not be easy, but the fight has been started. My plan is to finish it. I pray that will eventually mean the freedom of Ravenshire."

Barrington smiled. "Spoken like a true warrior, Novak. I must say my men and I have had a feeling something would happen now for several months. God was evident in many ways. When we heard of the victory in Xylor we knew the season of change was at hand. When we heard four strangers appeared to be the catalyst for this victory, we knew God answered the prayers of his people throughout the realm. As news of this victory spreads, I venture to say it will rally more troops to the cause. For you to be here now asking my assistance is no coincidence. It is a call to my men and me. Shall we now shirk from service after so many have valiantly gone before?"

"Does that mean you will help?" Novak asked.

Barrington pounded his fist into his palm enthusiastically. "We are at your service. Service is the highest calling one can aspire to. Service to God first, and then service to one's nation, there is no greater method for maintaining virtues of integrity and honor. Once a people become slothful and self-serving, they are on the path to destruction."

Novak was relieved. His mission was finally going in the right direction. After the shipwreck and the Trepanites he was starting to wonder.

"I hope you are right. I hope the victory in Xylor holds, and more come forward to fight. Maintaining control of Xylor is the beginning of the end of the realms servitude to Kelterland." Novak reiterated his intentions.

"You are correct Novak," Barrington pronounced as a matter of fact. "A loss now may demoralize the resistance throughout the realm. We must not yield that victory."

Rathbone shook his head dismayed at recollections of how the territory came to its present state. "A large portion of my generation turned against the values that served us so well for hundreds of years. That rebellion was borne out of pride. It is pride that compels one to reject tried and true values in favor of the latest fashion. Once a man creates his own set of morals, he has invariably pronounced himself a god. For only God has the right to decide what is good and what is evil. It is the ultimate in pride. And 'pride goeth before destruction and a haughty spirit before a fall.' Regrettably it is the children, your generation Novak, who paid the heaviest cost. Yours was the innocents who inherited the disorder earned by the poor decisions of others. In the span of a generation the land was turned from moral unity to self-serving pursuits. For hundreds of years the standard of living improved with each generation. For the first time in the history of the Astorian Realms a generation was handed less. It could be argued that instead of handing the realm to the next generation, it was yielded to the Kelterlanders."

The Major stood straight and tall with complete command presence. "But my men and I am not the yielding sort. We will never surrender. The Dales shall once again be free, and Her Majesty's rightful heir returned to the throne!"

A shout erupted from Barrington's men. They were in clear support of the Major, and his speech was a call to arms. They jumped to their feet and pumped their fists in the air.

"God save the Monarchy! God save The Dales! God save Her Majesty's Army!"

Dantes took in the scene quietly until now, relieved to be released from hanging by his feet. He noticed Cedric often referred to 'Her Majesty' as he spoke. Dantes held a different recollection of events. "Forgive me fer asking, but thar be some scuttlebutt circulating that the Queen of The Dales be killed some years ago."

Sergeant Greystoke turned salmon red and took a step toward Dantes. "There's no proof of that mate! I'll never believe…"

The Major silenced his Sergeant by placing a hand on his shoulder. "I dare say there is some truth to both statements. While we have yet to see Her Majesty, Queen Audrey of the House of Astor, since the fall of our capital, her exact status is as of yet unknown. She may indeed have been killed, certainly if the Kelterlanders found her that would be the case. Official protocol dictates Her Majesty remain in hiding until she can be safely retuned to the throne. My men and I intend to see to that very task."

"Here, here!" A shout erupted from Barrington's men, and they pumped their fists in the air. Their loyalty to the crown was unwavering.

Barrington was pleased by his men's outburst, and continued. "Regrettably, not all of the royal heirs are currently among the living. And one day not only will a rightful heir of the House of Astor be returned to the throne, but we shall reclaim our rightful capital. For far too many years it has been in the hands Kelterlanders. Astoria shall once again fly under the banner of The Dales!"

A round of cheers rose from Barrington's men. Novak estimated them to be about two hundred in number. Gloved and gauntleted hands clapped together enthusiastically in unison. The men rallied around their leader, showing their total agreement with his vision for The Dales. Most were half the Major's age, but there were a few long time veterans.

Barrington looked to his men with a fatherly pride. For five years they had been faithful. Now it looked as if the moment all had waited for was cresting the horizon. A tear welled in the Major's eye as he watched his men cheer in loyal allegiance to a nation whose future was far from secure. These few; these tattered rag-tag few; the forgotten ones of a forlorn generation; the ones who had little reason to serve a cause greater then self, would be the ones to fight for the freedom and redemption of their people. It moved Barrington deeply. Where were the men of his generation; when Kelterland started this God awful bloody war? The thought saddened and sickened Barrington. Many of his boys would die in the months and years to come. It would be a tragedy. For it would have taken less bloodshed to maintain freedom then it now will to reclaim it. These boys would do what his generation wouldn't.

The Major cleared his throat and wiped his eyes. "I say Novak, shall we proceed. We can make Stonebridge by nightfall."

Barrington motioned to one of his men and three horses were brought forward. Novak, Dantes, and Emerald mounted up, and the entourage headed northwest. Barrington rode with the three newcomers, and struck up a conversation with Dantes. He wanted to know about the blockade. Novak evaluated the country for landmarks. He liked to know where he was. The Dales were a green, forested territory much like Ravenshire; only Ravenshire was far more mountainous. The Dales contained small rolling hills.

Novak inhaled a deep breath of pine-scented air. It smelled like home. Off in the distance was a jagged rock outcropping. It was a large mound of boulders with a rocky spire jutting up from the center. It reminded Novak of the Alcazar in Ravenshire. When Kelterland seized control of his homeland they built a fortified compound in a clearing along the river to the northwest of Saltwater. The Alcazar had a ten-foot stonewall around the perimeter, and a castle with a giant tower from which the Kelterlander brigades could keep watch against trouble. It was a looming structure out of place among the smaller structures that made up Saltwater. From the outpost Kelterland controlled access to the territory. It was at the Alcazar Novak first met Cad.

Cad, like a good many residents of Saltwater, had been forced to build the Alcazar. Kelterland had a policy of "hiring" citizens into the King's Service. The King's Service consisted of compelled temporary jobs for which the enlistee was paid roughly one-third of a days wage for each day of work. In reality Kelterlander troops would enter a town and round up a number of citizens and put them to work. It usually involved strenuous labor. To resist meant to be killed on the spot. The meager pay offered was to add a semblance of legitimacy to the servitude. It sounded better then "slave labor". In this particular incident Cad had been caught in the Kelterlanders decided "hiring" spree. The Kelterlanders wanted their wall complete before the first rains. Novak went by the fortification to spy on the progress in order to exploit any possible weaknesses at some future date. On this day Novak noticed something about the thirteen-year-old Cad that caught his attention.

The lean, blonde haired youth was giving orders, directing the construction of the wall. Cad no longer performed the actual labor, but now supervised the project. Cad consulted charts and papers, pointing out details to his work crew. In a month, Novak saw Cad work his way from brick hauler, to brick layer, and now to project supervisor; an impressive feat for a thirteen year old boy. At the same time the Kelterlander guards seemed to endow Cad with more and more trust. His work was impeccable and he was given latitude to finish the wall without being under constant watch from the guard. Now the guards came by twice, maybe three times a day to see how work progressed. It was one of these times when the guards were away that one member of the work crew decided he had enough with taking orders.

"I don't know about you men, but I've had enough of this boy ordering me around." The man grumbled. He was a grizzled man with thick black unkempt hair. His forearms were thick and hairy, with two huge fists at the end. His voice was rough, and sounded like gravel in a gristmill. His clothes were soiled with food stains and his dark eyes were perpetually bloodshot. Normally he barged goods up and down the river. He was loosing considerable money being in the King's Service, and had been irritable and crotchety since the start.

"Just get back to work mate. This blooming project will be done soon." Cad advised. He had places he'd rather be also.

The man glared at Cad. "Well ain't that something; a little pipsqueak giving orders. Who made you king?"

Cad took a deep breath. He didn't want any trouble. "Look mate, no offense but I just happened to know how to read the plans, and I come from a family of architects. That's the only reason they picked me. It was nothing against you or anyone else."

"Ooh, mister fancy pants," the man rolled his eyes and made sarcastic expressions toward Cad. "The boy knows how to read and his daddy is an archer tick. I don't care if your daddy can make arrows, that don't give you the right to be in charge."

By now work on the wall came to a halt. The work crew watched to see what would happen. A few glanced nervously in the direction of where the guards would come if they should decide to pay a visit.

The man put down his handcart of bricks and took a few steps toward Cad. "I say I should be in charge." The man searched the eyes of the work crew. "Who's with me? Are any of you tired of being pushed around by a boy?"

No one else spoke. For the time being they waited to see how Cad handled the situation. Cad knew he had to act quickly.

"Get back to work mate! Or I'll have you off the crew."

"I'd like to see that; if you feel man enough." The man growled and assumed a fighting stance.

Cad's anger boiled. As a result, boyish exuberance got the best of his mouth. "You can't even stack the bloody bricks properly! Look at that heap of rubbish way over there. You have one simple job; bring the bricks and stack them neatly…and close to the work site. A blind chap could do better! And you want to be in charge? You're not even qualified for mindless tasks!" A chuckle erupted from some men on the crew.

A puzzled look came over the man and then realization slowly donned on his countenance. "Are you saying I'm too stupid to be in charge?"

"Did you figure that out by yourself mate? Or did someone help you?" Cad let out an exasperated laugh. "We could have been finished with this bloody project if not for you. It's easier for the masons if they get the bricks from a neat stack close by, then walk forty yards and sift through a heap. I've been telling you that for a week. But you're so blooming dense…a mule is easier to work with."

The man's face turned crimson. "Prepare for the beating of your life, you little…" The man proceeded to curse a string of expletives at Cad as he stomped toward him. Someone came forward to stop the man.

"Listen Stultus, we don't need trouble. In a few days we'll be done and then we can go home."

"I aim to teach this boy a lesson, now get back." The man growled. "And besides, why does anyone care about how good we build this wall. Let the wall collapse. He sounds like a traitor to me."

Cad took offense to that comment. "I am no traitor!" He had secret reasons for allowing himself to be used to work on the wall. Cad could have run off at any time and not been found by the guards. His motives for staying were much the same as Novak's.

"We're almost done Stultus. You're making a mistake." His friend tried to reason with the burly man.

"I said stand back!" The man growled and pushed his friend.

The friend grew angry but knew better then to physically try to stop the burly man. "I'm getting the guards."

The man glared at his friend. "Alright, I'll hold off on the boy." The man was unconvincing.

The man's friend smiled. "You're doing the right thing Stultus."

When the man's friend turned to go back to work, the burly man blindsided him with a massive blow to the side of the head. The friend dropped like a sack of grain to, unconscious and bleeding from his temple. The burley man turned toward Cad, hatred on his face.

"You're very brave when a chap has his back to you." Cad gave the man a look of disdain and grabbed a nearby shovel. "You've been itching for a fight, and now you've got one."

The man grabbed a rake from his cart and charged Cad. Anger coursed through the man's veins. He swung his rake with a grunt for Cad's head. Cad ducked and slammed his shovel against the man's left shin. It made a thick cracking sound upon impact.

The man let out a howl and spit curses at Cad. He limped toward Cad for another try. This time he swung at his chest.

Cad blocked the blow with the handle of his shovel. The rake cracked against it with tremendous force; enough to send Cad back a few steps. The man swung the rake downward trying to impale Cad's foot with the prongs. Cad shuffled to the side and the rake imbedded itself into the ground. With a jerk, Cad thrust the tip of his shovel into the man's belly. A burst of hot breath spewed from the man's mouth. The rancid stench of stale ale and an abscessed tooth stung Cad's nostrils.

"Whew! Your misses must suffer terribly mate. Your breath would drive a dog daft." Cad jeered as he brought the shovel down hard.

The man blocked the blow with the handle to his rake. "I've had enough of your mouth. It's time to learn some manners." He slashed at Cad's face with the prongs of the rake. Cad dodged and blocked the blows with agile dexterity. He used his shovel handle like a sword. He hacked at the man's limbs whacking the meaty portions of thigh and upper arm. The man may have been a fighter, but a swordsman he wasn't. Cad seized upon his advantage and thrust the handle into the man's solar plexus again. Again he elicited a deep guttural grunt.

"That smarts a bit mate, doesn't it?" Cad asked in the most sarcastic voice he could muster. The rest of the work crew drew closer to get a better vantage point on the action. A few shouted, encouraging the combatants.

The man turned four shades of purple. He glared at Cad, cursing him so vehemently spit sprayed from his mouth. He grabbed bricks from the cart and hurled them forcefully. Cad darted around to avoid the incoming projectiles. One glanced off his shoulder sending a sharp pain jolting down his arm. The impact caused him to lose his grip on the shovel. The man's face lit up when Cad let out a painful groan.

"Ha! Let that be a lesson to you." The man relished his small victory.

Cad decided to play out a hunch. He made no effort to pick up the shovel, and instead massaged his shoulder, feigning his injury to be greater then it was. Like a true coward, the man jumped from behind the cart emboldened. Cad turned aside keeping an eye on the man from the corner of his eye. All the while he groaned and held his shoulder. It was all the man could do to contain himself. An injured and inattentive opponent was an easy victory. Logic would not interfere with his moment of glory, as if a man fighting a boy could claim such a moment as a victory.

Cad's ploy sucked the man right in. He waited for his attacker to get within range, and then sprang like a cat. In one swift move, Cad stepped on the tip of the shovels blade hard causing the handle to hop upward. Cad grabbed the handle, raised it like a club, and brought the spade against the man's forehead with a crack.

The man stopped dead in his tracks. His face went blank, a barely audible groan escaping his lips. Slowly he sank to his knees, and then plopped face down in the dirt. Cad lowered his shovel, confident the man would not arise anytime soon.

Three of the work crew came forward. They didn't look happy with what happened. "You tricked him. You didn't fight fair." One accused.

"He started it." Cad pointed out.

"He was only fooling with you." Another protested.

"Coming at a chap with a rake isn't fooling around." Cad looked the three men in the eye. He had seen that look before in the soldiers that burned his home down. It was the bloodthirsty look of revenge.

Cad backed up still clutching the shovel. He kept turning and shifting, refusing to allow the men to triangulate on him. "We have no quarrel. Just go back to work. You only have a few more days."

"Look what you did to our friend. We can't let that go unanswered."

Cad was frustrated. No one took his side. The other men in the crew were staying out of it. The fallen man and his friends were bullies and the rest of the crew was afraid to get involved. Their cowardice sickened Cad. The burly man's other friend lay unconscious on the ground. Did these three think the burly man wouldn't have done the same to them? Why were they being loyal to a disloyal friend?

"Is there anyone who will stand for what is right?" Cad asked the rest of the work crew. "This bloke started the fight and lost. His three thick skulled friends can't see that. They want to go at it three against one like true cowards. And none of you have the courage to back me. What's wrong with this bloody world?" The rest of the work crew cast their eyes downward in shame.

"I'll stand with you." A voice came from behind Cad. He turned and saw a towering teen with well-muscled arms crossed across his chest.

Cad gave a nod of thanks. "Glad to have you mate. Thank you."

Novak glared at the three men surrounding Cad. "Now it is a fair fight."

The three men weren't as sure as they were before, but stubborn tenacity refused to let them back down in front of the crew they bullied for nearly a month.

"You two take the big one; I'll handle our 'boss.'" One man ordered his friends to take the more daunting task.

The two friends charged Novak, somewhat leery, but bold in their two to one advantage. One threw a punch, catching Novak on the chin. His head snapped to the right. Slowly he brought his face back facing the front, a grin spreading on his lips.

"Are there any men to fight?" Novak taunted. "You remind me of my grandma."

The man who struck Novak fumed and took another swing. It was a roundhouse. Novak blocked it with his left forearm, and then propelled his right fist forward in a swift jab. Bulbous knuckles impacted crooked teeth buried under a thick brown beard. The man's head lurched back amidst a flash of light. The rest of the man's body followed his head's momentum causing him to stagger backwards and fall to his posterior. Blood dripped from the man's chin whiskers.

Novak felt a blow to the side of his face. Another glanced of his muscled shoulder. Yet another caught him above his left ear. All of the blows came from behind. Novak reeled around in time to dodge a fourth blow, and leered at the other man.

Novak wiped a trickle of blood from the corner of his mouth and shot the man a blow to the temple. This man didn't go down like his friend. He was a brawler. Novak noticed the man's crooked nose and cauliflower ears; badges of many dockside fights. Novak shot the man two quick jabs to the face. Though he bloodied the man's nose, the seasoned brawler took it in stride.

"You'll find I'm not your grandma." The brawler grinned revealing several gaps in his teeth and came at Novak.

The two men circled each other and exchanged blows. Novak was younger and stronger, but the brawler could take the punishment. The brawler landed several hits on his young adversary. Soon Novak's ribs were burning with pain. Novak retaliated ferociously, ducking and throwing punches continually. The brawler would block a punch occasionally, and absorb the rest. He wasn't a skilled fighter. His strength seemed to be in his ability to take the pain. Novak pummeled the man's face until it was a bloody mess, and still he fought on. It was impressive. Novak had never seen anything like it. The brawler landed another punch on Novak. This one sent a sharp pain through his side. When the man connected, it was a good hit.

The two continued for another minute this way. The man grew tired, but refused to yield. Novak continued to land blows to the man's head fairly easily, almost too easily. Suddenly Novak realized something. The brawler kept his abdomen well guarded, preferring to leave his head unprotected. Novak seized upon the realization. The next time the brawler threw a hook, Novak drove a fist into the momentary opening catching his opponent in the gut just below the ribs. It was a powerful blow that raised the brawler an inch or two off the ground. A forceful gasp of air escaped the brawler's mouth as air vacated his lungs. The man froze mouth agape and unable to even moan. His eyes rolled up into his head, his arms cradling his midsection. Slowly the man sunk to his knees and collapsed in a heap.

Novak looked with satisfaction on his two fallen opponents. The first man scrambled back to the work crew. Cad stood over his opponent, a small rock in his hand. His attacker lay on the ground with a bulging knot on his forehead, a shovel clutched loosely in his grasp. Novak studied the scene while rubbing his knuckles. No other men came forward to take a shot at Cad or his new friend.

"Let's finish this wall and go home." Cad instructed the work crew. The men realizing the action was over reluctantly went back to work.

Cad turned to his large friend. "Thanks again mate. I appreciate it. There are not a lot of blokes now days willing to take a stand; especially when outnumbered."

"It was my pleasure." Novak shook hands with Cad. "I saw what they were doing, and it wasn't right. I am tired of men like that. They are just as bad as the Kelterlander soldiers."

"I'm with you on that mate; though I don't imagine too many people give you much trouble. You're one big chap." Cad smiled and introduced himself.

"You handled the first guy fine," Novak replied. "There are not many people brave enough to take a stand like that; especially when they are smaller. You're one of the few I've seen since Kelterland took over."

Cad shook his head in agreement. "I know what you mean mate. Ravenshire has gone daft. It makes me sick. There was a time when we were an honorable people who wouldn't stand for such a thing."

Novak was visibly impressed with what he heard. "Do you mean that?"

"Absolutely," Cad replied vehemently.

"I have a friend," Novak explained. "We have plans to change things in Ravenshire some day. We don't know how or when, but someday Ravenshire will be free from Kelterland once and for all. Maybe the three of us could meet and talk about it; if it's something you'd be interested in."

Cad's interest was held. He glanced around quickly because what Novak was saying would be considered treason and punishable by death.

"Well since you bailed me out of a bit of trouble I suppose I can trust you. Let's talk about it."

Cad and Novak quickly found out they had a common bond. Both of their fathers had been killed and were Ravenshire Knights. Both shared a common faith, and a desire to see their homeland restored to its sovereign state. Novak realized Cad would be a formidable addition to the clan. For six months it had been him and Scorpyus. Novak didn't know it at the time, but the next few months would see the addition of Zephyr. Together the four would form the Clandestine Knights.

XV

"CADWALLADER," THE NAME was spoken in soft urgency by a voice in the doorway.

Cad immediately stopped his conversation with Abrams and turned to see who was addressing him. Very rarely did he hear that name come from lips that didn't belong to his mother; and even she used it only occasionally.

"Oh, hello there," Cad was unusually surprised to see Cyrus. "You're back so soon?"

Cyrus took a deep breath, let it out slowly and entered the small room Abrams used as his office. He seemed heavy hearted, and looked tired. His thinning hair was unkempt and bore the mark of having been under a helmet. A day's growth of whiskers replaced his normally clean shaved appearance.

"I think I found one," Cyrus gravely reported. "But we have to hurry. I don't think any of them stay in one place long."

"Well done Cyrus," Cad stroked his goatee, concern written deeply on his face. "Take me to it at once."

Cad placed his helmet on his head, and picked up his shield. "Shall we take a squad of men?"

"I think the two of us will move with more stealth. Surprise will be our greatest asset." Cyrus offered his opinion.

"Very well." Cad made final adjustments to his armor then turned to Abrams. "Wish me Godspeed in this matter."

Abrams swallowed hard. Beads of perspiration trickled from his brow though the temperature was quite cool. He clasped Cad's hand in a handshake, and placed his other on Cad's shoulder.

"I'll be praying for your safe return. And remember; what is out of our control is in God's control. Listen and the Spirit will guide."

Cad nodded appreciatively. "That's good to know; for little has been in my control since the Valkyrie's arrival." Cad paused and then smiled weakly. "And I shall be praying for you. Your task is as…precarious. Filling in for Thadus won't be easy, especially at a time like this. The people are counting on you. What better hands could the people be in then those of the Master's Shepard? At any rate, I must be going. Rest assured, my friends and I will do our part…God willing."

"Take care; I've lost one too many close friends today."

The two men embraced momentarily like a father seeing a son off to war. Sorrow hung thick in the air. The pained look on Abrams's face betrayed his thoughts. A part of him wondered if he was saying a final farewell. Cad felt Abrams could very well be right. The future was far from certain, especially where a Valkyrie is concerned. Time would not permit a lengthy goodbye.

Cad walked out of Abrams office with Cyrus close behind. Quickly they went to the main gates. The sentries opened the gate for the departing twosome. Cyrus grabbed a torch from the sconce at the guardhouse.

"Any word from Scorpyus?" Cyrus asked.

"Not recently, but I have every confidence in him. Nothing short of death will keep him from the mission." Cad continued out the gate once the sentries had it open.

The two walked at a brisk pace, Cyrus leading the way and carrying a torch. Night fell and the fog was thinner than it had been all week. This wasn't necessarily a good thing. Fog worked both ways; it concealed Cad as well as his enemies.

Cad looked skyward. The moon was as of yet obscured. He estimated it was approaching midnight but couldn't be sure.

Cyrus led Cad to the docks. They passed all of the taverns on the south end of the port where the bulk of the ships were docked. Both walked to the northern most piers. The north side of the port normally had several ships docked, but now was virtually deserted.

"We're getting close." Cyrus pointed to the last pier.

"Where?" Cad eyed the wood planks stretching over the water.

"At the end of the pier is a wide spot with a small warehouse. It's been deserted for quite sometime, even since before the blockade." Cyrus wiped his brow. He was sweating profusely in the crisp cool air. He squinted into the fog, a pained look on his face.

Cad stopped before taking the pier. His own heart beat loudly in his temples. Facing a Valkyrie was stressful no doubt, but Cyrus seemed to be having difficult time with it.

"Are you going to be alright mate?" Cad asked, concerned.

Cyrus sucked in a deep breath and let it out quickly. "I'll be better once this is over."

"You'll do fine mate?" Cad managed a small grin. "This will work."

"When I was your age I was fearless like you." Cyrus swallowed hard. "But now I'm nearly forty, and that's not the right age for taking after Valkyrie's."

"There is no right age for tangling with a blooming Valkyrie." Cad replied.

Cyrus let out a chuckle. "You may be right about that."

With a nod to the other, the two started walking down the pier to what lay at the end. Both walked slowly, placing their feet down carefully on the wooden planks so as to not make noise. The rotted wood of the pier was slick with moisture, and it creaked with each step. No amount of care toward stealth could overcome that.

Cyrus winced with each creak of the boards, feeling like a man on his walk to the gallows. He stepped over a hole in the pier where the rotted wood gave out under some previous pedestrian.

Cad scanned the pier as it slowly materialized from the mist with each step he took. He decided to slip his sword from its sheath and Cyrus followed suit. His ears searched for the slightest sound as he padded his way to whatever lay at the end of the pier.

A dark object darted from the fog directly for the twosome. Cad and Cyrus both tightened in a quick flinch bracing for the unknown. A muffled squeak came from the object, which moved rapidly toward the two.

"Bloody rat." Cad relaxed and watched the rodent scamper down the pier, going right between him and Cyrus.

The two continued their trek, methodically making their way around missing planks and holes in the pier. Soon the pier widened and a rickety structure emerged. It was as dilapidated as the pier was. Several shingles were missing from the roof revealing black holes into nothingness beneath. In the middle of the structure were two doors. One door was unhinged and laying flat on the threshold. Several boards were nailed in place across the shutters. It was a good place to hide and by the looks of things, few had ventured down this pier in years.

Cad motioned for Cyrus to go to the right of the doors, and he would go to the left. The place looked deserted, but every instinct told Cad otherwise. His eyes searched in the flickering torchlight for what had to be there. Listening intently he could only hear the sea gently sloshing against the pier supports.

Cad peered into the doorway. Sawdust about an inch thick was on the floor. It was darkened with age, but it had been disturbed recently revealing lighter colored sawdust from beneath.

Cad looked toward the ceiling and could just make out the structure's rafters.

Suddenly Cad froze in a panic. The scent of lotus blossoms wafted near his nostrils.

There was a tremendous crash as black feet shot from the top of the doorway and impacted into Cyrus's chest. Cyrus was knocked to his back, the torch clattering from his hands and across the deck. Cad found himself one foot from a Valkyrie that swung down from the rafters. Instinctively he brought a metal gauntlet into the Valkyrie's gut eliciting a deep grunt. It fell from the rafters back into the darkness.

Cad backed from the doorway and braced himself. A shadowy foot appeared on the threshold and he swung his sword for the opening. His blade crashed into the rotted wood of the standing door, severing it in two and sending out a shower of splinters. The shadowy figure was gone, but a few drops of blood were speckled onto the sawdust.

Cyrus scrambled to his feet and picked up the torch.

"Throw me the torch!" Cad yelled and shifted his sword to his shield hand.

Cyrus complied. Cad grabbed it and flung it into the warehouse. Immediately the sawdust floor burst into flames, and firelight ate at the darkness. Cad saw a figure move to the corner. Another figure stood clearly visible in the light. It was the first time Cad saw a Valkyrie up close. It quickly headed for the opposite corner. Before Cad could formulate a plan of action he heard a scraping on the roof. He looked up just in time to see yet another figure leap at him from atop the roof. He braced himself and brought his shield up over his head at a forty-five degree angle. With a thud the Valkyrie landed, and then tumbled from Cad's sloping shield crashing to the docks. Quickly Cad took a swing with his sword, but in a flash the Valkyrie rolled from the blade.

Cad took several more slashes at his elusive enemy, cutting only air. The shadowy figure sprang to its feet and came at Cad. He shoved his shield into the cursed thing keeping it at bay. The Valkyrie hopped back and snapped its fists up. Cad could see a thin wire stretched between its hands. The Valkyrie crouched and started to maneuver. Cad kept an eye on his enemy while glancing about trying to locate the other two Valkyrie's. They were nowhere to be found.

Cad did spot Cyrus standing in the distance, light flickering erratically on his face. He seemed to be pulling back, watching the fight rather then intercede. It struck Cad as odd, but something else was even more bizarre. His mind analyzed the strange data. Not only was there an abnormally incandescent light flickering both upon Cyrus who was some twenty yards away, and the Valkyrie who was shuffling from side to side, but there was also a significant amount of heat coming from behind Cad.

The Valkyrie prevented further thought on the matter. Like a leopard it leapt up and nearly over Cad's upraised shield, whipping its arms and the wire over Cad's head. The two became locked in a morbid, grappling embrace, a shield sandwiched between them. Both wrested in a twisted dance of death. Cad felt a biting sting on the back of his neck as he shoved at the Valkyrie trying to break free from its clutches. His attacker was so close he could hear it panting as it struggled to employ its garrote in a more lethal manner.

Cad spun trying to shake the menace and started ramming the hilt of his sword into the Valkyrie's spine. The close quarters of the fight prevented him from getting a crippling blow. The Valkyrie clung on ever the more fiercely, its teeth gritting in determination as it tried to ensnare Cad's neck in its garrote.

And then Cad felt the Valkyrie's foot against his as he shuffled to the left. Immediately he smashed his boot down fiercely three times in rapid succession. He caught a foot under the stomp of his heel, hopefully fracturing an arch. Several pained grunts emitted from beneath the black mask that was inches from his face. In response, the Valkyrie tried to knee Cad in the groin, but caught him in the inner thigh instead. Cad spun to the side, his leg throbbing, and shifted his shield to protect himself. The Valkyrie's knee came up again, this time crashing into sturdy metal. A yelp of pain pierced the air bringing a grin to Cad's lips.

Cad felt the Valkyrie slump and become heavier around his neck. With a growl, Cad tried to fling the unwanted baggage from his person. Though he was the larger of the two, and able to turn about and spin, the Valkyrie clung like a leach. It continued to try and circle a loop of its garrote around Cad's head, fortunately unsuccessfully. Still Cad could feel the thin wire cut into the back of his neck.

When Cad spun he noticed the warehouse fully engulfed in flames. The fire ate greedily at the dry wooden and sawdust-laden structure. Smoke billowed skyward. The smell of burnt wood wafted in the air. Firelight lit up the whole pier. The flames were so bright that Cyrus was clearly visible, though now forty yards away. Cad recognized he was fading from the scene like a thief in the night.

"You bloody coward!" Cad was furious. He looked toward Cyrus with a sickened scowl. He hated deserters, and traitors were even worse. He was now alone in this fight. A cold chill swept Cad's soul. Scorpyus was barely able to beat one Valkyrie, and he was a faster more agile fighter. Even though Cad was strong, he knew the likely hood of defeating three Valkyrie's was beyond remote. This road Cad would walk alone.

Cad felt the presence of someone behind him. A shadowy arm grabbed his sword arm. Simultaneously another arm came over his left shoulder and wrapped around the front of his neck in a chokehold. A second Valkyrie was on him! Cad brought his chin toward his chest as the arm tightened around. He gnashed into the cotton fabric in front of his mouth, clenching his teeth bitterly. The taste of blood graced his tongue. A shrieking wail warbled from behind his head. Cad would not go quietly. The Valkyrie's may win this battle, but they would pay for victory with blood. The first Valkyrie continued jerking at the garrote violently. Cad could feel blood trickle down the back of his neck. For some reason he was without worry. Cad was completely beyond panic and at peace with whatever lay ahead. Even though imminent death or capture waited, he felt a renewing of his spirit.

Forcefully, Cad's head butted the Valkyrie that grappled him from the front. There was a considerable crack as his helmet smashed against whatever facial part lie beneath the black hooded cloak. A bit of tension went out of the wire biting at the back of his neck. It would be a short-lived victory.

Cad felt a blow to the back of his legs. The next thing he knew he was face down on the pier, his helmet clattering from his head. Fists from the shadowy attackers started pummeling him. Lights shot through his head with each blow. Blood dripped from his nose. He could feel rope being wrapped around his legs. Cad prayed. It was all in God's hands now.

Cad fought valiantly resisting until he could no more. The Valkyrie's continued their pummeling, enjoying their work. Cad felt consciousness slip away. He felt blood flow from his brow, and into his hair. His arms grew heavy and unable to move. His peripheral vision started to blur and darken, and the pier began to wash away. Wearily he waited for all to go black, his face pressed against the planks of the pier. Fragments of thought flashed through his mind as the warehouse burned brightly in the background. Cad thought of Novak, Zephyr, and Scorpyus. He wondered if he made the right decisions. Perhaps continuing on in Xylor was a mistake. He thought of Ravenshire, and of Ingrid. Cad could picture Ingrid clearly in his mind. No beating could ever drive her from his memory. He could still see her golden locks, her fair skin, and those deep blue eyes sparkled like a million stars when she laughed. Cad made himself a promise. If he lived to see Ingrid again he would propose to her.

Cad bathed in a cold sweat. He couldn't feel the blows as the Valkyrie's continued their brutal work. He began to pray again. It was the most sincere and heartfelt moment of prayer Cad had in a long time. At the times a person is at their weakest, God shows himself His strongest.

Cad saw something and squinted his blurring vision into focus. He noticed a man in a sand colored robe standing on the pier. The man looked on the spectacle undetected by the Valkyrie's though he made no effort to conceal himself. A golden sash held the man's garment at the waist. He stood cross-armed, his feet shod in sandals. The man stood there, a mysterious look in his eyes. It was the last thing Cad saw before loosing consciousness.

...*and precious shall their blood be in His sight.*

XVI

A LARGE DROP of blood gathered and swelled before cascading from the tightly clenched fist. It landed with a splatter on a mud-encrusted boot. The fist, a left one, was wrapped snugly with a red soaked bandage on the palm. Dried blood around the fingernails bore evidence the wound was not new, and at one time had stopped bleeding. Now crimson droplets oozed from between tightly clasped fingers, knuckles white with the effort. Another drop collected below the little finger before it too plunged downward, again striking the tall muddy boot. The boot faltered forward in a pronounced limp as the right hand pushed away a small branch providing for a better view. Confident all was clear, the boot, now joined by its mate, alternately limped and stepped forward.

Sergeant Greystoke motioned for his small squad of men to take a brief rest. They had been patrolling the Dales-Kelterland border for several long hours now and were getting hungry. Removing his helmet, he wiped his brow and scanned the clearing ahead. The tall grass blew wistfully in the breeze, and a vulture rode the currents above. Cocking his head to the side, the Sergeant listened intently for a moment. Birds chirped in the distance, and the light wind cut through the trees. Satisfied there was no danger lurking about, Sergeant Greystoke moved his men into the clearing but stayed near the shade of the trees. After posting a sentry he opened his pack.

"I'm having me a jam buttie! One of you lads fix up a pot of tea."

One of the men retrieved thin sticks of wood and scraped a clear spot in the dirt with his foot. The others rummaged through their packs for a quick bite to eat. Sergeant Greystoke took a savory chomp of his jam buttie thoroughly relishing every morsel. The sun would soon wane on the horizon, after which the patrol would start back for Stonebridge. There would be no trouble to report for a change.

Sergeant Greystoke looked contently on the countryside, his eyes misting up. He loved the land, and took great pride in the small part he played in helping to provide security for his countrymen. Kelterlander patrols would plunder the border villages at will; if the Sergeant and his men could stop some of the suffering then so much the better. He was happy to cause Kelterland some casualties.

When the tea was ready, Sergeant Greystoke poured himself a serving into a metal goblet and took a sip. Nothing went better with the cool damp air of impending nightfall then a bit of Black Astorian tea. Life was about enjoying the simple pleasures.

Sergeant Greystoke started to take another sip but the goblet froze part way to his pursed lips.

"Did you hear that?" He asked realizing his men also paused from their meals and silenced their light bantering.

He heard the noise again. It came from somewhere behind his squad. It sounded like something large rustling against dry brush. It managed to sneak dangerously close before being detected. The Sergeant and his men readied their crossbows and aimed them toward the clump of brush. Then all was silent, the rustling ceased.

Tension rose in the squad. Something was just there. It didn't just disappear. The whole squad couldn't have been mistaken. The Sergeant glanced at his men uneasily. The squad eyed the clump of brush nervously.

Sergeant Greystoke ordered his men to fan out. In unison they walked to investigate the source of the noise. White knuckled hands grasped drawn crossbows, and fingers rested delicately against triggers as the squad moved on a possible threat. Ears strained for the faintest tell tale sign of danger. The air was unbearably silent.

Sweat trickled from the Sergeant's brow and he swallowed hard. The clump of brush made not even the slightest noise or sign of movement. Finally a scraping sound emitted from an adjacent tree. Immediately six crossbows pointed out the location like well-trained hunting dogs.

"Behind the tree," Sergeant Greystoke whispered to his closest man and motioned for him to circle around in order to flank whoever was there. The rest of the squad aimed their crossbows covering the threat.

"We know you are there. Come out like a good lad before things get nasty." The Sergeant ordered. His command was met with silence. Jittery tension energized the squad with anticipation. Lesser-trained soldiers may have accidentally discharged a bolt toward the tree in nervous reflex.

"Hold your fire!" Sergeant Greystoke ordered as a black, mud caked boot slowly emerged from behind the tree. It was soon followed by another boot. Eventually a haggard man with black tussled hair emerged. He had a bandage wrapped around the palm of his left hand, which he cradled close to his side. He clearly had been in a terrible altercation, and looked to have gotten the worst of it. His nose had dried blood at the nostrils, and his cheekbone badly bruised. A purplish red mark ran across the breadth of his throat like a ghastly scarf. The rest of the man's chiseled features gave evidence of a recent beating. One lip was a little swollen, and several slashing smudges of dried blood were evident on his left brow and cheek.

"Come all the way out from behind the tree." Greystoke ordered.

The stranger complied and came completely out in the open. He carried himself gingerly with a pronounced limp and noticeable exhaustion. Was this man a robber who finally met his match against an unwilling victim? Or perhaps this beat and tired man himself had fallen prey to highwaymen. Something was amiss, and Greystoke aimed to find out what.

"Who might you be?" The Sergeant motioned for the man to raise his hands.

"I'm looking for Barrington Rathbone," the man replied in a tired voice and rolled the 'r's' in Barrington Rathbone noticeably.

"Well isn't that a grand notion," Sergeant Greystoke replied sarcastically. "That still doesn't answer my question now does it mate?"

The man took a deep breath, clearly irritated. "Can you tell me where Barrington Rathbone is, or not? I don't have a lot of time or patience right now."

"Are you daft? You're in no position to make demands. Identify yourself, lest I assume you are an enemy in my land and be done with you." The Sergeant demanded a response, growing frustrated himself. He leveled his crossbow at the man in a threatening manner to add weight to his words.

The man glared at the Sergeant with cold dark eyes, eyes that could penetrate a person's soul. A chill ran down Greystoke's spine.

Though the man was outnumbered he did not appear to be intimidated. In fact, if the truth were known, the man was too exhausted to care, much less be afraid.

"If I thought it would end the questions I would have already told you my name," the man replied tersely. "But I know it is merely the first in a series of questions. Now please sir, I see you wear the surcoat of the army of The Dales; I can assure you, one who wears that surcoat has nothing to fear from me. I have been through quite an ordeal and am pressed for time. If you please Sergeant, tell me where I might find Barrington Rathbone and I will leave your land at once. If you can't do that then perhaps you might know where I might locate Novak Reinhardt. I believe him to be near this…"

"Novak Reinhardt? Are you a friend of his? Well why didn't you say so." Greystoke lowered his crossbow. "How is it you know Novak?"

The man was taken aback by the rapid change in reception. He softened a little. "He's a friend of mine from Ravenshire."

"You're not one of those knights are you?"

The man hesitated. "What knights are those?"

"The Clandestine Knights; you know, like Novak."

"Um, yes, actually I am. I'm Scorpyus Verazzno." Scorpyus decided anyone wearing a surcoat of the army of the Dales couldn't be all that bad. No one would wear one who wasn't, especially this close to the border of Kelterland.

"Well then," Greystoke smiled. "I suppose I can take you to Novak. But if you don't mind my asking, what bloke did you tangle with? I'd like to avoid him." The remark elicited a chuckle from his men.

"If your fortune holds you'll never have to find out. Pray you never do. I pity the man who must face what I have. Surely this enemy was conjured from evil." Scorpyus's voice was grave with trepidation and dripped with foreboding. He knew few could understand the gravity of the matter from his perspective. His words were spoken like that of a survivor rather then a victor. The comment drew a curious silence from the men.

Greystoke's brow furrowed in puzzlement, and then a dawning realization swept his countenance. He knew of few things that could chill a man's blood so thoroughly.

"A Valkyrie or Trepanite?"

Scorpyus raised an eyebrow. "It was a Valkyrie. You've heard of them?"

Greystoke's nodded affirmatively. "Unfortunately I have. I've never seen one though, and that's the way I aim to keep it."

Scorpyus smiled. It hurt his mouth. "I couldn't agree more."

Sergeant Greystoke had one of his men extinguish the small fire, and the rest start their preparation for the ride back to Stonebridge.

Greystoke continued. "And since you've interrupted our tea we may as well start back now."

Scorpyus paused momentarily. He didn't want to disrupt anything.

The sergeant smiled at Scorpyus and extended a hand. "Don't worry. Any friend of Novak is a friend of ours."

A look of relief washed over Scorpyus. It was good to hear Novak was making a good impression. But then again he always made an impression of some sort or another; a good one on those that were friendly, and a deep one in those jaws that were not.

⸻

"Sir, the patrol is back!" A soldier anxiously reported to Barrington Rathbone. "And they have someone with them."

"Really?" The Major was mildly surprised. "Perhaps they acquired an unsuspecting prisoner; a foolhardy cutpurse who traipsed upon an outlying farm in order to pillage what he may."

Novak overheard the exchange and followed Major Rathbone to Sergeant Greystoke. The squad was unsaddling their horses. They were dusty and saddle weary after their long patrol. A few were drinking generously from their water skins.

Sergeant Greystoke, upon seeing the Major approach, stopped what he was doing and immediately approached his superior. He stood smartly at attention.

"Major, the patrol is reporting in as commanded. All is quiet along the border in our sector, but…we do have an unexpected guest."

Barrington eyed the olive skinned and bloodied man standing next to his sergeant. "And who might this be?"

"Scorpyus!" Novak blurted out much to Barrington's surprise. "What are you doing here? What happened to you?"

"I feel like I've been beaten with a shovel." Uneasiness was evident in Scorpyus's voice.

"Ya, I believe it." Novak looked over his battered friend. Emerald couldn't believe her eyes. She wouldn't have recognized Scorpyus.

"You know this chap?" Barrington asked.

Novak nodded, and studied his friend. His surprise quickly turned to concern. Something was wrong. He could read it in Scorpyus's mannerisms and shifting glances.

"Something's happened. You were not supposed to arrive yet."

Scorpyus looked down and shook his head. "I have some… bad news."

"What?" That familiar look of anger flashed in Novak's steely gaze.

The Major sensed the gravity of the situation and made an offer of privacy. "Perhaps you would like to confide with Novak in my private quarters."

Scorpyus contemplated and collected his tired thoughts. "Thank you, I think I will…and…has Novak talked to you yet?"

"Yes, Novak and I have discussed creating troublesome diversionary attacks on Kelterlander troops in order to give Xylor needed time to stabilize." Barrington admitted. "With any luck the King will be forced to utilize his new conscripts here. If Xylor remains free it should boost the morale of resistance fighters throughout the Astorian Realms."

Novak indicated assistance had indeed been secured to carry out Cad's plan.

Scorpyus managed a weak smile that hurt his swollen lips. "Well then, if you don't mind, you may want to join us. What I have to say may concern you after all."

"Very well; I shall join you." The Major smiled. Novak had a puzzled look on his face. He could see the gears turning in Scorpyus's mind.

"Good," Scorpyus replied. "I have an idea for our first… project."

"I'll see you soon." Novak smiled at Emerald.

"Alright," Emerald replied with a worried tone. She didn't want to know what Scorpyus had to say. All she knew was whatever he said, it was sure to somehow involve Novak risking his life. She wondered if she would ever be able to come to grips with the thought.

Novak, Barrington, and Scorpyus retreated to the Major's private quarters and situated themselves around a small table. His quarters were a small stone room underneath the bridge for which Stonebridge was named. At one time it had been an office for the toll master of the bridge. That and a few other structures were all that remained of the one time trail stop on a now forgotten highway. Now the place served as Barrington's command post. A small cot and trunk stood in one corner; a table and four stools in the other. A cloak lay draped across the cot. By no stretch of the imagination was the Major living a luxurious lifestyle.

Novak introduced his two friends. "Scorpyus, this is Major Barrington Rathbone. Major, this is Scorpyus Verazzno.

"Please, call me Barry." The Major shook hands with his new guest.

"Pleased to meet you."

After proper introductions, Scorpyus was ready to convey his news. "There's no easy way to say this." He directed his conversation to Novak.

"Shortly after your departure, Zephyr was taken captive by the Valkyrie. I think she may still be alive, but I can't really say much of anything for sure. God only knows."

Novak's jaw tightened and the vein in his temple throbbed in unison with his quickening pulse. Barry cast his eyes downward, a pained look on his face. He knew firsthand the difficulty of these situations. Then again, all in the realm did.

Scorpyus took a deep breath, waiting for Novak to take in his statement. What he had to say next wouldn't help matters.

"And Cad has been taken prisoner." Scorpyus continued.

As predicted, Novak fumed and stood forcefully. "Where are they now? The Valkyrie's will pay for this, I will not let this go unanswered."

Scorpyus motioned for Novak to sit back down. "Hear me out first."

"Is that how you were wounded?" Barry pointed to the bandage on Scorpyus's hand.

Scorpyus nodded and related a quick account of events. "Cad was captured at the docks in Xylor. It was on a deserted rickety pier by an abandoned warehouse. I trailed the Valkyrie's to a ship of known pirate's; a real hardened bunch for hire to the highest bidder. I saw them change from their black clothing to regular fashions. They were looking worse for the wear, and anxious to be leaving. Someone met them at the docks with a large wooden crate. They shoved Cad inside bound and gagged. They paid the pirates to take them to Kelterland, no questions asked. I disguised myself as a villainous type and paid for a trip to the mainland also. I told them I needed to leave discreetly as the law was looking for me."

Novak controlled his inner rage enough to sit back down and take in the account of events. He listened intently to Scorpyus, his brow furrowed into an angry crease. Barry listened quietly.

Scorpyus cleared his throat. "Anyway, the ship dropped us off at a small cove about five miles north of Astoria; at some obscure village. The Valkyrie's took Cad out of the crate, placed him in the back of a hay wagon and set out for Astoria. I followed them secretly from a distance, or so I thought. Now Novak, you know how well I can go unseen in the shadows; I've been able to follow people in *plain sight* without them knowing it."

Scorpyus spoke with exasperated surprise. "But somehow the Valkyrie's knew. I can't for the life of me figure out where I went wrong. One of the Valkyrie was able to slip from the others without my getting suspicious, and lay in wait to ambush me."

Scorpyus threw his hands up, at a complete loss for an explanation. "I still don't know how they did it. Unfortunately, I don't think we've seen the end of them."

Scorpyus took a deep breath and paused. "I thought it was over Novak. The Valkyrie almost killed me. Before I knew what was happening that garrote was around my throat…again. My vision started to blur and I was going unconscious. Somehow I was able to work my left hand under the wire. This hardly helped. The Valkyrie continued to choke me with my own hand. He pulled with so much force the garrote cut deep into my palm. Finally I was able to slip out of the stranglehold, and the real fight was on. The fight went on and on, both of us exchanging blows, death hovering overhead like a vulture to take the first to make a fatal mistake."

Scorpyus stared blankly at the table for a moment. "And then it happened; something…I can't say why, but the Valkyrie stopped for a second. He moved a little to my right like he was looking at someone behind me. Whoever it was must have looked intimidating because he definitely caught the Valkyrie's attention if only for a second. I didn't expect whoever it was to actually help but welcomed the distraction. I slashed the Valkyrie across his inner arm by the armpit. It was the fateful blow. The Valkyrie started to bleed profusely, its arm hanging limp by its side. Rather than continue the fight, the Valkyrie decided to hastily retreat. By this point I was too exhausted to do anything but watch it fade into the forest. I was glad it was over, and I was still alive. When I turned around to see who came up behind me, there was no one there. It was a miracle."

By the end of the story, Novak had calmed considerably. A sickening worry oppressed his appetite. His mouth was abnormally parched, his lips clinging to his teeth. He heard more then the tale of Scorpyus's survival against tremendous odds. Novak heard the haunting narrative that had always lain dormant in the farthest reaches of his mind; the possibility he never allowed himself to think about, the literal end of the Clandestine Knights. In the span of a few short days it almost came down to Novak alone. It was a horrendous proposition.

Barry let out a whistle. "I say, you are indeed quite fortunate. I have yet to meet anyone who has survived such an encounter. Clearly, it was not your time. There are some unfinished tasks yet for you to finish."

"Do you know where Cad is now? And what about Zephyr?" Novak seized on what hope could be found in this dim tale. He was alive. Scorpyus was alive. There was reason to believe Cad was alive albeit imprisoned. And there was no proof of Zephyr's death.

"After my fight with the Valkyrie I went to Astoria. Cad is being held in the main prison. Dungeon would be a better name for it. Zephyr was being held there also, but she is very sick. Information on her is a week old. That place is disease ridden and fowl. You can smell the stink just by getting near it. They are both to be executed in two days. For Cad and Zephyr they seem to be rushing the execution." Scorpyus related.

"So we will believe Zephyr is alive." Novak stated matter-of-factly, and shook his head in disbelief. "I leave and everything falls apart."

"You're partially right Novak," Scorpyus looked directly into Novak's eyes not wanting him to miss what he said next. "But this is also an 'Alcazar' episode."

Novak did a double take, a light of awakening dawning in his eyes. He mulled it over in his head for a minute. "It sounds too risky."

Scorpyus couldn't argue. "We didn't see any other way."

"So be it." Novak said reluctantly. "But you also said I was partially right. And I sense there is more to tell me."

Scorpyus sighed and proceeded to fill in Novak about all the unfortunate betrayal and subterfuge Natasha was a part of. He left no detail untold, including his part in Natasha's death.

"So the Order of the Valkyrie employs both men and women." Barry blurted out amazed at the discovery and joyous over the victory. "And you were successful in killing one? I say, perhaps there is indeed hope for the Astorian realms to regain their former splendor. For years now the Valkyrie's have been Kelterland's assassins for hire. A few of our notable leaders met their death at their hands just as significant resistance was beginning. That is why they were sent to dispatch you. The Clandestine Knights have been victorious, and a Valkyrie has been slain! This is certainly a good sign. Perhaps we are on the eve of a new beginning." Barry was oblivious to the exact nature of Natasha's relationship to the Clandestine Knights, much less Scorpyus. He couldn't help but take the news with great euphoria. Scorpyus and Novak did nothing to diminish his joy over the occasion. Lord knows anyone involved in resisting Kelterland could use all the morale they could get.

"Then Cad was right," Novak observed. "Xylor is rid of the Valkyrie's."

Scorpyus nodded. "It happened the way he and Hester predicted. A Valkyrie was killed; the rest retreated to regroup and nurse their wounds. Yet they left only after they thought they had finished their assignment."

"Their only admirable quality being their dedication to the task." Barry observed.

Novak cut the fancy speech and went to the crux of the matter. "The first thing we need to do is get Cad and Zephyr, and then start killing the King's brigades. That will give Xylor time to stabilize. Let's plan this out. I am ready to fight."

"Ahh," Barry drew a logical conclusion from what he was hearing. "Our first act of insurgency shall be a prison rescue."

"That's what I was hoping, and why I asked you to this meeting." Scorpyus was relieved to see Barry willing to lend assistance. "But we have to hurry. Cad and Zephyr are to be executed soon."

"Then we don't have much time." Novak gave Scorpyus a slap on the shoulder. "It's good to see you Scorp. Not all hope is lost. I bet Thadus is happy to be rid of the Valkyrie's. And now Cyrus will have his chance to command the troops with Cad being captured. They'll keep things under control." Novak was ready for a little good news before taking on the daunting task of a rescue. It was not to come.

Scorpyus had a pained, contorted expression on his face. "Now is the time to pray things get better; because we might not be able to bear it if things got much worse."

Novak and Barry looked at each other curiously. Neither had heard of Thadus's assassination yet. Both sat in numb disbelief as an exhausted Scorpyus labored through the rest of the story.

———◆———

Cad was forced to the chopping block for his beheading. The hooded executioner forced him in place roughly, pressing him down with a boot. There was little point in resisting. Armed guards stood all around the platform. Cad felt the jagged groves of the chopping block scrape against his face as a gruesome reminder of where a sharpened blade had plunged many times before. Not too far in the distance a bell started ringing incessantly.

Towering above, the executioner braced himself in a wide legged stance for a mighty hack with his razor sharp battle-axe. Cad drowned in the gloom of the executioner's shadow as the burly man readied for his merciless deed.

"No! No!" Zephyr wept bitterly and struggled to assist Cad. Thick hairy forearms held her tight in a menacing grasp. She could only watch as the executioner raised his axe waiting for his signal to proceed.

"You stupid ox! May God reserve a fiery judgment for what you are about to do. I tell you he is innocent!" Zephyr was hysterical and struggled against her captor. In her weakened state it was all in vain. Her overloaded senses coupled with her weakened state gave way, and Zephyr collapsed on the scaffolding.

With a shout, the hooded executioner tapped his foot twice and then brought his axe down on Cad with such velocity it whistled as it cut through the air. With a dull thud, it landed hard cutting clean through its intended target, and sinking deep into the wood of the chopping block. A gasp of excitement erupted from the crowd, and all leapt for joy in unison.

Quickly, the executioner placed one boot on the chopping block and worked the blade of his axe free. Without hesitation, he turned and buried the blade deep into the chest of one of the guards. Blood gushed from the cleaved gaping wound. Another guard collapsed, the blade of a dagger sunk deep into his left armpit. Felix, the High Cleric of Balar, dislodged the dripping dagger from the guard's armpit. His aged and slow movements were now swift and full of the youthful dexterity of a man less then half his age. The rest of the guards on the scaffolding stood bewildered, trying to process the chaotic events unfolding. Were their eyes deceiving them, or did Felix and the executioner begin an attack on the guards. It made no sense. The guards wasted valuable seconds not wanting to believe the impossible was indeed happening.

Cad sprang to his feet, the chain to his wrist shackles severed. He wrapped his hand around the chain near his wrist and flailed the iron links like a whip. He ferociously brought the chain against the face of the guard that mistreated him earlier. A series of red oozing welts appeared on the guard's cheek and brow like a grotesque constellation in a white sky. This was payback for two weeks in a filthy cell; two weeks of near starvation and beatings. Cad determined to balance the account. Four lashes of chain later and the guard crumpled into unconsciousness.

The executioner tore his hood off to reveal the thick neck and muscled jaw of Novak. Fire was in his eyes; every sense on high alert. Novak felt his heart racing. Power surged through his body. He fed on the mix of excitement and fear coursing through his veins. He breathed in the scene before him. A guard started climbing onto the scaffolding. Before he went too far, Novak brought his axe down hard on the man's helmet. The guard's armor saved his life, but the force of the blow rattled his brain enough to put him to sleep for a while.

"Let's move faster." Novak advised his friends. The guards around the scaffolding unsheathed their weapons.

Cad slipped a sword from the sheath of a dead guard. Shrieks erupted from the gathered throngs as fear spread like fire through dry grass in a high wind. The masses, once eager to see death, now wanted no part of it.

Like cattle, the citizens started pushing and shoving, trying to escape the packed courtyard. People screamed in fear and panic as hundreds pressed towards exits that were clogged with disarray. Within seconds the crowd was in a full stampede, and people were trampled underfoot. Mothers fought to hold their children as many got swallowed up in a tangle of legs. Pickpockets and cutpurses worked the crowd, taking advantage of the disorder.

"Guards! Sound the alarm! Treachery afoot!" The lord mayor yelled, pleading for assistance from anyone willing to render it.

"Scorpyus, get Zephyr," Cad swung the chain across the forehead of the guard restraining Zephyr. The man grimaced in agony as three link size swellings formed above his brow.

Scorpyus, still in cleric regalia, pried Zephyr from the guard's loosening grasp. "Zephyr, we're here for you, but you'll have to stay awake. We'll need your help." Scorpyus planted a boot in the gut of an approaching guard sending him back down the scaffolding stairs.

The commotion and yelling aroused Zephyr's state of alertness. "Scorpyus?" She squinted at the aged cleric. Behind the face of Felix's features was the unmistakable obsidian glare of Scorpyus's eyes.

"Oui, Scorpyus, it is you!" The sight of Scorpyus meant there was hope for rescue, and revived Zephyr further from her fever.

More guards came running from the prison. Their progress was slowed by having to weave and shove their way through the chaotic throngs. A few loyal citizens made their escape and ran to alert the King's Brigades. Others went to the nearby rooftops to watch the bloodshed.

Novak slammed the executioner's axe against another guard. This one almost got out of the way in time, catching a glancing blow to his right forearm, splaying his flesh open.

"Dantes better hurry!" Novak glanced around apprehensively as he defended the scaffolding. It was a small island on which he was trapped.

Scorpyus nodded his agreement as he wrestled the sword from the arm of a guard who was about to strike Cad.

"You will all be put to death for sedition!" The lord mayor shouted as he cowered against the wall as far from the edge of the platform as he could. "You'll never get away with this. You will be hunted down and dispatched like the despicable dogs you all are. It will be…"

Novak's fist silenced the annoying and idle chatter. The lord mayor collapsed and Novak threw him from the scaffolding. He was the last enemy to occupy the platform. Novak, Cad, Scorpyus, and Zephyr spread out to defend their small-elevated haven. The lord mayor landed on the ground with a dull thud, providing an opportunity for unsavory sorts. Within the span of twenty seconds he was relieved of the contents of his pockets and his shoes.

A wagon appeared from around the corner. The two horses pulling it were rearing a bit, spooked by the noise and press of the crowd. The driver pushed the team into the throngs, the horses shoving through those who were too slow to get out of the way.

"Dantes is here." Novak announced as he swung his axe, keeping the guards at bay.

Cad turned and saw a wagon mow through the stampeding people. One person went down and was lost between the hooves and wheels. Others scurried out of the way, some diving aside. Nothing parted a crowd faster then horses. Cad could see two men on the wagon. One was a bearded burly man who held the reigns. The other was a ruddy-faced man who shed his cloak to reveal a green surcoat. Three other men simultaneously shed their cloaks to reveal green surcoats also. They rode in the back of the wagon, and were firing crossbows at the guards. Two guards dropped, their hands cradling their chest, crossbow bolts sticking from their rib cage.

"Who are these blokes?" Cad didn't recognize anyone.

"They're here to help." Scorpyus stated. He noticed the remaining guards formed a half circle around the scaffolding, no longer trying to obtain a foothold on the platform. It was a bitter lesson that cost three of their comrade's lives.

A blast from a trumpet echoed through the courtyard. The crowd flinched in unison and attempted to flee faster. Dantes snapped the reins down hard on the team of horses, coaxing them along against their will. The mob was frightening the animals, and both were starting to rear terribly. It was everything Dantes could do to keep them under control.

The wagon stopped in front of the scaffolding and the men in green surcoats jumped out and engaged the guards in combat. The guards were taken by surprise and quickly found themselves no match for Barrington's men.

"Make haste lads!" Barry shoved citizens away from the horses.

Zephyr leapt the five feet into the wagon. The leap caused her to feel light headed; enough so she sunk to her knees.

Novak backed up against the wall on the platform in order to get a running jump at the wagon. Movement overhead caught his attention. Looking up he saw archers on the roof of the prison. In unison they drew back their bows aiming downward.

"Archers!" Novak hollered a warning he knew would be too late. A slew of arrows came shooting downward. Three citizens dropped like sacks of grain, arrows sticking from their torso. One of Barry's men hollered in pain. Scorpyus jumped to the ground and rolled under the wagon coming up the other side. He reached into the wagon, retrieving his bow and quiver.

"What's taking so long? Zephyr, grab your bow." Scorpyus notched an arrow and loosed it toward the roof.

A corpse landed with a thud on the scaffolding next to Novak as he took his running jump to the wagon. Looking back he noticed an arrow protruding from a Kelterlander archer. Novak scurried off the other side of the wagon just as the Kelterlander archers loosed another volley. Dantes screamed out in pain, an arrow through the side of his forearm. Screams echoed through the courtyard, the people in a terror filled panic. All civility was lost. Men punched women, the strong knocked the weak aside, and mothers abandoned children, all in a desperate attempt save themselves. All knew too well the Kelterlander archers would give no regard for innocent bystanders.

"Let's get this bloody wagon moving," Cad crouched behind the wagon as it lurched forward slowly. Barry's men soon joined him after dispatching a few more of the guards around the scaffolding. Dantes crouched under the seat and drove the team from his awkward position.

Another volley of arrows hurled downward searching for targets to sink into. One pierced the wagon near Scorpyus as he loosed another arrow toward the enemy.

"Dantes hurry!" Scorpyus notched another arrow.

"The animals be getting spooked. Thar be too much noise, and the people be blocking the path." Dantes growled, frustrated with the skittish animals. The horses reared and whinnied, frightened in place. They were beasts of burden, not trained war animals.

"Help me clear a path." Novak motioned to Greystoke. Together they ran in front of the wagon and started shoving people aside. Another volley of arrows thudded all around. A few more citizens dropped having been struck by the flying projectiles. Women ran screaming, children cried; men scampered away shrieking. It was a despicable display of cowardice. One woman dragged her four-year-old son by the hand, an arrow embedded deep in his hip. His leg hung limp, his pant leg saturated and crimson. He wailed terribly as his frightened mother pulled him along.

Novak felt a thud to his back as an arrow took him square in the cuirass. He ignored it and grabbed one horse by the bridle, pulling it with one hand and shoving a path with the other. Finally the wagon rumbled onward making better progress. Out of the corner of his eye Novak saw the woman loose her grip on her son. Almost instantly a wild-eyed man clawing through the crowd stepped on him. The boy shrieked as two hundred pounds pressed into his arrow imbedded hip breaking the shaft near the skin. The man continued on unfazed. As the man ran by Novak, he shot out a fist catching the coward in the jaw by the ear. There was an audible snap and the man dropped in a heap. Novak shoved him out of the wagon's path with a foot.

"My son! My son!" The mother cried and bent down to help her child who was wailing in utter agony. Another woman turned and tripped falling to her back. She was stepped on by several other citizens.

"I say there! You two provide some protection for Novak and Greystoke. And be quick about it." The Major ordered once his men finished with the last of the prison guards. His two men ran over and stood with raised shields between the archers and Novak and Greystoke. They tried to provide some cover from the incoming projectiles.

Scorpyus and Zephyr fired as fast as they could notch their arrows. Zephyr was in the back of the wagon. She was in a cold sweat but fully alert due to the gravity of the situation. She crouched as low as she could behind the two-foot high sidewall of the wagon. Zephyr felt terribly exposed but could do little to help it. Scorpyus stood on the side of the wagon, firing over it. Both concentrated solely on the Kelterlander archers trusting the others to watch their backs.

"Don't get daft; easy boy." Greystoke snatched the other horse by the bridle and forced it onward. One of his comrades held his shield in the trajectory of fire. An arrow slammed into the upraised shield; another creased Greystoke's neck.

"Blimey! We can't bandy about any longer!" Greystoke touched the side of his neck and felt a sticky warm fluid.

Cad helped Barry lift his fallen man to the wagon. The wounded man grimaced as he was dropped on the hard wooden surface, an arrow in his side. The projectile penetrated his chain mail shirt. Chain mail was not a guarantee of protection. That's why Cad wore a cuirass.

Novak had enough. He reached down and took the unconscious coward by the nape of the neck and the seat of the pants. With a guttural yell he raised the man over his head and heaved him towards the panicked crowd knocking two men down. Both were stepping on a fallen woman. Novak ran to the woman and jerked her to her feet. Immediately she fled. He then took up the wounded boy in one hand, and grabbed his mother with the other. Without explanation he carried them to the wagon, the mother barely touching the ground as she found herself moving. Effortlessly, his muscled shoulders plopped both into the back of the wagon.

"Keep down. We will get you out of here." Novak instructed and resumed his place at the horse's bridle.

The frightened woman cradled her son in her arms as the wagon rolled toward the courtyard's exit. She crouched low, bewildered by the flurry of activity around her but relieved to be on her way out of the mayhem. A wounded man lay groaning near her feet, and a woman fired arrows from above her head. A man stood next to the wagon and fired his bow over her. He looked strange. A white floury-like pasty substance was all over his face making him appear wrinkly. It had been scrapped from his right cheek to reveal younger looking olive skin. His black hair was matted, a gray wig laying in the wagon near him. Dark eyes under prominent eyebrows sighted arrows along their shaft before loosing them skyward. Two other men walked along the side of the wagon. It was the most chaotic and bizarre thing the woman ever witnessed.

"Hiyaa!" Dantes roared so loudly the woman's heart leapt within her. He snapped the reins down on the horses back. Novak and Greystoke pulled the animals by the bridle. The wagon rumbled forward cutting a swath through the masses.

"I tell you, we are almost out of arrows," Zephyr proclaimed. Suddenly the wagon lurched forward causing Zephyr to fall to her side. One of the horses erupted with a loud whinny, the shaft of an arrow protruding from its left flank. The other horse picked up the pace in unison with its wounded mate. Both trotted for the exit.

Somewhere in the not too far distance was several blasts from another trumpet. Cad and Barry shot each other a knowing glance. That could only mean one thing; more troops from the King's Brigade.

The wagon tore out of the courtyard at a trot. Citizens flooded out behind it. Novak, Greystoke, Cad, Scorpyus and Barry climbed aboard. Dantes sat back up, holding the reins with his good arm.

"Quick, turn right on this next street," Cad pointed to the right as he climbed over everyone and into the seat next to Dantes. "And slow the wagon down. We don't want to look like we are running away. We're just some blokes out for a ride."

Dantes rounded the corner a little too fast forcing a couple crossing the street to give him a dirty look. He smiled apologetically and reined the horses in to a walk. Scorpyus and Zephyr lowered their bows. Everyone in back tried to look composed and indifferent, trying not to garner too much suspicion. It was near impossible, and the group drew many curious glances; especially when the wounded boy cried out in pain.

"Let me have the reins mate," Cad noticed people looking at Dantes bloody arm with the arrow through it yet. "Cover that up if you can."

Dantes snapped the tail feathers of the shaft off, and then grabbed the arrowhead pulling the rest of the shaft from his forearm.

"Briny barnacles!" Dantes yelped. "That smarts just a wee bit!"

Zephyr handed him a strip of cloth from the wounded soldier's surcoat. Dantes wrapped it around his throbbing forearm. Trumpets still sounded in the distance. All knew it would be only a matter of time before the king's brigades tracked them down. Astoria was a huge city with many eyes and ears. Kelterlander soldiers were everywhere.

Cad turned down another street then stopped the wagon after four blocks near an apothecary. "No more passengers," he motioned to Novak.

"Here take this," Novak pressed three shillings into the mother's palm. "Find someone to help your son." He lifted the woman and let her down outside of the wagon.

"Thank you," the mother replied as Novak placed her son in her arms. She was relieved to be away from the chaos and now able to afford medical care for her boy.

Novak smiled weakly as the wagon started up again. He watched the mother enter the apothecary. The boy was pale and wounded terribly, but he was young. His survival was very questionable. All those in the wagon said a quick prayer for the innocent child.

The wagon rumbled two more blocks in nervous tension. Barry tended to his wounded man. All other eyes glanced around apprehensively.

The sounds of hooves on cobblestone echoed from the far end of the street where the group had just been. To everyone's horror, cavalry troops from the King's brigades rounded the corner. There were about twenty horsemen in all. The cavalry stopped, one of the horsemen questioning a passing citizen. There was a brief conversation after which the citizen pointed down the street toward the wagon. Novak could see one of the horsemen sit up straight in the saddle and look his direction with a hand over his brow to shield from the sun. A second later a trumpet sounded and the mounted soldiers galloped in the direction the citizen pointed them.

"They found us." Novak announced what all realized.

Immediately Cad turned the wagon down another street and brought the horses to a momentary trot. He went one block and turned yet again. Quickly he brought the wagon to a stop.

"We'll never escape cavalry in this bloody wagon. Our best chance is to go on foot." Cad hopped down from his seat. The others followed suit.

Scorpyus was in agreement. "Let's find a narrow alley; hopefully a cluttered one with many doors."

The party quickly assembled themselves retrieving what little possessions were in the wagon. Novak helped the Major with his wounded man.

"It will be easier if I carry him alone." Novak offered.

"I say Novak, that won't be necessary. I'm afraid he has already passed." Tears welled in Barry's eyes.

Zephyr looked at the pale lifeless corpse as Novak set it down in the street. "I am so sorry Monsieur."

Hastily, the Major called for the nearby shopkeeper. "Here is five shillings. Bring this chap to the river by Waldorf Grove at midnight. I'll send someone to meet you. There will be another five shillings for you then."

The shopkeeper's eyes lit up at the thought of earning what he felt were a king's ransom for one day's work. It was a price Barry was counting on to assure loyalty, if only for this one task. The man greedily took the money. Barry helped get his fallen comrade in the store. The shopkeeper hid the body in a back room.

The second the transaction was over the party set off in a run for the nearest alley. Fear now erased all traces of the fever from Zephyr. The rumble of hoof beats clattered as the last of the group rounded the corner.

The cavalry tore around the corner and reined to an abrupt halt next to the wagon. The shopkeeper was scrubbing the wooden planks of his store with a brush. A basin of water stood nearby.

"Where are the people who were in this wagon?" A lieutenant in the king's brigade demanded of the shopkeeper.

"Uh, um…" The shopkeeper stuttered nervously as he stood from his labor.

"And if you tell me you haven't seen them, I'll kill you where you stand." The lieutenant barked. Blood dripped out of the wagon onto the street. There was a small pool on the walkway in front of the store also. The shopkeeper froze speechless.

"Answer me! Lest your blood joins the traitor's whose is spilt on the walk." The lieutenant clasped the hilt of his sword.

"They went down the alley." The shopkeeper pointed pale as a ghost, his knees knocking together.

The lieutenant led his men thundering down the alley. Due to the restricted confines the horsemen had to go single file and weave between stairs and obstacles. A man coming out of an alley door was forced to press himself flat against the wall as the cavalry passed by.

"There they are at the end of the alley!" The lieutenant roared. "Sound the trumpet." He spurred his mount on as fast as it could negotiate the narrow corridor.

Scorpyus wheeled around at the sound of the trumpet, its haunting melody echoing down the street. "They're very close. The leader will be upon us soon."

The others nodded their agreement. Without hesitation they bolted as fast as their legs would take them. Cavalry was the best motivator of those on foot. Zephyr, with bow tight in one hand pumped her arms furiously as she ran. The cool air rushed through her sweat soaked hair and across her clammy brow.

A man stepped from an alley doorway right into Novak's path. He was unarmed and clearly not a threat. Novak tried to sidestep but was unsuccessful. At a full run, Novak collided with the man sending him into the wall. With a terrified look, the poor fellow bounced off the wall, spun and then staggered back toward the center of the alley directly into Cad's path. Before Cad could react he too collided with the man, this time knocking him to the ground. He was lost under a tangle of feet.

"I am sorry monsieur." Zephyr apologized realizing she stepped on someone. She looked back to see the man roll out of Scorpyus's path in the nick of time. The man rose to his feet, dusted himself off momentarily, and then starred slack jawed at the approaching horse soldier's charging his way. With a whimper, he ran for the door he just exited hoping to find solace.

The party continued down the alley and soon came to the end where it branched either right or left. To the left was a large wagon that just unloaded its supplies. It effectively blocked the pathway. The party went to the right and resumed their frantic pace, boot steps resounding off the stone structures looming on either side. Before they made it forty paces a man stepped out of a doorway and stood blocking their path. He wore a sand colored cloak with a white rope sash. Scorpyus recognized the man as the one he had seen before in Xylor and again at Hester's cabin. Cad recognized the man from the docks. And Zephyr recognized the man as the one she saw in the woods shortly before her capture by the Valkyrie's. Unlike the previous incidents when the man was unarmed, this time he held up a sharp two-edged sword. It was dazzling, brightly polished and silver. It seemed to radiate light. On it, inscribed in large eloquent letters was the words 'El Shaddai.'

"Who are you mate?" Cad screeched to a halt and eyed the man warily. For some unexplained reason, something he felt deep down, Cad wasn't alarmed by the man's presence.

The man looked at Cad with compassionate clear mahogany eyes. The white of the man's eyes were a brilliant ivory color and almost translucent. Without fear, without malice, he stood there with upraised sword. He carried himself with confidence and purpose.

"I am Caelestis. Peace be to ye who have found grace. Fear not the men who pursue you. They shall not pass." The man spoke with authority and motioned for the party to continue on.

The beating of horse hooves grew louder and louder. There would be no time to linger and contemplate a decision. Certain death would be upon them soon.

"We better go." Cad stated flatly, fixated on this stranger.

The others agreed. Reluctantly the party forged on, propelled by the urgent need to escape and yet unexplainably drawn to stay. Everyone felt at ease. It was impossible to explain. Normally, the thought of one man facing twenty horse soldiers was tantamount to suicide. Yet all concerned felt an unexplainable confidence. The party raced to the end of the alley. There was a sound like a still small voice on the breeze, a calming whisper of a mysterious presence. A feeling of repose bathed the party. It stirred emotions of serenity; like those a lost child would feel upon finding its parent. Zephyr shot a glance back as the party was about to turn onto a small side street. The man stood, sword raised, blocking the path down the alley. The first of the cavalry soldiers was seconds from a collision course with the man. The lieutenant rode, leaning to the side with upraised sword as if he would strike the man down as he galloped by. It was the last Zephyr saw of the man.

An explosive boom of thunder crashed overhead like mountains colliding. The report rolled through Astoria, echoing through the stone structures with such ferocity the ground shook. The sound reverberated deep within the party's chests like the thump from a giant drum, practically knocking them from their feet.

"Briny barnacles, the wrath of God be upon this place!" Dantes stumbled but caught himself. He heard no argument to the contrary from the others. His wide-eyed countenance glanced skyward expecting to see a manifestation of the thunder. There was but a few puffs of clouds in the sky; certainly nothing resembling a thunderhead or approaching storm.

Barry caught up to and ran along side of Novak. "I say there Novak, follow me. This street goes to the river."

Barry and Novak were in the lead and turned left down another street. The street soon dead-ended at a long series of stairs that gradually descended downward toward the river. The party descended them quickly brushing past a few citizens. Barry and his men drew a few stares. Their green surcoats were peculiar. Many citizens did not recognize them, but others did.

"You better get some cloaks." Novak paused and pointed at a vendor. The Major quickly bought and donned cloaks for him and his men.

Barry was perturbed. "We had cloaks. In our rush to assist our fallen comrades they were forgotten in the wagon. My apologies."

"Why not leave them on?" Novak asked. Certainly Barry knew the danger of being seen in a surcoat of The Dales.

The Major stiffened up as if he heard an absurd statement. "I say there Novak; I want it to be known to the Kelterlander soldiers I fight that it is the army of the Dales who has just taken them in battle. My men feel the same way."

"Ya, that is a good reason as any. But you trade off stealth." Novak replied.

The party continued on. At one point the stairs leveled out at a small footbridge spanning a tiny tributary, the waters underneath splashing over stones as they made their way to the river.

The party crossed the footbridge uneventfully. Hurriedly they took the stone steps as they came to a small amphitheatre at the rivers edge. The amphitheatre was packed with people. All were gathered and engrossed with what was happening on the opposite bank. Across the river was a small platform with black curtains for a backdrop. A stage play was in progress. The actors were in a pivotal point in the production that had the audience in silent anticipation.

"Shh!" An angry woman elegantly dressed turned to Barry and Novak as they stomped to a halt at the rear of the amphitheatre. The rest of the party came to an abrupt and noisy halt behind them. Several patrons of the play turned to glare at the arriving party. All had a look of displeasure furrowed into their brow.

Cad motioned to the cobblestone walkways at the front of the amphitheatre. They stretched along the riverbank in both directions.

"We will have to walk through the crowd." Novak loudly whispered to Cad.

"Shh," the woman gave Novak another nasty look. He nodded apologetically.

"What choice do we have?" Cad whispered back.

Novak shrugged his massive shoulders and then started working his way through the crowd. It was a difficult task. The amphitheatre consisted of a series of stepped shelves that served as seats. There was no aisle to go down and people were not sitting in any organized fashion. Novak had to find spaces to step between people, usually places barely big enough to place his foot. Patrons angrily moved and made room for the party to pass. The commotion quickly drew the curious glances of armed soldiers assigned to the amphitheatre for security.

Zephyr looked at Scorpyus, motioning with her eyes in the soldier's direction. For the time being the soldiers just eyed the party as latecomers.

"They don't know us, keep going." Scorpyus whispered. Zephyr continued on, following behind one of Barry's men.

"Oww that was my hand!" A slight man in scarlet apparel shrieked. A dozen heads turned at the outburst. One of the actors glared angrily out into the audience.

"I am sorry monsieur." Zephyr apologized. She stepped on without looking back.

The party weaved their way through the seated audience. The patrons were irritable at being bumped and disturbed during the climax of the play. One of the stage managers petitioned the soldiers to do something about the disturbance. Reluctantly the soldiers got up and started making their way to the party.

Cad saw the soldiers to the right and motioned to go to the walkway on the left. Still trying to draw as little attention as possible, the party made their way in the opposite direction.

"Hey, you knocked my tankard over." A young man in an ornately decorated tunic complained. More shushing and the wagging of several heads followed his outburst.

Novak tossed a coin in the man's lap. "So buy another." Novak's patience in this matter was waning. Yet he made an effort. Cad was impressed; not so much with Novak's restraint, but in the young man's courage. Few would dare speak to a man twice their size in such a tone. Then Cad changed his mind. Talking roughly to an armed stranger twice your size when you are unarmed was unintelligent.

A theatre patron rose abruptly in protest of all the distractions. As he stood he bumped against Dantes accidentally, yet forcefully. A sharp pain shot through Dante's wounded arm eliciting a yelp. The patron looked aghast at the blood spot on his immaculate linen tunic, and then cursed Dantes as a bumbling idiot. Dantes cradled his sore appendage and moved on, ignoring the patron. The exchange was not lost on the approaching soldiers. Cad saw a look of realization materialize on a young soldier's face. He tapped a sergeant on the arm and pointed in Dante's direction. The sergeant signaled his men and all of them picked up their pace. They were now blundering and jostling their way through the crowd in an effort to further investigate this suspicious circumstance.

Cad witnessed the whole thing. "They've seen us. Let's make a blooming run for it."

Novak turned around and shot a glance at Cad. He could tell his friend was serious. Like a charging bull, Novak tore trough the crowd. All courtesy evaporated. Novak shoved and tossed people aside, stepped on hands, laps, food; anything that didn't move fast enough. Before anyone could protest, he was well past them.

The others followed close behind in the path Novak was cutting through the theatre patrons.

"Watch where you're going!" An angry man rose to protest. Barry's scabbard had clunked him on the head.

The Major shoved the man down. "I say there chap; stay seated." Barry spoke with absolute authority.

The man saw the green surcoat showing from under Barry's cloak. His eyes grew wide with recognition.

"Sound the alarm! Traitor afoot! This man wears the sur…" The Major's fist silenced the man.

The Kelterlander soldiers followed suit. They were shoving their way through the theatre crowd, many of whom were now scrambling for an exit themselves. The Kelterlander soldiers looked like they were headed for a fight with these rude and noisy strangers. Their indiscriminate battle tactics were to be avoided at all costs.

The play came to an abrupt halt. The actors stumbled on their lines amidst the growing chaos. Part of their audience was fleeing the amphitheatre. The rest had their attention diverted elsewhere. For the moment the actors became an unwilling audience, and the audience became the play; a play with an ensuing fight sequence by the looks of it.

The party reached the bottom of the amphitheatre at a dead run. Several patrons became stampeded in the process of their escape. Many stood, mouths agape, at the uncivilized display of rudeness. Most were among the wealthiest Astorian classes and thought themselves to be a step up from the barbaric peasantry they judged Novak and his entourage to be. How dare anyone disrupt a stage play? For the patrons, it was one of the most incredulous events they had been privy to witness. They hissed and harrumphed as Scorpyus, who was bringing up the rear, ran by. Before the patrons could resettle themselves the soldiers took their turn coursing through the theatre. The hissing and harrumphing started again but soon fell silent. The soldiers were quick to slam a gauntleted fist into those to slow to get out of the way. The snobby citizens started to move like they had a purpose. Those who didn't were struck down and trampled.

Novak was the first one to the walkway. Coming to flat ground he was able to stretch out his stride. The others followed single file and spaced ten feet apart. Couples on a leisurely walk along the river scurried from the large man charging along the walk. Many stepped into the lush flora growing along the river, or behind the occasional tree. One man decided to put on a display of bravery for his lady. No socially inferior brute would force him and his lady from the path. After all, he was an accomplished swordsman. The man drew his sword.

"Stand aside my dear," he said to the lady. "This shan't take but a moment."

Novak pulled his sword, a smile appearing on his face. The man's confident smirk vanished as Novak got closer. He was a lot bigger up close. Nevertheless, he raised his sword in the proper sparring fashion. Unfortunately for him, Novak wasn't going to spar.

In one swift move, Novak swung mightily catching the man's sword near the hilt and sending it sailing through the air. Novak didn't even break stride. As he passed the man, he rammed a shoulder into the center of his chest.

"Ahh," the man billowed as he tumbled into the river. The lady gasped clutching her kerchief to her bosom. Cad laughed. What was the man thinking?

The party sprinted a quarter mile down the walkway eventually coming to an outdoor café. The café was nestled in a small clearing by an arching stone bridge that spanned the river. Several people were enjoying an afternoon luncheon along the river under the shade of the trees. Servers from the nearby kitchen were taking trays of food and beverages to the seated customers. Many glanced up when Novak and the others came to a halt before entering the area. Clearly these strangers were not of the social stature to dine at this establishment.

Cad caught up to Barry and Novak. All three surveyed the cafe. The scene before them was that of a regal gala. Cad and Novak had never seen anything like it. They must have come upon the King's court.

"Blooming aye, people live like this?" Cad took in the eloquent decorations, the impeccably dressed people, and the shear grandeur of the café setting. Gold and silver place settings, fine linens, and lavish floral arrangements graced the entire area.

"I say, this must be the Café Argenteus. It is a favorite establishment of the nobles." Barry deduced.

The awe and wonder of the café was soon interrupted by the sound of the pursuing soldiers. There was only one course of action for the party. The walkway was lined with flowers and wound its way through the center of the café. It ended at the stone bridge that spanned to the other side of the river. Atop of the bridge was stationed a half dozen soldiers from the king's personal guard.

"We will have to fight our way out of here." Novak felt the anticipation pumping through his veins.

"The king must be dining here." Barry pointed to two other soldiers standing next to a young man with a scarlet robe. He was surrounded by sharply dressed servants waiting on his every whim.

"Stop those men!" The lead soldier yelled as he lumbered up the walkway toward the café, his chain mail slinking with every bounce of the foot.

The soldiers on the bridge looked toward their approaching comrades. The two with the king immediately came to arms and shielded their liege with their lives.

Scorpyus gave Zephyr his last two arrows bringing her total to five. He tossed his bow aside and drew his sword. Zephyr notched an arrow, her only weapon. All prepared for what would surely be a pitched battle.

The party broke into two ranks. Cad, Novak, Barry and one of his troops concentrated on the soldiers running from the bridge. Scorpyus, Zephyr, Dantes, and Greystoke faced those coming up the walk.

"Surely thar must be a better idea." Dantes growled, a sword in his good arm, the other held close to his side.

"I'll let you know when I think of one mate." Cad replied. "I am open for suggestions."

Before anyone could voice an idea, soldiers swooped from two sides upon the party. An angry grinding clang of metal shattered the elite luncheon. Close quarters combat erupted, the pounding crash of sword on sword sending sparks shooting like tiny comets.

A soldier charging toward Dantes lurched backward suddenly, the shaft of an arrow protruding from his throat. Zephyr drew first blood. The soldier faltered forward, frothy sputum gurgling from his lips. He collapsed a few feet in front of Dantes. Zephyr already had another arrow notched.

Scorpyus swung at the first soldier to reach him, and heard the twang of a bowstring to his right. He heard a thudding sound nearby. He blocked the thrust of his opponent's blade then stole a quick glance downward. A soldier lay dead on the floor, an arrow shaft sticking from deep in his right eye. Zephyr couldn't miss at this close range.

Novak smashed his blade against the first enemy to reach him. The soldier blocked the blow with his shield. Novak locked blades with the man who proved to be a skilled fighter. A second soldier joined in the fracas, swinging at Novak's neck. Novak ducked and then shot out a sidekick to the man's groin. Instinctively the man's hands reached down to protect his lower portions. Novak broke away from his first attacker and then ripped his weapon through the air catching the man on the neck of his chain mail hood. The man's armor prevented Novak's blade from slicing into his flesh, but it could do little against the ferocity of Novak's powerful blow. The impact shattered the man's neck bones knocking his head over his right shoulder. The head flopped lifelessly on the man's torso like that of a chicken that had its head wrung. After a few seconds the corpse collapsed to the floor. By that time Novak was again engaged with his first attacker.

Barry skillfully parried with his two attackers. Little did they know they were up against a veteran Knight of Astor. Barry's falchion was light and well suited for multiple attackers.

"All right, who wants some falchion?" The Major taunted. He swung his blade knocking two separate thrusts aside simultaneously. Quickly he brought his sword from bottom left to upper right slashing one opponent across the thigh. Crimson droplets flung from his blade into the dining nobles. A lady shrieked, sprinkles of blood doting her face. Her lady friends fanned themselves in horror. One fainted at the sight going limp in her chair.

Greystoke took careful aim with his crossbow. Methodically he squeezed the trigger sending a bold on its way. It slammed into the shoulder of an advancing soldier, an anguished scream piercing the air.

"Blimey!" Greystoke exclaimed and swung his crossbow against an advancing opponent. The rest of the soldiers were upon him before either he or Zephyr could loose another volley.

"Nice try, but pathetic; much as one would expect from the army of the Dales." The soldier taunted, noticing Greystoke's surcoat. "That's why you lost the war now isn't it?"

Greystoke turned purple with rage. How dare anyone, much less a Kelterlander insult his country. He tore his sword from its scabbard and hurled the blade against the soldier's midriff. The Kelterlander dove aside hurriedly, unable to block the blow in time. The blade whooshed inches above his head. With a thud, he landed belly down on the ground, and flipped to his back just in time to meet Greystoke's blade bearing down on him. A shower of sparks flew as steel grinded into steel. The soldier dug his heels in and started sliding himself along his back trying to escape. Greystoke brought his sword down, repeatedly pummeling at his foe. It was everything the soldier could do to stay alive. He must have slid twenty feet, Greystoke hammering at him all the way, before he came to a stop against the leg of a table. The soldier's eyes widened in panic. It was near impossible to protect himself. In the tangle of blades, the table jostled about spilling the contents of several tankards on top. With a lurch, the soldier shifted to the side and then slid himself under the table with his feet.

"Who is pathetic now?" Greystoke swung at his opponent as the soldier crawled between the legs of those seated at the table. His blade knocked the table over spilling the contents on the patrons who were attempting to flee the area albeit a little late. A holler erupted from one of the patrons as hot soup spilled onto his lap scalding his inner thighs.

The soldier stood up knocking over a lady in a twist of overturned chairs. Without hesitation, the Kelterlander ran further into the café managing to stay one step ahead of Greystoke's blade. Greystoke had him in a full retreat. Had it not been for Greystoke's vehement reluctance to injure bystanders, the soldier would have met his demise.

"Stand still you coward." Greystoke yelled, still enraged at the earlier insult. The soldier managed to stir up a hornet's nest this time.

With Greystoke chasing a soldier through their midst, the café fell to pieces. Terrified patrons, once content to be spectators at a sporting match were now put to flight. The sound of ceramic shattering and the clanking of metal resounded throughout the café. Chairs scrapped against cobblestone as people scattered from the premises. The chaos played in the favor of the party.

Cad just finished off an attacker when he heard the raucous from the café. He turned in time to see the king being rushed

from the scene by his personal guards, a sizable entourage
following behind him as swiftly as they could muster. To his rear,
Scorpyus, Zephyr, and Dantes were being swallowed up in a sea
of enemy soldiers. Much to Cad's dismay, another contingent
of soldiers approached the bridge from the opposite bank of
the river. His stomach knotted up in an iron ball. The chance of
escape waned even further. He motioned to Novak and Barry
about the approaching soldiers from the opposite bank. Novak
shrugged his shoulders and pressed his attack on his opponent.
His blade glanced off the soldier's helmet.

Scorpyus was lost within a swarm of bodies, completely
surrounded and each with a blade hungering for blood. Ducking,
dodging, and maneuvering his blade like lightning he fought
his way out of the pack of ravenous swords looking like a man
flailing away at a swarm of bees. As he stepped over an overturned
chair, he brought his sword up hard into the groin of one of his
pursuers. A shrill cry pierced his ears as the soldier clutched his
groin and sunk slowly to his knees. Scorpyus continued into the
café shoving his way through fleeing diners. Once he felt he had
gone far enough, he turned to access the situation.

Several soldiers were working their way through the tangle to
come after him. There had to be about two dozen enemy soldiers
still fighting; far more then was in the amphitheatre. Where these
additional soldiers came from he had no idea. Perhaps the king
had a contingent in reserve nearby. Whatever the reason, Scorpyus
knew when his position was about to be overrun.

Worry creased Scorpyus's brow as he searched for the others.
Dantes was hacking his was to the café and would be there soon.
Novak and Barry were already inside the tangle of overturned
chairs and tables, fighting to keep the advancing soldiers at bay.
Cad and Zephyr were still without the dining area somewhere.
Scorpyus quickly glanced behind him. The view was bleak. He
was a mere few yards from a short two-foot high stonewall that

bordered the riverbank. Over the wall was a three-foot drop to the greenish water.

Zephyr raised her bow and diverted an incoming blade. Suddenly an arm wrapped around her neck from behind and a dagger pressed against her throat.

"Drop the bow lassie. I wouldn't want to kill you. We have better uses for young women." A laconic voice breathed words heavily near her ear. It sent a chill down Zephyr's spine, and brought a flood of revolting, sickening memories to life. She smelled the same musky stink, and heard the same throaty breathing. Zephyr's eyes iced over with fear. A familiar dread hung repressively in the air; a dread that was loathsome and reminiscent of demons walking the earth. Tears welled in Zephyrs eyes. The remembrance of such things, things no woman should have a memory of, caused her to nearly wretch. A cold sweat formed on her brow and her heart began to pound. Zephyr would die before living through such an ordeal again.

Mustering all of her courage, Zephyr lurched like a cat giving no regard for the dagger at her throat. She sunk her teeth deep into the flesh of the forearm before her throat and slid her dagger from its sheath. Dropping her bow, she gripped the wrist with the dagger and brought her own dagger up. With a fierce determination Zephyr sawed her razor sharp dagger back and forth as if she were attempting to sever a tree asunder. Her attacker howled in agony and pulled away with all he had. Zephyr bit and sawed with an even fiercer determination. Something came over her; some deep-seated fear propelled her onward, filling her with a powerful hatred to her attacker. Her attacker struggled, trying to free himself, but Zephyr unleashed all she had. She bit so hard her teeth hurt. Blood ran down her chin, the grotesque taste on her tongue. She worked her dagger like a butcher.

In a fit a fury, Zephyr threw off her attacker. "No!" Her voice echoed through the air. The soldier who attacked her fell backwards groping his wrist. Zephyr stood panting, blood smeared on her face and chin. She looked slowly to her hands. One clutched a bloody dagger; the other held a severed hand. The hand still held its own dagger. Zephyr let the appendage fall to the ground, turned toward the dining area and spit as much blood from her mouth as she could. In shock, she made her way toward Scorpyus who was clashing swords with a bearded soldier. Before she took two steps her path was blocked by a formidably large foe. Much to her relief the shaft of a bolt appeared in the center of the man's temple. Turning, Zephyr spied Greystoke standing atop the stone wall at the river edge, his crossbow having just been released. Barry was standing before him fighting off two attackers. Like a true warrior, Barry stood his ground firmly in protection of Greystoke so the sergeant could concentrate on providing effective crossbow fire.

Suddenly the head toppled from a Kelterland soldier and thudded to the ground. The headless torso jerked and staggered violently until at last it finally flopped over. The corpse twitched in spasms like a fish on the shore.

"Ya, take that!" Novak growled, fury etched on his brow. He quickly joined Barry at the wall who gave a nod of appreciation.

Dantes was being driven backward by two youthful soldiers who effectively took advantage of their wounded opponent's weakness. Both wore decorative cuirasses in contrast to their comrades. Dantes panted furiously, clearly in a lot of pain. Each blocked blow of a sword sent a bone-jarring jolt through his wounded arm. Cradling it close to his side provided little relief. The two soldiers grew excited sensing victory.

Dantes stepped backward and blocked another swing of the sword. Sweat trickled into his eyes stinging them. His left sleeve soaked with blood; a trail of red drops spotted his left pant leg. The two soldiers lunged forward for a lethal blow. Rallying the remainder of his strength, Dantes hopped rearward. His feet became entangled in the legs of an overturned chair. Dantes went down in a heap landing on his back, his elbow in a bowl of gravy. The fall knocked his sword from his hand. The two soldiers scampered around the chairs to come in for the kill. Dantes looked to his left and grabbed the closest thing he could find; a wooden serving tray. He raised it in time to stop a blade from cleaving open his abdomen. Dantes shifted and positioned the wooden tray using it as a shield against the flurry of incoming hacking blows. He made sure to keep his fingers as close to the edge of the tray as possible. Sliding himself along the ground, Dantes tried to escape the deadly deluge.

One of the young soldiers raised his sword high in preparation of imbedding it into Dantes skull. Half of the blade of a sword suddenly disappeared into the soldier's armpit. A look of shock formed on the soldier's face and he coughed, a tinge of blood spilling over his bottom lip.

Cad pulled his sword from the soldier's armpit and then swung it hard at the other. The two exchanged a few blows then Cad lowered his sword providing an opening to his right side. The other soldier seized upon the opportunity and raised his right arm over his left shoulder in preparation of hacking at Cad. When the soldier raised his sword, Cad unexpectedly stepped into his attacker and planted a dagger in his ribs just above the cuirass. The second attacker fell in a clump.

Cad turned to Dantes and stretched forth his hand. "Let's go mate. This is no time to rest."

Dantes grinned and grabbed his friend's wrist with his good hand. Cad pulled him to his feet. Both joined Novak, Barry, and Greystoke at the wall. Greystoke fired another bolt into the melee. Cad joined the fight, and Dantes retrieved Greystoke's sword.

"Do you have any other ideas?" Novak asked while swinging at an attacker.

"No, not besides jumping in the river." Cad swung hard at a soldier. There were five soldiers at the wall with several more on their way. "We'll jump as soon as Scorpyus and Zephyr get here."

A piercing scream shattered the air. A woman stood from her table in horror, a severed head in her lap. One of Barry's men had just been killed.

Pain etched lines on Barry's face. Losing another man cut to his very soul, but he forged ahead like a good soldier. "I say, we better hurry. We haven't much time."

As if on cue, Zephyr erupted between two soldiers, slashing one on the side of the neck as she did so. She jumped over the fallen man and took her place at the wall.

"I tell you this is not good." Zephyr quickly glanced up and down the wall. "Scorpyus is not here yet?"

"No but he's on his way." Cad stated.

Scorpyus ran for the wall through a tangle of soldiers, fleeing citizens, and disheveled furniture. His sword was nowhere to be seen. As he neared his friends, a soldier sprang into his path and took a mighty swing with a battle-axe. Scorpyus swerved to his left behind a panicked citizen who was turning to find a way to escape. The blade of the axe smashed into the citizen's back and a cry of pain shrieked through the air. Scorpyus shook his head in disgust. How could a soldier have absolutely no regard for their fellow citizens? The soldier was unfazed by the event. He merely placed a boot on the citizen's side and shoved him from his axe. By the time he was ready for another swing, Scorpyus was well past the soldier.

Scorpyus bounded toward his friends and motioned for them to jump.

"Dantes, you and Greystoke jump. Then the rest of you follow. I will wait and jump with Scorpyus." Novak instructed.

Dantes and Greystoke didn't have to be told twice. With a splash both disappeared over the wall. Zephyr and Barry followed suit. When Scorpyus was yards away, Cad and Novak took their turn. In a running dive, Scorpyus hurled himself over the short wall amidst a hail of sword swings. He landed with a splash in the green waters. With a gasp, Scorpyus surfaced and slicked his hair back. The soldiers at the wall were parting to make space for others who had crossbows. None ventured into the river after the party. The current already carried him ten feet from where he dove over the side.

Novak hit the bottom of the river some five feet below the waters surface. He shoved himself back toward the top with his legs. His head briefly broke the surface, enough for him to suck in a breath of air, and then the weight of his armor pulled him back under. Novak didn't panic. He methodically jumped toward the opposite shore taking a gulp of fresh air each time he surfaced. The current still forced him down stream making it an arduous task. When Novak reached the opposite shore it sloped upward toward the bank. He walked up the underwater hill until his head was above the surface. Novak caught his breath and assessed the situation. He noticed that Greystoke and Barry were having a similar problem, their heads occasionally appearing for short gasps of air. The others were safely afloat and drifting ahead of the three burdened with armor. Several soldiers drew back crossbows on the opposite shore.

"Shoot them! Don't let then escape!" An officer yelled at his men. Quickly the men placed bolts in place and released them at the party. A dozen projectiles soared through the air.

Scorpyus caught up to Zephyr. He shoved her under the water as a few bolts impacted the water overhead.

One of the bolts shot at Novak missed and hit a man on the opposite shore who was about to join his friend in a small boat. The man collapsed griping his thigh. Novak treaded over to the boat and gripped the side of it with one hand. He grabbed the man by the tunic and launched him from the boat to the shore.

"Sorry, but you need to help your friend." Novak capsized the boat and shoved it to the river's center. He used it as a flotation device as he drifted away from the enemy crossbows, and made sure to keep his head down.

Amidst a hail of projectiles Barry and Greystoke made their way to Novak's makeshift solution to staying afloat with armor.

"I say Novak, good thinking. I was about to abandon my armor." Barry replied, winded from his struggle. "Fortunately the river is relatively shallow."

"But still deep enough to drown," Novak added.

"Help me get this bolt out will you." Greystoke winced and then sank beneath the surface. The bolt of a crossbow was stuck in his shoulder. His chain mail was penetrated.

The Major helped his faltering comrade. He submerged and assisted Greystoke up under the air pocket formed by the overturned boat. "Grab the seat with your good arm. Stay with me sergeant. We've come too far to part now." Barry helped his friend keep his head above water.

Cad waited for the crossbowmen to reload and then swam to Scorpyus and Zephyr. It was one of the few times he was glad to be without armor. Dantes was already with them.

"Is everyone accounted for?" Cad asked.

"The others are all back with that boat." Scorpyus pointed fifty yards up stream.

Cad looked and saw Novak hunker down amid a slew of incoming projectiles, several of which slammed into the boat. Soon, they would all be out of crossbow range.

"Does anyone know where this bloomin river flows?" Cad asked, satisfied that the danger would soon be over.

"As long as it is away from here I do not care." Zephyr answered. The others couldn't argue with that statement.

The four floated onward, Novak and the others following close behind. Soon the party passed under another stone bridge that spanned the river. After they passed under Cad looked up and saw a lone man standing on the bridge watching the party as they floated by.

"There's that chap again." Cad exclaimed.

The others looked to where Cad directed them. There, standing on the bridge mid-span was the man they had all seen in the alley with the sword. The man just watched them, expressionless as they drifted by.

"If there was any doubt that God was with us, I tell you it is gone now." Zephyr spoke for everyone. She stared, unblinking as she drifted around a bend in the river until she could see the man no more. A line of scripture came to mind: 'He shall redeem their soul from deceit and violence…'

------◆------

Iris paced the wooden floor of her small cottage. There had been no word from Cyrus for what seemed like an eternity. Minutes agonizingly turned into hours, and hours twisted painfully into days. For all Iris knew he had been killed. A part of her felt he might have wanted it that way. He certainly wasn't acting himself the last time she saw him. Cyrus had been heavy hearted.

Thinking of all the possibilities swirled together in a mind-numbing tangle of gibberish. It was enough to make Iris feel as if she were loosing her mind. And then out of the corner of her eye she spied Cyrus's letter on the mantle. Iris stopped pacing and starred at it. Should she open it? Cyrus left instructions that it be opened only if he should be killed. But what else was Iris to think; all this time and nary a word from him. The waiting, the uncertainty was killing Iris. She had to know something. The letter wouldn't answer the question of Cyrus's whereabouts, but maybe it would provide some information to sooth her soul.

Iris snatched the letter from the mantle and fingered the red wax seal. Dare she read it? A part of her felt she should wait longer. That was her brain talking. Her heart said open it now. Iris thought about it but chose to follow her heart.

Iris slipped a finger under the fold in the parchment and broke the wax seal. She quickly unfolded the letter and started to read it before she changed her mind.

My dearest Iris,

If you are reading this letter it means I have met my end. For that I am terribly sorry. I pray you will find comfort in the fact that one day we shall meet again. My only regret is we were not able to share a life on earth. You are a good woman Iris, and a strong one. You must carry on no matter how hard it may seem. I know it won't be easy, but keep the faith and carry on the fight you have so valiantly begun.

I feel I must explain why I couldn't stay with you. Now that you are left alone, I feel I owe you at least that much. Well, as you were aware a group of assassins have been plaguing Xylor. These assassins are called Valkyrie's. They have killed many citizens, and have even captured Zephyr. Novak had been sent to the mainland secretly leaving only two of the four knights. In other words things were looking grim for Xylor's future. The Valkyrie had to be stopped in order to protect the people. The task fell to Cad, Scorpyus and I. Cad and Scorpyus worked tirelessly, and at a great risk to their lives to gain information in order to defeat these assassins. Iris, I will tell you this; the Clandestine Knights are the most selfless people I have ever had the pleasure of working with. One would have to search far and wide to find heroes of such caliber as these four souls. I truly believe they are who the realm has been waiting for. They accept their calling, and undertake the tasks that have befallen them with the utmost diligence and honor. We all owe them more then we could possibly ever repay.

At any rate, Cad came up with a plan. I am to make contact with the Valkyrie under the guise of betraying Cad and Scorpyus. I am to arrange for Cad to be handed over to the Valkyrie's in exchange for the Valkyrie's leaving Xylor. Cad thinks they will agree to this settlement. Scorpyus will then track Cad and find out where he is being held. We hope it is the same place where they are holding Zephyr. Scorpyus will then contact Novak in order to prepare a plan to free Cad and Zephyr. I am to join them on the mainland as soon as I can. I know it sounds terrible but Cad thinks it will work. He is staking his life on it, and will do anything to rescue his friend. Cad thinks that the Valkyrie's are only after the leaders, and once they are gone they will leave Xylor. Scorpyus managed to kill one, and another has been wounded. It is believed that the Valkyrie will want to end this while they can still claim victory. Shortly after delivering this letter I would have left to implement my part in this plan. If this plan should fail there may be a lot of rumors about my being a traitor to the knights. I write this letter to you so that you may know the truth. I care little what others may think of me, but I would not want you thinking me a traitor. I agreed to this plan because it is my duty to protect Xylor. If I can best do that by sacrificing my life…or my reputation, then so be it. The Clandestine Knights have already risked all to do the same and they are from Ravenshire. They are true Christians. Abrams once said, 'a lot of people will assist those who are in a position to return the favor some day, but it is a true servant who lends assistance to those who have no way to return the favor. These four are true servants. I will do my best to assist them; for the sake of the next generation, for the sake of the innocent citizens, and for the good Xylor, and for the good of the entire realm. May God be with us. Without you, I would have never found the strength to undertake such a daunting task. For it was the hope of being with you that propelled me to fight for our future. I am truly sorry that in doing so our future together was sacrificed. Our love was a considerable gift to sacrifice on the altar of freedom. I only pray that it wasn't in vain. Continue the goof fight. My love will be with you always,

Cyrus

Iris began weeping uncontrollably, and clutched the letter to her chest. She was overcome by the urgency and emotion of Cyrus's words. Truly she indeed found an honorable man. She loved Cyrus even more if that were possible.

A tinge of guilt crested Iris's heart. She read the letter in violation of Cyrus's instructions. Iris had no proof that Cyrus had been killed. Cad's plan was not without risk, but it could easily account for the time lapse since she had last seen Cyrus. If he went to the main land then his absence was still rather short.

Iris felt silly for letting her emotions run away from her. Her mind told her she overreacted and worried for nothing. She had no reason to believe anything, good or bad, had happened to Cyrus. But in her heart she was glad she read the letter. And Iris was one to always follow her heart.

XVII

$$\text{———} \bullet \diamond \bullet \text{———}$$

THE SUN BURNED brightly illuminating the half dozen
structures that had once been Stonebridge; a long forgotten
haven on a long forgotten trail. The structures bore the design of
centuries old architecture, and would have long since crumbled
had it not been maintained as a hidden base by the knights of
Astor. Now, with the fall of The Dales, it served as a refuge for a
small remnant of the army of the Dales. Or so Scorpyus was told.
He never heard of the place before recently, and now that he saw
it with his own eyes, it was scarcely more believable. A hidden
village, its stone structures all over grown with moss, a furlong
from a stone bridge on a lost trail; it was the stuff legends were
made of. But yet here Scorpyus was, deep in the woods at a secret
location. It stirred within him an excitement he had not felt since
he was a teen exploring Ravenshire with Cad, Novak, and Zephyr.

Scorpyus leaned against the rail of the balcony of the largest
structure in that hidden outpost; and at two stories it was the
tallest. From his vantage point, Scorpyus had a view of the whole
area, his friends and Barry's men milling about below. With
boyish glee, Scorpyus peered through his spyglass taking in the
scene below.

"I say there Novak, where are you off to from here. Have you and your mates made any plans?" Barry asked his new found friend.

"We have decided to go to Ravenshire for a rest. It's been too long since we've been home. We need to get things in order before we continue with the war. And we will probably take a small job; we still need the money." Novak clearly looked forward to the trip.

"What kind of job do you have in mind?"

"The easiest to find is protecting shipments from being robbed. Merchants are always looking for help getting their goods to other towns safely." Novak wasn't sounding enthusiastic. "Unfortunately escort details don't pay much. Hopefully something else will become available."

"You mean something more exciting?" Emerald chided. Novak grinned sheepishly.

Cad explained further. "But our first priority will be to look into fortifying our homes. The island is reasonably secure right now, but with those bloody Valkyrie's about; I would feel better if there were back up plans in place for our families."

"Do you really think they will be a problem?" Barry asked.

"Scorpyus thinks so. He did see one's true identity. They could very well be back." Novak looked around for his friend. He was nowhere to be found.

"There is a reason so little is known about them. We have to prepare. I recommend you chaps do the same. We certainly haven't made friends within the Kelterland regime." Cad advised.

"I fear you are dreadfully right Cad. Indeed we have become a larger threat to the king. We shall have to be even more careful as we venture forth." Barry waved his arm in a sweeping motion. "We are isolated here as well, but my men are in the process of constructing observation placements on the trail. I agree. Securing our positions is the first step we must all take. Fortunately for us, finances are not a problem. We enjoy a fair deal of support from the citizenry. It's not a lot, but enough to suffice our operations."

"And then we need to plan our strategy and build the army. As we discussed, starting in the Dales is the most logical choice." Cad sighed heavily and shook his head. "Unfortunately I don't think Ravenshire is ready yet, and it pains me to say so. What it will take to motivate my country…I can't say. Ravenshire suffered the most throughout the war with Kelterland, and yet many people are still paralyzed with fear. What resistance we do have is unorganized. We had hoped Thadus would be able to help with that, but now…"

"My father wanted nothing more then to be able to repay you for what you all did in Xylor. But everything happens for a reason." Emerald started to tear up. The news of her father's assassination hit her tremendously hard, as it did in most of Xylor. But his death was not in vain. Already it hardened the resolve of fellow Xylorians. More then what could have been imagined two weeks ago, Xylor was united. For the first time in a long time Emerald's people were ready to stand against Kelterland. The idea that King Phinehas Faust would send in assassins to kill Thadus was bad enough. To know the king was more then willing to have random citizens killed was a painful revelation for Emerald's countrymen. A Xylorian life was worthless to the king. Emerald felt it was about time all Xylorians stood together. She wondered what took so long. Redland had been killing people for years and the people tolerated it. Emerald guessed that when shadowy figures sneak around assassinating people like self-proclaimed grim reapers, somehow it was different. She thought it unfortunate it took that kind of horror to motivate her fellow Xylorians to take a stand. She hoped Ravenshire would learn from Xylor's slothful response.

Novak felt bad for Emerald. With the loss of her father and uncle, she now had no family. It further filled him with a fiery resolve against Kelterland.

"Things will get better." Novak clasped one of Emerald's hands. The size of his hand dwarfed hers. "Thadus is a hero. One day you will see him again."

Emerald sobbed gently and nodded her agreement. She was dealing valiantly with one of the most difficult moments in her life. If it had not been for Novak arranging for her to visit Ravenshire she didn't know what she would do. Going back to Xylor would be too painful. Emerald would be staying with Novak's sister Ingrid, and meeting everyone's family. It was a small consolation in the midst of her tremendous losses, but it was far better then going back to Xylor alone. Novak seemed happy about the decision, but Emerald had a lot to think about. How she handled Novak leaving on his next mission would largely decide her future. In the meantime the two enjoyed their time together.

Barry waited appropriately for Emerald to regain composure before continuing the conversation. "I dare say, I hope to have further resistance organized by the time you return. My men tell me news of what happened in Astoria has traveled fast. I hope to make contact with other bands of resistance. Lord willing, we shall be ready to place a rightful heir on the throne once again here in The Dales."

"I pray you are right Barry." Cad smiled. "First we fortify; then we plan and organize. Before we start we must be ready. The king's brigades are formidable blokes."

"And then we fight." Novak added enthusiastically. This drew a laugh from everyone except Emerald who shot him a look that was half frustration and half worry.

Greystoke spoke for the first time during the conversation. His left arm was in a sling. "You know Major, I was from Ravenshire.

Barry looked surprised. "I've always thought you to have been native to the Dales."

"I've been here most of my life. But I was born in Ravenshire. I was brought to the dales when I was ten…I think. It's been so long ago I can't really say."

"What part of Ravenshire?" Cad asked.

"I was from Saltwater."

"Blooming aye!" Cad stood amazed. "That's where we're from. How did you end up here?"

"I was captured. My parents were killed by enemy soldiers and they brought me here as a slave. They sold me to some nasty cobbler who worked me mercilessly. I finally escaped." Greystoke recounted the tale with disgust.

Cad's face bore a look of amazement. "That's bloody incredible. It sounds like exactly what happened to me. I was twelve and in the woods with my dog; on my way to a friend's house; when I saw thick smoke rising from the general location. Well, I'm not daft. I knew what that meant. So I ran home as fast as I could and told my mother. We tried to escape but the enemy soldiers caught up with us."

Cad's voice trailed off and he grew silent. Everyone waited quietly for him to continue. Novak fidgeted nervously. When any of the four talked about their childhood it would drudge up emotions for the others. That's why they seldom spoke of such things.

Cad inhaled deeply. "I lost Thomas, my older brother that day; and my dog. My father; all of our fathers died shortly thereafter. It was a miserable time. One for which the Kelterlanders have a fight coming. They must be stopped lest the whole realm fall to the same evil."

"Ya that's right!" Novak added fervently.

Greystoke thought on Cad's words. "That sounds familiar. The enemy soldiers were bandying about all of Saltwater on their tirade. I had a friend also. After I was captured, the soldiers were taking me on the road that led to his house. We came across his brother who killed two of the soldiers before he was killed."

A look of reckoning came to Greystoke's eyes. "Now that I think of it, I seem to remember a dog also."

Both Cad and Greystoke erupted with a look of bewilderment. Each searched their memories for more recollection.

Revelation shone in Greystoke's eyes. "Was your dog named Nixy?"

"Yes he was." Cad looked at Greystoke, searching for some sign of familiarity but there was none. Cad pondered the possibility. Greystoke looked nothing like his childhood friend Morton. Besides that, Morton stuttered at times of stress. He had yet to have heard Greystoke stutter.

"Is your last name VanKirke?" Greystoke asked.

"Yes but…" This couldn't me Morton, Cad thought. "My friend was named Morton Standish. Your name is Greystoke, isn't it?"

"Well I'll be a jam buttie! It is you!" Greystoke exclaimed with such excitement he was practically jumping about.

"My father died when I was a baby. His name was Greystoke. My mother remarried a bloke named Standish. Most people knew me by Morton Standish." Greystoke explained.

Complete shock registered on Cad's countenance. "Well bloody aye lad, it's a small realm, but what are the odds. I never thought I would see you again."

"I've changed a lot since then, and I don't stutter anymore."

Cad and Greystoke gave each other a firm handshake and a slap on the back. Immediately the two engaged in conversation about childhood antics. Each would laugh raucously as the other brought to mind some event the two shared as children. Novak listened with interest. He knew little about Cad before the age of twelve when the Clandestine Knights were formed. The whole thing was an amazing coincidence.

"What's everyone laughing about?" A familiar gravely voice sounded from Novak's left. Novak turned to see Cyrus.

"Cyrus, it is about time you show up."

"Following Scorpyus is no easy task. It took me two days to find passage here from Xylor. By the time I got to Astoria you had already broken Cad and Zephyr out of jail." Cyrus smiled.

"I'm kidding. We didn't know when you would arrive. We didn't want to wait with Zephyr sick." Novak shook his friend's hand.

"Cad's plan worked." Cyrus admitted with relief.

"Did you doubt it would?" Novak feigned surprise.

"Actually for a while there at the abandoned warehouse I did. But it looks like everything worked out for the best." Cyrus looked around at the joyous gathering. Everyone was enjoying the moment.

"Cad's plans usually work." Novak bragged about his friend.

"I'll say so." Cyrus replied with a hint of awe in his voice.

"What does that mean?"

"Do you remember the cavalry soldiers that were chasing you?" Cyrus asked. Novak nodded in the affirmative.

Cyrus explained, his voice filled with wonder. "Well every one of them was found dead in an alley; and their horses."

Novak's brow furrowed. "They were all dead?"

Cyrus nodded. "All of them and their horses. They were collapsed dead right where they stood. The Kelterlanders are trying to hide what happened. The whole area was closed off for two days while the bodies were removed. The King doesn't want news of this or the prison break to spread."

Novak smiled with deep satisfaction. "Is that possible?"

"No, all sorts of rumors are spreading; everything from sorcery to poison. The official story is the king killed the Cavalry squad as traitors. There are even some who are starting to believe God had a hand in all this. It's making the Balar worshipers nervous."

"Good, they should be nervous." Novak looked Cyrus in the eyes. "God did have a hand in this. We never fought the cavalry soldiers. If they are dead, it is of God." Novak remembered the man in the brown cloak he saw in the alleyway.

"By the way where is Scorpyus?" Cyrus asked searching the gathering for his friend's familiar features.

"I don't know." Novak looked around. "Zephyr went to find him. He was here earlier."

Through his spyglass Scorpyus watched everything; animals, people, trees, anything of even the slightest interest. Two chipmunks fought over a morsel of food. Horses stood patiently in a corral, their tails whisking at flies. Soldiers milled about relaxing or chatting over their morning meal. Cad and Novak were talking to Barry and Greystoke. Even Cyrus showed up. He couldn't hear what they were saying, but judging from the smiles and laughter, they were having a good time. They had every right to be enjoying themselves. They all made it through another ordeal, this one even more trying then the last. Things seemed to be happening quickly. Spirits were high as many anticipated a change for the better, one that would free the occupied territory from the shackles of Kelterland. A lot of people had their hopes and prayers pinned to the Clandestine Knights and their new friends. The burden of that thought slowly erased the smile from Scorpyus's face, and he lowered the spyglass. God knew that was a tremendous pressure, one Scorpyus had trouble with. Why would God chose an unwanted half-breed, a gypsy who few found any use for, the object of a lifetime of scorn, and use him and his friends to help His people in their time of need. That was undeniable now. After their recent deliverance from Kelterlander troops in Astoria, even the most hardened skeptic couldn't argue. Scorpyus thought of the mysterious stranger in that alley, 'El Shaddai' emblazoned on his sword. Without a doubt Abrams was right. He made a prediction about the uprising that began in Xylor. He thought it was the dawning of a new time, and soon 'the whole earth shall know that there is a God in heaven.' Scorpyus felt in awe to be a witness to it all. To be a participant was an even more staggering thought.

Scorpyus lifted his spyglass again and studied the scene below. Novak came into view. His big friend was listening intently to Cad, no doubt reliving recent events. Emerald was by his side. A more loyal friend wasn't to be found. Novak was the type who would die defending a friend. Quiet, given to few words, Novak spoke volumes with his presence. Underneath the imposing exterior was a soft side. Emerald recognized that. When it came to fighting, Novak was fearless. He had complete confidence in his abilities. Scorpyus remembered once, right after he first met Novak, something he said. Novak long felt God made him a tremendous fighter and blessed him with size and strength for a reason. He felt it was to help out those who were weaker, and hoped it was to help free Ravenshire. He said it was his secret to being a successful warrior. Novak had absolute faith that God would see him through any fight. Why else would He have made him so much bigger and stronger? Scorpyus couldn't argue that. Novak didn't dwell on endless strategic possibilities. It the fight was good, he was in. Sometimes that meant being arrested. Novak's passion to fight a good cause sometimes outweighed his judgment, but he had the faith to back it up. It made him a good warrior.

Standing next to Novak, as usual of late, was Emerald. Scorpyus wondered what would become of this relationship. Emerald had changed recently. Seeing the horrors of war was one thing. Becoming a participant was another. Something happened to Emerald while she was on her mission with Novak and Dantes. She lost her father and uncle, and had to fight for her life against a Trepanite. Much to Novak's relief, Emerald was dispassionate to the idea of going on any other adventures. Scorpyus deduced the two were at a crossroads in their relationship. If Emerald could live with the knowledge of what Novak would be facing while he was away, the two would survive. Emerald had some soul searching ahead. For now, she enjoyed this moment of peace and celebration.

Scorpyus moved the spyglass until Cad appeared in the lens. Cad was deep into one of his stories, describing something using his hands, often going into great detail. Cad did everything in great detail. He prided himself on studying all the possibilities, and was a gifted strategist. Some of his ideas were unconventional, but they worked. God blessed him with intelligence. It was a trait that occasionally gave way to remarks with a slight bite of condescension. Cad used it to anger opponents in the hopes it would cause them to do something rash. Decisions made in anger were usually wrong. But deep down Cad was humble. When things didn't go according to his plans, he quickly accepted responsibility. Cad made no excuses and shifted no blame. Mistakes weighed on him heavily, sometimes to a fault. Scorpyus knew Cad was taking the mutilation of the wounded at the battle of Hyssop Creek Oratory extremely hard. It wasn't his fault. No one could have foreseen the utter depravity with which some of the enemy soldiers would sink, but Cad blamed himself. Scorpyus wondered if his friend would ever get over it. He felt deep responsibility for every decision he made. It was that kind of concern Cad caught criticism for in Xylor. When the Valkyrie's struck, he made a decision to only send Christian troops out on patrol. The non-Christian felt cheated out of combat experience, and the Christians felt their lives were being unfairly risked. When pressed for an answer, Cad replied: "I'm not going to bloody well let a lost man die and go to hell to gain my freedom if I can help it.". His remark shamed the soldiers who were complaining about always going on patrols, but he earned a lot of respect by saying it.

Scorpyus searched for Zephyr. She was nowhere to be found. He wondered where she was off to, probably visiting Dantes who was in bed recovering from his wounds and unable to join in the celebration. Of the four, she was the one who kept compassion within the knights, though she didn't want to admit it. Oh she would try to be hardened, sometimes even very convincingly. It was necessary in battle. She could perform her duties as a knight if she had to, but killing, albeit necessary, didn't sit well with her. Sometimes Zephyr would pretend it didn't bother her, but Scorpyus knew otherwise. Zephyr cared about life. It bothered her evil people lurked about to victimize others. It was a sad state the whole realm had sunk into. It was frustrating for her, and caused her to loose trust in her fellow man. Circumstances in her past forced her to withdraw within. God only knows the hell Zephyr had been through in her life. All of the Clandestine knights had seen terrible times. And Zephyr had good reasons, better then most, to be distant and cold. But she wasn't and didn't want to be. That's what Scorpyus liked about Zephyr. She actually cared.

Scorpyus envied that. He had to pray for compassion. He found it hard to care about anyone, sometimes even himself. Sure, thanks mostly to God he came a long way since his childhood, but it was a constant battle. Gypsies were hated. Scorpyus had been abandoned by his parents. The two people who took him in and accepted him were murdered. It was a hard battle to fight. But Scorpyus knew that therein lay his strengths also. His task within the knights involved a lot of isolation and risk. Being distant was a good quality for a spy.

God took all of the evil that happened to the knights in their childhood and used it to mold the four into something useful. God didn't author the evil, but since it happened, He was going to use it for a greater purpose none could foresee. Each harsh trial was in reality a lesson to be gleaned from. Everything, from the four meeting, to their early adventures, their individual strengths; it was all a preparation for what would come. It reminded Scorpyus of the story of Joseph. God had been with them through it all. It wasn't always easy to see, but now it seemed so clear. For the first time Scorpyus felt at ease with his lot in life. His childhood shaped him into who he was today. Scorpyus always felt that if by his life or death the cause of good would be furthered, then he was ready to perform his duty. But now he meant it for the right reasons. He brought the spyglass up to his eye again. Before he could focus on anything, a noise startled him from behind.

"Here you are." Zephyr stepped out onto the balcony as Scorpyus spun around.

"You shouldn't sneak up on people who are armed." Scorpyus said sheepishly, embarrassed to be caught off guard.

"I tell you this, it is a wonderful day. To be able to rest a little is a blessing." Zephyr stepped to the rail and enjoyed the elevated view. She saw the others gathered in the distance. She also noticed Scorpyus fumbling with his spyglass.

"Are you spying on them?"

Scorpyus shot Zephyr a sideways glance. "No, I'm not spying. What's to spy on anyway? I was just looking around and thinking. There is a lot of that to do from here. This view begs contemplation."

Zephyr understood completely. Being alone with majestic scenery was tantamount to being alone with God. A heartfelt appreciation of the creation should naturally lead to a deep appreciation of the Creator. That's why Zephyr loved the outdoors.

"How's your fever?" For some reason Scorpyus fumbled nervously with his spyglass.

"I am feeling well. I should. I slept for one whole day." Zephyr watched Scorpyus fidget with the spyglass. "I have been meaning to ask you; where did you get that anyway?"

"What this?" Scorpyus extended the spyglass and showed it to Zephyr. "I found it on the ship when we first arrived in Xylor; right after Novak's arrest. I didn't think I would ever see it again."

Zephyr looked at the brass cylindrical object. It was aged and worn but due to the rarity of the object; she knew it was a valuable piece. She noticed 'V. V' engraved on the side. "Are you telling me you have seen this spyglass before?"

Scorpyus nodded in the affirmative. "Yes, do you see the engraving?"

Scorpyus waited for Zephyr to acknowledge then continued. "That stands for Vassilli Verazzno. This was his. It disappeared when he was killed."

Zephyr knew of Scorpyus's family and that the woman who took him in as a child also had an adult son that served as a father figure for him. Though she never met Vassilli, she knew he had been a Ravenshire knight, and had been killed when Scorpyus was young. "That is incredible! And you found it now after all of this time?"

Scorpyus smiled. "Yeah, I was surprised to find it. Vassilli used to let me use it as long as I didn't take it out of the house. I remember sitting in front of the window for hours and just looking at things; imagining I was on some adventure. I almost forgot about it. Seeing it again reminds me of all those times; before the war; when life was still innocent. It was the last time I remember being…" Scorpyus's voice trailed off.

"God knew I would need it." Scorpyus replied after a pause.

The lighthearted mood of the conversation shifted to the serious. Scorpyus and Zephyr looked at each other in an awkward silence. Both knew where the conversation was heading. Both were trying to avoid it, but also knew where it would eventually stray.

"About back at Hester's…" Scorpyus started to say.

"You do not have to say anything." Zephyr was afraid of what would come next so she changed the subject. "What did Hester give you before we left?"

Scorpyus sighed heavily and cleared his throat. "Nothing; it was just a letter."

"What did it say?" Zephyr asked curiously.

Scorpyus cast his eyes away from Zephyr. "It was a poem about a dream."

"A dream?" Zephyr was puzzled.

"It was about a dream…a dream of another time; of another place; of another life; of what could have been. This war and the Valkyrie's have changed all that."

Zephyr sensed a deep sadness come over her friend. She turned Scorpyus so she could look him in the eye. "What is it Scorpyus?"

The two looked deep into the others eyes. They had known each other for so long now that words couldn't have communicated any more then their body language. The way they stood close, the way their eyes met, spoke more then a thousand speeches. Without so much as a word, the incident at Hester's spilled to the surface.

"Where do we go from here?" Scorpyus asked, gently moving a lock of Zephyr's hair from her face.

A tear welled in Zephyr's eye. "I have been thinking about little else and it…I just…I do not know if I can. I tell you sometimes I do not want to do this anymore, but I see no end. We have been called to do this, and I do not want to let God down. I cannot take any more. To always be worried; to be afraid; it is bad enough now as it is; and loosing friends. I have lost my father and my brother. To lose another even closer…I could not bear. But life is passing by." Tears flowed from Zephyr's eyes.

"Must we four suffer for the whole of Ravenshire? Many do not help…" Zephyr stopped herself and wiped tears from her cheeks.

"That is why we made the rule, is it not?" Zephyr continued. "I remember at the compound when the others and I thought you had been killed; it was hard to fight on; for any of us. To lose you as…"

Scorpyus placed his hands on Zephyr's shoulders. She glanced up at him, her lip quivering. "It's alright Zephyr; I know."

Scorpyus managed a smile through all the sorrow weighing on him. He had been haunted by thoughts of his own. He could feel a shudder ripple through Zephyr's shoulders. He choked back emotion and forced reason out of his brain. It was like squeezing water from a rock.

"After you were captured I saw one of the Valkyrie. I think it was the leader. And I know she saw me." Scorpyus stated. A puzzled look appeared on Zephyr's brow.

Scorpyus continued. "I think they will try to find us again; at least me. This may never be over for us. I fear things will become worse, and there are many battles before this war is over. That fact alone may cloud the future."

Zephyr placed her head on Scorpyus's shoulder and held her arms to her bosom, sobbing quietly. Scorpyus comforted her gently. With great blessing comes great responsibility. To those who were given much, much is often required. But God does not forget those who make the sacrifices.

"They say the winter rose is rare. It blooms only one day a year, and then only if it snows. Its blood red petals evidence a glimmer of life in an otherwise bleak white void." Scorpyus whispered.

Zephyr quickly looked up catching his gaze. The words were not lost on her. "I tell you this; the thought of such a winter is not without hope."

EPILOGUE

AGED HANDS GENTLY gripped the armrests of an old, well-worn rocking chair. The dark wood creaked with contentment as the chair swayed back and forth in front of a crackling fire. Thin feminine fingers curled around the end of polished armrests like they had on many other evenings; so much so the finish bore the darkened impressions of where fingers frequently rested. Like all hands they told a story. These soft but sure ones, now aged but still displaying evidence of a former beauty, spoke untold volumes. They told of a woman who had seen many years, some good and some bad, but years that had been lived to their fullest. A scar ran the length of the right thumb from just below the fingernail to near the base of the wrist. These hands had seen war and as a result became acquainted with heartache and sorrow. They witnessed the passing of friends and enemies alike, and never got used to either. They fought valiantly to preserve their existence in a world that in times past wanted to see them cold and lifeless. These were the hands that held new life conceived from their owner, wiped its share of tears, both from children and now even grandchildren. In fact they had seen a lot of tears. They cared for the sick and dressed wounds. These hands knew love, the shudder of a soft touch, and the feel of a husband. They were fortunate to enjoy many moments of happiness, and knew of countless blessings. They also sorrowfully clung to a husband's hand as he passed from this earth, and sometimes searched for him in the dark of night hoping to find him still in his place on the bed. Tearfully they cradled a child who died in infancy and carried flowers to the grave where that baby was laid to rest. They gently stayed strong for many grandchildren, and worked tirelessly to ensure those grandchildren had what war stole from her; innocence. And these hands could often be seen holding a Bible under the dim and flaring candle light.

No, these were no ordinary hands; they survived the bloodiest war the realm had ever seen; one fourth of the population perished as a result. They could never properly tell the story of the elderly lady who possessed them, nor accurately relate the seventy plus years of joy, sorrow, and abundant life they had seen. They were the hands of a survivor, and belonged to a woman who hailed from a generation of heroes. And now, as they clasped the worn and weathered armrests, they served in a much-loved capacity. They joyously illustrated stories of the elder lady who employed them so well.

"Boy grandma, you sure did see a lot of things when you were young," her eight-year-old grandson exclaimed. The boy and his two older sisters sat in rapt attention as their grandmother related stories of days gone by. This was the second night in a row she spoke of those days before and during the war. It was a subject her grandchildren hungered to learn of, and one she felt it was time they learned.

"So you see children, freedom came with a price. Let us never forget those who sacrificed all so that we may enjoy what we have today. That is why we celebrate the March Octave. Each year we take eight days to honor the sacrifice made by so many, and the blessings given to us by God. It was forgetting that started our problems in the first place." The elder woman smiled warmly at her grandchildren. She loved them dearly, and was proud to see them so interested in family history. But more then that she prayed there would never come a day when they would have to make a similar sacrifice.

"I still can't believe it. It seems so incredible." The twelve-year-old granddaughter was elated. "And to think Grandpa was a Clandestine Knight!"

"That means we're related to a Clandestine Knight!" The eight year old drew a laugh from his sisters.

The elder woman chuckled, "Yes, but remember to be modest. Your grandfather always felt uncomfortable with the praise heaped upon him He would remind others thousands fought for the realms freedom, and it was God who gave the victory." The elder woman spoke in a soft loving voice, a gleam in her eyes.

"Did Morton join the Clandestine Knights?" The twelve year old asked while brushing brown curly hair from her face.

"No, his loyalty was with the Dales. But he did work with the knights many times through the years."

"Was that grandpa's sword? Did he kill anybody with it?" The eight year old pointed to the weapon that hung above the fireplace. Like all boys, he was fascinated by the weapon and had been looking at it frequently as his grandmother recounted her stories.

The elder woman glanced at the sword. It bore the marks as having been used in battle. "That is a falchion. Major Barrington Rathbone gave it to your grandfather as a gift. He gave all of the knight's one after the Hellbourne Manor venture. Your grandfather hung it there a long time ago. He never used it that I'm aware of."

A sixteen-year-old girl with long blonde locks sat near her grandmother. She took in the evening's story with great enthusiasm. She noticed her grandmother's eyes would mist up whenever she talked about the knights; usually when recounting a happy moment. For this reason, the sixteen year old debated

CHRONICLES OF THE CLANDESTINE KNIGHTS

weather or not to ask a question that had been gnawing at her. Not knowing her grandfather was a knight until the prior evening made her all the more curious. If he had been a knight and she not known it, maybe she knew the others too without ever realizing it. She couldn't help but ask her question.

"Grandma, are any of the other clandestine knights still alive?"

The elder woman smiled and nodded her head. "Yes, there is one yet who lives. The others I am sorry to say have passed on to heaven. You will see them again some day."

The eight- year-old's eyes lit up. "That's true. I forgot about that!" He was excited at the prospect of meeting those he heard so much about.

"Wait a minute grandma," the sixteen-year-old had a wry smile on her face. "You said meet them *again*."

The old woman chuckled warmly. "Yes dear, you are right. I did say that. You have a good ear."

"That means we have already met all of the knights then doesn't it?" The sixteen year old wasn't going to let the question go unanswered.

The older woman laughed joyously. "I suppose you'll not let me out of this one. But yes you have met all of the Clandestine Knights." The grandmother pointed to her grandson. "But you young man may not remember one. You were just a baby when the first one passed."

A sad look came upon the old woman as she reminisced this fact. "You should remember the others though."

"Who were they?" The three grandchildren asked in unison. Each was eager for more. They knew their grandpa was a knight. If they knew the others only half as well, then they indeed did know the knights; better then most people in the realm. It was an idea with endless excitement.

The grandmother remained silent, and looked lovingly at her three grandchildren. Again she was pleased to see her grandchildren so happy and proud of their heritage. And it was a heritage to be proud of. All she could hope and pray for, was that her grandchildren live for God with the same honor and integrity as the knights had done. She couldn't help but wish her husband could have been here to see this moment.

"Who is the knight that is still alive?" The eight year old asked.

"Tell us more!" The twelve year old beckoned.

The elder woman leaned forward to get closer to her grandchildren. She placed her arms on the shoulders of the two nearest her. "Now if I told you any more children; we wouldn't have anything to talk about tomorrow."

About the Author

AFTER SERVING IN the U.S. Air Force, Tony Nunes graduated from California State University, Chico. He resides in northern California with his family, and is currently employed as an Officer with the California Highway Patrol. This is his second book in the Chronicles of the Clandestine Knights series. Also available is book one of the series *Hyacinth Blue*.

Coming in the Future

---◆---

**Look for the third book in the Chronicles of the
Clandestine Knight series:** *Hellbourne Manor*

This book finds the knights venturing to the dreaded Ethereal
Region; a land shrouded with mystery and legend. Little is known
of the Ethereal Region, but what is known is to be avoided. It is a
land where some say the very wind groans out a warning, where
mysterious noises and wailing screeches can be heard in the
distance. It is a land filled with strange tales; tales of a barbaric
people called Trepanites, and a misty dead forest. It is a place
where most dare not go.

   The long lost heir to the throne of The Dales disappeared,
and with it the hopes of the rebellion. The Clandestine Knights
are called upon to find the heir. It is a task by which the very
balance of the war hinges. Once again Cad, Novak, Scorpyus, and
Zephyr find themselves in harms way. In order to track down the
missing heir, they must travel to the Ethereal Region and find
the lair of an evil warlord. But doing so will require unwavering
bravery, and the utmost intelligence. The knights must overcome
many perils and sift through many myths. They must confront
one of the oldest legends know to the world; that of the Holy
Grail.

   Join the knights on their next adventure…if you dare!